Killing for England

Also by Iain McDowall

A Study in Death
Making a Killing
Perfectly Dead

Killing for England

Iain McDowall

First published in Great Britain in 2005 by
Piatkus Books Ltd of
5 Windmill Street, London W1T 2JA
email: info@piatkus.co.uk

The moral right of the author has been asserted

A catalogue record for this book is available from the British Library

ISBN 0 7499 0724 X

Set in Times by
Action Publishing Technology Ltd, Gloucester

Printed and bound in Great Britain by
William Clowes Ltd, Beccles, Suffolk

For Jake

Prologue

New Year's Day

Despite the strong current, the body hadn't travelled far. There'd been a storm – and storm damage – back at the start of December. Uprooted trees had been washed down from upstream, junk of all sorts following in their wake. On the stretch of the River Crow that flowed eponymously through Crowby itself, debris still clogged the banks. And debris had halted the progress of Darren McGee's corpse, had held it fixed between sodden oak bark and the twisted remains of a rusted mountain-bike.

The Crowby Diehards made the discovery, had called off their famous swim for the first time in their history as a mark of respect. For fifty-one years, they'd gathered at the same spot at the same time. New Year's Day, Riverside Walk, eight thirty am. Across from the Riverside Hotel and just to the side of the Memorial Bridge. Twenty or so swimmers plus a small crowd of supporters. Their numbers had fluctuated over the years but three of the original members still turned out, still flourished. *We wore nowt but swimming trunks in those days*, Harold Fletcher, the oldest of them, and not the slowest, was fond of saying. But nowadays, like every other Diehard, he wore a wet suit – while a support team stayed close with a motorised dinghy in case any of them got into difficulties. Even Fletcher conceded that it was common sense. The River Crow was wide and as cold as ice – cold enough for cardiac arrest – cold enough for unconsciousness and death.

Fletcher hadn't been the first to see it though. That distinction had gone to Gemma Reed – the Diehards' New Year's Day swim had long since ceased to be a single-sex tradition – and Gemma Reed had usefully been a probationer, six months uniformed service in. She was working a shopping-centre beat, kids nicking fags and dropping litter, but she knew an opportunity when she saw one. Everybody away from the edge except you, Geoff, and you, Keith. Everybody else stay back. Who's got a mobile handy? Give it here for Christ's sake. She'd dialled the number and then the three of them had hauled Darren McGee on to the bank. His head had been face down and submerged lower in the water than the rest of his body so that she knew he was dead – at least knew it theoretically – before they'd even touched him. But she remembered her training, remembered her lectures. The pulse-taking and the check with the mirror were what you did first. No matter what. Always. Invariably. *The immediate priority is to take what life-saving measures may be necessary or possible.* It was only secondly that you thought about preserving a potential crime scene. *Thereafter avoid all unnecessary further contact.* OK, that's it, he's a gonner. Everybody just stand clear till the experts get here. They'd laid him out on the bank and then kept their distance. *Establish an interim cordon as soon as possible.* It was her first dead body, apart from the obligatory training visit to the morgue. But that had been different, had been anticipated, planned for. This was unscheduled, out of the blue, the real thing. She'd had to stay closer than the others of course. They were her mates but they were also civilians. She was the professional: the one who had to keep guard, the one who had to keep looking.

His clothes were wet, green-weeded, yet there was something almost neat about the way they clung to his tall, gangly frame. She knew he hadn't been in the water for long. There were no bite marks on the face, no sign yet of the head swelling, the trunk bloating. What there *was*: a welter of bruising, ugly and scarring. Probably from collisions with rocks and the remains of trees, or maybe from hitting the bridge supports, if that was the way he'd gone in. And as she'd stood watching, something foul and slug-like had crawled out of his left nostril. Oh Jesus, please don't let me be sick.

Chapter One

Wednesday April 20th

Chief Inspector Jacobson left his office on the dot of six o'clock, glad to be going. His cases right now were routine, low-level, tedious. It was one of those interludes when real badness had slipped off the radar, biding its time, drawing its breath. As a citizen, you welcomed its absence. But as a copper, you twiddled your thumbs, rearranged your desk ornaments, watched and waited. He bought a copy of the *Evening Argus* from the news stand in the pedestrianised square which filled - or compounded - the void between the comforting geometry of the Town Hall and its unlovely neighbours: the Divisional building, the public library-stroke-NCP multistorey, the pimply, unwashed rear of the shopping centre.

'There's nothing in it, mate,' the vendor told him despondently.

It wasn't the best sales technique Jacobson had ever witnessed. He pocketed his change and folded the paper under his arm. He was headed across the square in the direction of Silver Street, the fastest route he knew to the dark, smoky interior of the Brewer's Rest.

There were daffodils blooming in the floral borders and overhead the early evening sky was irritatingly blue. To the conventional mind, spring was a Good Thing, a harbinger, something to be looked forward to after the grey months of an English winter. But Jacobson had never really cared for it, thought that it was probably his least favourite season. The sudden brightness of the days startled you like an alarm clock you'd forgotten had been set. And there was too much that was transitional about it, too much that was uncertain. You never knew whether to grab your coat or leave it at home. You never knew whether the sun would shine or the rain would piss down. How completely and utterly marvellous the season of renewal was, according to the greetings card industry and the more sentimentally-inclined nature poets. Sap rising. New life spilling forth all over the shop. As if there wasn't enough of the bastarding stuff around already. Bristling, seething, greedy. All of it eating the other bits. Or being eaten by them.

He let Henry Pelling, the *Evening Argus*'s chief crime reporter, buy him a drink. The quid pro quo was a wary, mutual update that consisted of not very much on either side. But then Pelling's regular work cronies poured in, brimming over with office politics and professional jealousies. Although the *Argus* was located out at the Waitrose complex these days, the journos preferred to be downtown of an evening. There was a new face amongst them. Male, twenty-something, smartly dressed. Jacobson paid him no more attention than he did the others except to clock that he was black. Rationally and intellectually, Jacobson was the precise opposite of a racist. But he'd still lived all his life as a white man in England. The labels of his school shirts had proclaimed Made In The British Empire. He still noticed Otherness, couldn't not do. Scrupulously, he ordered another Guinness for Pelling and then extricated himself to a quiet corner with his second pint.

The Brewer's Rest was selling genuine Czech Budweiser on draft now – a brew not to be confused, in Jacobson's view, with the better-known 'Bud' favoured by teenage hoodlums and no-taste Yanks. It was a significant compensation in the face of the BR's latest measures – karaoke, a big screen PlayStation – to weather the competition from the fun pubs, sports bars and pole-dancing clubs which seemed to be taking over the night life of the town centre. Jacobson sipped his beer, glanced at the court reports. His B & H packet and his silver lighter were secure inside his jacket pocket and he was making an attempt – with how much seriousness remained to be seen – to leave them that way as much of the time as possible. The figure might have been standing there whole minutes before he finally glanced up, took it in that somebody wanted to speak to him.

'Chief Inspector Jacobson?' Pelling's new arrival asked.

Not nervously exactly. More that the speaker was conscious of a level of importance which would attach itself to any further interchange.

'Who wants to know?' Jacobson challenged, taking another sip.

'My name is Paul Shaw,' Paul Shaw said.

He produced ID from his wallet, passed it over: an NUJ card. It was up-to-date, the genuine article as far as Jacobson could tell without fishing his underused reading glasses out of his spectacle case. He handed it back with his left hand, continued to hold the *Argus* in his right.

'Old Henry usually introduces his new lads to me personally—'

Shaw had pulled out an empty chair from the table while Jacobson had studied the press card. Now he sat down abruptly, pulled it back in.

'No, Chief Inspector, that's not it. I'm not with the *Argus* – I'm freelance, from London. I've never even been in Crowby until this last week.'

'Congratulations on that score. So why spoil a good track record now?'

Shaw coughed, cleared his throat. His suit didn't look cheap, neither did his shirt, the collar fashionably open, the top button undone. He placed a laptop case in front of him. The kind that held the computer secure but still left ample room for other essential stuff: documents, mobile phones, sandwiches from Prêt à Manger. He unzipped a compartment, produced an *Argus* of his own, held up the front page. It was an old copy from earlier in the year. *January the something* was all that Jacobson could make out for the date without his specs. He really needed to get into the habit of wearing them when he was reading. But at least he could see the headlines without any difficulty. *New Year's Day Tragedy: Drowning Was Suicide, Says Coroner.*

Paul Shaw smiled the way you did when your cat had just died or your wife had just left you for the woman next door.

'I want to tell you about a murder, Chief Inspector. Here in your town. A black man murdered by white racists.'

Chapter Two

'Darren McGee?' – Jacobson put his own *Argus* down on the table, didn't look any closer at Shaw's – 'An unhappy young man to say the least. Mental health problems leading to suicide. DCS Salter himself handled the police investigation.'

He drank another mouthful of beer, fell silent. In the age of nanotechnology – cameras and microphones the size of a gnat's penis – you were careful what you said to the press. Especially press you'd never met before. Shaw kept up his anguished smile.

'I'm aware of the official verdict, Inspector Jacobson. I've read the coroner's report. The transcripts of the hearing as well.'

'And?'

'And they don't tell the real story. They don't even get close.'

Jacobson thought about knocking the embryonic conversation on the head right there and then. He'd been on annual leave when the young man – yes, the young *black* man – had been fished out of the River Crow. Fished out dead. Because of his absence, smooth-arse Greg Salter had assumed the role of senior investigating officer in a suspicious death inquiry for the first time – hopefully the only time – since he'd taken over as Crowby's chief of detectives. But not even Salter could blunder a case that had been textbook simple. Even though everything had been done and dusted before Jacobson had returned to duty, he'd checked the files as a matter of course. Well, he'd done more than that to be honest. There would have been a modest, professional pleasure in pronouncing Salter's investigation as flawed and incompetent. But the facts had suggested otherwise.

McGee had had some trouble with his neighbours and his workmates it was true. And there had been racism in the mix all right. But the overwhelming factor had been his mental condition. He'd been sectioned more than once, diagnosed as schizophrenic. He'd only fetched up in Crowby in the first place because he was on the trail of a girlfriend who'd given him the elbow, who'd reported him as violent, who'd gone to court for a restraining order. The forensics read the same way, pointed in the same direction. No compelling evidence of injuries sustained before he hit the water. Definitely no evidence of ligatures or weights on the body. Plus the diatoms swimming microscopically in his lungs had matched convincingly to the diatomic population in the stretch of the river where his body had been found.

No, he almost decided, Shaw wasn't worth listening to. He was either on the make – hungry for a byline regardless of the evidence – or an obsessive, a conspiracy nut. Or quite possibly both. On the other hand, there was hardly a great rush to get home to an empty flat and a Chinese takeaway. Why not hear him out while he finished his pint?

He checked his watch. Then:

'You've got five minutes of my time, Mr Shaw. Don't waste it.'

'Darren McGee was my cousin, Mr Jacobson. It's not a story that I'm after here. It's the truth – justice. Darren moved to Crowby in November. He was dead in January and he was dealing with racist threats every day in between.'

'Every day? That's as maybe. But racist attitudes *were* mentioned at the inquest, old son. The coroner criticised those responsible, commented that the hostility Darren McGee experienced was an added stress factor against his mental stability.'

Paul Shaw didn't have a drink with him, didn't produce any cigarettes, gave the impression that he ran mainly on his own, twitchy energy.

'Especially at the moment he was being thrown off a bridge by racist thugs. Held over, then dropped.'

Jacobson studied Shaw's face. He didn't *look* like any kind of nutter.

'The only racism that got mentioned at the inquest was just everyday, ignorant harassment,' Shaw continued. 'I'm talking about what got left out. The serious threats that were made against Darren. Really serious ones. Threats that were finally acted on.'

'If you've studied the evidence like you say, Mr Shaw, then you already know that the forensic team searched the bridge from end to end for any indication that there'd been a struggle, that Darren McGee *hadn't* just tipped himself in. Evidence of a scuffle. A significant shoe mark or a tread. They found precisely sod all.'

'Maybe they didn't look closely enough,' Shaw countered. 'There wasn't what you might call any political will to get to the truth. Darren's mental history made it too easy – too tempting – to write his death off as a suicide. I don't expect your boss, Chief Salter, was over-keen to prove otherwise. It would have meant a lot of hard work and unnecessary bad publicity on his patch to track down the killers.'

Jacobson took a deep mouthful of beer. Shaw had evidently mastered the basics of his trade at any rate, had done his homework before he'd made his approach. Not only had Henry Pelling or one of his colleagues pointed Jacobson out for him, they'd also marked Shaw's card about the non-Love-In between Jacobson and Smoothie Greg.

'That's a serious allegation, Mr Shaw. And one I'm

prepared to pretend I didn't hear. In any case, like I say, there's not a shred of forensics to back you up.'

Paul Shaw smiled politely on.

'Professor Merchant did the post-mortem. From what I hear, the local force are always a lot happier when Peter Robinson's signature is at the bottom of the report.'

Jacobson took another mouthful of beer before he replied.

'Professor Merchant was regarded as one of the half-dozen top forensic pathologists in the country.'

'But he hadn't exactly been very hands-on in recent years, had he?'

Not in the way you mean, old son, Jacobson thought. Something featuring duck from the Yellow River takeaway followed by an hour in the company of a decent book had suddenly regained their appeal. Here he was, in his own free time, stuck with defending the reputation of two of the biggest prats he'd ever had the misfortune to work with.

'Why the sudden interest now anyway?' he asked. 'The inquest was in January. Why wait till now if you had concerns to raise?'

'I've been busy working on other projects. And I was out of the UK in January. This is the first opportunity I've had to look into what actually happened to Darren.'

Shaw had started unzipping another one of the compartments in the front of his laptop case. Jacobson glimpsed a wad of documents inside.

'Hold it a minute, old son,' he said. 'Why tell *me* all this? Apart from the fact that I'm not DCS Salter's best mate – which is hardly the scoop of the year.'

'Because you have a reputation for fair play, Inspector. I thought maybe if I could show you what I've found out, *you* might see a way to reopening the investigation.'

Shaw had his pile of documents halfway out of the case. He pulled a single sheet of paper all the way out, placed it down neatly next to Jacobson's beer glass. The sheet contained a single, typed list. Four first names and four surnames. Jacobson gave the names the barest glance, none of them meant anything to him.

Shaw glanced around the room, as if suddenly remembering he was in a public place. His voice, never loud, lessened to a whisper.

'These are the four who killed him. They threatened him that they'd do it, they promised him they'd do it – and then they *did*.'

Jacobson's mind replayed the forensic highlights like a mantra: no signs of a struggle, no prior injuries and, most of all, no witnesses.

'These threats were made exactly how?'

'In his face mainly – on the street. Although sometimes they'd call his mobile too. Plus each one of the four's connected. The far right, you know? I'm not sure with what exactly. Not the BNP or the NF anyway, maybe some new group.'

'And you can provide me with corroboration of these threatening incidents?'

Shaw paused, took another look around.

'Not so far. The people I'm speaking to – third parties – they don't want to go on record. Not yet at least – I'm still working on them.'

Not sure. Not so far. Not yet. That capped it. That plus the glancing, whispering and pausing. It had been a mistake after all inviting Shaw to ramble on. The guy *seemed* normal. But he was evidently as demented as his terminally wet cousin. Jacobson finished off the rest of his beer in one long, practised gulp.

'This is still a free country, Mr Shaw,' he said when he'd finished drinking, 'despite the best attempts of the Home Secretary. Wander around Crowby as takes your fancy. Contribute to the local economy by all means. But don't bother me again – unless or until you've something more persuasive to offer than a roll call of lippy local bigots and fantasists.'

Jacobson stood up, leaving the sheet of paper where it

was on the narrow table. Finally, just in the remote case that Shaw wasn't bonkers, he took a card out of his inside pocket, placed it on top of the list of names.

'And next time - if there *is* a next time - try and go through the proper channels, old son. Call me and make an appointment first.'

Chapter Three

Thursday April 21st

Thursday dawned. Bright. Sunny. But not all that warm. Jacobson took a shower after his breakfast and shaved more meticulously than usual. He always wore a suit on a working day. And a tie. But not usually a black one.

The main event had been scheduled for ten thirty. Too late in the morning to make it possible for him not to go into the Divisional building beforehand. Entirely typical: Merchant had succeeded in being an irritating, irksome bastard right to the very last. Jacobson straightened the tie in his hall mirror and decided not to risk the day without his overcoat.

He drove into town with the *Today* programme on the radio, was at his desk by ten to nine. He studied the overnight incident sheet and then dug out his notes on the Sheila Cassidy case which was finally going to trial the next week. The unfortunate Mrs Cassidy was a middle-class housewife straight out of the TV commercials: except that she'd stabbed her husband to death in an argument about her cooking. Hubbie had complained about her 'obsession' with the River Café cookbook, had demanded bangers and mash over her customary *bacalà con carciofi* just one time too often. She hadn't meant to kill him, of course. She'd phoned the police after she'd called the ambulance, had made an instant, anguished confession. In all probability, she wouldn't have done it at all if the physical circumstances had been different. If the shouting match hadn't happened in the kitchen. If there hadn't been a shiny row of Sabatier carving knives standing handily between her and her husband at the time. If she hadn't had the bad luck to slice straight through a major artery. But the law still had to take its course and Jacobson, who'd conducted the interviews and put the charges, needed to make himself available as a CPS witness.

He worked on until just before ten. DCI 'Clean' Harry Fields was one of the passengers in the lift which he caught down to the ground floor. Fields offered him a lift and Jacobson was fool enough to agree, leaving his own car behind in the Divisional car park. The quickest way to the crematorium was out past the hospital and then via the bypass. But Clean Harry had an idiosyncratic route of his own which involved an additional, unfathomable detour through Longtown. There were only minutes to spare when Fields and Jacobson finally slipped into the back row of the chapel of rest.

Merchant's family had been paid up C of E and there had been a full church service at the parish church in Wynarth before the funeral cortege had headed over to the crematorium. By all accounts, Merchant had barely set foot in the place but his wife, Elspeth, was apparently a stalwart attender. Jacobson's unkind funeral thoughts #1: married to Alasdair Merchant, the poor woman would've sorely needed the solace of religion – or, better still, the ecumenical, all-embracing solace of half a dozen religions.

He looked down across the packed pews. Elspeth, right at the front, decked in black, visibly leaning on the eldest of her three sons for support. Relatives and friends around her: two or three rows' worth. Then came the massed ranks of those who'd known Merchant only professionally, who had to be *seen* to be here for their own professional reasons. Medical colleagues, the local legal establishment and, of course, the police. Dudley 'Dud' Bentham, the Chief Constable, had decreed a three-line whip on attendance. Everybody down to the rank of Inspector and no excuses accepted other than urgent operational ones. Jacobson's unkind funeral thoughts #2: there was never a psychopathic serial killer around when you needed one. He clocked Greg Salter, squeezed on to the end of the pew occupied by Bentham and his entourage of Assistant Chief Constables. Predictably, Salter was the only Super who'd managed to get so close to the source of power and preference. The legal great and good included Alan Slingsby and his ever-growing band of associates. Amongst the medical contingent, Jacobson made out the back view of Peter Robinson's unruly ginger hair. Robinson was Crowby's assistant pathologist, Merchant's junior: at least officially and theoretically.

The music started as the coffin was carried in by the bearers. Jacobson recognised it as something familiar but he had to look to the order of service to discover that it was the Sanctus from Mozart's 'Requiem in D Minor'. He'd heard that the family had paid out for two consecutive spots in the crem's schedule. It was the only way, seemingly, to stop the stewards hustling you rapidly out into the garden of remembrance at the end of the committal – before the second half of the deceased's desert island discs had got a decent spin on the PA – on a busy day, before the curtain was even fully across the furnace. The vicar was at the lectern now, shuffling her notes. Soon the music would stop and she would start up. *We are gathered here today, etcetera, etcetera.*

Jacobson didn't bother to listen, found himself trying to remember the last time he'd actually spoken to Merchant. He worked out that it must have been around six months ago – Merchant, he thought, had carried out the less-than-challenging post-mortem on Sheila Cassidy's husband – but he realised that he could barely recall a word. No doubt Merchant had sneered and patronised, no doubt Jacobson had been rude and abrasive. They'd never hit it off since day one and in recent years they'd actively avoided each other as much as Crowby's murder rate permitted. Merchant's frequent invitations to the international conference circuit had been helpful to both of them in that respect. The rot between them had really set in over the Roger Harvey case – when Merchant had deliberately failed to mention certain pertinent facts upfront for fear that the stale news of his obsessive philandering would finally get back to his remarkably credulous wife. Jacobson still regretted not shopping Merchant's professional misconduct and thereby knocking the sheen off his exaggerated reputation. Conversely, Merchant had hated it that, from the Harvey case on, he was firmly in Jacobson's debt – that Jacobson definitively had his number.

He felt Harry Field's elbow nudging his arm. They'd got to the hymn singing. Or more precisely to Psalm 23, 'The Lord's My Shepherd'. Fields, naturally, could render any of the psalmist's Greatest Hits without the aid of a crib sheet; and probably to any of the variant tunes and settings. But Jacobson had to read the verses – even to be able to mouth silently along. On one of the few occasions that Jacobson had ever achieved a meaningful conversation with him – when they'd both been less than sober at a police function – Merchant had revealed himself as a fervent atheist: *We're just meat, Frank,* he'd said, *and then we're just dead meat*. Jacobson smiled inwardly at the memory. Given that Merchant's marriage had been one long double-life of deceit it was entirely appropriate that his final send-off should be completely at odds with his real beliefs.

He watched Elspeth after the service, accepting condolences from well-wishers, a brave glint in her eyes. The official story was that Professor Merchant had suffered a heart attack in his hotel room at the end of his successful visit to a forensic convention in Chicago. The story doing the rounds of the Divisional building was that Merchant had died *in flagrante* and that a young pathologist from Milan had caught her flight back home to Europe a sadder and a wiser woman.

Jacobson eluded Fields for the drive back into town. He wanted to get to the Riverside Hotel before the vol-au-vents ran out. And he was gasping for what – incredibly – would be his very first cigarette of the day. He cadged an alternative lift from Brian Fairbanks, a harmless if tedious traffic superintendent, who qualified on both counts. He lit up one B & H for Fairbanks and then one for himself as the traffic cop eased his personal vehicle, some kind of customised saloon, into the stream of departing mourners. The sudden intake of tar and nicotine made Jacobson cough. Merchant had been more or less his own age. But tall, lean, fit. Jacobson was distinctly average in height. And overweight, out of condition. You'd have looked at both of them together – if they'd ever latterly been seen together – and unhesitatingly picked Jacobson as the first one to go. He took a second, less thorough puff. Merchant's unexpected death was a blip, an anomaly, totally contrary to the general facts of health. He promised himself there and then not to let it lessen his current resolve to smoke less, to use stairs more often.

The après-cremation bash was in the Flowers banqueting suite. After the food and the tributes, the mourners were at liberty to mingle. Jacobson caught up with Peter Robinson in one of the side bars. Robinson had married the previous summer and had brought his wife along with him. Like her husband, she was in her late twenties. Unlike him, she was dark-haired, pretty and visibly pregnant. Jacobson hoped their marriage would be a truer partnership than Merchant's. Or his own come to that. He knew Robinson well enough by now not to have to hide behind the conventional proprieties when they talked.

'They're offering you the job then, Peter?' he asked.

'They're encouraging me to apply anyway,' Robinson answered.

'Make sure you do, old son. You don't want some outsider waltzing in.'

'That's just what I've been telling him,' Mrs Robinson commented, her fingers wrapped proprietorially around her husband's left arm.

Inside CID, Jacobson had more or less allowed Greg Salter to do just that. At the time, he'd thought Robinson hadn't wanted the job. Later he'd realised there was not wanting a job and there was preventing an idiot from grabbing it from you.

To divert his mind from a sore point, he mentioned his pub conversation with the journalist from London. Robinson told him he remembered the main details of the Darren McGee case even though it had been Merchant who'd performed the autopsy:

'Truthfully, in the last year or so, I've been in the habit of diverting the Prof's reports before they were officially filed. He was a gifted pathologist – there's absolutely no doubt about that – but he could cut corners if he thought an examination was too boringly routine or if his mind was elsewhere.'

'Elsewhere meaning his research and his conference papers?' Jacobson asked.

Robinson nodded, taking a mouthful of his gin and tonic.

'Darren McGee got his full attention of course.'

'Why of course?'

'Death by drowning,' Mrs Robinson answered, nursing a tonic – but no gin – in her free hand. 'The pathologist's equivalent of football or politics as a perennial topic of conversation. Peter's certainly.'

Robinson smiled down at his attractively petite wife. His marriage wasn't likely to do much for his bookish stoop, Jacobson thought.

'That's why, Frank,' he said. 'Bodies in water are one of the most difficult categories when it comes to identifying the precise cause of death. Or – as the textbooks like to say – drowning lacks unique pathonomic characteristics.'

'Rather them than me. So the case wasn't beneath Merchant's dignity then?'

'Definitely not. He'd pulled out all the stops as far as I could see. A thorough piece of work by anybody's standards.'

'And sufficient to prove that Paul Shaw's story is completely off beam?'

Robinson took another sip, hesitated. Then:

'No. Not actually. Not strictly speaking. The circumstantial evidence and the deceased's psychiatric history did that. Theoretically, McGee *could* have died the way your journalist says that he did.'

Chapter Four

Detective Sergeant Ian Kerr had set off from the Divisional building and driven out of Crowby on the Wynarth Road too late to witness the stately crawl of the funeral cortege in the opposite lane. He circled the market square twice before he managed to grab a parking space from a departing Range Rover. He locked his car and walked over to the Bank House. At a mere hundred and twenty-odd, it was the youngest building in the centre of Wynarth. For most of those years it had actually been a bank. Nowadays, though, one half of the building was occupied by a firm of estate agents cum property developers and the other half housed Kerr's destination: the Viceroy Tandoori.

Kerr knocked on the front window, just above the laminated menu. The Viceroy opened for business at twelve noon, still half an hour away. Kerr could see a couple of waiters inside, busy setting the tables for lunchtime. Plus the proprietor, Randeep Parmeer, hurrying towards the door. They talked in the back office. There'd been trouble with thugs on a couple of recent Friday nights. But now Parmeer had reported receiving death threats on his home telephone and the situation had mutated from one for the plods to keep an eye on into a potential CID case.

Kerr accepted a cup of fresh tea but passed on a tray of samosas. Like any ex-beat officer, he was no stranger to the kind of piss heads and/or pill heads who descended mob-handed on ethnic restaurants from time to time intent on mayhem. Winding up the waiters, throwing the food about, arguing about the bill if their meal actually progressed that far. *Fucking Paki this* or *fucking Chinky that. Fuck off back to your own manky country.* Fighting with other customers. Fighting with each other if all else failed. You expected it in Crowby. You didn't expect it in a rural idyll like Wynarth with its complacent demographic of antique dealers, retired pop stars, vegetarian accountants and Reiki practitioners.

Randeep Parmeer had brought his answerphone in from home. He connected it to a socket at the side of his desk while Kerr stirred his tea.

'Ready?' Parmeer asked.

He was a short, dapper man in a dark blue suit. Kerr made him thirty-five, maybe forty.

'Sure,' Kerr replied, putting the spoon down. 'Go ahead.'

Parmeer pressed play on the machine. The sound quality was good. And what there was to hear came through loud, ugly and clear.

Not answering tonight, Parmeer? You're still a dirty little Paki, Parmeer, whether you answer or not. Do you know that? A dirty, filthy little Paki. You've no business to be in our country, you Paki scum. You and your fat wife and your Paki whore daughters. We know where you live, you piece of shite.

Kerr shook his head. The human race had discovered DNA and walked on the surface of the moon. But the world was still full of ignorant, stupid, malicious bastards.

'And this was the third call you've received, Mr Parmeer?'

'That's correct,' Parmeer replied. 'Sunday night was the first. Then Tuesday night. Then last night. Only this time I didn't pick up.'

'And always around twelve thirty?'

'Yes. Each time. Not long after I got home from the restaurant.'

Kerr put the obvious questions. Had anything like this happened before? No, it hadn't. Did Parmeer recognise the voice? No, definitely not.

He tried a sip of tea: Earl Grey at the perfect strength.

'And you say your number is ex-directory?'

Parmeer nodded.

'That's the worrying thing, Sergeant. Apart from a few business associates, only my friends and relatives have that number. So how can these – these racists get a hold of it?'

'That's something we might need to look at further, Mr Parmeer.'

Kerr put the cup down, took out his notebook and a biro. The public – especially the anxious public – found it reassuring if they could watch you scribbling while they talked. He asked Parmeer about his household.

'There's my wife and myself. And our three daughters, ages eight, ten and seventeen. I've a lad too. Ashraf. But he's in Leeds, studying medicine.'

'And have there been any other incidents, anything involving your wife or your daughters?'

Parmeer looked freshly worried by the thought. But he said that there hadn't been, that he'd checked and double-checked:

'Only these sick calls – and the yobbos of course.'

Kerr repeated the apology he'd made in the doorway on behalf of the force. There was no sub-station in Wynarth these days and only one over-stretched patrol car per shift assigned to Crowby's rural hinterlands. Both times that Parmeer had called in the presence of unwanted thugs at the Viceroy, said thugs had disappeared howling and guffawing into the night before Crowby's finest had finally shown up. There was a complicated history of lunatic Home Office funding decisions which, once impartially digested, explained why none of this was really the force's fault. But Kerr realised that this wasn't the moment to run it past the Viceroy's owner. He made a few more scribbles, took another sip of tea. Then:

'This is probably just some sick nutter, Mr Parmeer. Harmless in the sense that he has no intention of ever actually carrying out what he says. All the same, you and your family need to be extra careful for the time being. Especially yourself by the sounds of it. You could consider varying your routines. Always leaving here at the same time and late at night – that's none too clever for a start.'

Parmeer had an old-fashioned gold cigarette case on the top of his desk. A collector's item: the kind with a built-in lighter. He opened the lid, offered one to Kerr – which Kerr declined – and lit one for himself.

'You don't think the phone calls are linked to the trouble we've had in here then?'

'Obviously that can't be ruled out. But a nuisance caller is very likely a different kind of offender from a Friday night yobbo. As far as that goes, what I suggest is that we arrange a time for you to call in to Divisional HQ in Crowby, have a look at some mug shots, see if any of our, eh, customers look familiar to you.'

Parmeer puffed lightly on his cigarette.

'Any time you like, Sergeant. The sooner the better. These morons – my family are from Mysore. I've never set foot in Pakistan.'

Parmeer was politely soft-spoken, only the slightest trace around his vowels of his second-generation Birmingham origins.

'Fine,' Kerr replied, still scribbling. 'I'll sort something out, give you a call back later today hopefully.'

It was something the plods should have already set in motion, he thought. Though, realistically, you couldn't blame them for not bothering. Neither the Viceroy nor the Market Square outside it had CCTV. Supposing Parmeer *could* identify the thugs, there would still be the whole difficult matter of finding additional witnesses and sufficient corroboration for the CPS to bring a court prosecution. From the overworked plod perspective, it was a lot easier – and a lot less time-consuming – to chase up unpaid parking tickets than to pursue more complicated cases that might never lead to a quantifiable result.

'And the phone calls?' Parmeer asked.

Kerr put his notebook and pen away.

'Let's take it one step at a time, Mr Parmeer. If there are any more calls, I'd suggest leaving the answerphone to deal with them so we get a nice record of the voice. There might be a point where it could be worth putting a trace on the line. But I don't think we've reached that stage yet.'

Kerr took another sip of tea, asked to hear the existing answerphone message again.

The voice was male and deep. Other than that there wasn't much to say. The accent was local but not uneducated. Not obviously young. Not obviously old. Somebody you could walk past in the street any day of the week. The bloke standing in front of you at the supermarket checkout or sitting at the next table in the pub. You'd watch him buying his groceries or drinking his beer. And never catch a glimpse of the fucked-up cesspit between his ears and under his scalp.

He waited until he was outside the Viceroy Tandoori before he called Rachel, mobile to mobile. It was one of their rules that he should never just turn up unannounced, not even when – like today – his work had put him legitimately around the corner from her flat in Thomas Holt Street. But she was on the train to Birmingham anyway, she told him. She was meeting an old art college friend for lunch at the Ikon Gallery. A friend who was doing well, she said, who'd just landed a major exhibition at the Custard Factory. Kerr guessed from her careful avoidance of any gender-specific description, that the friend was probably male, was conceivably even Tony Scruton, the man Kerr had replaced in Rachel's affections but hadn't entirely displaced from her life. He of the country cottage, the splodge-filled canvases and the infuriating, neatly-trimmed goatee beard. Rachel's platonic friendship with Scruton troubled Kerr far beyond the fact of the more recent lovers she'd taken up with and then dropped in her intermittent attempts to end their affair. Scruton was Rachel's *type*, led her kind of life and – outside of the bedroom – Kerr knew that he wasn't, knew that he didn't. The first time she'd mentioned the Custard Factory to him, for instance, Kerr had thought that she'd meant just that, a custard *factory*, had never before heard of the city's fashionably arty hang-out.

His wife, Cathy, would be busy too. A situation that it didn't require a phone call to confirm. Now that the twins had settled in at the nursery school, Cathy had taken her old office job back on a part-time basis that fitted with their hours. She'd argued that they could do with the extra cash. Especially, she'd pointed out, after the winter holiday that had turned out more expensive than they'd expected. What it really was: she needed to be out of the house, needed to spend time in the real world, needed to feel like an independent adult again.

He drove back towards Crowby the same way he'd driven out – via the Wynarth Road. But this time he detoured to his empty family home on the Bovis estate. He fixed himself a couple of bacon sandwiches for lunch. When he'd upgraded the hi-fi system in the lounge with a new CD player and a nice pair of Celeston speakers, he'd moved the old player and speakers into the kitchen. He shoved Lucinda Williams on for company – *Essence* – and sat down to eat alone. At least the cat was pleased to see him. She'd left off sunning herself on the porch roof to follow him inside. He'd treated her to some fresh milk and the fatty bacon rinds which she liked so much that she could barely chew them for purring.

After he'd eaten, he phoned the control room back at the Divisional building, asked for Amanda Singh's telephone number, gave her a speculative call. She said she had a window at two o'clock. He told her great, that would be fine, he'd be there. He checked the morning's post before he left the house. Bills, Cathy's bank statement, a holiday brochure from the travel agent they'd used at Christmas. They'd spent ten days in Florida, baking in the sun. Kerr would rather have been somewhere else - New York or San Francisco or cruising the interstate across Arizona. But at least it was better than Crowby in the pissing rain and/or ice and/or snow. And the twins had loved it, which had really been the point. Disneyland especially. It was the kind of family time he'd tried to fix in his memory for later. One of these days, he firmly believed, Cathy would find out about Rachel and then he'd lose them, end up seeing them once a month or once a fortnight. He'd become one of those desperate Saturday afternoon dads, spoiling his kids with Big Macs and cinema matinees, trying to compensate for hurt and turmoil and absence.

Chapter Five

Jacobson wasn't sure how he'd get back to the Divisional building. Maybe he'd call a cab or see if there was a bus due. It was always theoretically feasible that he could walk. Theoretically. That had been the word that had captured his imagination and caused him to linger in the vicinity after the wake had broken up. *Theoretically, McGee could have died the way your journalist says that he did.* Of course, Robinson had qualified his surprising comment with a concise reminder of the governing principle of forensic post-mortem examinations. Or a reasonably concise reminder anyway: *All the pathologist can do, Frank, is establish the parameters of possibility and impossibility. It's for the police – bearing those parameters in mind – to work out what actually happened.* When Jacobson had asked him what he'd *thought* about the police explanation in this particular case – a question that Merchant would have treated with snide contempt – Robinson had been adamant enough that suicide was the best empirical fit to the available facts. Even so, Jacobson had felt a sudden impulse to look at the scene of Darren McGee's demise for himself.

The Crowby Riverside Hotel was a mile and a half from the town centre. The hotel's private gardens led down to its private stretch of the riverbank. Alternatively, as Jacobson had just done, you could stroll over the Memorial Bridge to the other side of the water: Riverside Walk – a street of large, well-preserved Victorian mansions facing on to a tree-lined colonnade which gave access – via two smaller footbridges – to the Memorial Park. Jacobson didn't walk that far along. Instead, just to the side of the Memorial Bridge, he negotiated the series of broad steps that led down to a small, wooden jetty, maintained and made use of by the Crowby Rowing Club. It was also the spot where the masochistic nutters who swam the Crow every New Year's Day gathered. The banking next to the jetty looked neat, newly tended, in the cool April sunshine. But it would have been wild and unkempt and muddy when the Diehards had fished out the corpse.

A couple of swans had shown interest at his approach. Jacobson regretted that he hadn't filched something for them courtesy of the banqueting suite. He checked his watch. Less than four and a half minutes since he'd walked through the automatic doors of the hotel's main entrance. McGee, of course, would have come out of the staff entrance around the side. Four thirty am, if Jacobson remembered correctly, was when he was supposed to have left the Riverside Hotel's kitchens, where he'd been working as a kitchen porter. And only just holding the job down by all accounts. The belief of Greg Salter's investigation – ultimately, the belief of the coroner's inquiry – was that McGee had walked on to the bridge and deliberately thrown himself in.

Jacobson watched the swans glide off huffily. The Crow was quick-running year round. In January it had been a torrent and tricky with the cross-currents that had swept McGee's body towards the bank. On a calmer river at that time of year, the body would have sunk all the way to the bottom, would have stayed sunk for a couple of weeks, maybe longer. Putrefaction creates the build-up of internal gases which causes bodies to resurface. But putrefaction is much slower in cold temperatures. Jacobson had read somewhere or other that in really deep, cold water – one of the Great Lakes over in Canada, say – dumped or drowned bodies frequently never resurfaced.

The thought made him shiver. He wasn't sure why he'd wandered down here really. All his investigations into death started at the place of death. But this death had *already* been investigated. And Jacobson had *already* privately reviewed the investigation to his own satisfaction. Maybe it was just that he had nothing more pressing – no, nothing more *interesting* – to be getting on with. Theoretically was the word to underline, the word to emphasise. Theoretically, Robinson had said, it was possible that if Darren McGee had been taken totally by surprise, he could have been dropped into the Crow without any obvious sign of a struggle attaching to his body or elsewhere.

He looked up at the bridge. It wasn't an easy theory to get enthusiastic about. For one thing, where did the mystery assailants spring from? A vehicle of some kind was the obvious, most likely possibility. But McGee would have seen it pull up – heard it – would've had some inkling, surely, of what was afoot? Even if he hadn't managed to get away, he would have fought back, would've got hurt in the process, might even have spilled blood – his own or his attackers. Yet nothing had been found. Of course, once a body hit water, the distinction between ante-mortem and post-mortem injuries blurred. Ordinarily, as Robinson had reminded him, the evidence of bleeding on a corpse pointed clearly to injuries acquired before death. But after-death injuries to a drowned body, buffeted by rocks and currents, could also bleed, sometimes profusely. Especially – as in McGee's case – injuries to the head and face. *It's why your journalist's theory isn't completely implausible, Frank. And why the science can't rule it out one hundred per cent.*

Too bad, he thought, that no witnesses had come forward, preventing any scope for any kind of doubt. It was hardly surprising though, given the presumed time of the incident. The hotel's New Year dinner dance, which McGee's kitchen shift had been catering to, had wrapped up at three am. The guests who were staying overnight were already in their bedrooms, the others had left by taxi or by designated driver. New Year's Eve bustled in the town centre. But over here, in the Riverside area, the parties happened behind closed doors. The party goers turned up well before midnight, strictly by invitation only.

He turned to go, deciding to walk. The bus was a daft idea and a cab was just sheer laziness, the kind of habit he was trying to lose. Paul Shaw was flying a great big kite, that was all. A veritable effing zeppelin. Even if he could substantiate his claims about death threats, that would still be a very long way from proving they'd been acted on. Jacobson reminded himself what it was that he did for a living. He was *police*, CID: he wasn't a philosopher inquiring after the ultimate truth of things. If an explanation was solid – if it didn't twist the facts or cause the innocent to get banged up – then it was good enough. And good enough was all he was paid for, all he was thanked for. On the rare occasions when he *was* thanked.

Amanda Singh was based at Crowby Central, the local nick on the other side of the town centre from the Divisional building. Kerr parked in the police car park at the rear of the Divi and made his way on foot, taking a short cut through the lunchtime crowds in the shopping centre. He got there early – barely ten to two – but she didn't seem to mind, came down to the front desk herself, invited him up to her crammed, cramped office space. He'd never met her before, hadn't expected her to be a looker. Blonder than Cathy. Taller than Rachel. He tried not to lech too obviously at her legs as he followed her upstairs.

The force's Hate Crimes Unit. Aka a single office that nobody else had a use for on the first floor. Aka one Detective Sergeant – Singh – plus two uniformed PCs to cover the entire county. Aka lip service. Aka doing the minimum. Some HCUs in some other forces were *operational*. Which meant they had the human resources – and the authority – to take over any investigation where racial, religious or sexual prejudice was judged to be a prime motive. The local HCU was at the other end of the scale. Singh and her scant team were mainly desk-bound, their time overwhelmingly taken up with *monitoring*: adding the details of a case to their files if it had a hate element, keeping the statistics up to date, liaising with Victim Support. The relative status of the unit was apparent simply from the fact that it was located here and not at the Divisional building or out at County HQ.

One plod was on the phone, the other was hunched over a computer terminal. Amanda Singh squeezed in behind her desk, Kerr selected one of two spare plastic chairs. The one nearest the window. The one furthest away from her distractingly blue eyes. There was a small framed photograph hanging discreetly on the wall behind her. Amanda Singh and a man with deep-brown skin splashing in the waves.

'Goa,' she said, following the direction of his gaze, maybe gauging his reaction. 'Our honeymoon.'

'My sister went there last year, loved it apparently,' Kerr replied, wondering if he'd passed her test, wondering if it *was* a test.

He told her the details of Randeep Parmeer's troubles with thugs and anonymous telephone calls. The plod at the computer clicked his mouse, swivelled his chair in Kerr's direction.

'Not counting Mr, eh, Parmeer, we've logged forty-three reported racist nuisance calls since January county-wide,' he said. 'Up three per cent from the equivalent period last year.'

Amanda Singh nodded.

'And what gets reported is probably a fraction of the real figure. People ignore it. Or learn to live with it.'

'So this particular case,' Kerr asked, 'would you say it's worth taking seriously or not?'

Amanda Singh didn't answer straight away. She looked at what she'd written while Kerr had been talking, scribbled another line or two at the bottom of a sheet of official-issue A4. Then:

'On a scale of one to five, I'd say it merits a three at least. You've got a caller motivated enough to get hold of an ex-directory number for one thing. A caller who knows stuff about the intended victim or, possibly worse, has taken the trouble to find it out. That he's got a wife and daughters for instance. So it's probably not just your standard phone book job.'

Kerr looked puzzled. The plod at the computer explained.

'A lot of nuisance calls of this nature are pretty much random events. A few bored, spotty teenagers going through the telephone directory, picking out any foreign names they can find.'

Amanda Singh nodded a second time.

'But it's possible that what you're dealing with here is specific *targeting*. Especially given the element of persistence – three nights out of the last four.'

'So you don't think the yobbo incidents in Parmeer's restaurant are coincidental then?' Kerr asked.

'It can't be ruled out obviously. But I'm inclined to bet that it isn't. Not when he's never had any similar trouble over there in the past.'

He watched her right hand put an expensive-looking pen down on her desk. Gold. Like Randeep Parmeer's cigarette case. Like the wedding ring on her second finger, the gold bangles on her wrist. He wondered if she'd volunteered for her job or if she'd been dragooned. A white policewoman, married to a Sikh, heading up the Hate Crimes Unit. The Chief Constable, 'Dud' Bentham, had milked the appointment for every drop of progressive community relations that it was worth. But you could look at it another way – and see something totally different. Something flat-footed and patronising. Something racist with a small, unconscious *r* all of its own.

He asked her about the unit's visual suspect database.

'It's still in the development stages really. But there's a beta version available if you were thinking of trying it out.'

Visual databases were the force's new big thing. All the specialist units had been charged with trawling their records, matching files to photographs. The idea was that eventually every computer on the force's network would be able to swiftly access the mug shots of anyone who had form for every class and type of offence.

'And I can access it from the Divi?'

'Sure. No problem,' the plod at the computer screen replied. 'I'll email you the password.'

'Thanks,' Kerr said.

Amanda Singh explained the criteria the unit was using to identify racially motivated offenders.

'We're not like drugs or fraud obviously. Charges and convictions under the specific anti-discrimination laws are a rarity – so it's not as simple a matter for us as it is for them. What we're doing is wading through case files for the categories of other offences that are likely to be relevant.'

'You mean like football hooliganism, pub fights, gang brawls?'

'Exactly. We look at the original witness statements – what got said or what got chanted. Where race-hate looks to be an element, we load the visuals on to the database.'

She paused, cleared her throat. When she spoke again, Kerr thought that her voice had hardened.

'Eventually, we'll flag up every toerag who's not only mouthed it about pakis and wogs – but who's committed an offence into the bargain.'

Chapter Six

Victoria Maxwell - Vicky - didn't answer the door, stayed upstairs in her bedroom until she was sure Paul Shaw had gone. She'd wait a few more minutes to be certain, then she'd go down to the kitchen, make herself a cup of tea. He'd have hung around near the school at lunchtime, watching for her. Then driven over here. He'd probably sit in his car next, hoping he'd catch her on her way back from wherever she'd given him the slip to. It was just as well she'd phoned in sick, taken the day off, not set foot outside the door. He was persistent all right. Doorstepping was what they called it, she thought. Doorstepping was certainly what he was doing. Getting people to talk who didn't want to talk. Winning your confidence. Winning you over. He'd phoned her mobile six times so far this afternoon, had left practically the same message each time. *Call me back, Vicky. Please. There's more I need to ask you. You owe it to Darren.*

She took the photo album out of the drawer where she kept it. Underneath a dissolute tangle of tired bras, unwanted knickers, redundant sweaters and old, odd socks. Not hidden exactly. But stored with discretion. Out of the way. She sat on the edge of her bed, turning the pages. Vicky and the man of her dreams: dark, handsome Darren. The whole history of their time together was there. Or one side of it anyway. The light but not the shade. What she liked best were the photographs of Darren on his own, undiluted by the presence of others. And especially the ones where she'd caught him by surprise, where he hadn't had time to pose – he could be such a poser – for the camera. Darren rolling a fat spliff in some pub on Camden High Street, directly under the sign on the wall that declared 'drug free zone'. Darren falling off a surfboard at Newquay. Darren in the mud at Glastonbury. Darren with his fire clubs on the Ramblas. Barcelona: even now any casual reference to the city she happened to overhear or read or see could pull her up, make her heart pound. Maybe if they'd been able to stay there or if they'd travelled on, stayed out of England anyway. Everything had fallen apart when they'd come back here. *It's my country, old England*, he'd liked to say. Proudly, like it was something to boast about. Bloody cold, drab, racist England. He'd thought he'd loved it. And in return it had killed him.

She closed the album by its green cover, put it back. She promised herself to try not to look at it again today. At least she could look at it without tears welling now, which might be some kind of progress. Before she went downstairs, she went through to her mum's room, risked a look out over the garden. His car was red, she thought. Expensive. Only don't ask her what kind, what make. As far as she could tell, it wasn't there. Maybe he'd got fed up with chasing after her. For the moment anyway. After she'd made the tea, she cut a slice of cheesecake to go with it. A lot of people didn't eat when they were anxious, over-emotional. With her it was the opposite. She'd cram it in: food as a comforter. Even so she never seemed to put on the pounds. Darren used to tell her she was too thin. *Like a white ghost, girl*.

She walked through to her mum's fastidiously tidy lounge, zapped a few channels. She selected a nature programme – wanted something restful – but kept the volume muted just in case. It had been a mistake to talk to him at all. And there was nothing she could tell him anyway. Nothing that would add substance to his mad theory. Look, just get lost, she should have said to him – leave me alone. He'd caught her in a weak moment that was all, had offered himself as somebody to talk to, somebody who understood. Plus there'd been the family resemblance, a little touch of Darren about his face. That look that Darren had had too, that made you feel you were the absolute focus of his attention, that he couldn't take his eyes off you.

She ate the last of the cheesecake slice, careful not to spill crumbs on the prize sofa. A wolf running against snow. She fiddled with the zapper, brought up the subtitles: *Any change to the fragile ecology of the tundra could spell the end of the line for the wolf packs.* Raking it all over again wouldn't help anyone, least of all her. The best thing she could do now was try to move on, try to put it behind her. Darren had been gone from her, lost, in any case; had been gone from her long before New Year's Day on the Memorial Bridge. Six wolves now, dragging dead rabbits it looked like.

She put down the zapper, slurped her first mouthful of tea. He was barking up the wrong tree anyway. The police had treated Darren's death as potentially suspicious, had looked into from that angle, hadn't found anything. The main cop, Salter, had been a smarmy piece of work. But that didn't mean he hadn't done his job properly. And some of the others had been fine, sound. The female detective, the one who'd said she was married to an Indian, had said to get in touch anytime, if there was any way she could help. Maybe she should call her, ask *her* to give Paul Shaw his marching orders. She slurped more tea. Calm down, she told herself, calm down. She could deal with Shaw on her own – if she could just get herself together, just stop acting so weak, so needlessly panicked.

She switched the wolves off, paced to the window. Nothing, although that didn't mean he wasn't parked further down the street where he could watch the house without being seen. She remembered that she had an A-level class in the morning. The kind of teaching that she actually enjoyed. What she'd do next, she thought, was take a bath. A long, hot soak with plenty of scented oils. And then do some extra preparation, deliver something brilliant. The last thing she needed right now was Paul Shaw and his crazy ideas. If he phoned again, she'd answer this time, tell him straight: if he wanted to take his daft story any further then that was up to him – but he could leave her out of it.

Shaw waited thirty minutes and then gave up, drove off. The estate – the Beech Park, wasn't it? – resembled a thousand others, was easy to get lost in. He doubled-back to the shops in the centre and followed a bus out to the main road. He took the only route he knew to the Riverside Hotel, though he doubted if it was the quickest way. He pulled up at the main doors. You could drive into the car park yourself or you could wait for valet parking. He always opted for the second option when it was available. Getting out, he grabbed his laptop case from the passenger seat, proffered his car keys and a two-pound coin to the porter. The guy knew him now, smiled. He was Polish or Hungarian or something. Over here to make his fortune, the way they all were, hopeful – any day now – for his first big break. He took the lift up to his room, ordered a ciabatta melt and fresh orange juice from room service. He left his mobile switched on but otherwise planned on lying low for an interval, considering his options. He took a shower, had only just stepped out, had to wrap himself in a towel when his order arrived. He doled out another tip, dried himself, pulled on the track suit bottoms and the old T-shirt he always brought with him when he was staying in a hotel room for a while. They were more relaxing to lounge in when you were alone and it meant you could keep your street clothes smart on hangers. Appearances were important in his line of work, vital. You had to look the part if people were to believe in you. If you told them their story was worth money, you had to look like money yourself, like someone familiar with its elegant cadences, close to plentiful sources.

He poured himself some orange juice, carried the glass over to the window. He'd asked for a room with a view over the river. He hadn't mentioned the bridge but, as his luck had turned out, he could see that too. This story wasn't one of those of course, not something he'd sell on to a tabloid rag just for the cash. This one was from the heart. He'd been truthful to the police inspector about that. A hundred per cent truthful. The *Guardian* might carry it, he thought, or the *Independent*. He didn't care, they could even rewrite it, bring it out under the by-line of one of their own reporters. All that mattered were two things. Getting the story out and – following on from that – getting the police investigation re-opened.

He'd been in the belly of the beast – America – when he'd heard about his cousin, interviewing black Britons who'd ended up on death row. That had been an important story too, the reason that had kept him from the funeral. But Darren's death had played on his mind nonetheless, something hadn't smelled right about it from the first time he'd heard the news – a garbled telephone call from Aunt Tilda. He'd promised himself he'd look into it when he got back to the UK, had been as good as his word. He'd made a mistake with the copper though – he could see that now. He'd gone to him too soon. And with speculation, not hard evidence. He'd let keenness get the better of his usual professionalism. Keenness driven by personal factors. Or one personal factor anyway: the guilt he felt about Darren's life as much as about his death. He was the clever one – the success story – against whose example Darren's problems and failures had stood out all the more, had been condemned in the family all the more. He sipped the juice, studied the solid contours of the bridge. But at least the situation with the police was recoverable, wasn't fatal. Everything could change – *would* change – once he'd dug deeper. The important thing was that his instinct about Jacobson had been correct. The guy was a straight arrow, a cub scout. He would be willing to take him seriously just as soon as he had serious proof to offer.

Somewhere in the distance he heard church bells chiming. Four o'clock already. It was still sunny outside, dog walkers and joggers were taking the air along Riverside Walk. A nice area. Calm, affluent, convenient for the centre of town but not too uncomfortably close. The kind of setup guys like Darren only ever experienced from below stairs: sweeping the streets, doing deliveries, sweating in the hotel kitchens. His girlfriend – Vicky – had been a real surprise in those terms. A graduate, a teacher – middle-class or very nearly as good as. Her background was pure white nigger admittedly – the cramped, neat council house, her dad's twenty years' hard graft in the paint factory before he'd pegged it early – but she was well on her way all the same. Give her another five or six years and she'd be there. A house in the suburbs, dinner parties, gardening catalogues, renting a gîte in the long summer holidays. And Darren would become nothing more than a bad, exotic memory.

He poured out the rest of the orange juice, finished it, put the glass down on the nearest table. Reflexively, he re-did the safety on the door, turning the lock, re-attaching the chain. You learned not to take chances if you sailed close to the wind. One black man dead and another black man nosing around, asking awkward questions. It was the kind of dangerous, extreme sport you couldn't get insurance for. Not that he didn't feel safer here than elsewhere, away from the streets, the bars, the night clubs, the grubby estates. He did. In any case, he'd never so much as whispered Darren's name in the hotel even though it was the place he'd worked in. He hadn't mentioned journalism either. As far as the hotel knew, he was just the normal type of customer from out of town. Here on straightforward, unspecified, money-making business. There were people here who'd known Darren obviously. The chefs, the waiters, the laundry maids. And the ones that were white had given him a hard time according to the police evidence at the inquest. But that didn't interest him, wasn't why he'd come.

Of course Darren's co-workers had taken the piss. Why wouldn't they? Darren's illness had made him weak, different. He'd act and sound crazy. Face it, he *was* crazy. And the healthy always gang up against the sick. They'd probably called him mental as much as they'd called him coon, would have called him a mad fat bastard instead of a mad darkie – if obesity had been his secondary, transgressive category. There was one exception to that situation of course. Someone in the hotel who'd meant Darren the worst kind of harm. But the police had never got to him, hadn't even questioned him. And Shaw had steered well clear too – once he'd grasped who he was. Luckily, he'd barely spoken to him before he'd known.

He tore an end off the over-fussy sandwich, broke it into two smaller pieces. He ate the first piece but abandoned the second, wasn't as hungry, after all, as he'd thought he was. What he was – suddenly – was tired. Even the shower hadn't revived him. If the police effort had been sincere – had been anything more than shoring up the suicide theory with a bit of appropriate background – then it had been wasted inside the hotel. The important questions about Darren weren't to do with the crap job he'd taken and the low-level harassment that had gone with it. They were to do with him chasing Vicky Maxwell back to Crowby – and the real shit, the really ugly shit, which that had landed him in.

He stretched out on the bed. A couple of hours would do it, get his energy back up and running. He'd try her again obviously, keep trying. What she'd told him – although she didn't know it – was the fulcrum, the link in the chain. He needed to get her to talk to him again. And on tape this time. She'd refused the tape before. But next time he'd record her anyway, surreptitiously if he had to. He'd talk her around again sooner or later. Meantime he'd carry on with what he'd already started. Scratching, ferreting, burrowing. Appealing to consciences when he found any. Waving cash around – waving lots of cash around – when, more frequently, he didn't.

Chapter Seven

Kerr drove home after work exactly like a million others. The congestion started at the Flowers Street traffic lights and didn't stop until he turned off the bypass at the North Crowby junction. In good traffic, you could do the journey in twenty minutes. But at the peak of the rush hour, you could triple that, occasionally quadruple it. He'd phoned Randeep Parmeer earlier in the afternoon and fixed up a time for him to look at the HCU's mug shots: tomorrow, one o'clock. It felt like the only useful thing he'd done all day. Otherwise he'd caught up with his form filling, tidied his files, put in the kind of shift that left you feeling like any kind of working stiff in any kind of job anywhere: tired, vaguely disgruntled, wishing you'd won the lottery – or at least got off your arse to buy a ticket regularly, at least give yourself a chance of winning. Policing was more unpredictable than most occupations. The element of surprise was one of the reasons you stuck with it, even though the surprises were rarely less than filthy and nasty. But it wasn't unpredictable all the time. Not every day. Not every week. Not even every month.

He'd run into Jacobson on his way out of the Divisional building. Jacobson had been headed, as he frequently was, for the Brewer's Rest. Inevitably, he'd invited Kerr to join him. He'd heard himself saying no thanks, playing the family man card. In all honesty, he wouldn't have minded stopping on in town, maybe even getting plastered. But he'd promised Cathy he'd leave on time for once. And he *did* want to see the twins, that much had been true. He turned up the volume on the in-car, drummed the steering wheel through the guitar breaks: *Californication*, his favourite Chilli Peppers album, the one he played too much.

There was a queue of cars waiting at the right-hand turn that brought you on to the Bovis estate. There were queues of cars going home all over the western world, he thought, allowing for time differences. Blokes not so dissatisfied with their lives they were about to do a runner. But not delighted either. Not ecstatic. Not shouting for joy at the top of their voices. And then there were young men in third-world shanty towns watching the car ads on satellite TV channels, thinking that if they had that kind of life, a life like Kerr's, the one that bored him so easily, that he took so much for granted, then their dreams would be fulfilled, their existence would be transformed and perfected. Ending oppression was one thing. So was getting enough to eat, achieving a decent standard of living. But beyond that there was the same kind of delusion that he had himself about a lottery win. The bigger house, the better car, the permanent holidaying - and then what? Sooner or later, time would hang heavily on your hands until you'd long for a daily grind to crawl back into.

To be alive was to be dissatisfied. You faced up to the fact if you could. If you couldn't, you went mad or bad. Or you tried for the jackpot: both together.

Four streets away, Rick Cole stood on the patio of his Bovis semi and answered his ringing mobile. Cole's house had four bedrooms, one more than Kerr's. And a bigger garage. It wasn't as well located though. Cole's looked on to other houses front and back while Kerr's still had the solace of open fields at the bottom of his garden. Not that this mattered. Not that Cole knew Kerr or Kerr knew Cole.

The number-withheld caller was from the Party. Cole recognised the voice instantly but was careful not to speak the name. The venue for the meeting had been switched at the last minute – the way they frequently were.

'Cheers mate,' Cole said, memorising the new details.

The caller ended the call as abruptly as he'd started it.

Cole slid the door open and went through the kitchen and into the lounge in search of his *A to Z*. His wife, Wendy, and his daughter, England, were plonked in front of the telly: the Pingu tape that was the three-year-old's current favourite. The *A to Z* wasn't with the travel books and maps on the bookshelf, where he'd expected it to be. Eventually he tracked it down, wedged in the magazine rack between the money and sports sections of last weekend's *Sunday Times*. He flicked through the pages. The new meeting place was remote and rural. They usually were. Somewhere out past Wynarth this time. On one of the backest of the back roads.

The Bideford Arms was the name of the place. Cole smiled to himself, picturing some unsuspecting, hairy-nostrilled landlord, too busy shagging sheep to give a fuck *who* hired his upstairs room for a private meeting. Just so long as he was paid in advance and just so long as he was paid over the odds in cash.

He slung the *A to Z* on the sofa, checked the amount of shirt and cufflink emerging from under the cuffs of his suit jacket. Hugo Boss: dress to impress. You turned up smart to a Party meeting or you didn't turn up at all.

'Later, dolls,' he said, apparently satisfied.

Wendy smiled non-committally. England grinned from ear to ear.

'Daddy,' she said.

He lifted her up for a moment, stroked her curls, told her to be good.

The Wynarth Road was still busy. Fat cats heading home to their secluded country gaffs plus the teachers, social workers and allied communists chugging back in their clapped-out Skodas to Wynarth itself. *Darling, I'm home. Shall we knit some muesli or go out fund raising for al-Qaeda? Oh do let's.* He got lost twice but managed to make it to the venue on time – just after seven. He sat in his car for a moment, catching the tail-end of the news bulletin on Radio Four. There was always some handy bit of bollocks or other on there. The government giving lottery grants to homosexuals or making buggery compulsory in the army. He always found it useful to be able to drop something current into a conversation as and when necessary, demonstrate that he was well informed, serious.

The turn-out was reasonable if the car park was any guide. He recognised at least half a dozen familiar vehicles straight off, including the Stuart brothers' unmarked white van. Matthew Sutherland, the regional organiser, was ensconced in the lounge bar with the speaker. They were both on malts but Cole asked for a mineral water mixed with orange juice. He had no time for boozing anymore himself. Or pills. Although he was prepared to concede that either or both were helpful enough for the run-of-the-mill foot soldiers. The kind who might need firing up in the belly before a street operation. Personally, he preferred sobriety if he was going into action. He liked to feel alert, in control, his guard permanently *up*.

Sutherland did the introductions. Rick this is Martin. Martin this is Rick. And so on. They shook hands and Cole listened while the newcomer gave a précis of his planned talk. Martin Kesey – *Dr* Martin Kesey – looked to be somewhere around his own age. Older than twenty-five, younger than thirty. What pleasantly surprised Cole, impressed him, yes, was that the guy was big, imposing: six foot three, maybe four, and with a strong build to match. You always thought of intellectuals – even the ones on your own side – as weedy types. Poor specimens of the race. But Kesey was just the opposite. You'd trust him in a ruck. Plus his hair might even have been fair, blond, if it hadn't been neatly and recently shaved. His talk sounded like nothing special however. The latest evidence of the Home Office bending over backwards to let the gyppos from the old Eastern Bloc in. As if *that* was news.

They finished their drinks and Sutherland led the way to the hired room. Cole deferred to Kesey, followed upstairs as the last of the three. The content wasn't the point of course. What mattered was that a punter like Kesey was prepared to be here, was prepared to stand up and be counted. Carefully worded academic papers were one thing, addressing a meeting under Party auspices was another game of soldiers altogether. He enjoyed the creak of his shoes on the crooked, wooden stairs. The Bideford was an old coaching gaff apparently. Rundown maybe. But old and English just the same. The room was full when they reached it. Forty or more. Standing room only. The Stuarts, Phil and John, had set up a small table just inside the door. Phil sat behind it, counting the money they'd taken as a contribution for room hire. John stood behind Phil. A looming, solid presence.

The threesome made their way to the front where there was a larger table with three chairs, three tumblers and a single jug of tap water. There were no visible signs in the room of who was meeting there. No posters, no regalia. Phil Stuart had literature for sale of course. But none of it was on open display, was kept instead inside the thick cardboard box which he'd stashed by his feet. As the local node point, Cole had to open the meeting. As always he kept it short and sweet, didn't bother to stand up. Public speaking still made him nervous, though nothing like it had done at first. The leakage that he still hadn't learned to stem – that he still probably wasn't aware of – was all in his right leg, the knee of which bounced uncontrollably up and down under the table while he was talking. It was a relief when he could pass on to the main speakers, Kesey then Sutherland.

Kesey's talk was more impressive than Cole had anticipated. As Cole had guessed, there weren't many new facts, there wasn't much new analysis. But Kesey turned out to be the kind of confident, natural speaker Cole knew he could never be. And it was more than that, more than just his delivery. Somehow Kesey *reaffirmed* their beliefs, reminded them that they were right, that they, not their enemies, were the ones who understood the world correctly. Cole had no jealousy though. Each to their own: that was what a party - a *movement* - was all about. Bringing what you had to the table. Sharing it for the greater good.

Matthew Sutherland wound things up, gave an update on the general situation. Even here, where as far as they could possibly tell, everyone in the room was committed, loyal, sound, he chose his words carefully. You had to understand the code, had to be able to read between the lines to get the full meaning. Recruitment was steady in the initial target areas, he told them. The Midlands, the North-West, London. They weren't national yet, mightn't be national for some time. But that wasn't the point. *This* party wanted mainstream support - but not at completely any price, not by recruiting casual sympathisers with no political understanding (*laughter*). That was the road the BNP and even the National Front had taken - and they were welcome to it (*more laughter*). *This* party's job was at the cutting edge, would stay at the cutting edge, however big their organisation grew. And that meant quality in recruitment, not quantity. Lads - like themselves - who knew what they were about and *why* they were about it. Lads with a track record, lads who'd *proved* themselves.

The meeting broke up with proper discipline: no more than three or four vehicles to leave at a time. Even though the roads were under-policed out this way, it didn't do to take chances, advertise your presence unnecessarily. Cole and the Stuart brothers were the very last to leave. The three of them sat in the white van. Phil in the driver's seat, Big John and Cole sharing the passenger side unequally between them.

'Parker didn't show then,' Cole said.

He wanted to avoid the issue for a minute or two longer; the reason why they were still here, why all three of them had automatically lingered on to the end. It had been a good meeting. No, it had been a great meeting. He wasn't ready for problems, for reality, yet.

'Probably worried about getting back for his shift,' Big John commented.

Cole nodded.

'Yeah, course. That must be a downside in his line of work.'

He was trying to keep the unnecessary conversation going. But both of them ignored him this time.

'It was a fuck up, Rick,' Phil said quietly.

Cole stared straight ahead, feeling their eyes boring into him.

'What? Doing a nigger and getting away with it? That was a fuck up?'

'And there was no point to it. Not a political point anyway,' Phil persisted.

Cole saw red but knew there was nothing physical to be done. Not with John Stuart stationed between them, looking out for his brother.

The personal is political: the phrase leapt into his brain from Christ knows where. But he didn't utter it, didn't say anything. A minute passed slowly, silently. Of the three of them, it was Big John, unexpectedly, who finally got there.

'The thing is this, Rick. What the eff do we do now?'

Chapter Eight

Friday April 22nd

Kenneth Grant poured himself a second cup of tea and spread some butter on his last remaining slice of toast. The radio was quiet in the background – something by Sibelius – and the house was quiet in the background behind that. His wife was still asleep, would sleep on for another hour or so. But he liked to be up early, even though there was no practical need any longer, now he'd been retired these several years. The peace of early mornings had been a life-long pleasure for him. He'd always got up with his dad first thing when he'd been a kid. Ahead of his mother, ahead of his brothers and sisters. It had been a secret thing, him and Dad together, breakfasting while the rest of the world was asleep. When he was old enough, he'd mash the tea, fill the flask his dad carried to work in his haversack. He'd been a runner at university – long-distance – had sweated along the Cam every morning while the ex-public-school boys were still dreaming and snoring, still sleeping off last night's booze. The only time in his life he'd broken the habit, he often realised, was in the honeymoon years of his marriage. When there had always been a better reason to stay in bed than to get out of it. Later, when his own kids had arrived, and his job had turned large and bulky with the demands that promotions brought, early mornings had been his refuge – the sanity hour of peace and tranquillity.

He cleared the dishes from the table when he'd finished, stacked them by the sink. He wouldn't wash up now of course. Too noisy. He'd leave it till he got back, boil the kettle then too, take her up her early cup of tea. It was Friday, he realised, their morning for driving over to the supermarket in advance of the weekend crowds. He switched off the radio, found his jacket and the lead in the hall. Cygnus – *cyggy*, it was a kind of weak joke about her fear of swans and their broad, flapping wings – was crouched on the door mat, waiting. The dog was his wife's idea really. A good-natured, mongrelised terrier she'd rescued from the doggy gas chamber. She'd known, of course, that he'd insist on training it properly, that he would end up doing the lion's share of the walking and exercising.

They took the route they always did. Riverside Crescent, second left into Riverside Avenue and – *voilà* – Riverside Walk. He crossed the road near the floral clock, headed for the nearest footbridge into the Memorial Park. Cyggy strained at the leash when they set foot on the bridge. She always did at that point, knowing that once they were over, he'd let her off, set her free. But not like this. Not barking for all she was worth. Not this badly behaved. Afterwards, he could never understand what primeval instinct had kicked in, caused him to unleash her. But it had, but he did.

The approach to the footbridge was railed off on either side, the river bank curving sharply down to the water's edge. For a long time, it seemed, Cyggy would bound off to the right, flinging herself uselessly against the railings. Then run back, howling for him to follow. Then repeat the game. Finally he saw it, maybe five feet out, the current sweeping it closer. He fumbled in his pocket for the mobile phone that his wife insisted he always carry now that he was no longer a young man who might never need help, never need to summon assistance. It only looked like a bundle of old clothes to start with, billowed, air-filled.

Then you took in the shape, made out the way that the head hung down, the way that the legs dangled lifelessly underneath the brown water.

Exactly an hour later, Jacobson pulled up behind Peter Robinson's beat-up Volkswagen. Maybe the new job – if he got it – would lead to a new car. Or maybe, like Jacobson, Robinson had as much interest in cars as in eating worms. It was a coincidence, he'd thought sleepily, driving over; a body in the river only a day or so after the wild story Paul Shaw had tried to sell him in the pub. A body was all he'd been told first off. Then somewhere in the vicinity of Flowers Street, his mobile had rang again: Sergeant Ince in the control room. *We've a bit more detail for you now, guv. Male, twenties, IC4.* Jacobson had accelerated when he should have braked, had nearly caused a minor collision. Strictly speaking, IC4 denoted Afro-Caribbean. But – universally – coppers used it to indicate any kind of black.

The scene was already in some kind of order. Police tape along the outer cordon, a hastily erected tent-like tarpaulin down on the banking, shielding the body from casual gaze. Robinson and Webster were waiting for him in front of the railings. Webster was the chief SOCO, aka the Crime Scene Manager in the latest official nuspeak. Just along from them, a couple of council workmen were removing four of the metal spurs so that access could be gained through the railings rather than over them.

'Any ID on the body?' Jacobson asked.

Robinson and Webster shook their heads.

'Nothing so far,' Webster said, thinking it was an odd, first question.

He told Jacobson the story that Jacobson usually wanted to hear: when the control room had logged the call from the member of the public, when the body had been confirmed as dead, when— but Jacobson, he realised, was barely listening.

The workmen stepped back. The proverbial spear-carriers, two pieces of railing each.

Jacobson eased himself through the gap, might have sprinted down to the tarpaulin if the banking had been less steep. All the time he was telling himself not to be a fool, not to appear foolish. It was a coincidence right enough. But that was all it was, surely? A grim, unpleasant coincidence. Somehow he found the self-control to wait until the SOCO under the tarpaulin had completed filming the initial video record. Then he stepped forward, bent down, saw that it wasn't.

Chapter Nine

Webster, to put it mildly, was reluctant. He'd need virtually his entire team, he told Jacobson, when Jacobson clambered back up on to Riverside Walk and made his request: an immediate sweep search of the Memorial Bridge and the two footbridges. He'd have to take them away from other work, pull them off other cases. Robinson sided with Jacobson (while Merchant's ashes fulminated in their casket). Maybe it would be a waste of time, maybe Jacobson was making something out of nothing. But if one of the bridges *was* a crime scene, Robinson argued, any evidence which was still up there could be deteriorating, suffering contamination, minute by minute.

'Look just do it, old son,' Jacobson said impatiently. 'I'll sign a personal statement to the effect that Frank Jacobson is one hundred and ten per cent to blame for any abuse of resources.'

'I'll hold you to that, Frank,' Webster replied glumly.

They watched him walking back to the scene of crime van, mobile in hand, setting things in motion.

'So the MO – if it *is* an MO – is the same as for his cousin?' Jacobson asked.

'It's possible, yes,' Robinson answered, bleary-eyed.

The medical contingent had carried Merchant's wake on into the late afternoon apparently. And the hard-core – Robinson *sans* wife included – had reconvened for a further, extended session in the evening.

'Although to be fair to Jim Webster,' he continued, 'you probably *are* jumping the gun. Before the autopsy and the lab tests, we can't even be sure that drowning is the most likely cause of death. Or where – or how – the body entered the water.'

Jacobson wasn't bright-eyed himself. Not beer or malt whisky for once. He'd exited the Brewer's Rest after a modest two pints. But he'd stayed up late reading. Or re-reading to be precise. Schopenhauer: *The World as Will and Idea*. If philosophy was just a kind of intellectual football match, as some critics said it was, then the gloomy old German was currently ahead of Jacobson FC by a ten-goal margin.

'But the scenario's not impossible?'

'Well very little's impossible at this stage, Frank. Whether the injuries are ante-mortem or post or a bit of both. Whether there are other factors involved – drugs, alcohol. It could just be misadventure of some kind.'

Jacobson ignored the mundane options for the moment.

'He hit the water at much the same time of night, didn't he?'

Robinson glanced at his clipboard.

'Actually no. Probably an hour or so earlier. The old boy with the dog dialled 999 at ten past seven. I took the readings at seven forty-two – more or less as soon as the body was on shore – so I'd put the wide estimate as sometime between midnight and two am.'

He explained the science in straightforward terms (Merchant's casket shook mightily on its shelf). A body immersed in water cools about twice as fast as it does out of it. Roughly 5° Fahrenheit per hour as a rule of thumb. But when he'd first measured the corpse's temperature, it still hadn't dropped completely to the temperature of the river. A process which at this time of year typically took around five to six hours.

Jacobson turned his head and scanned the River Crow.

An army of swans this time, massing along the banks. Seeming to be curious at the commotion. But of course, not really. Nothing happening in their heads but feeding.

He called himself an empiricist, hated his hunches, tried to ignore them as much as listen to them. But it was only Wednesday when Paul Shaw had buttonholed him about the drowning of his cousin. And now, two days later, Paul Shaw himself was wet and dead in an identical fashion. No obvious signs of a struggle. No obvious signs of force. You didn't have to abandon reason, didn't need to subscribe to the *Fortean Times*, to think that the circumstances merited sticking a team of SOCOs in the vicinity – and issuing all of them with fine-tooth combs.

Chapter Ten

Robinson drove off, promising to schedule the post-mortem for later in the day. Jacobson used his mobile to get things moving and then drove off himself. He left DC Barber at the scene in the meantime. Barber had been the duty CID who'd answered the control room's original call-out. For which small mercy Jacobson gave his usual agnostic thanks. Barber was a murder squad regular, had prevented any forensic idiocies when the body was being fished out.

DS Kerr and DC Mick Hume were waiting outside his fifth-floor office when he got back to the Divisional building. He unlocked the door and they followed him in. The Town Hall clock chimed through his window. Nine am. He brought them up to speed and despatched them to join Barber. When they'd gone, he slid his illicit kettle out of the bottom drawer of his filing cabinet. It had just enough scaly water in the bottom to yield a cupful. He stuck it on and lit up an equally illicit B & H, did nothing but think for five minutes.

His conversation with Shaw justified the sweep search. But at this stage that was probably all it justified. Deploying Kerr and Hume, bringing them off whatever else they were currently working on, was a different matter. The best thing would be to keep Greg Salter in the dark for as long as possible. Come to think of it, that would always be the best thing. Kerr and Hume had looked pleased enough anyway. If you had the aptitude for it – and both of them did – murder squad work got into your bones, left you bored, flat, between cases. It wasn't a nice way to look at the world. But nice people made lousy detectives.

He needed to know who Paul Shaw *was*, beyond his name and the fact that he was from London, a shit hole with eight million inhabitants at the last count. He finished his last, unappetising mouthful of black instant coffee and stubbed out his cigarette on the sole of his shoe. He checked that the fag end had burnt out properly then transferred it to the re-sealable evidence bag he kept for the purpose. Henry Pelling over at the *Argus* probably knew enough about Shaw's background to make him the quickest information source. Unfortunately, Pelling would also gladly fill the lunchtime edition with the story – and string it out to the nationals too if he could get them interested.

He took a deep breath, rang Pelling's office number.

'I'm sorry. He's not at his desk.'

The voice was young, female, don't-bother-me bored.

Jacobson said who he was, gave the police identification code. Improvising, he told her it wasn't Pelling he needed to reach anyway. It was one of his associates, a freelancer just up from London—

'Oh, you mean Paul – Paul Shaw?'

The voice was less asleep suddenly, very nearly lively.

'That's right. Paul Shaw.'

Uselessly, she offered him Shaw's mobile number. Jacobson scribbled it down anyway. He asked her if she knew where Shaw was staying in Crowby, careful to stick to the present tense. Yes she did, she told him quickly, almost as if it was a matter of pride. The Riverside Hotel. Somehow the news didn't entirely surprise him. He asked her for her name and made a note of that too.

'Shall I let Henry know you called?'

'No. Don't do that, eh, Jane. No need. But thanks anyway.'

Jacobson put his phone down, grabbed his coat from his

precarious coat-rack, a low-grade hunch whispering in his ear. It had been sunny out before. But April was still the cruellest month, no time to take chances with the weather.

The desk clerk at the Riverside – no, update that, desk *manager* – was helpful but inexperienced, new. The good thing about his lack of experience was that he clearly had bog all idea what the police were entitled to do and what they weren't entitled to do. He tried Shaw's room number, obviously didn't get an answer, offered to show Jacobson the way before Jacobson had even asked.

They took the fast, comfortable lift. The cleaners were out in force along the corridor when they stepped out. Jacobson and the clerk negotiated an obstacle race of vacuum cleaners, piles of white towels, sacks of rubbish. There were cleaners in 313 and in 314 but the Goddess of Police Investigations had fixed it so that they hadn't got to room 315 yet. The clerk swiped his pass key, waited for the green light, pushed the door open.

Jacobson stepped in to chaos. Sheets and mattress on the floor, drawers pulled out, the wardrobe doors hanging open, clothes everywhere. He stepped back out, clicked the door shut behind him. Webster would really love him now, he thought. But it couldn't be helped. He needed another SOCO – ideally he needed another three or four – and he needed them five minutes ago. He also needed a uniformed patrol officer to keep the room secure until the SOCOs could get here. He took out his mobile and made the necessary calls. The clerk – Chris Finney, according to his name badge – stood watching agape. Jacobson explained to him what was about to happen and that Jacobson himself would have to stay put until other police arrived. Finney, still helpful, still not seeing the bigger picture, got out his pager: *Maybe Jacobson would like a cup of tea or coffee while he waited?*

The plod arrived ten minutes later. But needn't have bothered really – since two of Webster's SOCOs showed up just after; glad, probably, to be free of bridge-scrubbing duties. Jacobson and Finney went back downstairs and ran into to the Riverside Hotel's real manager, a forty-something blonde by the name of Alison Taylor who explained superfluously that she'd had a doctor's appointment, had only just come on duty. She'd evidently seen more episodes of *The Bill* than Finney had, mentioned something about a warrant. Jacobson told her that he didn't need one: there had been a dead body in the Crow – it was possible that the body was Paul Shaw's – Section 17 of the Powers of Search covered everything that he needed to do immediately.

The concept of a dead guest swiftly changed her attitude. The more helpful she was, she was probably thinking, the sooner the police would *go*. Jacobson asked to see whatever records the hotel's booking system contained about Shaw. She told him the computer in her private office would be quicker, seized the opportunity to get him away from the reception desk. She even encouraged him to read the screen while she printed out the details: Shaw's check-in date, his London address, his car make and registration, his American Express Platinum card number. Jacobson noticed that Shaw had signed in on the 14th, had been in Crowby just over a week. He asked her if she'd encountered him personally.

'No, I don't think so. But that's not unusual. Quite often I don't deal directly with a guest unless there's a problem of some kind.'

'And there wasn't in this case?'

'Not as far as I'm aware.'

Jacobson told her he might need to speak to the staff who'd been on duty the day before, especially last night.

She nodded, said she'd print out the roster for him.

'I take it you use security cameras here?'

Another nod.

'Twenty-four hour surveillance. All the entrances and exits, car parking, the reception area.'

'But nothing above ground level?'

Alison Taylor tried a smile that would have charmed some.

'This is the *Riverside*, Chief Inspector. We don't snoop on our guests.'

'I'm pleased to hear it,' Jacobson said unmoved, already headed for the door.

He took the fast lift up to the third floor again. He gave the plod Paul Shaw's car details and sent him down to the garage level:

'Locate the car if it's there, old son. If not, let me know *and* let the control room know - if it's not here, we need an alert out on it.'

He stuck his head into room 315. The SOCOs were doing what they could but Jacobson knew he was asking them for the next to impossible. A hotel room was living history: skin, fibres, prints, latents and general detritus deposited by guest after guest - all of it persisting and accumulating for weeks, months, even for years. Plus Jacobson didn't know what it was he was looking for. Just that later - maybe - something they found now could turn out to be useful, significant, even crucial. He asked them what was in Shaw's belongings at any rate. Another way that hotel rooms told stories was from the artefacts left lying around them: restaurant bills, taxi receipts, cinema tickets, night club flyers, scribbled names and addresses on headed hotel stationery.

The nearest SOCO, dusting under a modish bedside lamp, looked up.

'Nothing actually, Mr Jacobson. Absolutely sod all.'

'Nothing?'

'Well, there's all this expensive clobber in here. And there's a toothbrush and shaving gear in the bathroom. But otherwise the room looks like it's been deliberately cleaned out. Nothing that says where he's been, who he's seen. No ID either.'

'And no laptop computer?'

Both SOCOs shook their heads.

The second SOCO spoke up.

'There's a spare battery and a power cable in the bottom

of the wardrobe. But that's it, I'm afraid.'

Jacobson paced cautiously into the room and across to the window, careful not to touch anything, not to stray from the SOCOs' stepping boards. There was a clear view of the Memorial Bridge, currently closed to traffic at his request. His mobile rang: the uniformed patrol officer down in the car park, telling him that Paul Shaw's red Lexus wasn't on the premises. He'd spoken to a porter who'd seen it parked there yesterday afternoon. But the porter had clocked off at six, had said they'd really need to speak to the night staff. Jacobson made a snap decision. The lad seemed bright enough for a plod. He told him to stay with it, to find out exactly how the hotel's car parking system operated and who precisely the relevant night staff were.

'No sign of a forced entry, then?' he asked without turning around.

It was more or less a rhetorical question.

'Doesn't look like it,' the first SOCO answered. 'The door's not been tampered with. Nor the window. Although that's hardly a very likely route anyway – on the third floor with no balconies or ledges.'

Jacobson frowned, muttered audibly. *Shit*. The SOCOs exchanged glances behind his back. Jacobson was widely respected in the force. But he was also known to be unpredictable, unfathomable, best filed under Handle With Caution. *Shit*, he muttered again. He'd just remembered something. No, he'd just remembered that he couldn't remember something.

Chapter Eleven

Jacobson wandered out into the hotel gardens, sent a nervous squirrel careering up the trunk of a monkey-puzzle tree. He gawped at the flowers, stared at the goldfish pond, kicked at the harmless gravel. But none of it helped, none of it made the slightest difference. It was shit all right. But there it was. Inside his mind, he could *see* the single sheet of paper sitting on the pub table between himself and Paul Shaw. Yet he couldn't see – couldn't recall – a single one of the four names Shaw had typed out. All he could do was carry on. He phoned Kerr. Kerr, Barber and Hume were door-to-door along Riverside Walk, looking for someone who'd noticed something – anything – unusual in the early hours. So far they'd drawn a blank, Kerr told him. He found DC Emma Smith's number, dialled it, pulled her away from the nine separate forms she had to complete to process a straightforward charge of attempted burglary. He gave her Paul Shaw's details, told her to do the usual background trawl, locate whatever other electronic traces he'd left behind.

'A photograph would be handy as well, lass,' he added finally.

For one thing, without a photograph, the only copper who could reliably scan through the Riverside's CCTV footage was himself. But he could worry about that later. Right now – and regardless of what found its way into the

Argus – he still had Henry Pelling to deal with. Pelling might have some idea of how Shaw had spent his week in Crowby: where he'd gone, who he'd spoken to. He bit the bullet, tried Pelling's office extension again. Pelling was there this time.

'Frank, the very gent. Word has it there's been a drowning incident. Word also has it that your good self's involved from a murder squad point of view.'

Every hour, the tea boy and/or tea girl at the *Argus* crime desk had the job of phoning the Divisional building. And every hour the tea boy and/or tea girl in the Divi control room read out a carefully edited list of newly reported incidents. Pelling would know by now that there'd been a body fished out of the water. But probably, at the moment, that would be all he knew.

'Stow the crap, Henry. As it happens, you can probably help me out on this one,' Jacobson said, emphasising both pronouns.

He looked at his watch, it was near enough ten thirty already.

'I'll be in the Harvester at eleven. See you there.'

He ended the call before Pelling had the chance to go through the pretence of checking his appointments.

Rick Cole dumped the new boiler at the top of the landing for now and walked through to the bare room that would be somebody's front bedroom when the renovation was complete. He sensed a rim of sweat under his shirt from the exertion. Maybe he should've called on one of his cash-in-hand contacts to help him with the heavy lifting after all. But he preferred to work alone whenever he could. He found his flask where he'd left it, poured himself a cuppa and sat down near the window, resting his back against the neatly re-plastered wall. He only ever drank black tea, hated even the smell of milk near a cup, something fetid in it, something hinting at fleshy decay.

He hadn't chosen to be a plumber any more than he'd

chosen to live under the tyranny of the New World Order. It was the job he'd fallen into after various other plans, schemes and dreams had failed to materialise. But it suited him well enough. The money was good, he always had more offers of work than he needed and – most of all – he was his own boss. He worked as much or as little as he liked, chose *who* he worked for. The Rushtons, *père et fils*, were a case in point. They were smarmy bastards by necessity – they sold houses for a living after all – but they paid on time, never quibbled about using decent materials, and they were *white* – English through and through – when more and more developers were anything and everything but.

He turned his radio down to a whisper. Crowby FM – music for dead people. Or worse than that: music for *deaf,* dead people. It was the kind of station where they'd play Queen or Celine Dion – any of that middle-aged crap – without even blushing. Normally he'd tune to Radio Four or Five Live; anything with news, information, knowledge – even though you had to dig deep for the buried truth, cut through what Kesey had called the layers of ideology. It had a nice turn to it that had, he thought. Layers. But today wasn't completely normal. Obviously it wasn't. And he needed to know what kind of coverage there might be locally.

Nothing so far anyway. He blew across the surface of his tea before he took a sip. There was no more than another day's work in this gaff, he thought. Another day and a half tops. Clive Rushton, the son, had mentioned another couple of properties in the area though. *They should be coming onstream soon, Rick,* Rushty had said, misusing the world's greatest language as per usual. He'd see how much there was still to do by mid-afternoon, he decided, then maybe fit in the repair job he'd promised around the corner in Claremont Road. Cole still found it weird to think of Longtown as an up-and-coming area – or parts of it anyway. Gentrification, they called it, yuppification. The landlords turfing the students and druggies out of the bedsits and selling up to firms like the Rushtons. You only kept the shell in some gaffs, stripped everything inside. Then you hiked up the price to some IT geek or other who'd pay through the nose for a designer kitchen and a slap of white paint.

He checked his mobile. Still no daft calls or messages, thank fuck. All they had to do was sit tight for a while, he'd told them. Sit tight and keep it shut. No panicking. Nothing that wasn't their normal routine. There might be a bit more grief this time obviously. Even the thickos in blue might see *two* as a little bit more than a total coincidence. Especially when there were blood ties, family connections. He wasn't really worried about the Stuarts of course. Phil huffed and puffed a bit but both of them were a hundred per cent sound, a hundred per cent reliable. No, if there was going to be any kind of problem, it was going to be with Wayne Parker. They'd had to involve him a lot more this time and you could tell he wasn't happy about it, had been virtually crapping himself. Cole had tried to motivate him, rally him, remind him that taking risks wasn't something to run away from. Far from it. Coping with danger was key, central. You could sit at home - watching the lies on the telly, believing what you were told, sleepwalking through life - or you could do something, stand up for yourself. A warrior needed to fight, only advanced himself by taking action. To be in the vanguard took bollocks, courage. It wasn't meant for weaklings, for the useless, slavish herd. You were either part of the problem or you were part of the solution. *Your choice*, *Wayne*, he'd told him, *show you're committed or fuck off*.

He sipped his tea again. Still, Parker had done all right on the night. Just about. Maybe he'd call him later, make an exception, try and keep him geed up, steadfast. There was nothing else to worry about as far as he could see. Even if it went to suspicions, interviews, aggravation, there was still the small matter of proof and evidence. That was the beauty of the System, the built-in weaknesses it practically begged you to exploit. The way they stuck to their rules, didn't have a clue how to use their strength, their power. A *real* police force wouldn't muck about. They'd knock heads together, shove a few relevant fuckers up against the nearest wall, *have done*.

Chapter Twelve

'But the way Dickens thought about it, Vicky. There's folk today still think the same selfish way, don't they? Think we should sort out our own problems, help our own people, before we start worrying about others.'

Vicky Maxwell nodded encouragingly.

'That's why history's important, Barry. The past sheds light on modern times too, holds a mirror up to *us* as well.'

Barry Morton was definitely one of the brightest in the group, her A-Level British and Empire History class. He had several conditional offers from good, pukka universities, always grasped the point straight away. Carol Gray, who definitely wasn't, stirred herself in the back row.

'I think Dickens was a slimeball, Vicky, Thomas Carlyle too. What Governor Eyre done was wrong. Even by the standards of the day.'

What Eyre *did*, she thought, but couldn't find it in her heart to correct her *again*.

She kept the discussion going, throwing in loaded questions, subtly directing. The real slimeball had been John Edward Eyre of course. The worst kind of nineteenth-century imperialist. He'd suppressed the 1865 Jamaican uprising – the topic of her lesson – with a brutality that had shocked even mid-Victorian public opinion. Although not all of it. Charles Dickens had defended him. And so had Carlyle and John Ruskin. Parliament had sacked him from his post but it had been left to pinkos and do-gooders like J.S. Mill to demand, unsuccessfully, that Eyre stand trial for murder.

She glanced above their heads, suddenly noticed the jerky big hand on the ugly wall clock. There was barely enough time left to wind up. The session had gone as well as she'd hoped though. She'd held them engrossed, had been engrossed herself too. She asked Barry Morton to read the summary from the set text, found her mind spinning back reluctantly to the present.

She wondered if she'd finally heard the last from Paul Shaw. He hadn't phoned back again last night, hadn't troubled her so far today. Maybe he'd lost interest, even found a better, more promising story to investigate somewhere else.

The stakes were high on both sides. But it was the former slaves who paid the highest price. Four hundred of them had been hanged with dubious legality and no respite had been gained to the injustices of land-exclusion and oppressive taxation.

Barry was engaging, confident. You hoped, sensed, that life would turn out well for him. But you could never be sure. He had a good, clear voice, was nothing like as diffident about reading aloud – about performing in public – as she'd been when she'd been his age. When she'd been about to leave Crowby far behind, about to start everything over.

George William Gordon wrote to Queen Victoria on behalf of the black population. But the mother of the empire's reply commended to her children only the virtues of "hard work and industry".

The period bell dinned loudly and bitterly in her ears. Thanks Barry. Thanks all of you. Well done. And don't forget your essay plans are due in on Monday.

The Harvester was as bland a pub as you'd expect to be perched on the edge of the Waitrose complex. The hacks at the *Argus* detested it. But it was the nearest viable daytime watering hole to their equally bland and equally detested office premises overlooking the Toyota dealership. Henry Pelling must have been the first customer of the day, had already ensconced himself in a corner with his trademark pint of Guinness. Jacobson, by contrast, and contrary to rumour, rarely drank alcohol before midday. He ordered a double-shot expresso - the Harvester possessed a decent Gaggia, he'd give it that much - and walked over to Pelling's table. He waited until the waitress had brought him his coffee and departed again before he got down to business. Point one: the body fetched out of the Crow still needed to be formally identified but - informally - it was Paul Shaw, the black freelance journalist from London. Point two: Jacobson was treating the death as suspicious until he could establish otherwise.

Pelling absorbed the news in silence. But he needed three deep, swift mouthfuls before he was capable of speaking. And even then all he said was *Jesus*.

Jacobson told him how Shaw had tried to sell him his theory about the death of his cousin, Darren McGee.

Pelling took another mouthful. Then:

'Yes. I know his idea about McGee, the whole of the *Argus* does, I expect.'

'So he came to you as the local man, looking for pointers?'

'That's it exactly, Frank. Phoned me up last week. Thursday, I think. Invited me for dinner at the Riverside. On him. I think I was a bit of a disappointment though - I don't know a thing more about the case than came out at the inquest. He's called in to our offices a couple of times since then, of course - had a look at our back files, etcetera.'

'He didn't strike me as a nutter,' Jacobson said.

Pelling read the subtext adeptly.

'I don't think he was. The story was wild. But looked at from his point of view, the stuff he liked to cover, it probably seemed worth checking out at least.'

'He was some kind of high-flyer then?'

'He was certainly that all right. The *Sunday Times*, Channel Four, the Beeb – he's sold stuff to all of them at one time or another. *This* story will be big too once it gets out. The big boys always take an interest in one of their own.'

Jacobson reminded him that the meeting was off the record. All that was official so far was that another dead body had washed up in the Crow:

'Not much of even a local headline in that, surely, old son?'

There were three or four every year typically. Accidents and drunkenness, in Jacobson's experience, more than suicide or any kind of foul play.

Pelling feigned offence.

'I'll play it by the book, Frank. But once the wires start carrying the public fact that a well-known investigative journo's been washed up dead in Crowby, there'll be national interest whether you want it or not. If you offered me ten K and ten nights with ten different hookers, I couldn't put a stop to it.'

'You could leave the Darren McGee angle out though?'

'*I* could leave it out – but Fleet Street will only stuff it back in again. And quickly.'

Jacobson tried a mouthful of coffee. Not bad. Not bad at all. He could live without the big time media crawling around the case – if there *was* a case. But it was something to worry about later. Not right now.

'But you don't see anything in it yourself?'

Pelling grinned, shook his head.

'No, I don't. I'm sure you'd prefer it if DCS Salter had made an arse of the investigation. But as far as I know he didn't. Plus the inquest looked thorough enough to me – and I've seen a few, believe me.'

Mostly from the nearest public bar, Jacobson thought. But kept it to himself.

'Shaw actually showed me a list of names – the punters who were supposed to have done the killing.'

Pelling looked genuinely surprised.

'The first I've heard of it, Frank. He played that one close to his chest anyway. I don't expect you're about to share this intelligence with the local press?'

'Not at this stage, old son,' Jacobson bluffed, giving the answer he would have given in any case. He asked Pelling if he had any idea *how* Shaw had set about working on his story.

'Well, checking the inquest materials would have taken up a fair bit of his time—'

Jacobson had been about to take another sip. But now he left the cup exactly where it was, only kept some of the irritation out of his voice.

'Come on, Henry. You know what I mean.'

Pelling shrugged.

'I remember him saying that the police had wasted too much effort at the Riverside Hotel. I sort of got the impression that he intended to concentrate his energies elsewhere – but he didn't go into any details. That's about as much as I know. Sorry.'

Jacobson looked doubtful.

'Honest to God, Frank,' Pellling tried again. 'I didn't really take that much of an interest – I wish I had now, obviously. Plus this is a London-based journalist we're talking about here. A big fish. If he *was* on to something, he wouldn't have been about to share it with the Crowby minnows – now would he?'

Pelling took another mouthful of beer, wiped an inch of Guinness foam off his top lip afterwards.

'I'll ask around the office though. Straight up. It's always possible one of my esteemed colleagues managed to glean something more useful.'

'Thanks, old son, I'd appreciate it,' Jacobson said, slightly pacified. 'Incidentally, who's the female with the unfriendly telephone manner?'

‘Oh you mean young Jane? Jane Spencer – one of the graduate trainees they keep sending to try us with these days. A bright enough lass but a bit of a surly cow with it. Especially if you’re an overweight and over-fifty local press hack.’

Jacobson actually sipped his coffee this time – and upgraded his earlier hunch a level or two, thinking that Paul Shaw had failed to qualify under either undesirable category.

The lunch break at last. Vicky felt almost calm, almost normal. She decided it was time – high time – to get her life back in gear. Starting right now. She’d promised Susan Dunsfield, the head of the history department, that she’d join her and a couple of other teachers who were planning on a Friday lunchtime drink and a bar meal. But now she had a better idea. She’d drive into town, investigate some of the estate agents who specialised in rented accommodation. Eight months was more than long enough to be getting under her mum’s feet. And for her mum to be getting under *her* feet.

It was a fifteen-minute drive from the Simon De Montfort Comprehensive into the town centre. Vicky found a parking space for her six-year-old Clio on the top level of the NCP multistorey and took the lift down to the pedestrianised square. It was another sunny day and warmer than the day before. She crossed the square in the direction of the High Street. Darren, when he was well, liked to say that you made your own reality, made yourself happy or sad, brave or frightened. He was full of that kind of stuff really. Homespun wisdom, bits and bobs of New Age gobbledegook he’d pick up here, there and anywhere. But it was true to an extent, she thought. She could carry on being the victim of everything that happened to her – or she could choose herself another role, write herself another script.

She called in on three agents, ended up with four

appointments to view properties over the weekend. One tonight, the rest tomorrow. The guy in the last place had even tried his luck, invited her out for a drink. She'd said no. But the idea had intrigued her, had made her laugh, smile. Maybe she could get the hang of being ordinary, everyday, get the habit of it back. There was nothing written on her face that said, *My boyfriend was a schizophrenic who nearly killed me.* She'd thought she'd never last the first term out at De Montfort for instance. And now Susan Dunsfield was talking about her staying on – about converting her temporary appointment, under the graduate teacher programme, into a permanent one. None of it was the kind of life she'd seen for herself when she'd been with Darren. A schoolteacher in a provincial town. Worse, a schoolteacher in the school where she'd been a pupil herself. Renting a little flat. Probably buying one of her own later on, as another one of the agents had just suggested. Start down that road, girl, she thought, and even marriage couldn't be excluded. Marriage and kids and weekends shopping at Homebase. But their kind of life – his kind of life – hadn't remotely worked out. Least of all for him.

She was halfway along the High Street. She wondered if she had time to grab a proper lunch in Zola's Brasserie, just around the corner in Holt's Way, realised she definitely hadn't. She'd grab a sandwich from somewhere on the way back to her car instead, eat it in the staff room with a hurried cup of tea. She couldn't forget Darren, wouldn't forget him. But she couldn't spend her whole life in mourning. The Brasserie, like the S Bar next door and Club Zoo upstairs, hadn't been there when she'd left Crowby for London. The red stone building – the old Workingmen's College – had lain empty for years before it had been bought up, re-developed. There had used to be a way in around the back if you knew how. When she'd been a teenager but too young for the serious bars and nightclubs, it had been somewhere in town to smoke, drink, hang out.

Illegal, illicit, cool. Cole had known the way naturally, had always known that kind of thing in those days.

Cole would loom up from time to time, of course, if she stayed on here: swaggering down the street or ogling her out of his car window or pushing a shopping trolley around Waitrose in his new role as the family man. But Cole wasn't Darren. Cole she could forget, Cole she *would* forget.

Chapter Thirteen

One thirty pm. Jacobson caught up with DC Emma Smith in the police canteen. Smith's office space was an undersized desk in the fourth floor area which was officially and grandly known as the CID Resource Centre – in actuality, a crowded open-plan hell-hole where too many DCs fought over too few computers, too few telephones and too few working photocopiers. By contrast, the canteen was a haven of peace – and relatively leak-proof if you chose a quiet enough section of the room. Jacobson had driven back from the Harvester via the Riverside Hotel and Riverside Walk. He'd managed to pull a grateful DC Williams from a seminar on Recent Developments in Car Crime organised by the traffic division, sent him over to join Barber and Hume on the door-to-door effort. DS Kerr had ducked out to keep his appointment with Randeep Parmeer. Kerr had suggested postponing it for now but Jacobson had argued that if they ended up taking Paul Shaw's story about racists seriously then Parmeer's problems at the Viceroy Tandoori might turn out to be relevant in some way, might throw up a name worth talking to.

Jacobson tucked into a plate of egg and chips. Emma Smith had bought a mung bean salad from the salad bar. Both of them were on orange juice, both of them had a taste for decent coffee, both of them avoided the canteen's curiously disgusting version of the beverage whenever they could. When they'd finished eating, Emma Smith opened a red manila folder whose corners were creased and battered. Jacobson noticed that she'd scrawled the legend 'Paul Shaw' on the cover with a blue biro.

'A slight case of information overload, I'm afraid, guv,' she said. 'Type "Paul Shaw, British journalist" into Google and you get nine hundred and fifty one entries. He even has – had – his own publicity website. Recaps of the stories he's broken, how to contact him if you have a story that – quote – needs to be told. Etcetera, etcetera.'

'So no problem about a photograph then?'

'Well, strangely enough, there was. There's a note about it on his web pages, seems he was camera-shy for reasons of personal safety' – she pulled the wad of documents out of the folder – 'I did get this though.'

She handed Jacobson a colour photocopy of a camera still: Paul Shaw, smiling and wearing a dinner jacket, shaking hands with a tall, tanned figure in a linen suit.

Jacobson moved his orange juice out of the way, placed the copy in front of him. 'Isn't that John Pilger, lass?'

Emma Smith nodded, well-impressed. She'd vaguely heard of Pilger, had immediately thought he looked familiar. But hadn't been able to name him straight off.

'Right first time, guv. I found it on the Press Association members' site. They've got a gallery of snaps taken at some kind of awards dinner last year.'

Emma Smith handed him a second photocopy – where she'd evidently cropped the image, had sharpened and magnified Paul Shaw's face.

'Well done,' Jacobson said. 'So Shaw *did* move in exalted circles – Pilger's an acknowledged leader in the field.'

Emma Smith talked him through the rest of the details she'd accessed: Shaw's next of kin, the council tax banding of his London flat, his education – local schools in Camberwell followed by a scholarship to New College, Oxford – his last three addresses, the last four vehicles he'd owned. Quite a haul for an hour or so at the keyboard, Jacobson thought. It wasn't the comprehensive and instant Big Brother Is Watching You facility demanded by hysterical right-wingers everywhere - not yet anyway - but the force's competence with the nation's computer networks was moving steadily, inexorably, in that direction. From the CV that Paul Shaw had helpfully posted on his own website, Jacobson noticed he'd spent six months with the *Birmingham Post* as part of his journalist's training. It was still possible, he thought, that Shaw had been telling the truth when he'd said he'd never set foot in Crowby previously - there were plenty of Brummies who never had - but it was a complication all the same. Even without visiting Crowby as such, his time in the nearest big city might easily have brought him into contact with those who did.

'At least he wasn't married, Emma,' he commented. 'Better get on to the Met next though. We'll want Family Support in the relevant borough to get in touch with the parents. Once they're up to it, there's the issue of formal identification.'

He paused, took a sip of his fruit juice.

'After that I thought you and DC Williams could—' he started then didn't finish, suddenly remembering something else he'd forgotten, something a lot closer to home.

He took another sip, stalled for time, tried again.

'You and Williams, lass - you *can* still work together, I hope.'

Jacobson knew that he was no expert on the female mind, certainly not on the part of it devoted to sex and relationships. But, like everyone else in the small world of Crowby CID, he'd heard the consecutive rumours about the brief affair between the two DCs and its even quicker demise.

Emma Smith had coal-dark eyes that rarely flinched. And weren't about to now, she thought. Certainly not as a consequence of the error of judgement she'd made about Detective Constable Raymond Hywel mouth-and-trousers Williams.

'I don't have any problem with it if he doesn't.'

'Fine, great,' Jacobson said, not entirely reassured.

Randeep Parmeer apologised for the fact that he was more than half an hour late.

'The lunchtime traffic,' he said, offering his handshake.

'No problem, Mr Parmeer,' Kerr said, offering his own hand and then ushering his visitor towards the lifts.

In fact, Parmeer's unpunctuality had been useful, had meant that Kerr had been able to pay a quick visit to Steve Horton, the civilian computer officer. Horton's office was a danger zone – wires and cables dangling everywhere, the naked innards of computers sprawled across every available surface – Horton himself, crammed into his too-small chair in front of the three keyboards he'd recently taken to using simultaneously. But visiting it was usually worth the risk. Horton was an enthusiast, a proselytiser for the day when the geeks would rule the world, had been pleased to treat Kerr to a swift tutorial on the basics of using the visual database software. Enough, Kerr hoped, to give him a veneer of confidence when he sat down at his own terminal for real.

Parmeer and Kerr squeezed into the crowded lift. Kerr pressed the button for the fifth floor. Earlier, he'd thought that one o'clock Friday had been a strange time for Parmeer to want to call into the Divi. Wasn't that when they had Friday prayers? Then he'd recalled Parmeer's comments about Pakistan, had realised that he was Hindu not Muslim. Chicken tikka massala was the nation's single favourite dish, Bollywood films had started to chart at the box office. And yet most white Britons, himself included, lived in deep and blissful ignorance about Indian culture, its complexities, subtleties and distinctions. He'd recalled something his dad had said one time, in the middle of one his political rants: *Don't kid yourself that Britain's racially integrated, Ian. All that happens is that immigrants quickly work out our dreariest social rule: keep yourself to yourself.*

Kerr showed Parmeer into his office. As a DS, at least he *had* an office, albeit cramped and shared. His roommate, DS Tyler, wasn't around though, was working the evening shift again. Parmeer declined the offer of a drink, seemed keen to get on. Kerr booted up his computer.

'No more calls then, last night?'

'No, absolutely nothing. Do you think that's a good sign?'

Kerr managed to squeeze an extra chair in front of his machine, invited Parmeer to sit down.

'It's probably still too soon to say, Mr Parmeer.'

Unexpectedly, Kerr logged in to the Hate Crime Unit's database without a hitch. He brought four sets of mugshots up at a time, three images for each: face front, left side, right side. He showed Parmeer how to right-click on any image that he wanted to take a full-screen look at. Parmeer worked diligently, studying each one closely in turn. But after ten minutes, he hadn't got anywhere.

'No offence, Sergeant,' he said, glancing at Kerr, the hint of mischief in his eyes. 'But so many of them look exactly the same.'

Kerr cracked up.

'When you've see one racist hooligan, you've pretty much seen them all,' he said, when he'd stopped laughing. 'But you might as well have a look at the entire crew now you're here.'

Parmeer took another twenty minutes and ended up with a selection of six possibles that he narrowed down to a final two.

'You're certain?' Kerr asked.

'No, I'm sorry. I can't be that. But it *could* be one of these two. The unzipper.'

'The what?'

'The unzipper, Mr Kerr. That's what we called him. He complained that our lager tasted like piss, said he preferred the taste of his own.' Parmeer shook his head for emphasis. 'I fear he was going to take it out, wave it about. But one of the others told him to put it away, not to bother.'

Kerr sighed. What a national treasure the British yob could be.

He thanked Parmeer for his time, escorted him back down to the reception area, promised he'd be in touch. He told him that he'd requested that the rural patrol car kept an eye on the Viceroy this evening. Kerr wasn't over-confident the request would be acted on. But he kept his doubts to himself.

Back in his office, he pulled up the associated data on the two faces that Randeep Parmeer had eventually settled on. The first one fell at the first hurdle: he was currently banged up in Winson Green, on a stretch for GBH that had started back in December. But the second candidate remained a contender: Gary Bowles, currently at liberty, currently living locally, and with an extensive history for football violence and petty thieving. He'd made it on to the HCU's files because of a ruck in the Bricklayer's Arms, the non-salubrious boozer at the heart of the non-salubrious Mill Street area. Bowles looked to have come off worst in the incident but the court had still accepted the prosecution argument that he'd started the trouble. He'd accused a group of Asian drinkers of being – quote – *fucking terrorists who wanted gassing*. Kerr noted the essential details. As soon as he had time, he'd check the database again, study the fuller picture. Bowles, he thought, was precisely the kind of toerag it would be an unambiguous pleasure to put away. The kind of collar that even his dad would be proud of him for.

Jacobson paged him: the afternoon meeting point was the Bellevue, *as soon as*. Kerr recognised the name, though couldn't recall ever having been there previously. The drive took him ten minutes. Locking his Peugeot in the car park, he clocked another six vehicles, all but one of them belonging to members of Crowby CID's ad hoc murder squad. The Bellevue was a small private hotel at the far end of Riverside Walk. The proprietor, Bob Harker, was an early-retired ex-uniformed sergeant who'd been on the rugby team when Mick Hume had started playing. It was ideal for Jacobson's purpose: a briefing session not too far from the crime scene – if there *was* a crime scene – and handily away from official police premises. The room even had a flip chart and marker pens – the Bellevue having unfulfilled aspirations towards the business awayday market. Kerr was the last to make it, arrived just after Jacobson and Emma Smith. Harker had laid on a few bottles of lager and a pot of tea. Kerr helped himself to a cuppa and grabbed a seat.

Jacobson, B & H in hand, recapped swiftly. Paul Shaw had arrived in Crowby with the notion that his cousin, Darren McGee, hadn't killed himself but had been the victim of a race murder. Now, scarcely a week later, Shaw himself had met a virtually identical death. It was possible, even likely, that the post-mortem would be inconclusive, would back up a theory of accident or misadventure as easily as anything more sinister. That's what had happened in the case of McGee. But in that case there had also been good circumstantial evidence that had pointed quickly away from any idea of murder and towards suicide. McGee had been mentally unbalanced, had tried to kill himself on at least two previous occasions. Paul Shaw was a different kind of customer altogether. Nothing so far suggested that he was anything other than sane. Not to mention intelligent, successful and resourceful. Plus there were the indisputable facts of his missing car and his ransacked, cleared-out hotel room:

'Personally, I'm thinking suspicious with a capital S,' he concluded, 'but I need to know your views.'

'Maybe his mental health does need checking out though, guv,' Barber suggested. 'You do get copycat cases don't you? Shaw obsesses about his cousin topping himself, ends up doing the same.'

Jacobson nodded.

'Obviously that can't be ruled out without proper checking. We need to look into his medical history as a matter of course.'

Williams made the point that Shaw could have been killed – *if* he'd been killed – for reasons unrelated to the death of his cousin. He'd been an investigative journalist, his stock-in-trade was treading on toes, making enemies.

'Ditto,' Jacobson answered. 'That's another avenue that needs looking down thoroughly.'

There were no other objections. The general opinion was that two identically drowned, suicidal cousins was stretching the concept of coincidence too much.

Jacobson moved on to the immediate practicalities – the SOCOs had apparently discovered nothing of interest so far – or were keeping it to themselves if they had – and bog all was a polite term for the outcome of four plus hours of door-to-door inquiries.

'But it's still early days,' he added. 'Point one: Webster's a fastidious sod who likes to check and re-check his results, even preliminary ones, before he'll let on he's found any. Point two: the door-to-door's not complete. The next door you knock on could be the one where somebody saw something or heard something. Point three: we haven't even started on the Riverside CCTV tapes yet.'

He found an ashtray for his fag end.

'So none of that worries me too much. What *does* worry me is Greg Salter. He's likely to be our real problem. He'll seize on the pm report, if it turns out how we're expecting it to, argue that coincidences can and do happen.'

'You really think he'd nip a potential murder inquiry in the bud, guv?' Emma Smith asked. 'Just because it would make him look bad?'

'Looking bad is a bit of an understatement,' Kerr commented. 'The Met might've bungled with Stephen Lawrence and Damilola Taylor – but at least they didn't fail to notice that they'd been murdered in the first place.'

'Not nip it exactly, Emma,' Jacobson said, 'but he might be tempted to starve it of resources, encourage it to run itself into the ground. Suppose he restricts the team to just DS Kerr and myself. He could easily justify that officially.

Think about it: a team of two trying to delve into Paul Shaw's life, who he knows, where he's been, retracing his steps around Crowby – not to mention the small matter of completely reopening the Darren McGee inquiry.'

Mick Hume, for once, was the quickest on the uptake.

'So what you're saying, guv, is that we might need to be ready to work for you on the QT if it comes to it?'

'Exactly, old son,' Jacobson answered.

'I'm in,' Hume responded without a second's hesitation, waving his bottle of underchilled Heineken. And speaking for every detective in the room.

Chapter Fourteen

Jacobson reassigned the squad's tasks and drove out to Crowby General. Robinson had rescheduled his working day to fit in Paul Shaw's post-mortem. As the SIO - senior investigating officer - Jacobson was legally obliged to witness the dissection. He took the lift to the fourth floor of the new wing of the hospital with a familiar sinking feeling in his stomach. He could live quite happily without observing yet another medical horrorshow and he could do without losing around ninety minutes of valuable inquiry time into the bargain. He ran into Webster halfway along the yellow-walled corridor which led to the pathology department. The Chief SOCO was another one of the party guests who had no choice except to be there. Webster's team had completed their sweep, he told Jacobson, were currently bagging and logging samples. Jacobson extracted the promise of a personal update on what they'd got before the end of the day. Extraction was the operative term, he thought - or something more complicated, root canal work maybe.

He'd learned to blank as much as he could. But there were some sights, sounds and smells you couldn't blank. The buzz of the saw through the skull cap. The bile sacks which had a tendency to burst when the pathologist plucked them out of the body, although at least not on this occasion. And little details - the appliance of the clamp to the femoral artery was one of them – that made him wince every single time.

The autopsy was recorded on video and Robinson gave a verbal commentary as he worked. Even so, he was prepared – unlike Merchant would have been – to talk to Jacobson immediately after the event, to translate technical jargon into common sense if he could. They spoke in the Senior Pathologist's office, not yet completely devoid of Merchant's effects – his fading *Belle de Jour* poster and his Cona machine, for instance. Jacobson poured the coffee while Robinson slumped himself into a chair, willing himself to relax after the tension of his one-man show.

'So he *did* drown then? And he was alive when he entered the river?'

'Well, there's still the lab work to be done of course. But, yep, barring laboratory surprises, I'd say that much is pretty clear, Frank. Or as clear as a drowning case ever gets anyway. Foam in the airways – water, mucus, tinges of blood – and lots more extruding when I pressed on the chest. Evidence of *emphysema aquosum* in both lungs. Some shoulder-girdle bruising too.'

Jacobson passed him a cup.

'And that tends to suggest a struggle to survive in water?'

'Exactly. A drowning man thrashing around basically, fighting a losing battle with the currents. What you get – as in this case – are muscles rupturing and haemorrhaging. Especially the *scaleni* and the *pectoralis major*.'

'But you don't think that he struggled for long?'

'Not with severe head injuries like those. And – as we're assuming – the shock of a considerable fall.'

Jacobson latched on to the issue of the injuries to Shaw's head and face.

'Puts us right back to the problems on the Darren McGee case, doesn't it? Damage that could have been done when he hit the water – *or* sustained beforehand.'

Robinson slurped some coffee. Then:

'There's the rub, Frank. There are still some problems that science can't solve for you, I'm afraid. Not post-mortem pathology anyway. But if his head injuries were inflicted by human hands, there are going to be forensic indications *somewhere* – at the scene or on the perpetrators themselves.'

'So if there was an attack it has to have been by more than one attacker?'

Robinson stretched his long legs out in front of him, yawned.

'Mr Shaw was a young, strong man, just like his cousin. Unless suicide is the explanation after all, I'd argue it definitely took more than one person – more like a minimum of three or four – to get him into the water involuntarily.'

There was probably a zealot somewhere in the Home Office at that very moment, drafting legislation to prevent any tape anywhere from ever being overwritten or re-used. But meanwhile, in the real world, it was still left to private organisations to decide their own archiving policy. At the Riverside Hotel, Crowby, the approach was minimalist: the CCTV tapes were wiped clean every twenty-four hours at four o'clock in the afternoon. The viewing facilities weren't exactly state-of-the-art either. One monitor on the reception desk and another one in the manager's office – which Alison Taylor had cheerfully abandoned for the duration rather than run the risk of Mick Hume and DC Barber frightening off potential customers at the point of sale.

Barber munched on a complimentary chocolate biscuit and studied Paul Shaw's photocopied face while Hume got the playback up and running. Assuming this *was* a murder case, Barber thought, the chances were it that it was his last for Crowby CID. He'd finally passed his sergeant's examinations the previous year, was working out the last month of his notice period. On May 2nd, the day after the bank holiday, he was all set to become DS Barber of the City of Birmingham force. 'Fuck it,' he heard Mick Hume say, not especially quietly. One of the problems with security cameras was that you rarely ran into any two systems that worked identically. Every installation seemed to have its own idiosyncrasies. Hume was trying to synchronise the footage from the car park and the reception area plus half a dozen entrance and exit points. Barber finished his biscuit, scrunched the wrapper into the wastebin. 'About fucking time,' he heard Hume curse again, finally getting there.

Hume set the replay to run on a medium-speed fast forward. Only specialised CCTV recorded in real time. Most everyday systems – like the Riverside's – produced a limited number of still frames per second. The upshot was that viewing took a fraction of the time that had actually elapsed on film. But it was still a time-consuming process, Hume thought. Hume and Barber were taking the first stint, would hand over later to Emma Smith and Love Rat Williams, as he was currently dubbed. The first priority was to find a trace, if one existed, of Paul Shaw himself and/or his car. Whoever had ransacked his hotel room might've been caught on tape too. But that would have to wait. And might require help from the hotel's night staff. Whoever they were, they hadn't attracted any attention at the time, had probably been dressed appropriately smartly for Crowby's self-styled 'top hotel'.

'Too bad they didn't have the common decency to turn up wearing stocking masks, mate,' he said, continuing his thought out loud, 'and carrying bags marked swag.'

Barber moved his chair closer to the monitor.

'The odd Union Jack T-shirt wouldn't go amiss either,' he commented. 'That and holding a copy of *Mein Kampf* up to the sodding camera.'

Kerr drove over to the Woodlands, Crowby's second worst housing estate, as measured by local levels of crime, vandalism, drug abuse, child poverty – as measured by just about any social index of deprivation you cared to mention.

According to the HCU database, Gary Bowles' last known address was on Shelley Road: at the Woodlands' furthest, grimmest end. The street was a series of elderly, ugly, two-storey attached houses which dated back to the 1960s and which led, like a series of warnings on the path to hell, towards four damaged, leaking blocks of flats; medium rise, ten damp, insanitary floors each. Which of these was the least bad housing option was the kind of choice you hoped you never had to make.

He parked outside the two-storey gaff, number thirty-six, his hopes rising that the address details, always the weakest, least up-to-date police data source, were correct on this occasion. If Bowles didn't live here, whoever did certainly had something in common with him at any rate; along past the rubbish-tip garden and above the battered front door, he watched a red-and-white St George's flag fluttering from a bedroom window. There was a slogan stitched in blue letters across its centre: *England for the English*.

Kerr knocked on the door, then knocked harder. A thin, white-faced girl flung it open, gaped at his warrant card.

'Gary's at work,' she said flatly, before Kerr had even asked.

'I'm impressed to hear it. Mind if I check for myself?' Kerr said wearily, chancing his arm.

'Yes I flaming *do* mind. You've no right. He's working on a site over near Wynarth.'

He didn't press it.

'What's your name, love?'

She looked about eighteen, he thought. There were spoilt rich girls developing bulimia to look half as slender.

'Well, it's not frigging Jordan, is it? Living on Shelley flaming Road on the palatial flaming Woodlands estate.'

Kerr kept his temper. He didn't get further than the doorstep. But eventually he got the details he needed, buried in a job lot that he didn't. Bowles' previous girl-friend, in whose name the house was still rented, had effed off to Birmingham with her two effing brats and some bloke – a car frigging salesman – who was old enough to be her dad. She'd left Gary with five months' rent arrears and a pile of other debts. But Gary was getting it sorted, had got himself a job with a couple of painters – subcontractors. It was steady work, good money, and he was talking about renting somewhere decent – nowhere round flaming here anyway – as soon as they'd got a deposit together.

'Where was Gary last Friday night, Linda?'

'At home with me of course,' she answered as quick as a flash, giving Bowles an instant, valueless alibi. 'Same as most nights.'

'That's Gary's flag, I expect?' he asked neutrally, pointing upwards.

'Don't tell me that's against the law now,' she said, 'sticking up for your own.'

She glanced up and down Shelley Road with a look of disgust.

'They're all over this frigging place. Filthy black bastards. Women with them creepy hoods on.'

Involuntarily, Kerr looked around the street himself. But it seemed empty, the late-afternoon sun blinking gently above the four squat blocks of flats. His dad had brought him up to see the world very differently. But it wasn't in his job spec to demolish prejudice on a daily basis. And there weren't enough hours in the day anyway. He scribbled down the details of the building site where she claimed Bowles was working, left her standing sullenly in her doorway.

The quickest route was over to the North Crowby bypass and then straight along the Wynarth Road itself. Kerr knew where the site was: the retirement flats complex, carved out of two adjacent properties, both of them late eighteenth-century in origin, and rurally surrounded by landscaped gardens and ancient oak trees. Bowles would need to do an awful lot better than lugging a few paint cans around before he could look forward to that kind of contented old age.

Sixty apartments all told and a completion date in June, he remembered from somewhere: the property supplement in the *Evening Argus* most probably. He parked in the muddy compound near the site entrance, noticed that there were vehicles starting up and moving off all around. The Friday early finish, he thought. He might be unlucky after all, might just have missed him.

The painters were over in the solarium, a bluff, red-faced man in the site office told him, giving him a couple of gruff directions. As it turned out, the painters had finished up too. There were half a dozen of them walking towards him as he made his way past a large, unfinished swimming pool which was currently being used to store bags of cement and assorted timber. Bowles was at the back of the group. None of his workmates seemed to have a problem with picking him out to the police.

'A word, Gary,' Kerr said, waving his ID.

They stood by the edge of the pool, occasionally glancing over. Bowles denied everything. He'd been nowhere near Wynarth last Friday night. He'd been at home with his girlfriend, Linda. They'd rented a couple of DVDs from the Spa shop.

'They'll have a record of that on their computer no doubt,' Kerr commented.

Not that it would prove or disprove anything if they did.

'Fucked if I know,' Bowles replied. '*The Return of the King*, the extended version, that was one of 'em anyway.'

'A bit wholesome for your tastes, Gary, isn't it? Good triumphing over evil and all that.'

Bowles didn't reply. But shot him a puzzled look: what are you *on* about mate?

Kerr had detoured to the Divi en route to the Woodlands, had studied the rest of Bowles' form. He mentioned a few names that the HCU computer had linked him to in the past.

'Look, mate,'— Bowles was trying for friendly, but he was fairly crap at it.— 'I ain't seen any of those losers for months. Linda and me. It's a serious thing. That was all kids' stuff, the rucks, nicking – I'm twenty-three now, I ain't in any of that no more.'

Kerr watched a sparrow pecking uselessly at a cement bag.

'So there'll be other witnesses, apart from Linda, who can put you on the Woodlands last Friday night. And you wouldn't be even slightly worried about an ID parade?'

Bowles shrugged, bluffed.

'I went straight home after work. I got nothing to hide.'

'Nice flag at your gaff, Gary,' Kerr said, changing tack.

'What's it to you? It ain't against the law, is it?'

'It could be, Gary, if a court thought you were inciting racial hatred.'

Bowles guffawed, forgetting his humble pie act.

'There's a time when you've got to stand up and be counted, mate.'

'You mean like taking a leak on your lamb vindaloo for instance – show them who's the master race.'

Emotion splashed across Bowles' face for a second before he got it under control, masked it. Pride maybe – or anger. Whatever it was, it inclined Kerr to believe that Randeep Parmeer had picked out the right customer after all.

'I don't know what you're talking about. I swear I don't.'

'Any plans for tonight, Gaz?' he asked.

'The name's Gary,' Bowles replied, straightening his shoulders.

He wasn't exactly little. But he certainly wasn't as big as the chip on his shoulder. His only plan, he claimed, was to get blinkin' back home if his blinkin' lift hadn't gone already.

'My heart bleeds,' Kerr said finally. 'You're in the frame, *Gaz*. We'll talk again.'

Chapter Fifteen

Jacobson drove back to the Divisional building, parked, took the lift up to the fourth floor. Jim Webster's 'office' was a cubicle-sized area partitioned off from the smaller of the two Scene of Crime labs. Handily, Webster, who'd left the hospital straight after Paul Shaw's post-mortem, was at home, sitting behind his sparse, neatly ordered desk. Jacobson pulled out the one visitor's chair and plonked himself down.

'Whatcha got?' he asked, giving it his best Marlon Brando impersonation.

Webster never ever got the joke or the reference it was based on. Since he seemed to treat the entire world as if it was a giant, contaminated crime scene it was always possible that he'd avoided the cinema in his youth for fear of germs.

'Too much is what I've got, Frank,' Webster answered, 'Three bridges' worth of scuff marks, handprints, fingerprints, blood—'

'Blood?'

'On the Memorial Bridge. The KM test identified potential blood samples at two different locations. I wouldn't get your hopes up though. They could have been there for months for one thing. As I'm sure you know, as soon as blood dries, there's no scientific test for determining its age.'

Jacobson nodded. The Kastle-Meyer test turned a reagent purple-pink in the presence of blood. It was a standard, highly useful presumptive test – even if it did always make him think of a piss-awful Australian beer.

'But at least they must be more recent than New Year's Day – assuming, which I'm more than happy to assume, that your lads did a thorough job back then.'

Webster ignored the flattery, kept his face as deadpan as usual.

'That's a fair point, Frank. But it still doesn't prove that they were deposited in the last twenty-four hours either. I expect you want them sent on to the FSS lab for analysis?'

Jacobson nodded again.

'Yes, please. At least they can be compared with Paul Shaw's blood straight off. That would certainly be something to go on.'

He asked Webster about the other samples his team had detected.

'All pretty useless, Frank, until you come up with a suspect or suspects' – Webster allowed himself a rare smile – 'always assuming there was a crime committed in the first place.'

It was Jacobson's turn to ignore a subtext.

'Why useless, old son?'

Webster leaned back in his chair, stretched his arms behind his head.

'Stone bridges don't make great crime scenes. But even so, we've lifted a good old number of prints from rubbish bins, lampposts and the like. And shoe marks from all over the place. But we can't really do anything with any of it until you give us somebody to test against. And before you ask, apart from the putative blood samples, there's no DNA sources we can use – other than the contents of the rubbish bins again. Fag ends, bits of Mars bars, apple cores covered in saliva and what have you. But there could be samples from literally hundreds of people in there – and most of them co-contaminated anyway.'

Jacobson didn't comment, asked him about the search in room number 315, the Riverside Hotel.

'I'm still waiting on an initial report-back from the hotel team,' Webster replied. 'But you're probably looking at similar difficulties. Too *much* potential evidence rather than too little. And there'd be a need to eliminate a large number of hotel staff, previous guests, etcetera, etcetera. Greg Salter's never going to authorise expense on that scale without a lot more to go on than a conversation you had down the pub.'

'But if suspects *do* come my way, there could be corroborative forensics?'

Webster lowered his arms.

'It's not like you to look on the optimistic side, Frank. But yes, there could be. Say foreign fibres from the hotel room that match up to foreign fibres on Shaw's clothes – even to foreign fibres on Darren McGee's, if the case gets reopened.'

Jacobson brightened a little. Contrary to popular belief, fibres that had attached themselves to clothing before a drowning incident, could stay happily attached long after the clothing had been immersed in water.

He rose to go, only had one more question.

'So, do you buy it, Jim? Shaw's idea that McGee was murdered?'

Webster hesitated. Then:

'I can't rule it out. And I can't rule it in.'

It had all the makings of a gameshow catchphrase. Jacobson almost mentioned the notion but thought better of it. If Webster had time to watch TV when he wasn't too busy sterilising his kitchen, he was probably more of a Discovery Channel type than a quiz-for-morons fan.

He considered taking the stairs up to the eighth floor – the senior management level – but rejected the idea in favour of the lifts. Four floors was pushing it, he thought. Plus the last thing he needed was to be out of breath and flustered in the presence of Smoothie Greg. Salter had paged him three times during the afternoon and had left a message on his mobile while he'd been at the post-mortem: *We need to talk, Frank. ASAP.*

Jacobson straightened his tie and walked into the lion's den. Greg Salter was standing by the wall which had used to host his predecessor's pictorial history of the force and now boasted Salter's burgeoning collection of pie charts, bar charts and organisation charts. He appeared to be studying the force's mission statement with the kind of lecherous-seeming delight that most men reserved for female tennis stars and *GQ* models. One of his recent additions to the room was a low oval table and a matching set of low, soft-backed chairs which had been placed in a corner well away from his desk and his personal work area. According to DCS Salter, it was - quote - a more ambient space for discussion which promoted a less hierarchical interchange - unquote. Jacobson's view was that it just made it more difficult to snatch a glimpse of whatever confidential documents were currently lying around Salter's IN tray.

They sat down opposite each other and Salter poured out two cups of his admittedly decent - and fully authorised - coffee. He got to the point with less preamble than usual.

'The black journalist, Frank. Do you really think there's criminal involvement in his death?'

Jacobson restated his main arguments: the forensic and post-mortem ambiguities, the burglary in Shaw's hotel room, Shaw's missing Lexus, the suspicions that had brought Shaw to Crowby in the first place.

'I assume you don't take his story about Darren McGee seriously though?'

'I didn't until this morning. But now—'

Jacobson left his sentence to hang in the air. Salter kept his practised, professional smile up and running. But only with some difficulty.

'Coincidences *do* happen, Frank. Poor McGee was a diagnosed schizophrenic. He told his doctors there were angels in the room, said he talked to the Devil on a regular basis.'

Jacobson suddenly glimpsed a possible DCS-manipulation strategy:

'This isn't about Darren McGee though, is it? Not directly anyway. All I want to do right now is to investigate the circumstances of Paul Shaw's death as fully as possible.'

Which probably means reopening the Darren McGee case in all but name, he thought. But so long as that wasn't part of what was *officially* happening, there was a slight working chance that Salter would give the investigation his OK – for the time being at any rate – until something turned up that threatened to make his own prior investigation look sloppy.

Salter sipped his coffee, tried to look like whatever his idea was of the senior man looking seniorly thoughtful, drawing on his senior bank of senior experience. Jacobson mirrored him – as far as the coffee-drinking went.

'An open-ended investigation. But with no specific reference to previous cases investigated by this force?' Salter asked after a long moment.

'Exactly, *sir*,' Jacobson replied.

Salter hated to be called sir – maybe because it reminded him he was supposed to be a policeman, not a marketing executive – which was why, try as he might, Jacobson couldn't resist using the epithet at least once whenever they spoke.

He mentioned the blood samples again, went into more detail: he'd like the FSS laboratory in Birmingham to fast-track them over the weekend.

'Which would mean results by Monday?' Salter asked.

'Or Tuesday at the very latest.'

Salter did the looking-thoughtful thing again. Then:

'OK, Frank. We'll review the situation when the blood results come in. Meanwhile, you can continue to deploy the specialist officers – but only your core team mind, no extra bods. Not with the budget as tight as it is currently.'

'Thanks, *Greg*,' Jacobson managed, very nearly without sarcasm, thinking that if he gave a stuff about budgets, he would've gone in for accountancy or for some other less stressful, more remunerative occupation.

From the projection booth of the small purpose-built cinema at the heart of Crowby University's Media Studies Centre, Dr Martin Kesey dimmed the lights and started up the film. To the annoyance of the department's technicians, Kesey always insisted on using an old reel-to-reel version of his own and on pissing around with the projector himself. Admittedly it meant the duty technician didn't have to hang around during the actual showing. But that advantage was more than offset by the awkwardness of getting the old-style equipment out of storage and up and running in the first place.

Kesey couldn't have cared less. To understand a film – to understand any cultural artefact – you had to see it and experience it as close to the medium of its original transmission as was possible. And especially for this one. *Triumph of the Will*. Germany, 1934. Directed by Leni Riefenstahl. Kesey couldn't recall how many times he'd watched her astonishing, mesmerising portrayal of the Nuremberg Rally. But he found something fresh to marvel at every time. Even the reddest of his students – not that all that many of them were all that red these days – usually conceded the power of her film: its unique, disturbing ability to work on the psyche and on the emotions. There were forty or so of them scattered around the room. A reasonable attendance for the graveyard shift of late Friday afternoon – which was when his Sociology of Media Culture class, year three, was currently meeting.

The shadow of the Führer's plane coming in to land across the nearby countryside, the crowds – smiling, raucous, healthy – lining the medieval streets for a glimpse of the motorcade and, later, as light gave way to dark, the night rally itself: torches, marching soldiers, the hypnotic rhythms of the speeches. Nobody in the world denied that it was art. And numinous art at that. Dealing in archetypes, universal longings. The techniques the great Leni had pioneered were used nowadays for valueless purposes – to sell cars, beer, washing machines. But back then, Riefenstahl had sold a nation an image of itself, a dream of what had once been and might be again. The message of the *Triumph* was simple, he thought. And yet infinitely satisfying: join us and your life will have true purpose and meaning.

He noticed that Karen Mott had turned up, was sitting with her usual crowd of mates. They'd probably invite him for a drink in the student bar afterwards. They nearly always did. Or Karen nearly always did anyway, pointing her tits at him like an invitation card. He'd turned her down last week and the week before, needed to know how keen she really was. But he'd accept her offer this time if she made it, he decided. Tomorrow – Saturday – promised to be a difficult day, conceivably even dangerous. An evening's rest and recreation between long, splayed legs might settle his battle nerves quite nicely.

Chapter Sixteen

Jacobson parked on Riverside Walk and walked across the reopened Memorial Bridge towards the Riverside Hotel. Salter's easily given OK, although welcome, had foxed him. But only slightly. *We'll review the situation when the blood tests are in*, he'd said – or words to that effect. Meaning that Salter still reserved an absolute right to call a halt if he didn't like the way things were going.

The traffic on the bridge was chocka in both directions. But it was after six now, bang in the middle of the rush hour. Virtually every through-route in town was clogged up with going-home traffic. Once you got to seven or eight in the evening, the Riverside area returned to tranquillity. There would be dog walkers and strollers later of course. But fewer and fewer cars. After midnight – and certainly by one or two in the morning – it was all too believable that something bad could have happened to Paul Shaw out this way and be unwitnessed by anyone except the perpetrators.

He walked through the automatic doors, past the reception desk, and found all four of his DCs – Hume, Barber, Smith, Williams – crowded behind the desk in the manager's office. Hume and Barber were nearing the end of their stint with the Riverside's CCTV footage; Smith and Williams were about to start theirs.

The time stamp on the monitor screen read 20:09:01:12. Hume decided he might as well let the footage run on until it reached nine pm. Then he'd press *pause*, hand over to Romeo Williams and his ex-Juliet. He watched the digits flashing by. Nothing going on at the rear of the hotel. Nobody coming or going via the main entrance. 20:12:31:06. Movement down in the car park now – a car stopped at the barrier, a driver's hand leaning out of the window, pressing the button to summon the porter. Replaying CCTV footage was like looking for a needle in a haystack. Except that you had to examine every inch of hay into the bargain. He rewound twenty seconds' worth, slowed the playback speed. He rewound again, replayed again And then a third time. It was what they were after all right: Paul Shaw's Lexus GS, Paul Shaw's registration plate in full view, Paul Shaw still alive – waving a thank you to the offscreen porter as the porter raised the striped exit barrier.

'Useful as far as it goes,' Jacobson said, lifting the last complimentary chocolate biscuit from the plateful that Barber and Hume had steadily depleted. 'So now we know Shaw drove out of here just after eight last night. What we *don't* know yet is whether he came back at all – and whether he was on his own if he did.'

DS Kerr arrived. And then left again, accompanied by Barber and Hume. There were still houses that hadn't been reached by the door-to-door effort. And there were houses that had been reached but needed revisiting – because some or all of their inhabitants hadn't been conveniently at home in the middle of the working day. Williams and Emma Smith took over the CCTV replay. They turned the monitor sideways so that they could both look at it while sitting well away from each other on opposite sides of Alison Taylor's substantial, mahogany desk.

The biscuit turned out to be too sweet for Jacobson's taste. He binned it half-eaten and wandered through to the hotel's main lounge bar which was starting to fill up with customers: well-heeled locals mainly, plus eager, early-arrived guests for the evening's functions. A significant tier of the Riverside's clientele was absent though. The business and corporate crowd who used the hotel as their base when they were in the area tended to check out on Fridays, take themselves off home for the weekend.

Seeing as he was there, Jacobson ordered a Glenmorangie with ice but was careful to pay for it. He found an empty booth as far away as possible from the white grand piano and the white-jacketed pianist who had started to work his way, none too subtly, through *Your Hundred Blandest Tunes*, Volume Ten. The head barman, Jack Speirs, joined him as soon as he had a moment. By now everyone who worked in the hotel had heard the basic story: the guest known as Paul Shaw had washed up stone dead in the Crow.

'You've served Shaw in here then, Jack?'

Jacobson vaguely knew Speirs, who'd worked in the Brewer's Rest for a year or so a while back.

'Only a couple of times that I can definitely recall, Mr Jacobson. The first time was last week - Thursday night maybe. I remember it because he came in with Henry Pelling. You know, the reporter from the *Argus*? The world's greatest tipper - not.'

Jacobson smiled.

'And the other time?'

'That was just a couple of nights ago - Wednesday to be precise.'

'You're sure about that?'

'Definitely. He had a lass with him, young, quite a looker. They came in about nine, left about ten.'

Jacobson asked him if he had a description. He did. Jacobson pointed out that 'nice arse' and 'nice legs' were fuzzy, subjective terms - then had to explain what subjective meant.

'She had reddish hair, Mr Jacobson, if that's any more help to you. Not ginger - that sort of nice, deep red some of 'em have. Got through three Red Bulls with vodka.'

'And what about Shaw?'

Speirs scratched the side of his head. He was short, thin, wiry; the sort who could deal with half a dozen complicated rounds simultaneously while calculating the totals for half a dozen more.

'Orange juice, tomato juice, something like that. Not a proper drink anyway. Fancied his chances maybe – the girl was all over him as I recall.'

'Think they went upstairs then?'

Speirs inclined his head towards the doors.

'I reckon it's possible. But I wouldn't know – the corridor bends out there, so you can't really tell *where* the punters are going once they leave.'

Jacobson took a deep, fiery-cool mouthful.

'So you didn't really speak to him – other than to take his drink orders?'

Speirs shook his head: no, he hadn't.

'He didn't, for instance, mention Darren McGee?'

'What – the mad dishwasher? No again. Why – was there some connection there?'

Jacobson didn't enlighten him, asked him what he knew about McGee in any case.

Speirs leaned over the table, lowered his chirpy tones.

'Just like I say – mad as a hatter. You'd see him in the staff rest room, talking to himself like he was oblivious to his surroundings. He went for one of the commis chefs with a knife one time – took three of 'em to pull him away apparently. All that bollocks at the inquest, racial abuse and whatnot. Nobody gave a toss what colour he was, Mr Jacobson – they just didn't want to work alongside a certified nutcase. Who the hell would?'

Vicky liked the look of the place. A conversion halfway along Claremont Road – one of the old terraced houses reborn as two full-size flats and a smaller attic apartment. Not too far from the local shops and handy for the little pub on the corner. The pub was closed up but the girl who'd come out from the estate agents to accompany the viewing had said that it would be reopening again soon, once the new owners had carried out a complete redesign and refit. Now that the area was on the turn, she'd added, they were going for more of a wine bar atmosphere. The only real problem Vicky could see would be with parking. There were vehicles nose to tail along both sides of the street, including a couple of people carriers that were taking up half the pavement as well as the road. The girl had an answer for that too. The council had carried out a consultative exercise recently: there were plans to bring in a fully fledged residents' parking scheme before the end of the year – so it wouldn't be an issue for too long. Vicky asked to look at the attic flat again. The tenancy would be for six months in the first instance, the girl reminded her, leading the way, with a sum equivalent to two months' rent to be held as a security.

Vicky loved the kitchen and the bathroom. She liked the view from the wide front window too: street after street of terraced roofs – red, pink, occasionally grey – stretching into the distance, and a clear April sky, still light, overhead.

'I'll need to think about it,' she told the girl, 'I'm looking at some more places tomorrow.'

'No problem. But if you *are* interested, I'd advise you to let us know soon. These places usually go pretty quickly.'

They took the bright, airy stairs back down to the street. They shook hands and walked off in opposite directions to their cars. Vicky had managed to park her Clio around the corner in Claremont Avenue. She reached the corner just as it was being passed by a small blue van. The solitary driver slowed, looking straight at her: Rick Cole in his plumber's overalls, a wide, leering grin all over his face. He'd actually stopped now, was leaning across to wind down the passenger's window.

'Vicky, doll,' he said, his mouth still wide, 'we should talk some night, catch up.'

But Vicky already had her head down, was already

walking on. *What's past is past, girl,* Darren had said one time, *you've gotta walk and not look back – you know what I'm saying?*

Jacobson thought better of a second scotch, went off in search of Alison Taylor, the hotel's manager. He found her sitting over a pile of paperwork at an outside table in the hotel gardens. The evening was just about warm enough – or not cold enough – to make it a pleasant spot.

'The spreadsheet of the staff rosters for the last week,' she said, handing him half a dozen stapled sheets of A4. 'I've highlighted last night's evening and night cover in red. And I've attached the contact details as well – telephone numbers, addresses.'

It was more information than Jacobson had strictly asked for but he said thanks anyway. Better too much than too little.

She tried her usually winning smile on him again.

'I could do with getting my office back again soon, Inspector.'

Jacobson told her matter-of-factly that his team were copying the tapes as they went, which would at least minimise the need to view them on site again. It was still probable however that he'd want the desk staff and porters who were on duty last night to take a look through – in case any faces jolted their memory about something unusual or suspicious. Maybe the best thing would be to set aside one of the delegates' rooms in the hotel's conference area for the purpose, she suggested. It was an entirely reasonable suggestion: Jacobson could only nod and agree.

She had some kind of blue concoction in a long glass on the table beside her. Curaçao in the mix somewhere, he guessed. She watched him watching her idly swirling the contents with a cocktail stirrer.

'Business meets pleasure,' she said, still trying the smile, 'perks of the job.'

Jacobson didn't comment straightaway. He was starting

to realise why it was that she irritated him so much despite evidently trying to be helpful. Powder-blue suit, powder-blue eyes, neat blond hair: if his ex-wife, Janice, ever became famous, she had her look-alike ready and waiting in the wings. He wanted to ask her about Darren McGee, couldn't think of anything cleverer than a more-or-less direct approach.

'Not a stress-free job though, yours,' he said. 'Not with two suspicious deaths in four months – it'll work out at about six a year if the rate keeps up.'

Her smile fell away to nothing.

'But there's no connection is there? I mean – other than that they both drowned? And Darren – well, Darren was Darren.'

'I'm surprised he was still on your payroll from what I'm hearing,' Jacobson responded, ignoring both her questions.

She produced a packet of Dunhill, took one out, lit it. She offered one to Jacobson but he shook his head, even managed to keep his B & H in his pocket.

'He probably wouldn't have been for very much longer. There were starting to be just too many problems involved. The other staff weren't happy to say the least.'

Jacobson mentioned the incident with the knife that Jack Speirs had told him about.

'Well, that story was never really proven to my satisfaction, Inspector. If *you* pick up a knife, you're just picking up a knife. If somebody who's supposed to be mad picks one up, it's a dangerous incident.'

Jacobson's mental database accessed words such as litigation, compensation, terms such as employers' liability insurance.

'You were taking a risk employing him though, surely?'

Alison Taylor exhaled her cigarette smoke with a sigh.

'Schizophrenia isn't always the life sentence it used to be. You'd be surprised how many people have been diagnosed but go on to lead more-or-less normal lives. Provided they get the right support and the right medication anyway.'

Jacobson probably didn't keep the surprise from registering on his face. If he ever thought about the kind of people who ran hotels at all, he certainly didn't think about them as likely sources of expertise on mental illness.

'My brother was a sufferer from the age of twenty – until he died,' she added simply. 'He walked off a bridge too – the Clifton suspension, down in Bristol.'

'I'm sorry,' Jacobson said inadequately.

For years now, his job had meant looking beyond first appearances, probing for the real human being underneath. Yet he could still get it wrong, still jump to conclusions. He'd seen her as shallow: a pushy cow in a business suit. And maybe she was that – but it wasn't all she was. He watched her take a drink from her glass, follow it with another drag on her cigarette.

'It was more than ten years ago now. But I still think about him every day. We were close as kids. He was the next up in the family, two years between us.'

'So the new treatments didn't work so well for him then?'

'They worked very well for a long time. But he stopped self-medicating – it's always one of the biggest dangers. The next thing was he that he suffered a bad episode before anybody knew what was going on. Something similar happened to Darren, if you want my view. He was fine the first few weeks he worked here. No real problems at all.'

It was uncanny, Jacobson thought. Her resemblance to Janice. Although Janice hadn't smoked, had nagged him about his own habit.

'I assume you didn't know *why* he'd come to Crowby? Why he was looking for a job here?'

She shook her head.

'About his girlfriend you mean? No, I'd no idea until it all came out at the inquest. Obviously that would've made a difference if I had known. Even I probably wouldn't have allowed him to be taken on in that case.'

Chapter Seventeen

Kerr, Barber and Hume were working one property at a time each. Kerr pressed the bell on a gaff that called itself Radbourne. The middle-aged, middle-class couple wanted to be helpful but had to admit that they'd gone to bed at eleven o'clock, had slept soundly, hadn't seen or heard anything unusual or suspicious. Then the wife mentioned Arlette, the French exchange student who was lodged with them temporarily. The wife's younger sister taught languages at the university, she said, was adept at persuading her into taking in one or two foreign students for the second semester every year. Kerr had very nearly been yawning through the interview until the point where the husband added that Arlette tended to keep late hours and that she was staying up on the third floor. He'd studied the house as he'd scrunched along the broad, gravelled driveway towards the front door, had calculated that anybody looking out from the top level would have a clear, unimpeded view right across both the river and the Memorial Bridge.

Arlette Lefevre's student digs turned out to be substantially bigger than the poky Hall of Residence room that Kerr had put up with during the not very grand total of five months he'd endured at uni himself before he'd packed in higher education as a bad job. As well as her bedroom, Arlette enjoyed her own kitchen and her own bathroom.

Plus the lounge where she was currently sitting – watching an ancient episode of *Will and Grace*. Fortunately her English was an awful lot better than Kerr's holiday-phrase-book French. She'd been out with some friends at Club Zoo last night, she told him, had left early, around one o'clock. She hadn't wanted to walk the streets alone at that time of night so she'd taken a cab home.

'The cab would've gone past the Memorial Bridge then?' Kerr asked her.

She was a pretty enough girl. But her looks were dramatically boosted by the trace in her voice of that accent – above all others – which Kerr, like most British men, had a conditioned reflex to find sexy.

'Yes, straight past,' she said.

'Anyone around, any vehicles?'

It was the kind of situation where you tried to keep your questions vague and neutral, tried to avoid planting suggestions or giving mental cues.

'Not that I noticed. But later on there was a – what do you call it – *une camionette* – a van. Yes, a van.'

'You mean a van on the bridge?'

'*Vrai*. That's right. Parked on the bridge. I thought that wasn't permitted. I saw it when I was looking out of the window. I like to watch the moon before I go to sleep.'

Kerr found it an attractive enough image. He asked her if she could remember when exactly.

'Not exactly. But around about one thirty maybe.'

She had a description too: white, medium-sized, no windows on the side.

'Did you hear anything, Arlette? Then or maybe a little while later.'

She looked genuinely thoughtful.

'No,' she answered, shaking her head. 'Once I'm in bed it's out like the light, I'm afraid.'

Jacobson talked to the evening receptionist and the porters who worked the late shift. But there was nothing doing.

The porter who'd lifted the barrier to let Paul Shaw's car out of the car park remembered the fact, didn't remember him returning later in the evening. No one recalled seeing him later on. The receptionist – this one was accurately labelled as such, not as a faux manager – impressed Jacobson as having a good memory for names and faces. But she hadn't seen anyone around the night before who'd looked as if they shouldn't be there. Most of the hotel's bars and restaurants were open to the public and Thursday nights weren't the quietest nights in the week, she told him, early on anyway: other than the private residents' bar, everything closed before midnight except on Fridays and Saturdays – unless there was a function booked, which there hadn't been. The upshot was that there were lots of people coming in and out of the building who weren't registered guests. She hadn't noticed anyone suspicious headed for the lifts to the accommodation floors – *But what did suspicious mean anyway? In the hotel trade, you soon learned that appearances could be deceptive.* Jacobson could only agree, told her it was exactly the same for him. On balance, he thought, it was probably still worth getting the night staff to take a look at the CCTV footage. But it didn't feel like something to keep his hopes up about. Not something, as Greg Salter would say, to *prioritise*. What it all came down to right now, he concluded, was the night porter. He came on duty at half past eleven, clocked off at seven am. Between times, seemingly, he was a one-man security band. He controlled access to the front door for anyone without a guest key and he operated the car parking barrier – and the overnight exit shutters – as and when necessary.

He checked his watch: seven thirty on the nail. The problem with the night man was that he wasn't answering his mobile or his land line. It was possible that he was at home with his phones turned off. But it was just as likely that he was propping up a bar somewhere, or visiting his girlfriend, or wading through a bucket of popcorn at the multiplex. He phoned Kerr, delegated – just like the management textbooks said he should. Kerr reckoned the door-to-door would keep him going for another couple of hours anyway. Barber and Hume likewise. He didn't have a problem with talking to the night porter after that, even if it meant going home and then calling back out again later – *I'm not in CID for the regular hours, Frank.*

He looked in on Williams and Emma Smith. They didn't have a problem either. They were prepared to keep going until they'd replayed the footage all the way through – *As long as it takes, guv,* Emma Smith told him. He wandered out to the hotel gardens again, just wanting to enjoy the view across the river before he drove home. Alison Taylor had gone and the temperature had started to drop. There was a time, he realised, when he'd have hung around himself, getting needlessly in his team's way. But he trusted them implicitly these days, knew that they were every bit as keen for genuine results as he was. Even though, when they'd solved one piece of badness, all it really meant was that they could move on to the next piece – and then on to the piece after that.

Martin Kesey and Karen Mott sat next to each other. A thick lad called Alan something – with a Home Counties accent which sat incongruously on top of his *Free Palestine* T-shirt – got the drinks in. Or maybe not that incongruously. There was certainly a lengthy British tradition of young men from minor public schools playing at being revolutionaries while they were students. Some of them even stayed in politics of a kind for life – transformed themselves into mainstream cabinet ministers and backbenchers, the ones who were intermittently anxious that the embarrassing phase when they'd actually believed in something would be raked over sometime by a tabloid editor desperate for a story on a quiet day.

There were five of them around the table, not counting Kesey himself. Two lads and three girls. They were full of the *Triumph*, debating the pros and cons, whether art was subject to ethical imperatives or whether it floated free – above morality and governed solely by aesthetic considerations. Kesey sipped his beer, accepted a too-thin roll-up that Karen offered him after she'd made one for herself. Occasionally he'd ask a question or make a comment. The trick, as ever, was to lead the discussion without seeming to lead it. It almost didn't matter anymore what politics they had – as long as they had some politics at all. So long as they did, you could talk to them, argue, seek to persuade them to the correct point of view. The hardest to reach were the others: the grey, dozing, silent majority. The ones who never thought beyond their next shag or their next booze-up. The ones who were already cannon fodder for whatever the government and the multinationals wanted them to do with their malleable lives. He noticed that Karen was knocking back the vodka and Cokes and hanging on his every word whenever he condescended to utter one.

One by one they drifted off – until there were only the two of them left. Karen was brighter than she thought she was. Although she hadn't learned to play the game properly yet. She still voiced her opinions in normal English, had still to master the academic knack of jargonising common sense, of making the obvious appear complex.

'All those Teutonic musclemen,' she said, leaning close, so that he could smell her perfume and the hint of sweat underneath it. 'They must've made the *frauleins* as horny as fuck.'

He liked the way she said fuck, near-whispering the word in his ear, her breath hot, making it plain that her interest in the topic was a lot more than abstract.

Kerr, Barber and Hume met up in the Bellevue. It was a quarter to ten. Bob Harker had no more than half a dozen customers in his modest-sized lounge bar but he seemed cheerful enough. He was thinking of selling up, he told Mick Hume, effing off to Spain or Portugal, somewhere

where his pension would be worth something, where the necessities of life didn't cost an arm and a leg.

The three detectives carried their beers through to Harker's meeting room, compared notes in private. Arlette Lefevre was the only person remotely resembling a witness they'd discovered and her testimony, they agreed, didn't amount to very much. Barber and Hume called it a night as soon as they'd finished their drinks. Kerr's mobile rang: DC Williams with the news that they'd replayed to the end of the tapes and neither Paul Shaw nor Paul Shaw's car had put in a reappearance.

'Too bad, Ray, but cheers anyway,' Kerr said, 'see you in the morning.'

He didn't put his phone away, dialled Rachel's number.

There was noise behind her voice. Chitchat, laughter, bass-heavy music.

'Oh – Ian,' she said, as if his call had surprised her.

She was still in Birmingham, she told him. They'd run into even more college friends than they'd expected when they'd had lunch at the Ikon. And one thing had led to another. Drinks, a second meal, more drinks: *You know how it is*.

'Yeah, sure,' Kerr lied, not remotely knowing how it was and not enjoying his picture of how it might be in the slightest.

He asked her how she'd get home.

'Well, Tony will be on the train with me back to Crowby. Then we can share a cab back to Wynarth. Don't worry.'

So she *had* spent the day with Tony Scruton. It was a pity, he told her, *too bad* – he had a couple of hours free, he'd thought he might've been able to call over.

'Oh, I see. Yes it is too bad. Maybe there'll be another time over the weekend.'

'Yeah, I hope so. Look take care, Rayche, I've got to go,' he said, seizing what little psychological advantage he could from the situation by at least being the first one to hang up.

He drove back into town and then out towards the Bovis estate, telling himself it was no big deal. It was how their relationship worked. Snatched hours and afternoons – very rarely, days – grabbed here and there. Both of them put the other one a poor second to the rest of the stuff in their lives. It wasn't even an unspoken agreement, it was something they'd talked about openly, sometimes interminably.

He parked in the street outside his house. There was no point squeezing his car on to the driveway in front of Cathy's when he'd have to be driving back out again in an hour or so. He wasn't seriously jealous of Scruton, why the hell should he be? But he was in danger of letting himself sulk like a teenager. A quick screw would just have suited him fine – that was all there was to it. And come to that, the twins would be fast asleep in bed by now, he thought, stepping out of the car and locking it. He wasn't the kind of married bloke who looked to other women because his wife bored him. She didn't, she never had. At heart, he knew, it was really just a matter of greed, impure and simple, of grabbing what you could.

He turned his key in the latch, slung his jacket on the hook, walked through to his lounge.

'Michelle?'

He'd been expecting to see his wife, curled up on the sofa and waiting for him. Instead, Michelle, the quiet girl who was Cathy's most reliable babysitter, was poring over an A-Level text book, a re-run of *Friends* on low volume in the background.

'I don't know you how can study and watch TV at the same time,' he added, recalling Arlette Lefevre and masking his disbelief – but only a little.

'Well, the TV's always on at our place, Mr Kerr, so I suppose I'm just used to it. The twins are fine by the way – both snoozing their little heads off.'

The cat roused itself from the arm of the sofa, looked up at him, but evidently decided his arrival wasn't worth stirring herself for on this occasion. Michelle was known to make a fuss of her, had probably sated her immediate need for petting.

'Cathy's nipped out then,' he said superfluously.

He'd phoned her at tea time, explained that there was a new murder squad case, that he didn't know exactly when he'd be able to knock off. He couldn't recall her saying that she was going out anywhere.

'She phoned me up at short notice,' Michelle said, gathering her books together. 'I think a few of them from her office are meeting up for a drink. A bit of a girls' night out by the sounds of it.'

Kerr nodded, tried not to look too blank. After Michelle had gone, he checked on the twins himself. She'd been right, both of them – his son, Sam, and his daughter, Susie – were sound asleep. They had their own separate bedrooms now which meant that Kerr had lost the cramped box room he'd used as a den and which was now festooned with Sam's Bob the Builder paraphernalia. He closed their doors on them quietly, padded back downstairs, got himself a beer, killed *Friends* in favour of the History Channel.

It was gone midnight when he heard the CrowbyCab pulling up and then driving off. Cathy came in a minute later, her face slightly flushed. He'd already decided that if they were going to have a row about it, then it wouldn't be right now. He asked her if she'd had a good time, explained that he'd waited in for her but that now she was here, he needed to go back out again.

She was looking straight at him, still hadn't ditched her jacket. Her voice when she spoke had a terrible calmness to it.

'Off to see her, is it?'

Kerr just gaped at her. As if a bomb had just exploded – or the wings had just dropped off the aeroplane.

Chapter Eighteen

Saturday April 23rd

Saturday morning. Six am. Kesey would have preferred to spend the night in his own comfortable flat rather than in Karen's dilapidated student accommodation. But there had been other considerations. The biggest one being that he had to get up and get going early. He couldn't risk her hanging around his private space after he'd gone and he didn't want the hassle of turfing her out at the crack of dawn either. All in all, it had been easier to go back to hers. Even though the bed was soft and lumpy and her flat had a pervasive, indefinable dankness everywhere you went in it. There was also the issue of her flatmates. If you made a habit of shagging your students in the era of sexual harassment codes, you needed to exercise at least a modicum of discretion. But everything had turned out just fine. The others had still been out when the two of them had got back, certainly wouldn't be up and about now.

He watched her sleeping, her eyes tight shut, her hair dishevelled. He slid his hand between her legs for a moment just because he could. She gave a gentle little moan but didn't wake up. Reluctantly, he stole out of bed, pulled on his clothes, shut her bedroom door behind him slowly, quietly.

He drove back to his own place, showered, changed,

enjoyed a breakfast of grapefruit juice, toast and scrambled eggs. He was on the road by seven, heading towards the complex of motorways around the Birmingham conurbation. The route was simplicity until you turned off the M42 at the recommended junction and hit the network of twisting B roads that bisected the open countryside beyond. He made it with only one wrong detour, was pulling on to Matthew Sutherland's private land by eight thirty.

Sutherland, the Party's regional organiser, had made his money from builders' supplies, had forged a personal empire of trade-only outlets across the Midlands. When his company had grown big and flourishing enough he'd sold it on, lock, stock and barrel, to a national chain and promptly retired from the tedious, daily grind of working for a living. He played at farming and race-horse breeding but his real passions and interests lay in neither direction. There were some in the Party who didn't like him, who felt that his wealth gave him an undue, unearned influence over policy – but so far they'd been overruled by the pragmatists. Back in the 1960s, Colin Jordan's British Movement had been bankrolled by his marriage to Francoise Dior, heir to the perfume fortune. And even Hitler had needed the support of the men with money, would've lived and died as an unknown rabble-rouser without it.

Kesey drove slowly along the drive to the main house, knowing that his face and his licence plates were being electronically clocked and monitored every hundred yards or so. Sutherland's total pile was substantial – in excess of the forty acre mark – and all of it protected behind stout walls of Midlands red brick. He had plenty of woodland too, thick, green and sheltered from prying eyes. Even a simple briefing and training event, like this one, had to be planned and coordinated thoroughly. You were told when to set off and when to arrive relative to your journey – so that too many cars didn't show up at once – so that there was no perception in the area of an unusual volume of traffic. Once you got there, you parked in ample-sized barns that had been cleared out for the purpose, that hid your presence from the air as well as from the ground.

The meeting the other night had only been local but this was high level, Party-wide. There would be Party members here from right across the country. But only by specific invitation, only those who'd showed sufficient promise and sufficient dedication. For a recent recruit like himself, the invitation was seen as an ultimate privilege. In Party terms, Dr Martin Kesey had finally, indisputably, arrived.

Jacobson made himself some fresh coffee and drank two full cupfuls, standing in his dressing gown by the sliding glass door in his lounge, the one that gave access to his balcony and a view over Wellington Park. Unexpectedly, he'd slept like the proverbial log, was starting to feel that the works of Arthur Schopenhauer ought to be made available on prescription as a natural, organic alternative to sleeping pills. He'd spent another evening bogged down in *The World as Will and Idea*. Jacobson liked to restate concepts in his own terms, a technique he'd picked up from his OU studies – frequently he did the same with post-mortem and forensic reports – but he still hadn't got very far with the father of modern pessimism. Sometime around midnight he realised he'd been trying – and failing – to decipher the same three sentences for the last ten minutes. An object was entirely different from its representation (sentence one) except that an object and its representation were exactly the same thing (sentence three): that had been the moment of dis-illumination when he'd finally decided to hit the sack.

He shaved, showered, checked both his phones: no messages. He wanted to know what had happened with the night porter but decided it could wait until he clocked on at the Divisional building. He preferred not to call DS Kerr outside working hours unless he had to. You never knew if he'd be at home to answer his land line, never knew exactly what else he might be doing if he answered you on his mobile. Despite Schopenhauer, he'd actually gone to sleep thinking about Paul Shaw's shit-fuck piece of paper and the four names it had contained. He'd woken up thinking about it too, had lain in bed for a good half-hour replaying his conversation with Shaw over and over, trying to visualise the scene, trying to put himself back in to it. But nothing had come of it. *Rien de* bloody *rien*.

He took a clean shirt from a hanger in his wardrobe, couldn't decide which tie. All of a sudden, he realised he'd dreamt about it too. In the dream, he'd been seized by the conviction that he only had to look in the telephone directory. The four names were buried somewhere in his memory, he'd reasoned. If he flicked through the phone book, sooner or later something would kick-start his synapses, ring the necessary bell. He'd been in some kind of public building, large and gloomy, library-like. There'd been a whole room of directories, stacked high and elaborately bound. Shelf after shelf of them. He'd woken up briefly, he remembered now, with sweat on his brow. And the gilded pages of every big, heavy book he'd looked at had been completely and entirely blank.

Kesey helped himself to a second breakfast – bacon with his eggs this time – in the barn nearest the house which was functioning as an ad hoc canteen. He was relieved to see that Rick Cole, the local guy he'd met the other night, had already arrived. He thought he'd made a good impression on him at the Bideford Arms. Cole was sitting with the Stuart brothers, still more of an unknown quantity as far as Kesey was concerned. Although there was no reason to worry about them particularly, as far as he knew.

He carried his tray over to join them. They would be working in area-based units for the first half of the day which meant he'd be sticking with them in any case. Kesey noticed there was still a spare chair at the table after he'd sat down. He'd been told there would be five of them altogether – it looked as if somebody was missing.

'No Parker yet,' Rick Cole said, maybe reading his thoughts, more likely just thinking along similar lines.

'The guy is fucking us about,' John Stuart commented. 'If he doesn't show today, he's finished.'

'He's still not answering his mobile then?' Phil Stuart asked.

Cole shook his head slowly from side to side.

'Never mind his phone, mate. He's not answering his effing front door.'

'What? You called round there, Rick?' Phil asked again.

He was shorter than his brick-shithouse brother. And bespectacled. But he still didn't look like a pushover.

'Yeah. Last night. No worries, mate – Rick Cole knows how to be discreet. But the fact remains Parker can't be found.'

The three of them lapsed into silence. Kesey got on with his bacon and eggs. Whatever the problem was, it wasn't something they were sharing with him – not yet anyway. After a moment or two, Cole started the conversation back up again: he'd really enjoyed Kesey's talk, he told him, they all had.

'Thanks,' Kesey said, 'there's nothing better than an audience of like minds.'

He cut through a slice of bacon, wondered if the day would turn out to have been worth abandoning Karen Mott's warm, musty bed for.

Chapter Nineteen

Jacobson waited in his office for DS Kerr to put in an appearance. It was a few minutes before nine. Technically they were involved in 'preliminary inquiries' – the phase before the murder squad went into full-scale operation – so there was no question at the moment of setting up a dedicated incident room. Kerr apart, he'd instructed his team to stop at home but to expect a call-out from him first thing. He had to know what he wanted them to do before he asked them to do it, had never confused productive work with simply hanging around the premises. He picked up the photocube off his desk: his erstwhile family – his ex-wife Janice and his grown-up daughter, Sally. For more than a year now, he'd been telling himself it was time for Janice's photograph to go, although he'd hang on to Sally's, obviously. But whenever it came to it – now would be as good a moment as any, for example – he never seemed able to carry out the threat, to finally get Janice's image out of his daily life once and for all. He put the cube back down, at least made sure that it was Sally and not her mother who was in his direct line of vision.

Kerr made it on the dot of the hour, cursing the Saturday morning shopping traffic. As they often did, they dispensed with chairs, stood over by Jacobson's window as they talked, watching the crowds mass across the pedestrianised square towards the arse-end of the Crowby Arndale Centre.

Kerr's news was two per cent about the CCTV footage, eight per cent about Arlette Lefevre, and ninety per cent about the Riverside Hotel's night porter.

'So he didn't show? Didn't even phone in?' Jacobson asked.

Kerr ran through the story again. The night porter hadn't clocked on at the appointed time, hadn't shown up in the next half-hour, hadn't phoned in to explain his absence. The receptionist had disturbed Alison Taylor at home; Alison Taylor had put a call out to the local employment agency she used for staff emergencies. The guy that Kerr had talked to when he'd driven over there after midnight had been an agency stand-in and not the regular night porter – the one who'd been on duty the night before.

Jacobson lapsed into thoughtful silence. Both of them carried on gaping out of the window. Kerr was still trying to get last night's panic out of his head. He couldn't believe he'd got away with it. That he had – apparently – got away with it he put totally down to luck. If he hadn't been so gobsmacked, if he hadn't been stunned into silence, God know's what he might have said. It had probably been seconds only in reality. *Off to see her, is it*? Cathy had asked – and then she'd laughed. She'd been joking, making light of something that usually she found anything but funny: Kerr's job and its demanding, unpredictable hours, the disruptions it constantly made to their life. *Yeah, another blond one – just like you*, he'd said, recovering, *I'm meeting her over at the Riverside*. He'd told her why he really had to go there, kissed her, said he didn't think he'd be gone too long. It had taken him virtually the entire drive over to the hotel to get his pulse and his heartbeat back down to their normal levels.

'You checked his home address again, old son?' Jacobson asked.

'I cruised past,' Kerr said, pulled back to the present. 'I tried the intercom as well. Nowt.'

'And nothing on the PNC?'

'Ditto, not that that proves anything.'

'Proves absolutely bog all,' Jacobson agreed.

The Police National Computer was in a mess, he was always being told by those – like Kerr – who took an interest in technology. Years of accumulated human error compounded by technical glitches and out-of-date software. You could have a dozen convictions and not show up there. It was an essential first check but only an idiot regarded it as infallible. And besides, as every copper knew in his heart of hearts, there was no such animal as an entirely innocent member of the public: just miscreants of varying degree who hadn't been brought to book yet.

They headed off in Kerr's car. Jacobson used his mobile on the way, made his promised calls to the rest of his team. He wanted DC Williams to set something up at the Riverside Hotel: get the off-duty night staff in to take a butcher's at the CCTV footage. It would probably be a good idea to involve Steve Horton, the civilian computer officer. Now that they had their own copy of the footage, Horton might know some geeky way of speeding up the process. Barber and Mick Hume could take another – final – stab at door-to-door along Riverside Walk. As for Emma Smith, he had a different kind of task in mind altogether. Kerr drove on autopilot. He still wasn't doing too well at setting last night's near cataclysm to one side. The Riverside's missing porter's address put him on the wrong side of Midland Road. Not precisely Mill Street but barely a kick in the bum away from that area's rundown terraces and back-to-backs. He carried on past the place when they reached it, pulled up and cut the engine a useful hundred yards or so away. They got out and walked. The gaff itself was a modern block, privately owned. Three storeys of flats above half a dozen retail units. A bakery, a branch of Blockbuster and the Merry Fryer chippy amongst them. Visitor access was by entryphone. He pressed the number, wasn't surprised not to get an answer. He tried another number, said he had a parcel to deliver. The door buzzed and he shoved it open: they were in.

The night porter's address was on the top floor. Kerr pulled on the gloves he always carried on duty before he lifted the letter box and then peered though it into semi-darkness and silence. He made out three or four letters – junk mail by the looks of it – on an uncarpeted floor. The door lock didn't look up to much, looked like a standard-issue yale. He scanned Jacobson's face for a reaction. The porter had picked an irritating time to go absent without leave. But that was probably all there was to it. An irritating coincidence of the kind that happened to their inquiries with irritating frequency. But then on the other hand . . .

Jacobson nodded unequivocally. Kerr searched in his wallet, found the expired Visa card that he used for the purpose these days – ever since he'd knackered one of Cathy's customer loyalty cards against a raggedy doorjam out on the Woodlands. It was a thirty-second job, barely that. Jacobson followed him in and Kerr pulled the door shut behind them.

The place was small. Minimalist without being remotely fashionable. A single bedroom, a bathroom, a kitchen and a nondescript lounge. Kerr always felt uneasy about assisting Jacobson's recurrent, unauthorised fishing trips. But he had to admit that they were a quick option. Even in the simplest cases, it could take a couple of hours to get the due, legal authorisations. Or to get them refused. Jacobson's argument was that if you found out something worth knowing, you could go through the official channels later – and at least be sure in advance that you weren't wasting your time.

They worked their way through methodically. The post *was* all junk. You could tell just by looking at the outside of the envelopes. Kerr left it where he'd found it, interrogated the wall-attached land line further along the hall. There were only two messages on the answerphone: both of them from Alison Taylor, asking him to phone the hotel. He dialled 1471: the last call tallied with the time of her second message, left half an hour ago. Jacobson checked the bathroom and the bedroom. There was no shaving gear and enough gaps in the wardrobe to make recent clothes-packing a plausible scenario. Looking under the bed - sod all - he stubbed his toe on the biggest of the set of weights which had been dumped haphazardly at its side. He swore venomously under his breath - *bastard*.

They met up in the kitchen. A stack of dishes had been left unwashed and greasy in the sink but the litter bin had been emptied and the only correspondence lying around, if you could call it correspondence, was a red electricity bill and a meal deal offer from Pizza Hut. On the other hand, there was an elderly PC resting on the corner of the kitchen table. The keyboard was nicotine-stained and a few of the keys were missing or wonky. The machine had been unplugged from the nearby wall socket. Kerr re-plugged it, tried to boot it up. The error message on the black screen puzzled him for a minute or two. Then the penny dropped:

'Shit, Frank. Some bugger's removed the hard disk, just swiped the thing out.'

He took a closer look, noticed that the casing was loose and that there were screws scattered around on the floor under the table. He unplugged it, switched it back off. They moved on to the lounge. Chief contents: sofa, armchair, cheese plant, TV, DVD player. Jacobson scanned the dozen or so DVD titles. Although they looked harmless enough it was always possible that they weren't what they seemed, didn't contain what they claimed to contain. Especially in a gaff where somebody had thought that the hard disk on their home computer needed removing to protect it from unwanted gaze. He bunged a couple into the player at random. But *The Dirty Dozen* and *Catwoman* both did exactly what they said on the tin. There was no time to check them all in detail so he left it there, thinking that it was scarcely the scientific method in action. There were a handful of books too. Action adventures mainly. Plus a couple of tomes about the Second World War. Kerr lifted up Bullock's *Hitler: A Study in Tyranny*.

'The definitive study of AH, old son. Until Ian Kershaw came along anyway,' Jacobson said, reading Kerr's obvious thought. 'I've got both of them at home. And so have a million others. So far most of us haven't felt the urge to make nailbombs or sign up with Combat 18.'

Kerr put the book back where he'd found it. In just about anybody's gaff, from the grungy bedsit to the country house, there was a cabinet, a drawer, a hole in the wall, an old sock – some kind of concealed or unconcealed space where you kept your personal papers. Love letters and share issue certificates for the wealthy; love letters and DSS claim forms for the poor. Jacobson and Kerr were seasoned snoopers. But they'd found nothing in that line anywhere. Not so much as a holiday snap.

'So what do you reckon, Frank? If it's a runner it's a highly coincidental one.'

'I completely agree. The bugger of it is we've nothing to go on so far that would justify any kind of official alert. We'll need to keep it on the QT for now. Let's see what we can find out about Mr Wayne Parker without making too much noise about it.'

They heard a bed creaking through the far wall, someone switching on Crowby FM at a volume you wouldn't want to live next door to. Jacobson nodded towards the hallway.

'Let's get going before someone comes round to borrow a cup of sugar. If there *was* something here for us, someone's made bloody sure that it's not here any longer.'

They took the stairs down without encountering any of Parker's neighbours. Kerr slipped his gloves off on the other side of the front door, ran one of them lightly across the intercom buttons just for the conceptual, theoretical completeness of it.

Emma Smith drove the car to the hospital. Carole Briggs, the duty victim support stroke family liaison officer was in the passenger seat. Paul Shaw's parents were in the back. Nobody was saying very much. It was the best way until you were certain. The force got it wrong on occasion, brought the wrong parents to look at the wrong dead child or the wrong teenage heroin victim. And the relatives always clung to hope until the last minute, right up until the sheet was pulled back.

They took the lift up to the mortuary. Jacobson had sold her the job the way he usually did. It would be useful to observe the parents, the kind of things they said. Inadvertently they might give away some bit or piece of background that could turn out to be crucial. Emma hadn't argued, respected Jacobson too much for that. But she wasn't fooled either, didn't think he was faultless or that he escaped the limitations you'd expect in someone his age and his gender. Dealing with presumed innocent, unconnected relatives was women's work, something to wriggle out of yourself – especially if you happened to have a junior female colleague handy and available.

Linford Shaw, like his wife, Edith, looked to be in his fifties. Although Emma always found it hard to judge the age of black men accurately. Their faces didn't seem to age by the same rules as white men, didn't seem to crease and wrinkle and collapse so soon. He was a bus driver, he told her. Thirty years with London Transport. His wife was a nurse, a ward sister, at King's College Hospital. Emma sat with them in the windowless room reserved for civilian visitors while Carole Briggs sorted out the necessary arrangements. Somebody had tried to brighten the room with a vase of daffodils and a pile of magazines. But it had been a thankless, doomed effort underneath the buzzing strip-lighting and, most of all, in the face of the reason why anyone ever came in here. The wife – the mother – had barely spoken and you could tell that Shaw was holding himself in too, being strong for her.

Emma asked him when they'd last seen their son. It was still remotely possible that her questions were premature. But if they weren't, they were easier answered now than later.

'A fortnight ago this coming Sunday. He always comes to Sunday dinner when he's in London. Always.'

Emma was conscious of her use of tenses, unconscious of fidgeting with a button on her sleeve.

'He came alone? Or maybe with a girlfriend?'

Shaw was a tall man - like his son - his legs long and awkward between the low chair and the table with the bland, yellow flowers.

'I think Paul's too busy for girlfriends. Or not the serious kind anyway - the kind you bring home to meet your mother.'

'Did he talk to you about his work? I mean then - or in general?'

'Paul has a rule. He only talks about his assignments afterwards. Never before or during.'

Carole Briggs opened the door quietly: everything was ready.

'You must be proud of him, of his achievements,' Emma said, standing up.

It was a superfluous remark. Obvious, banal. But somehow she felt a need to say something positive - while they were still half-listening to her - something they might remember about her later.

Linford Shaw held out his straight, wiry arm, helped his wife to her feet.

'If my son's lying in there, miss,' he said, glancing out of the tiny room and across the corridor at the scuffed yellow doors they needed to walk through next, 'then this world has lost a *man*.'

Chapter Twenty

A guy from Coventry that none of them knew was depositioned to join them in Wayne Parker's absence. Going first wasn't an easy gig, Phil Stuart had complained when the batting order was announced. But Cole had just ignored the comment. Easy gigs didn't interest him. The rest of his life was an easy gig. His house, his job, his wife. Cole was here because he wasn't frightened of a hard gig, wasn't a fat-arsed laze-around stooge. Never had been, never would be. The body armour was a tight fit and unfamiliar, made it difficult for him to swing his arms. But he'd manage. Just watch him manage.

The five of them were part of a bigger group, twenty in all. The task was to hold the line in front of a row of tall oak trees which were doubling as an inner-city blockful of asylum seekers. They had riot shields, helmets, batons and half an hour to prepare for the onslaught of the superior force. The idea behind the exercise was simplicity itself: to put yourself into the mental space of the boys in blue. If you learned how you'd react in their shoes, you had a better idea of knowing how they'd react the next time you were up against them. The Coventry guy, the Stuarts, Cole and Kesey were right in the centre of the line. A megaphone was passed along. Someone was wanted to play the officer-in-charge, the prick who bellowed at you that you were unlawful, that defending your own people wasn't British anymore. Cole passed it to Kesey.

'You're the man with the vocabulary, mate,' he told him.

Kesey took it from him with a show of reluctance but Cole noticed that he didn't pass it on. He watched him step forward, try it out for volume.

'Now, you men,' Kesey shouted, turning to face them and adopting a comic, upper-class-twit voice, 'I want you to stand fast and I want you to dispel this mob. There are darkies here depending on you. Some of them haven't shagged a white woman in weeks. And it's up to every man jack of you to make sure that once again the streets are safe for the darkie pimps and the darkie drug dealers.'

Cole shook his head, laughed with the rest. Kesey had style, there was no doubt about that. Kesey spoke into the megaphone again, serious this time: '*Whatever happens, keep the formation tight, move forward on the signal.*' He rejoined the line just as the first brick landed a few yards short of its target. There were still supposed to be ten minutes left in the half-hour. But the opposition were starting early. Either that or the half-hour rule had been disinformation: a ploy, a first test. They were charging towards them now: chucking more bricks at them, stones, a hail of milk bottles that would be petrol bombs in the real situation. Cole kept his shield up, held his place in the line, waited.

The opposition were keen. But their strategy was bollocks. They'd used up their volley in the first five minutes and now they had nothing, only their fists and boots. This was their chance, Cole realised. Kesey seemed to realise it too, bellowed into the megaphone again. '*Batons out, lads. Lay into them.*'

It was too easy after that. In a real ruck, they'd have put half of them in hospital. As it was, there were a few nasty cuts and bruises around the field and a few scores set up that might need settling later. Even when they were pulling their punches, guys like John Stuart could inflict heavy, unpleasant damage. The Crowby contingent stayed in the thick of it, gave better than they got. Kesey, Cole was pleased to see, had his shit together, wielding his baton like a samurai and not above stomping on the heads of the fallen. In this context, of course, you only pretended to stomp, only made it clear that you had your opponent where you *could* stomp him.

Matthew Sutherland himself blew the finish whistle. There would be only fifteen minutes this time, he told them, to change sides and regroup – and then a new twenty would take on the police role. Sutherland's wife, Nora, was standing next to him, camera in hand, making the video record they'd study later, picking up pointers about what had worked and what hadn't. She was a tall, blonde woman who must've been quite a looker in her prime. Sutherland gave Cole and the Stuarts a friendly nod as they filed past. Nora, Cole thought, was probably the sole female presence on site other than the couple of local, trusted wives in the kitchen. When the Party went public – next year was the currently rumoured date – it would be theoretically open to women. Not to mention gays. Not to mention certain kinds of immigrants under certain kinds of circumstances. But all of that would just be camouflage, just for minimal conformity with the System's rule books and so-called laws. You could be pretty certain that the first poof or the first black to turn up at a Party event would also be the last. And you didn't need women doing men's work. That wasn't their place. That was one of the problems with the world that needed fixing. Besides, the command structure would be completely in place by then. Solid, strong, unbreakable. And built up entirely from men. Real men. The backbone of the race. Its real, proud warriors.

Cole eased off the riot kit, glad of the room to swing his arms properly again. Men like himself obviously. Men like the Stuarts. Men, by the looks of it, like Martin Kesey.

Vicky had started to dread weekends. Her mum had a new boyfriend. Stan, her third or fourth since her dad had died.

Or the third or fourth that she knew about at any rate. Not that she minded that part of it, which wasn't any of her business really. Her mum had been barely forty when the paint factory cancer had claimed her husband and from what Vicky remembered they hadn't had the closest marriage anyway. Just one of those dreary, rubbing-along relationships born of habit and circumstance that so many endured. Not unhappy enough to make either party quit. But not exuberant either. Not warm, not close. No, good luck to her on that score. The problem with Stan was just that he was here so often. He worked up in the North-East during the week. Somewhere near Newcastle. But he spent his weekends in Crowby: Friday pm right though till Monday am, hogging the bathroom, the television, the washing machine, getting in the way in the kitchen. It wasn't deliberate, she was sure. She was the real interloper after all, landing back on her mother, when it had seemed to her that there'd been nowhere else for her to go, nowhere else where she could have got through the lonely, empty days. And Stan had tried to be kind to her in his way, had trodden around her on the same eggshells her mum had. But for all that, his presence irritated her, cramped her. The more she thought about it, the more she knew it was time to be living in her own, exclusive space again.

She slid out of bed, pulled on her dressing gown, stood behind her door, listening. Silence. They'd been out late last night, at somebody's wedding anniversary or somebody's birthday party, she couldn't remember which, were probably still fast asleep. With luck she could fix herself some breakfast before she ran into either of them. She more or less crept downstairs, more or less crept back up. But ten minutes later she had her bedroom door closed and a breakfast tray poised on her duvet: a pot of coffee, toast, jam, a fruit yoghurt. She put Dido on quietly in the background while she ate. Easy listening. A sign of age for sure, she thought. But she'd grown tired of rebel music a long time ago. Before she'd even left Crowby. She demolished the toast then moved on to the yoghurt. When she'd finished eating, she poured coffee into one of her mum's overly decorated mugs. A ghastly flowery design: like drinking out of a bereavement card. She sat down at the desk by her window. She'd worked here when she was studying for her A-levels. Only now she was the teacher. It was nearly ten o'clock and the first of her three flat-viewing appointments wasn't until twelve thirty. Her plan for the next couple of hours was to get some preparation done for next week's lessons. Then she'd take a shower and wash her hair before she drove back over to Longtown, always assuming Stan wasn't having a bath or, worse still, shaving – clogging up the sink with scummy water and grimy dots of grey stubble.

The Empire History class had gone well yesterday. She wanted to build on it, keep their enthusiasm going. Something about the 1919 riot in Liverpool would probably make a good case study, she decided, provided she could put enough resources together in time. She lifted the lid on her laptop, switched it on, sipped her coffee while it loaded up.

There had been race riots at half a dozen British ports in the wake of the Great War, mainly aimed against black seamen. Glasgow, Hull and Cardiff had seen trouble too. But Liverpool, uniquely, had played host to the country's first lynching. Charles Wootten, a West Indian sailor, had been chased into the Mersey by a 200-strong mob. Once they had Wootten in the water, the crowd had kept him there, pelting him with stones until he sank and drowned. There had been a police presence at the scene. But they didn't bother to intervene. And they didn't bother to arrest anyone for the murder. She scanned through her files, hoped she still had enough materials. The contemporary newspaper reports of 'the black menace' made interesting reading. So did the understated letter from F.E.M. Hercules, Secretary of the Society of Peoples of African

Origin, to the Secretary of State for the Colonies politely requesting an inquiry. A request which – naturally – was rejected out of hand.

She worked on steadily, the contours of the lesson starting to take shape. Darren had hated her interest in black history, had walked out on her for three days the first time she'd asked him seriously about his own family's story. She wasn't only interested in black history, she'd told him. She was interested in history full stop. She was a history student for fuck's sake. But Darren hadn't been pacified. She'd made him feel like a specimen, he told her when he finally came back, near enough calm again. Everything in the past had been shit, hadn't it? But it was long gone, over, best forgotten. *Why would you care, girl? You ain't even black.*

They'd still been living in St Peter's Street then, just along from the Duke of Cambridge. Vicky had been staying there instead of the usual grot student deathtrap through sheer luck and chance. Her first week at University College she'd rescued a girl called Barbara from the pawing clutches of an overbearing postgrad who'd gatecrashed the Freshers' Ball and had plied her with way too much to drink. Barbara, frankly, had been rat-arsed, and Vicky had half-walked, half-carried her back to the safety of her Hall of Residence, Ramsay, next to the Post Office Tower. Barbara – sober – had turned out to be Barbara Malhoney, an Anglophile from New York with an English mother and a rich, all-American daddy. When Barbara had wanted to move out of her UCL digs during their second year, Daddy had forked out the substantial readies for the Islington flat and Vicky, by now her closest London friend, had followed her there on a ludicrously cheap, virtually token rent.

Darren had come into her life that summer, the interlude before her final year, via the top deck of a number seventy-three – Victoria to Tottenham – that she hadn't planned on catching. Except that the pollution as she'd walked up Pentonville Road on the hottest day in July had been unbearable, had made even the inside of a London bus resemble something like a safe haven for her lungs, her eyes, her throat. Mainly people don't believe in love at first sight. Lust, yes. But not love. Not full-on, unadulterated passion and madness. Yet there Darren was, seeming to be already smiling at her before she even saw him for the first time – when she sat down across the aisle from him in the last free seat. They didn't speak, didn't even glance at each other all that much, both of them observing the unwritten survival rules of London Transport journeys. She'd got off at the stop on White Lion Street, thinking that she'd try walking again. She'd noticed that he'd still been smiling when she'd got up to leave, noticed that he'd got up to leave after her. She'd stepped into the Nag's Head when she got to Upper Street, telling herself she was obeying the recommendations of the London Student Women's Committee – if you think you're being followed, head for a safe, public place – but not telling herself all that earnestly.

She'd completely ignored their advice to be honest. Had let Darren pay for her drink. Then buy her another. Barbara was with her mother for the week – in Rome – so the flat had even been empty when she'd let him walk her over there an hour later, had let him pad in to the long, sunlit hallway after her. He'd been telling her about fire juggling while they'd been walking, about how you went to another place in your head, another level of perception, slowing time to the point of stillness you needed. But Vicky hadn't really been listening, had only one thought in her mind: *Oh, it's him.* They'd sat in the lounge for a moment, Darren preparing to go through the usual motions. *A cup of tea would be nice*, he'd said. *English afternoon tea, girl.* But she'd pretended she hadn't heard, had just taken his hand instead, pulling him directly towards her bedroom and her unmade, sheet-furrowed bed. No messing when it's real love. No worrying about past mistakes. No clumsy fucking about.

*

Jacobson's mobile rang as Kerr pulled out into the stream of traffic: Sergeant Ince in the control room – there was a burnt-out Lexus on the Woodlands, it was possible that it was Paul Shaw's missing vehicle. Jacobson noted the location while Kerr executed a risky U-turn to point the car in the right direction. When they got there, he took a route along the main drag, Shakespeare Road, and past the Poets, the estate's solitary boozer. There was some kind of semi-legal boot sale occurring in the pub car park. Stolen goods endlessly recycled. Maybe even the odd, legitimate article being sold on in the desperate hope of a quick fiver or a tenner that could be put towards the weekend's groceries or the weekend's oblivion supplies – the cheap Dutch speed, for instance, that was Crowby's current flavour of the month according to 'Clean' Harry Fields.

'*Caveat emptor*, old son,' Jacobson said as they drove past.

A circling wasteground bordered the Poets. Muck, weeds and doomed patches of grassland. The burnout was up ahead, maybe ten or so yards from the road. The uniformed patrol who'd called it in had parked up nearby, were waiting inside their patrol vehicle. The driver got out to greet them while his oppo took the last bite out of his late breakfast, a cold, unappetising individual pork and apple pie he'd bought in the Spa shop and lived to regret. Jacobson took the driver's word for it that the burnt-to-the-metal structure he'd spotted was the right make and model.

'No reports from concerned citizens of when it got here or when it was set alight, old son?'

'Not as far I know, guv. A burning car on the Woodlands isn't exactly man bites dog.'

Jacobson could only nod in agreement. Cars nicked for joyriding were abandoned and trashed out this way on virtually a daily basis. If you had a more sinister purpose in mind, it was the ideal dumping ground. And although half a dozen high-rise blocks had a clear view over the wasteland, the odds against a witness coming forward were of lottery proportions. *I wouldn't piss in your ear if your brain was on fire* was the kind of response you were likely to get on the Woodlands if you asked any kind of police-related question that you couldn't back up with a threat or a bribe of one kind or another. Somebody would need to check thoroughly with yesterday's uniformed patrols to see what had or hadn't been sighted before this morning. Yet if the car had belonged to Paul Shaw, the reality was that it could have been brought here anytime since he'd been recorded driving out of the Riverside Hotel on Thursday night.

They trudged across the muddy ground to take a closer look. There was no telling what a decent forensic examination might reveal but there were no secrets being instantly given away to the unskilled naked eye. Jacobson called back Sergeant Ince in the control room, told him he needed the SOCOs out here pronto, asked him to arrange it, authorised him to disturb Jim Webster at home if necessary. Kerr got closer to the boot than he would have risked if there had already been a SOCO around. The heat had twisted the lid right back. He peered inside: nothing – or nothing that was recognisable as anything. He did the same with what was left of the interior, achieved another non-result. Jacobson asked the plods to wait with the wreck until the SOCOs turned up. If they had nothing urgent doing after that, then maybe they could ask around the high-rises across the way. He wasn't expecting they'd find out anything much, he told them, in fact he wasn't expecting they'd find out anything at all. But sometimes police work was all about going through the motions – just in case.

Every space in the Market Square had gone but Randeep Parmeer had managed to grab the last three yards of car parking space around the corner in Thomas Holt Street. He felt almost optimistic, walking towards his restaurant. There'd been no more unwanted telephone calls since Wednesday night and no nuisance customers last night.

He'd worried that the trouble on the previous two Friday nights might've had a bad effect on his weekend takings. But that hadn't happened either. The restaurant had been pretty much full of normal, more or less civilised diners and there'd been no real problems of any kind. Maybe the policeman, Kerr, had been right after all when he'd suggested that the calls were just from some pathetic, harmless lunatic. And maybe the yobbos had just got fed up, moved on to some other target. If so he'd been lucky. But it wouldn't do to take any more chances. CCTV was the key, he decided. He'd get a few quotes, get a system installed, maybe have something done at home too. When you had a wife and daughters to think of, it didn't do to take needless risks. He'd get it sorted today. In fact he'd get it sorted next, make a few calls as soon as he'd got the place opened up. Wynarth got busy on Saturdays and he liked to have everything up and running on time. Hordes of shoppers drove over from Crowby, browsed in the antique and New Age shops for an hour or two and then – bless them all – they got hungry for lunch. He stopped outside the estate agents for a minute, the other half of the Bank House building, the window crowded as ever with property for sale. All shapes and sizes as usual – and every kind of price. The English loved their property nearly as much as they loved an over-spiced curry and too much lager. He took the thick bunch of keys from his pocket, approached the front door of the Viceroy. He undid the locks, pushed the door open. It was mainly the smell he'd remember later. That and the way his hopeful mood had vanished in an instant. It was thanks to the smell hitting his nostrils that he didn't step into the mess. Dog shit probably. Or cat shit. Shoved through the letterbox in the middle of the night. Animal dung splattered on his door mat – courtesy of some unknown piece of all-too-human excrement.

Chapter Twenty-One

Jacobson's mobile rang again as Kerr drove them back towards town: Henry Pelling at the *Argus*. He'd been as good as his word, he told Jacobson, had asked around the newspaper office about Paul Shaw.

'Jane Spencer might be worth half an hour of your time, Frank. The rumour is she was getting more than professionally friendly with Shaw. She turned as white as a sheet when she heard the news about the drowning, looked like she was close to fainting – I was there at the time, saw that much for myself.'

'She's a redhead, isn't she?' Jacobson asked, recalling his hunch of yesterday morning and his later conversation with Jack Speirs, the Riverside Hotel's head barman.

'That's right, Frank. I didn't know you'd met her.'

'I haven't yet, old son. Is she at the *Argus* offices this morning?'

'She should be. She's supposed to be sitting in with one of the subeditors on the Saturday edition, learning the ropes. I'm working from home though – so I don't know for certain.'

What Pelling meant by 'working from home' was that he was hungover after a night on the piss, would drag himself into his office just in time to scribble something together for the lunchtime deadline. Jacobson's phone broke up as Kerr crawled the car under the railway bridge in the midst of a queue of shopping traffic. When it came back Pelling was asking for his pound of flesh: the latest news on the case. Jacobson fed him the possible discovery of Shaw's vanished Lexus and grossly exaggerated the amount of useful information the find might lead to once the wreckage had been forensically examined. If someone had burnt out the car to cover their tracks, it wouldn't do any harm to convince them into thinking that the boffins could *un*cover them – whether they actually could or couldn't.

'And the body's been ID'd?' Pelling asked.

'In the process of, Henry. There'll be a mention in the control room's incident list once its official.'

The drive out to the Waitrose complex and the *Argus* building took half an hour – into the town centre and back out again. But at least Jane Spencer had turned in for work. They talked in a quiet corner of the staff canteen. Kerr and Jacobson on one side of the table, the girl on the other. She'd be twenty-three on her birthday, she told them, the *Argus* was her first proper job after uni. The shock of Shaw's death seemed to have taken the edge off her surliness.

'So you got to know Paul Shaw while he was in Crowby?' Jacobson asked.

'It's not what everyone thinks,' she said, drawing on a Superking.

There were No Smoking signs in every direction. But the room stank of nicotine and there were hacks lighting up regardless everywhere. Remarkably, Jacobson didn't follow suit.

'What does everyone think, lass?' he asked.

'That I was throwing myself at him, that I was some kind of groupie.'

She pulled the saucer out from under her cup of coffee, ready for use as a makeshift ashtray.

'But that wasn't the case?'

'No, it wasn't. He liked me for myself and I liked him. There was a real connection. It wasn't just shagging.'

Jacobson nodded, deadpan. When he'd been young, several thousand geological ages ago, otherwise-polite middle-class young women rarely used words like shagging – not even while they were.

'So when did you last see him?'

'Thursday night. He came over to my flat. The other nights I'd gone back with him to his hotel and I thought it was about time he stayed at my place. Especially as my flatmate had to go to London for her job so I had it to myself for a couple of days. I cooked a meal and everything.'

'When did he get there?'

'About half past eight, I think.'

'But evidently he didn't stay all night.'

'No. He got a call on his mobile about ten thirty – and after that he told me he had to go. He said it was a big lead.'

Jacobson asked her whether she'd overheard the phone conversation.

'Only one end of it, Paul saying *yes, where, I'll be there* – that kind of thing.'

'And all he said was that it could be a big lead. No details?'

She flicked ash into the ad hoc ashtray.

'He never told me details about his story, just vague, general stuff. And I didn't want to push it – you know – give the impression that I *was* only interested because he was a big name and such.'

Kerr looked up from his notebook. She was putting a brave face on things, he thought. Even if you'd only just met, nobody liked a lover to drop dead on them. He asked her how much time she'd actually spent with Shaw, apart from Thursday evening.

'Saturday night, Tuesday night, Wednesday night. Plus I'd see him now and again when he was around here, looking at the archives. That was how it all started really, a conversation at the photocopier.'

'But he didn't involve you in his investigation in any way?' Jacobson asked.

She shook her head slowly from side to side before she answered. Jack Speirs had been right about her hair at least, Jacobson thought. Deep red. The colour of autumn leaves.

'He told me he liked working on his own, he said it was why he'd gone freelance in the first place.'

Kerr asked if they'd been anywhere else together, apart from the Riverside.

'We had a meal in Morricone's, Saturday night, but we didn't stay long. Tuesday we arranged to meet in Zola's. We had a few drinks there before we left. Well, I did anyway, Paul doesn't – didn't – really touch alcohol. Otherwise no.'

Jacobson fidgeted with a salt cellar in lieu of lighting up.

'You said he talked vaguely about his story? How much did you really get to know?'

'That he believed his cousin, Darren McGee, had been murdered. That some far-right nutters were involved. Some new group. That's all he ever told me. Honestly.'

'A new group?'

'Not the BNP or the NF. Something newer, potentially more dangerous. Those were his exact words. But I couldn't get him to say more than that. Not a word.'

'And you've no idea where he was spending his time around the town – when he wasn't with you and when he wasn't here in the *Argus* building?'

'No I haven't. I could tell he was cut up about Darren though. It wasn't just another story for him. He said they'd been close as kids but had lost touch when they'd grown up. He reckoned Darren's mum had been too hard on him, too strict, that maybe that had been the start of his problems. I think he felt guilty in some way – like he'd had all this success and Darren had been left stuck at the bottom of the heap.'

Jacobson gave her his card when they were going, thanked her for being helpful, though in point of fact she hadn't been especially. Or not as much as he'd hoped.

'Telling the truth, you reckon, Frank?' Kerr asked him, when they were back at the doors of his Peugeot. There'd been no spaces near the *Argus* offices - and in the end they'd had to park outside Homebase. The whole setup was a far cry from the newspaper's glory days when the journos had worked from a solid, elegant Victorian building which had been promptly sold off when the *Argus* had been taken over by one of the big media conglomerates.

'Pretty much,' Jacobson replied, clambering into the passenger seat. 'The picture we're getting all round is that Shaw preferred to work alone, kept his discoveries to himself.'

'But he sought you out with his list of names,' Kerr objected.

'Only because he hoped I'd reopen the case - or at least share some police intelligence with him.'

Kerr started the car, steered it carefully around an abandoned shopping trolley.

Jacobson rolled down his window, decided to treat himself to his next cigarette at last. He lit up, thinking about what Jane Spencer had said about a new far right group.

Just what the world needed: a fresh bunch of racists, Holocaust deniers and thick-as-shit boot boys.

Emma Smith grabbed a table upstairs, which was otherwise empty, and where they could talk without fear of being overheard. Linford and Edith Shaw followed her, Carole Briggs had volunteered to go up to the counter. They were in the Costa coffee franchise at the railway station concourse. The next London train was scheduled to depart at twelve thirty, just over half an hour away. Linford Shaw had asked earlier about making the funeral arrangements, about getting his son's body out of the morgue. Emma had explained that no decision could be taken before Monday at the earliest - when the coroner would formally convene an inquest into the death. Carole Briggs had offered to help them arrange accommodation locally if they'd wanted to stay on until then. But Linford Shaw had said no, they'd be better off at home where they had their friends and relatives around them.

Carole Briggs came up with a tray of hot drinks. Emma helped her set it down, helped her pass the drinks around, lifted up a too-hot Americano for herself.

'So you'd no idea that Paul was looking into what happened when his cousin died?' she asked, directing the question at Linford Shaw.

His wife had sobbed her heart out when the sheet had been pulled back. But after that she'd lapsed into silence again. As if breathing and moving around were as much activity as her brain and nervous system could sustain for the time being.

'No, miss. None at all,' Shaw replied, 'although it seems obvious now. I mean – why else would he have come to your town?'

'You must have discussed Darren's death in the family though?'

'Of course. But Paul was in America at the time Darren died. My son's no fool – but nobody in the family put him up to this. Everybody just thought Darren had finally succeeded.'

'In killing himself?'

Linford Shaw nodded.

'Even Tilda believed so – my sister – Darren's mother.'

Emma stirred her coffee with a green plastic stirrer. It was a daft habit she had – stirring her coffee, even though she always drank it black and without sugar.

'You don't think that's what Paul did too?'

Edith Shaw let out a moan that the word anguished didn't begin to cover.

'I'm sorry,' Emma added. 'It's my job to ask these questions.'

Linford Shaw took his wife's hand, held it gently.

'Why would my son take his own life? He had everything in the world to live for. Darren was gone in his head, you know? Paul was saner than me – saner than you.'

'But Darren had always been ill?'

'Not always. Or not that we knew about anyway. Tilda kept him on a close leash when he was younger, you see. Darren had to get away, find his feet. And that was when his troubles seemed to start.'

Edith Shaw managed a sip of tea at last, dabbed at her eyes with a handkerchief.

'Too tight a leash.' Her voice was quiet, strained. 'The boy couldn't breathe. An' religion. Morning, noon and night.'

They waited for her to continue. But that seemed to be all she was going to say for the time being. She dabbed at her eyes a second time, gripped her husband's hand. After a moment, Linford Shaw took over again as her official spokesman.

His sister, Tilda, was a Baptist, he told them. Old school. Darren's father had walked out when the lad was barely three. She'd struggled, bringing him up on her own. Yet what Edith had said was true. Tilda had been over-harsh, always on the lad's back, hadn't spared the rod. Maybe she'd been well intentioned but it had all had the wrong effect. As soon as he looked old enough, Darren had taken off, scarpered over to the West End. He'd started living on the streets when he was about fourteen, maybe fifteen. The family had tried to watch out for him but he'd been determined to go his own way. When or where his mind had flipped though – that was something they'd never got to the bottom of, probably never would.

Upstairs started to fill. Two youths and their girlfriends plonked themselves down at the next table, texting manically on their phones simultaneously to telling each other crude, unfunny jokes. Emma told them to shut it, enjoyed seeing the cockiness drain out of their faces when she brought out her ID. Carole Briggs diverted the conversation back to neutral topics. The unreliability of trains, how long it would take them to get from Euston to Camberwell. Linford Shaw made a noble attempt to humour her. But although you could take the bereaved father out of the mortuary, you couldn't usually persuade him to leave the memory of the corpse behind.

Kerr drove them back to the police car park behind the Divisional building. Kerr made for the rear entrance, Jacobson walked across to his own car, started it up and headed straight out again. He wanted to find out what he could about Wayne Parker, the Riverside Hotel's AWOL night porter. Kerr was going to check the PNC for a second time. Plus the force's localised intelligence database. Plus any other accessible electronic sources he could think of. Jacobson planned to stick to traditional methods: pay another visit to the hotel, see what he could glean by the quaint technique of talking face-to-face to living human beings. He'd considered walking but there were nasty-looking clouds banking overhead and he'd got the spring weather wrong as usual, had left his coat at home because he hadn't needed it yesterday.

Shiny, happy Chris Finney, the clerk from the day before, was behind the reception desk, *managing* it presumably. He assumed Jacobson was there to see DC Williams and Steve Horton. Helpful as ever, he pointed out the way to the conference room that Alison Taylor had made available for them. Jacobson didn't disabuse him. Just asked casually if there was any word yet from the regular night porter.

'Wayne Parker? No, there hasn't been. Mrs Taylor's not best pleased. Not many people like night portering. If you get someone reliable, you don't want to lose them.'

'Not turning in on a Friday night doesn't *sound* very reliable, old son.'

'It's never happened before. Apparently he's been here eighteen months without any problems.'

'You don't know him too well then, I take it?'

'I've only been here a month. He always does an efficient hand over if I'm on early days. But he doesn't say very much that he doesn't have to.' Finney paused, stared into the middle distance until he found the positive spin he sensed was out there somewhere. 'You'd need to be a bit self-contained, though, wouldn't you? Working on your own in the middle of the night.'

Jacobson ignored Finney's directions, made for the main lounge bar instead. The white-jacketed pianist was at it again – *Now That's What I Call Bland*, Volume Six – and the lounge was only medium busy, which made it harder to ignore him than it had been the night before. Jack Speirs offered him a drink, insisted it would be on the house this time. Jacobson asked for another Glenmorangie with ice, reckoned that a second exposure to the Elton John songbook easily justified the partaking of a remedial whisky. Speirs joined him in an empty booth as soon as he had a minute.

'Wayne Parker,' Jacobson said simply.

'Never showed last night,' Speirs replied, 'caused a bit of a rumpus.'

'And we still can't get hold of him, Jack. Which is effing annoying, given that he was on duty at your front desk while one of your guests went for a terminal swim.'

'You're not saying there's a connection, surely?'

'No, I'm not. I'm certainly not saying that officially and publicly. But I would like to *talk* to the bugger. If anyone saw anything here that I need to know about, he could very well be the one.'

Speirs had poured himself a glass of pineapple juice, probably with a surreptitious dash of something stronger. He took a rapid sip.

'You wouldn't have any ideas where we should be looking for him, old son?' Jacobson asked.

Speirs put his glass down. The pianist abandoned Elton John but only to start into an Andrew Lloyd Webber medley.

'With most other regular staff the answer would be yes. But not with Strange Wayne.'

'Strange Wayne?'

'That's what we call him. The international man of frigging mystery. Comes in, does his job, buggers off again.'

'Nowt wrong with that surely?'

'Not as such, Mr Jacobson. But it's a hotel, isn't it? Most people who work here are a bit lively, aren't they? Even your average night porter usually likes to have a chat or share a joke in passing. But Strange Wayne doesn't want to know. I couldn't tell you if he's single, divorced, lives with a blow-up doll - or what.'

Jacobson drank his whisky. Speirs had poured a generous measure, he'd give him that much.

'Any idea what he was doing before he started work here?'

'Supposed to have been with one of the big London hotels. I've heard that he was in the army before that. Don't know where he let that slip from though - or whether it's true.'

'But until last night he'd been a reliable worker as far as you know?'

Speirs finished off the rest of his juice quickly. The bar was getting busier.

'Yeah, to be honest. Mr frigging reliability himself.'

Chapter Twenty-Two

Rick Cole, John Stuart and Phil Stuart gave Martin Kesey and the guy from Coventry the slip in the half-hour of free time that followed lunch. They had nothing against either of them. Nothing at all. But they had urgent issues to discuss amongst themselves. And only amongst themselves.

Even when there weren't clouds in the sky, the daylight wouldn't penetrate too deeply into the densest parts of Matthew Sutherland's thick woodland. They stopped in a gloomy clearing where there was no one else around in any direction. Even so they kept their voices down. And kept a constant listen, a constant look-out.

'So far, so good,' Cole said, hunching down on a yard of felled timber.

'You think so, Rick?' Phil Stuart asked sarcastically. 'You really fucking think so?'

Like his brother, he seemed to prefer standing.

'They hadn't even identified the body, the last I heard on the radio. Exactly the same in the *Argus*.'

'That's because the media can't use the name till the relatives are informed and all that,' Phil Stuart persisted. 'You can bet your life the plod already know who he is – *and* the reason why he was in Crowby.'

'And they're going to take that seriously, are they, Phil? They'll look fucking clever on *Midlands Today* admitting that they got the first one totally wrong. Plus which half of them think exactly the same as we do. Total, sound racists most of 'em. Nobody's going to make a fuss over a dead ethnic. Especially when he can be written off as another unfortunate suicide. Driven to it by the pressure of being a successful black bastard in a white society, I expect.'

John Stuart tore a branch covered in newly budded leaves off a beech tree.

'It's not funny, Rick. This isn't just having a laugh like the old days. This is two blokes dead. It's fucking years inside if we're caught.'

'Timothy McVeigh didn't worry about doing time, mate,' Cole replied, without looking up. 'I thought you guys were serious, committed.'

Big John pointed his foot at the tree but held off from kicking it.

'Timothy McVeigh is dead, Rick. Executed. And America's still run by the Jews and big business. Not to mention the Saudi royal family.'

The three of them fell silent. There was birdsong in the distance and the noise of some kind of animal less far off, cracking its way through the ferns and bracken. Phil Stuart was the first to speak again.

'Look, Rick, it's not about the politics. It's about covering our backs. We're prepared for the war when it comes, just the same as you. But we want to be in on the action when it does. Not banged up somewhere.'

Cole smiled insincerely.

'Exactly, mate. Covering our backs is exactly what we've done. Tipped him in the water, destroyed his fucking laptop, settled his fucking hash. All we've got to do now is sit tight, carry on with our normal routines.'

'And supposing Parker *has* done a runner? It's not true what you say about the plod. Not the top rankers anyway. Not the kind who investigate murders. Half of *them* are knobhead graduates – ex-commies, Socialist Worker types, all bloody sorts. They're going to focus in on Parker if he's legged it, they'd have to be complete fuckwits not to.'

Cole stood up. He was taller than Phil when he did so. But still dwarfed by John.

'OK, fair point. But we've followed Party discipline from day one, remember? No careless pub talk, no home visits, no casual social contacts between members who weren't previously known to each other.'

'There's been a few phone calls, Rick. And you went round there last night. You told us—'

'That was different. A one-off. I made sure I wasn't seen.'

'All the same, maybe we need to go for the hat trick,' Big John said, throwing the branch to the ground.

'You're joking,' Cole said, realising that he wasn't.

This was what he loved about these guys. They blew hot and cold. But at the end of the day they always came through.

Phil Stuart spoke again.

'John and myself talked about it on the way over, Rick. Parker's a weak link, always has been. You've said so yourself before now. If the plods do manage to pick him up, he'll squeal like a little piggie, probably try and cut a deal for himself.'

Big John broke off a second branch.

'But not if we get to him first, Rick,' he said, splitting it neatly in two and chucking it in the same direction as the first.

Jacobson located Alison Taylor in the hotel gardens. She'd been sitting at the table he'd found her at the previous evening. But now she was gathering her latest bunch of paperwork together, getting ready to move indoors – out of the way of what looked like impending rain. He noticed that she was still in blue, noticed that she'd tied her hair back, something Janice had used to do if she was in a hurry in the morning, no time to fix it properly. She treated him to her white, professional smile. The Riverside Hotel seemed to be smile city – the occasional race murder victim apart.

'It's a pity my colleague couldn't talk to your night porter last night,' he said, matter-of-factly. 'He hasn't rung in yet by any chance?'

Wayne Parker was a tricky item. He needed to know more about him but couldn't be too open about the fact yet.

'No, I'm afraid not. I've tried his land line and his mobile – but no luck. It's odd really. We do get staff who just pack it in suddenly, don't bother to let us know. But Wayne's been steady up till now. He hasn't even pulled a sickie that I can recall.'

'Ex-army too,' Jacobson commented. 'Ex-servicemen are usually reliable, aren't they?'

She didn't ask where he'd got his information from. Or contradict it. Jacobson slid the door open for her that led back inside.

'That's what I mean. Maybe I should check the hospital.'

It was something DS Kerr had already done. Last night and again this morning. Jacobson followed her in, told her there was no need, he already knew that Parker wasn't there.

'You really *do* want to speak to him,' she said.

This smile was less wide, less impersonal. Jacobson thought he liked it better.

'Paul Shaw's room was ransacked,' he replied. 'It could have happened any time from about eight fifteen on Thursday night. But common sense says it happened later that night rather than sooner. If any of your staff saw anything relevant, the night porter's the most likely candidate.'

They started to walk along the long corridor that led back to the reception area. Jacobson was distracted by the click of her heels on the polished pine, overlaying the rhythm of his own stolid, broguish steps. All that was telling against Wayne Parker was pure coincidence – apart from what he'd seen on the illegal fishing trip that he'd have to keep permanently under wraps.

'I could do with looking at his staff file,' he said,

deciding to take a chance, deciding he had nothing to lose.

She stopped and turned to look straight at him.

'You think he's involved in some way, don't you?'

'I didn't say that, eh, Alison. But we're assuming the room was ransacked quietly. And there was no sign of a physical break-in.'

Something passed between their eyes. Something Jacobson could scarcely remember, something he'd buried in days of work and nights of booze and serious reading, something he'd buried in the almost comforting notions that he was out of shape, no catch, past it.

'I can't let you see confidential hotel records without proper authorisation.'

'I haven't got any right now. I won't tell if you won't.'

She smiled at him again. It was the first time he'd said her first name, he realised. They walked on. And then he remembered what smiley-face Chris Finney had said: Mrs Taylor isn't best pleased. *Mrs* Taylor.

She switched on the computer when they got to her office, accessed Wayne Parker's details, found a fern in need of watering while Jacobson studied the information. It wasn't over-enlightening. Parker was mid-thirties, unmarried; according to his previous employment data, he'd served ten years in the military and then had had a series of hotel jobs, nearly all of them night portering. The big London hotel Jack Speirs had mentioned turned out to be illusory. Parker had worked in London all right but somewhere Jacobson had never heard of. Alison Taylor lifted her head up from her plants when he mentioned it, told him it was a budget place just behind Russell Square, aimed at downmarket tourists. Jacobson clicked successfully on the link that brought up Parker's MOD reference, albeit at the third attempt.

Parker had seen action: a tour of duty in Northern Ireland and peace-keeping in Bosnia. But for all that, his testimonial wasn't glowing. Reading between the lines of official-speak, Parker had been Private Average. If he'd never put a foot seriously wrong, he hadn't covered himself in glory either. As to education, he'd left school when he'd been sixteen – without bothering to collect a leaving certificate.

'I think he was brought up in care – foster homes and so on,' Alison Taylor said, unprompted. 'Maybe that was the appeal of the army – more regimentation.'

Jacobson scribbled down anything he thought would be useful – Parker's precise date of birth, his national insurance number.

'Any idea why he was in Crowby particularly?' he asked.

He'd noticed that Parker's secondary school had been in Wolverhampton. He didn't seem to have any obvious roots in the local area.

She shook her head.

'He told me he was looking for somewhere smaller, quieter, to live, said he wanted to get out of London. He was experienced for the job, had reasonable references – that's all I was bothered about to be honest.'

'A big responsibility, I suppose, running a place like this,' Jacobson said, stuck for words now that she'd told him as much about Wayne Parker as she probably knew.

'You mean for a dizzy blonde woman?'

Jacobson moved away from her computer. Her window looked out at an angle on to the gardens.

'I mean for anyone. And long hours too, I expect. Anti-social.'

She looked at him again the way she'd looked at him before.

'It hardly matters when you've no one waiting at home.'

'You look a lot like my ex-wife,' Jacobson blurted, instantly feeling stupid, instantly wishing he'd kept his trap shut.

'You don't look at all like my ex-husband,' she replied. 'Not remotely. So that probably balances out, don't you think?'

Jacobson's mobile rescued him from finding a suitable

response. DC Williams: something had turned up with the CCTV footage after all. Jacobson explained he was already in the building, told him he'd be with him in a minute or two.

'My team,' he said, 'a new development. I have to go.'

'Of course. See you later.'

'Yes, later,' he said, not entirely sure what either of them actually meant by the word.

He gave her his own smile, rarely seen, and turned towards the door.

DC Williams and Steve Horton were hunched over Horton's sleek-looking laptop and a couple of connected peripherals that might have boiled tea or scanned the skies for signs of alien life – or both – for all Jacobson could tell about their purpose just by looking. He'd expected they'd have had some of the night staff with them by now. But they were clearly still working on their own. Horton explained what they were up to. One: they'd copied the CCTV tapes on to computer memory. Two: they were running through Thursday night's post eight pm footage from the camera positioned at the hotel's main entrance. Three: Horton was using software which enabled him to discard the yards of dead film; the interludes where no one was coming or going. The end result would be a set of digitised stills of every face that had entered or exited the building after Paul Shaw had been last seen there.

'That way, Mr Jacobson, the night staff can take a look in rapid time. Probably no more than half an hour to clock anyone who came in or went out.'

Jacobson nodded. Even he could appreciate that it was a clever idea, one that would speed the process overall.

'Great, Steve,' he said. 'But Ray said that something had turned up.'

'It *has*, guv,' Ray Williams said. 'Steve just thought you might want to know the background steps, how we got there.'

Which was exactly what Jacobson didn't want to know.

But he kept the ungrateful thought to himself.

Horton clicked his mouse, made some quick keystrokes, brought the original footage back on to the screen. Even with enhanced resolution, it was poor quality – grainy and snowy. Not that there was much to look at immediately, anyway. Just the motionless automatic doors at the front of the hotel, no one going in or out.

'The thing to keep an eye on is the time stamp, Mr Jacobson,' Horton said.

He was salon-tanned and muscled under his neatly pressed T-shirt. Jacobson never understood why he wasn't in a boy band. Or at the very least, coining easy money as a male stripper: give it up, ladies, for Steve Horton, the world's first Geek-o-Gram. Jacobson watched the digits rolling on the top-right corner of the picture. Eight minutes before one am. Then seven minutes before. Then six. Then one thirty-two am. Horton rewound the sequence, replayed the really crucial seconds again.

'You see it, guv?' Williams asked. 'The time stamp jumps straight from twelve fifty-four till gone half-one. To be more precise, there's thirty-eight minutes' worth missing.'

'So the tape's been what? Cut? Spliced?'

'I doubt if it's anything as technical as that, Mr Jacobson,' Horton said. 'It looks to me as if the system was just switched off – and then switched back on again later.'

'How come we didn't notice this last night, old son?'

'We should have done, guv. But we didn't,' Williams said frankly.

Horton attempted some damage limitation.

'In fairness, Mr Jacobson, it's not so easy to spot when you're watching on fast forward – *and* trying to follow more than one feed at a time.'

'And we were pretty much focused exclusively on Paul Shaw, looking for signs of him or his car,' Williams added.

'I hope that's what you were exclusively focused on, old son,' Jacobson said.

The Williams-Emma Smith situation worried him. They were both good 'tecs. But it wasn't easy to put mutual bad feeling to one side, keep totally concentrated on the task. Not when sex and – apparently – broken promises were involved. Williams didn't reply. He tried to keep the colour from rising on his cheeks, didn't entirely succeed.

Jacobson decided to let it go for now.

'Presumably the night porter's responsible if there was a switch-off?' he asked.

'He's certainly the only one with legitimate access to the system at that time of night,' Williams said, trying to recover some ground. 'Of course there's nothing to say that it wasn't just accidental. Maybe some kind of fault. An unlucky coincidence.'

'Nothing at all, old son,' Jacobson said evenly.

But thinking – very nearly knowing – the exact opposite.

Chapter Twenty-Three

It was already raining in Manchester. Wayne Parker found a noisy, ordinary-enough looking pub not far from the Chorlton Street coach station. The kind that was full of big groups of Saturday lunchtime booze-heads, most of them too absorbed in having a good, matey time to pay any attention to a solitary drinker at the end of the long, dark bar. He nursed a pint of Boddingtons, tried to rehearse the kind of thing he might say when he made the phone call he needed to make.

He'd left Crowby late yesterday afternoon. Packed what he really needed into his old, army-days rucksack, stuffed everything he didn't want – but didn't want to leave lying around – into a black bin liner. He'd worried about the motor of course. A K-reg Fiesta, an absolute crock of shit. There was something wrong with the timing and it drove like mud until you got it above fifty and kept it under seventy-five. But at least it had got him there in the end. He'd taken the direct route to North Wales – across to the M6 and then on to the M56, had wanted to make sure that the journey would be clocked, recorded and monitored all the way. Friday night he'd spent in the Bangor Travel Inn, had made a point of chatting to the girl on the reception desk, selling her his cover: he had an old mate in Dublin who was finally doing the decent thing, finally tying the knot – he was catching the ferry over there for the wedding, might stay on a few days afterwards, take in the sights. Not only that, he'd paid for the room by credit card, had done precisely the same when he'd filled up at the Keele services.

The Travel Inn was located out at the business park, the way they frequently were. He'd spied building work on the way in. A half-completed office unit with several waste skips lining the road alongside. Once it was dark, he'd taken the Fiesta into Bangor, bought a McDonalds, tipped the bin liner into one of the skips on the drive back and covered it over. He hadn't slept too badly, all things considered. Admittedly, he'd brought a bottle of Bell's along from home which had probably helped do the trick. There'd been a bloody Paki on the desk, though, when he'd handed in his room key this morning. But he'd managed to bite the bullet, had given him a cheery nod – and the same crap about Dublin. After that it had been on to Hollyhead. The Fiesta had shuddered and struggled but somehow he'd coaxed it along the last twenty-odd miles and into the long-term car park. He'd locked it, paid for a week's parking, caught the shuttle bus over to the main terminal building. He'd used the same card again, bought an open return and then headed for the bog. When he came out, he'd done the risky thing, taken the gamble he couldn't avoid, had joined the stream of returning passengers on their way out towards the railway station. *A single to Liverpool, please mate.* Paying cash this time and making straight for the platform.

He decided on a second pint, thought it would help the words flow when he phoned. The train had taken for ever, had sat in the platform at Chester for a good half-hour while something was cleared further up the line. Debris chucked by vandals apparently. He'd ducked out of Liverpool Central as quickly as he could when they'd finally got there. The plan wasn't perfect, couldn't be perfect. Any road journey, any big town or city street, you lived your life on candid camera these days. But he'd led them as much of a dance as was possible. Making sure he was traceable as far as the ferry port, trying to stay invisible thereafter. The taxi driver who'd brought him over to the Norton Street bus station had been another Paki of course. He'd taken him the long way round, stoking up his meter. Parker had played dumb, had played along, had even tipped the bastard: not so much or so little that Gunga Din would be particularly likely to remember the fare. His luck had been in at that point anyway. National Express were running as late as the trains. He'd made it on to a delayed coach which was just leaving, hadn't had to hang around the bus station for more photo opportunities. He'd paid in cash again, found two empty seats at the back, plonked his rucksack on the one next to the window.

He asked the barman for change from a tenner when he paid for his drink, wanted to use the cigarette machine. The twat positively twinkled at the cash register, fiddling with the red diamond studded into his ear and patting down his hair-do with one hand while he fished out the coins with the other. Bent as an effing nine-bob note. There was a lot of that up this way apparently. Perverts. Filth. Gas chamber material. The Gay Village, as they called it, was hardly a kick in the arse from where he was stood right now. He switched on his phone, checked that he still had the correct number in the memory, switched it back off. He'd drink his second pint, have a cig, before he tried. Now that he was here, funnily enough, he felt in less of a hurry. The important thing, the urgent thing, had been to get out of Crowby, to put a comfortable distance between himself and the scene of the crime. Well, crimes really, to be exact. The cigarette machine was maybe ten feet away from his pint and his luggage. He kept an eye on both while he extracted some over-priced cancer sticks. He didn't really smoke that often anymore. Certainly not as a regular habit anyway. But he could hardly be blamed right now, could he? Not in the light of recent effing developments.

The phone connected after only two rings when he finally found the courage to dial. He turned away from the bar, wanting to keep the conversation to himself.

'Hello, mate, long time no see,' he said, knowing at once that his voice was instantly recognised, but unsure if it was instantly welcomed.

The man from the property agency had called to apologise. He'd been held up with another client, but he'd be there as soon as was humanly possible. Inside ten minutes he'd promised. Vicky left her cellphone switched on in case there was a further delay or another message. She'd managed to park in Claremont Avenue again, squeezed in between an old-style Beetle and some kind of big four-wheel drive monster. The sort of vehicle you wouldn't bat an eyelid at in Texas. But just looked worse than stupid on a narrow English street. The more she thought about it, the more the attic flat she'd seen last night seemed just right. She might as well take a look at the others first though: it wasn't as if her weekend was crammed with activity otherwise.

She switched on the radio. Moby on Crowby FM: *Why does my heart feel so bad?* You heard Moby everywhere these days. On crap radio stations like this one. Even on dull telly dramas and furniture ads. But he'd been cool back then, the business. Barbara had liked to play him loud; too rich, too sure of herself, to give a toss about the neighbours. Vicky had worried – needlessly – about how Barbara and Darren would get on when he'd moved in with her. But they'd hit it off from the start. Darren had his looks and his edgy charm and Barbara had loved it that he'd been from the street, was part of what she called 'the real London'. 'The real London' – like 'the real England' – was Barbara's thing, the reason she was here and not at some upmarket 'school' in Boston or Connecticut. They'd become something of a threesome – at least socially. Pub-crawling along Upper Street or wandering up to Camden Lock in the warm summer evenings. Darren still had his pitch at Covent Garden then, fire juggling for the tourists. Occasionally, Vicky and Barbara would take the hat round, vamping it up in short, spangly skirts. Sometimes they'd get pissed upstairs in the Punch and Judy afterwards, squeezing through the crowd on the terrace to gaze out over the balcony at the even bigger crowds swarming in every direction underneath. Barbara always insisting on paying, sometimes needing to be prevented from giving out ludicrous tips if she happened to fancy whoever was behind the bar. *It's only money, Vix*, she liked to say, *stolen from the wretched of the earth – and returned in person by my good self.*

It was the kind of summer that surely every life had the right to – at least once. Sex that was more than just sex. Fun that was more than just fun. And the autumn and winter that followed too. Darren liked to meet her outside the Senate House library when she was finished studying for the day, liked to spend as much time with her as he could, would probably have sat in on her lectures and seminars if she hadn't put her foot down – much as she loved all of his attention at first. It was a time when she'd hardly thought about Crowby, about what had happened there, had hardly thought about the future either – or, if she did, only to hope that it would be some kind of extended version of the present: waking up with Darren just so she could spend the day with him and then go to sleep with him again.

Moby turned into something she didn't recognise, something new and tedious. She turned the volume down, checked her watch. She was half-tempted to drive off. Why should she hang around if he couldn't get here in time? She could just see Barbara calmly putting up with lateness in any situation where she was the customer. Like hell. In a way, of course, it would have been better if Barbara hadn't taken to Darren, had frozen him out instead, even barred him from moving in. Their friendship would have been over. And Darren would probably still have lost it. But at least there wouldn't be a cold, irrational pulse in her veins that still blamed Barbara for everything.

*

Nevil Drury told Parker to stay where he was. He'd come and fetch him – save him the cab fare. Cheers, mate, Parker had said, relieved there'd be no cabbie to recall the fare and the address – but also sussing that Drury had his radar up and running, must've worked out straight off that the unexpected visit wasn't social, wasn't about looking up old mates. Parker offered to buy Drury a beer when he showed but Drury said no, leave it for now, best get going.

The gaff was on the edge of Rusholme. A long, grey street of over-sized villas which looked like they'd mainly been built in the 1930s. A few had struggling, hopeful gardens outfront. But most, like Drury's, had been concreted over, the odd rose bush or sliver of ivy apart. If you'd been beamed down from a spaceship, you wouldn't have had a clue where you were: Northampton, Swindon, Manchester, London, Crowby. Streets like this, areas like this, looked the same everywhere you went. Whether the locale was aspirational or dead end was entirely relative to where you'd come from, where you might be going to next. Parker suspected that Drury had been winding him up with regard to his choice of route: taking an unnecessary detour along some other street altogether – one that had crawled with Indian restaurants and saree shops, hordes of ethnics everywhere he'd fucking looked. But he didn't mention it. They didn't talk much at all in fact until Drury's motor was locked on his driveway and they were safely on the other side of his discreetly strengthened front door. Parker had commented on the vehicle though, a Volvo. Upmarket and reliable, Drury had described it as. But not showy. Showy was the last thing he said he needed.

Parker slumped into a sofa in the front room. Drury brought a couple of chilled Kronenbourgs through from his kitchen, lobbed a can into Parker's hands. A neat, slow parabola.

'Fancy a smoke?'

Parker declined the offer with a shake of his head. Drury shrugged, took his ease in the armchair nearest the window, rolled himself a thin, elegant joint.

'You've got yourself into a scrape then, mate?'

Parker nodded, proceeded to tell him the highly edited, highly imprecise version he'd been rehearsing since Hollyhead: some lads he was associated with had taken a particular situation too far – and he didn't see why he should spend the next twenty years in jail alongside them.

Drury lit up with a red Zippo.

'No more can I, Wayne. I said this to you years ago. Forget the fascist groove thing. Get yourself a *life*.'

'It's *been* my fucking life, mate. Comradeship, solidarity. All the stuff that nobody else gives a monkey's about. Patriotism.'

Drury ignored the opportunity to debate the state of the nation.

'But now you want out?'

'I'm not proud about it, Nev. But I know I couldn't hack it – not double figures.'

'And it would go to that? Double figures?'

Parker pulled back his ring-pull.

'Conspiracy to murder. Maybe even murder. And Christ knows what else – these fucking anti-terrorism laws they've got now. They apply to us as well as the Pakis.'

Drury took a deep draw, flaring his nostrils on the in-breath.

'Enough, mate, enough,' he said after a moment. 'I really don't need the details. You're welcome for a few days, you know that. But you need to think through your options.'

'There's only one option, Nev. I need a new identity, I need to skip.'

'You could take it to the plod yourself, couldn't you? The full story in exchange for lighter charges. Especially if, like you say, you were peripheral to the main action.'

'If I go inside that way, I come out in a box, believe me.'

Drury smoked the joint down, drank his beer, idled with the TV remote.

Parker drank too, watching and waiting. Drury owed him, freely admitted it. The only question was how much – at today's prices.

'It's not as easy as it used to be,' Drury said finally. 'The checks they got against forgeries now, you would not fucking believe. And it's not my area. Not my area at all.'

'Yeah but you got the contacts, Nev. You must have in your line of business.'

'You got cash?' Drury asked.

'Three grand maximum,' Parker lied.

He'd hit all three of his credit cards before he'd left Crowby. Two grand only each – in case they were thrown out as unusual transactions. Six thou in total.

'Leave it with me. I'll look into it – but no promises yet,' Drury said in a tone that suggested meeting concluded, no other items.

He wandered back through to the kitchen, came back with more beers and with a takeaway menu, dog-eared and battered.

'The Royal Naz, mate,' he said, 'Wilmslow Road – where we drove past before? They do the best grub in town if you're hungry – assuming a decent curry's not against your effing oath of effing allegiance.'

Chapter Twenty-Four

Jacobson convened another semi-official briefing in Bob Harker's meeting room at the Bellevue Hotel. The team paid for their drinks this time and took a collection for Harker's trouble. Jacobson positioned himself in front of the flip chart, the others sat facing him in uncomfortable chairs. The kind where the right arm folded out into a mini-desktop so you could take notes or doodle or suddenly remember what it felt like when you'd been trapped in a boring lesson at school.

'We could get used to this, guv,' Mick Hume said, balancing a pint glass expertly on the narrow surface, 'the murder squad's awayday.'

Jacobson allowed himself a laugh. He'd lit up a B & H but he was making up for it by sticking to the Bellevue's over-stewed coffee even though Jack Speirs' substantial dram had all too easily put him in the mood for another.

Hume gave the first report back. Short but not sweet. Arlette Lefevre apart, no one along Riverside Walk had anything suspicious to report from Thursday night. There were a few houses where they were getting sick to the teeth of Crowby CID, where Hume and Barber had knocked on their doors three times now.

'And I thought the middle classes were worried about law and order, wanted the force to be more visible,' Jacobson said. 'But we'll leave them in peace for now anyway. You've done what you could I'm sure.'

Emma Smith recapped on her morning with Linford and Edith Shaw: even though they were proud parents, they weren't convinced by Paul Shaw's theory about his cousin. The family view was still that Darren McGee had taken his own life. DC Williams went next. He'd sat himself at the back of the room, conspicuously well away from Smith. Steve Horton had his stills ready, he told them, and he – Williams – had contacted the night staff, had arranged a timetable for each of them to take a look-see. They all seemed happy enough to help out, especially as the hotel manager had authorised overtime payments for the loss of their free time. All apart from Wayne Parker who still couldn't be contacted. Jacobson asked him to outline the theory about the missing thirty-eight minutes of CCTV footage for the benefit of the others.

Jacobson finished his coffee, started to use the cup as an ashtray.

'I'm asking for permission to kick in Parker's door next,' he said when Ray Williams had finished, 'and I'll be asking Ince to circulate Parker's details nationally if he's not at home. I think we can justify that now, yes?'

None of them disagreed. Kerr was sitting with his chair arm unfolded. There'd been no tea available – Kerr rarely touched booze in the daytime – and he was the only one without something to drink. There was definitely nothing on the PNC about Wayne Parker, he reported, nothing on Crowby's localised database either. He'd even taken a look at Amanda Singh's HCU system just on the off chance – nothing again.

'He's listed on the electoral register at his current address. And you'll be thrilled to know that Equifax rate him as a low-to-medium credit risk. No outstanding debts or CCJs—'

'Lucky old Parker,' Mick Hume interjected between mouthfuls of beer.

'The only useful thing really, Frank,' Kerr concluded, 'is

we've got a car reg for him now from the DVLC – assuming that the details are up-to-date of course.'

Jacobson cut to the chase.

'What's important is not to lose the big picture here. Let's assume the wildest story is true for the sake of argument – that Darren McGee was murdered and Paul Shaw was on to the killers. Then what?'

'He's contacted by them – or somebody close to them – on Thursday night, lured out somewhere in his car,' Emma Smith suggested. 'Then they repeat the trick they'd already used with Darren McGee. Stage his murder to look like a drowning, burn his car out to cover their tracks.'

'Plus remove anything sensitive from his hotel room,' DC Barber added. 'Which they did with inside help from Wayne Parker during the half-hour the CCTV system was down.'

Jacobson stubbed his fag out, put the cup and saucer down on an empty chair.

'And for all this we can prove exactly what?'

'If Parker *has* gone AWOL,' DC Barber commented, 'it's a reasonable inference that he's involved with *something* – nobody accidentally switches off security cameras, do they? Plus there's a good possibility the SOCOs will find bits of Paul Shaw's laptop in the burnout for instance.'

'Most probably evidentially useless bits, old son,' Jacobson said. 'But there's still nothing in what any of you are saying that amounts to proof at this stage.'

'The white van, guv,' Mick Hume offered. 'It fits the time frame both for the drowning and for doing over the room.'

'And if we get positive results back on the blood from the Memorial Bridge—' Williams tried, but left the sentence unfinished.

Jacobson summarised the points they'd made on the flip chart. The task didn't take long. He tackled them one by one – without the benefit of the second B & H he was highly tempted to light up but equally determined not to.

'Blood and fibre comparisons – that's in the lap of the FSS laboratories in Birmingham. Ditto anything substantial from the car wreck. The white van we can do something about ourselves. There's no CCTV on the Memorial Bridge or in the Riverside area in general. But there *is* in town. The van had to get there – and leave again. If we're lucky there might be something on camera elsewhere that ties in time-wise, maybe even a number plate. Paul Shaw's previous investigations still need looking at – is there any motive there for someone to want revenge? The same goes for his medical history – that's still outstanding too. Everyone's telling us that he was Mr Sanity – but we need to know it for a fact.'

'And Wayne Parker, guv?' Mick Hume asked.

'The usual stuff, Mick. Neighbours who might've encountered him, places he's associated with he might be likely to return to. And phone checks if I can screw the authorisation out of Smoothie Greg – who he's been speaking to, who's been speaking to him. The same goes for Paul Shaw's mobile – I've already asked for the authority on that one. I've also requisitioned the Darren McGee files.'

He paused – needlessly – for effect.

'We don't know yet who Shaw spent his time talking to while he was here – but in all probability at least some of them would already have spoken to the McGee inquiry team. It could give us the start we need.'

'So you think that Darren McGee *was* murdered then, Frank?' Kerr asked.

'I didn't say that, Ian. What matters right now is that Paul Shaw *thought* that he was.'

'That's what we're telling DCS Salter anyway,' Mick Hume commented to general laughter.

Jacobson didn't contradict him, started to tear the sheet he'd written on from the flip chart. Plus the one underneath – just to be on the safe side.

Drury insisted on using plates for the takeaway. He had a

woman living with him at the moment, he'd said: a nurse at the eye hospital, he had to keep the place a little bit neat.

Parker smoked a cigarette after they'd eaten. Drury found another couple of cans, rolled himself another joint.

'You're still doing all right then, Nev, by the looks of it.'

'Steady, Wayne, steady. That's the key to this business. Don't get over-ambitious, don't get too greedy.'

Drury's mobile rang.

'Yeah? Yeah? What time? OK. No probs.'

He plonked the unlit joint on the edge of his ashtray. The table was a curiosity. A round glass top and the sexy plaster figure of a slapper underneath holding it up: down on all fours – tits, arse, stockings and suspenders – the lot. Drury had said it was art, worth a bob or two. A replica according to him. But in a seriously limited edition.

'I've got to nip out, Wayne. Maybe an hour. Make yourself at home. I'll give Teresa a bell on the way. Don't want you to frighten her if she gets back before me, do we?'

Parker cleared the plates and the remains of two lamb passandas once Drury had gone, wanted to show willing. There was a dishwasher in Drury's kitchen but Parker felt happier with plain old washing-up liquid and hot water. He turned the tap on, bunged the first plate in. The kitchen wasn't the one the house had come with, that was obvious. One of those modern jobbies instead. With the sink and such moved over to the middle of the room. A workstation, he thought they called it. Something like that. Gold plating everywhere. Lights that adjusted themselves automatically to the time of day apparently. Drury was doing all right, he thought. Enough home comforts to be going on with. But nothing over-loud, nothing to call too much attention. He'd put together a regular, low-key business and he'd probably got smart enough to be salting it carefully away, planning for a nice early retirement. Even a bird who lived in: one he seemed to be taking seriously.

All change since the army days then. Lance Corporal

Nevil Drury had been shit-reckless back then. And thank fuck for that. Otherwise there would be nothing owing between them now, no unpaid debt for Wayne Parker to finally collect on.

Chapter Twenty-Five

Parker rented his flat but couldn't be contacted. Which meant that his landlord could legally give consent to the police accessing the property for the strictly limited purpose, under the PACE guidelines, of establishing whether Parker, missing from work and a potential witness in a serious inquiry, was still alive and well. Jacobson and Kerr located said landlord via half a dozen calls to the local letting agencies. He'd sounded a lot less than delighted at the prospect of having his Saturday afternoon interrupted – until Jacobson had pointed out that if he was to let them in with his key then Jacobson's officers wouldn't have to damage the door or any of its fittings. It was a uniformed task really, wasn't even a typical job for a detective constable – let alone for a chief inspector and a detective sergeant – but it was always possible that they'd need a forensic search *chez* Parker at a later stage. If that did happen, it would be highly useful to have a legitimate explanation in place for any forensic traces that either of them might have deposited earlier.

'So much for speeding things up with a fishing trip,' Kerr had said on the drive over.

Jacobson had left his car at the Bellevue for now, would need to collect it later. He hadn't replied – although he could see that Kerr had a point. Especially now that there was an internal campaign underway for all serving police officers to volunteer their DNA to the national database for ease of elimination at crime scenes. So far nobody in Crowby CID had volunteered. Not even 'Clean' Harry Fields. But making it a compulsory obligation was probably only a matter of time.

They went in and out as quickly as they could. The place hadn't been disturbed since they'd broken in. Jacobson thanked the landlord for showing up. He'd turned out to be a surly old sod with an unattractive habit of picking ear wax out of his left ear. He hoped there wasn't a problem, he told them, Parker had paid his rent promptly, took care of the place, hadn't caused any trouble as far as he knew. Mick Hume and DC Barber had followed them over in Barber's car. More door-to-door work for the wicked, Jacobson thought, leaving them to it, not envying them the task.

Kerr tried to keep his temper in the snarled-up traffic, his mind lost, or so it seemed to Jacobson, in one of his gloomy CDs: all thrashing guitars and despondent lyrics. At least he'd stuck it on a low volume. Not that Jacobson was any kind of an expert or really in any kind of informed position to judge. His tastes had been old-fashioned and terminally out of date even when he'd been young. While his mates had been grooving to Pink Floyd and Jimi Hendrix, Jacobson's Dansette player had played uncool host to Chuck Berry, Little Richard, Buddy Holly - even to Sinatra and Peggy Lee on occasion. It had been something Janice had gently mocked him about when they'd first met, had claimed he'd been born a decade too late.

When they arrived back at the Divisional building, Kerr persuaded him to take the stairs to the Central Records Office on the basis that it was only on the second floor. The summary files and major witness statements were ready for Jacobson to collect, should be enough for them to go on for now, he hoped. There would be hours of reading and note-taking ahead if they ended up having to delve back into all of the raw data. A police force was a bureaucracy first and foremost. Even the simplest case generated a mass of cross-referenced paperwork. Greg Salter's inquiry into Darren McGee's death was on the minimalist side by the typical standards of serious incident investigations. But that still made it quantitatively a lot more like *War and Peace* than a nice, slim volume of haikus.

Jacobson insisted on the lift up to the fifth floor. He unlocked his office and they got to work, taking a pile of documents each and swapping them over as they went. Jacobson awarded himself his third B & H of the day. If he could put up with Kerr's thump-thump-I'm-so-miserable music, then Kerr could put up with a modicum of secondary nicotine. They worked on for an hour, Jacobson reminding himself of the main details, Kerr studying them for the first time.

'The girlfriend as priority – or Pete Bradley's place?' Kerr asked when they were done.

'Bradley's cesspit's closer. Let's try that first,' Jacobson replied, reluctantly swinging his feet off their comfy position on the top of his desk and back on to the worn, standard-issue carpet.

Pete Bradley had just about kept himself on the right side of the law for the last three or four years although his name still came up regularly in one local court case after another. One of the bouncers from his door-security firm getting over-eager in the crowd control department or one of his tenants nicked again for shoplifting, dealing or breaking and entering. The word was that his door licence was very unlikely to be renewed beyond the current period. Which would leave Bradley with the eight gloomy bedsits at number ten, Derby Crescent, as his sole legal source of income apart from his half-share in a less than flourishing minicab firm.

Kerr kept his CD player switched off this time. Derby Crescent was off Mill Street, not far from the old grain store. The last juncture Jacobson could recall being there personally had been when he'd been looking – in the wrong place as it turned out – for one of the suspects in the Dave Carter murder. Another case that had involved a deliberate torching. Except that what had been burned on that occasion had been human flesh and bones. Darren McGee had spent the last nine weeks of his life at Bradley's gaff, up on the top floor. Greg Salter had taken half a dozen witness statements at the address, all of them testifying to McGee's oddness: talking constantly to himself, complaining about his voices, on one occasion allegedly barricading himself in the bathroom because the TV in his room had become 'possessed' by demons. Kerr parked up behind Bradley's vehicle – if the PNC was to be believed. A beamer. But ten years old and pockmarked with rust.

Bradley answered the door in person. He'd had a rep as a hard man once upon a time but a fondness for booze and pills had taken their toll. Nowadays he looked like forty going on sixty-five: muscle melting into laze-around fat, and with the kind of bald head that would look better with a rug stuck on top – to distract your eyes from the eczema. The downstairs was his own live-in area. Bradley also had a fondness for female teenage runaways, always carefully over-age. But when there wasn't one in residence both his personal appearance and his living quarters degenerated from untidy to squalid. Jacobson and Kerr were happier than Bradley realised to talk in the hallway, not to needlessly venture any further in.

'I've been expecting you lot,' Bradley said, scratching his armpit through a grubby sweatshirt.

'And why's that, old son?' Jacobson asked.

Bradley disappeared into his front room – from where Sky Sports was booming out – and came back with a copy of the *Argus*. The lunchtime edition: but already food-stained and grimy. *Police Launch Inquiry as Top Journalist Found Drowned* was the headline story. Jacobson took it from him and found his reading glasses. Henry Pelling had dug up the same photograph Emma Smith had discovered – Shaw shaking hands with John Pilger. His report was accurate enough but thin. Relatives had identified yesterday's drowning victim as Paul Shaw, a leading investigative journalist, blah, blah, blah. The police inquiry into the drowning was being conducted by officers from the Murder Squad. DCS Greg Salter, Crowby CID's senior officer, had refused to speculate on the scope of the investigation in advance of forensic test results and the coroner's inquest which had been scheduled to convene on Monday. DCS Salter had also refused to comment on claims that Paul Shaw was the cousin of another drowning victim, Darren McGee, whose body had been fished out of the Crow at the same spot on New Year's Day.

Jacobson handed the newspaper back to Bradley.

'So why would this bring us round here, Pete?' he asked.

'I assume because you're checking what Paul Shaw was up to in Crowby—'

'And?'

'And he's been here. Spoken to me, spoken to a couple of my tenants.'

'Suppose you take it from the beginning,' Jacobson told him.

They followed him into his lounge. Bradley turned the telly volume down a fraction. Before he loafed back on to his sofa, he cleared a pile of magazines from an armchair. But both Jacobson and Kerr preferred to stand. Bradley's story appeared to be straightforward: Shaw had wanted to speak to anyone who'd had contact with Darren McGee while he was staying in Derby Crescent. Unfortunately, nearly all of the tenants who'd been here then – and who'd given statements to Salter's inquiry – had moved on. *Nobody stops here for long* – Bradley's words – *I mean – would you?* Shaw had interviewed the two who were still on the premises. And had interviewed Bradley himself. He'd been here twice. Last Saturday and again on Monday night.

'What did he want to know?' Jacobson asked.

'Whether I'd ever seen anyone make threats of violence

against McGee – or heard him speak about threats. That was the thing he mainly seemed interested in.'

'And had you?'

'No, I hadn't, mate – but I *had* heard McGee claiming it. He'd say he was getting jostled in the street, that somebody was hassling him on his mobile.'

'Did he say why?'

'They don't like black people round this way, that's what he used to say. He told me he'd been warned to get out of town – or else.'

Bradley drew the flat of his hand across his throat by way of further explanation.

'That's not in the statement you made at the time, as far as I recall,' Jacobson said.

'Probably not. But I only answered the questions your lot asked me. Like, did I think McGee was bananas – which he definitely was in my view.'

'So you didn't take his story about race threats seriously?' Kerr asked.

'Not particularly. This is a guy who gets messages from his dead relatives on BBC effing One. Not exactly a reliable witness, is he?'

Bradley's – or somebody's – cat brushed against Kerr's leg. Untypically, he ignored it.

'What about Paul Shaw then? Was *he* the full shilling?'

'Smart as paint. And professional – he put up a hundred quid just for talking to him. He said there could be a lot more – big sums – if I asked around, came up with anything of interest. I didn't bother though. I've got my own problems without sticking my nose in where it's not wanted.'

Jacobson checked the list of witness statements which Salter's inquiry had taken at Bradley's gaff, put a cross at the two names who were still supposed to be living at the address.

'I don't expect you know where your ex-tenants have moved on to?' he asked but wasn't remotely surprised at the answer.

'Nope. I never want to know. Just so long as they leave with their rent paid up to date.'

Kerr nipped upstairs. But neither of the two long-term inmates appeared to be at home. Jacobson told Bradley they'd be back, would need to call back until they could speak to them.

'Please yourself,' Bradley shrugged, but didn't volunteer when a good time to catch them might be.

Jacobson paused in the doorway.

'What's your own view of coloureds then, old son? A lot of people think there's far too many of them here nowadays.'

It wasn't a brilliant trap and Bradley didn't fall into it.

'Live and let live – that's always been my motto, mate,' he said, with neither too much nor too little enthusiasm to be unbelievable.

They discussed the encounter inside the car, ignoring the rat-a-tat drumming on the roof. While they'd been indoors, the rain had arrived with a vengeance.

'Lying, isn't he?' Kerr suggested.

'Lying about something – or not telling us the whole story anyway. If Shaw *was* prepared to put serious cash about, Bradley's exactly the type who'd go after it.'

Kerr started up the engine, wheeled the car back in the direction of Mill Street and the routes out of town. Jacobson used his mobile on the drive over to the Beech Park estate, caught up with the rest of his team. Emma Smith told him he'd she'd eventually managed to raise Paul Shaw's London GP. He'd been shirty about medical confidentiality but he'd been prepared to state off the record that Shaw had been, quote, *entirely fit in mind and body*. She was looking at Shaw's previous investigations now, using his website as her departure point. The Riverside's night staff had got nowhere with the security camera stills, DC Ray Williams told him, couldn't associate anything unusual or suspicious with any of the faces – although the last of them, the receptionist, had only just turned up, had still to take a look. Jacobson phoned Mick Hume last: Hume and Barber hadn't had much joy with Parker's neighbours although they had found out that he was a semi-regular drinker over at the Bricklayer's Arms in Mill Street. Did Jacobson want them to look in there? – only right now they were heading over to the surveillance OCS in the town centre.

'No, you're all right, Mick,' Jacobson said, ending the call, 'I'll keep the pleasure of the BA for myself and DS Kerr.'

Kerr drove straight to the address, knew the Beech Park estate like the back of his hand. His father, Tom, had led the family a yo-yo existence when Kerr and his sister had been kids, flitting between Crowby and Scotland – and back again – as the mood took him while they'd been growing up. But the Beech Park estate had been where Kerr had spent most of his teenage years; hanging around the shops and the youth club, snogging in the bus shelters, drinking cider and cheap wine at the far end of the scrubby park. Jacobson rang the doorbell. When he didn't get an instant response, he kept on ringing, rattled the letter box for good measure. Sharon Maxwell, Vicky Maxwell's mother, answered the door a full minute later. She was wearing a red silk dressing gown, still tying the cord around the middle. Jacobson showed her his ID, asked if Vicky was at home. She invited them in. But didn't look very pleased about it.

A male voice resonated from upstairs.

'Who is it, Sharon?'

'It's nothing, love,' she shouted back, 'carry on with your – bath.'

She told them Vicky was out, looking at flats – she didn't know when exactly she'd get home.

'You don't know if anyone's been trying to talk to Vicky recently do you?' Jacobson asked. 'About Darren McGee?'

'Darren?' She pushed dark hair back from her forehead. 'Is that what this is all about? Vicky needs to forget about him – not have his name dug up every five minutes.'

'So someone has been asking?'

There was a framed photograph of Princess Diana resting on the mantelpiece, a few letters and postcards stuffed behind it. Sharon Maxwell flicked through them, found what she was looking for, handed him Paul Shaw's business card. Jacobson studied it closely: Shaw's mobile number plus a fax number and an email address.

'Mind if I keep this?'

'Be my guest,' she said huffily.

He told her that Paul Shaw was dead, had been fished out of the Crow like his cousin, that they were trying to retrace the last few days of his life. She didn't say anything but she sat down, pulled the dressing gown tighter around herself. Jacobson asked her again – directly this time – if Paul Shaw had talked to her daughter about Darren.

'He called round last Sunday. Vicky wouldn't speak to him at first but he kept phoning her after that. Eventually she met him in town – Tuesday after she'd finished teaching, I think. Just to get rid of him – to put a stop to him pestering her.'

'Any idea exactly what they talked about, Mrs Maxwell?'

She had the air of a smoker who didn't smoke anymore, who wasn't sure what to do with her hands. Her fingers played with the cord of the dressing gown.

'No, not exactly. Vicky told me he had a daft story that Darren – that it wasn't suicide although it had been made to look like it. She was fuming, really angry. *If he calls again, I'm out, Mum.* That's what she said when I saw her afterwards.'

He asked her if her daughter had a mobile, if she could let them have the number. She looked around for a pen, something to write on.

'It looks as if his story wasn't rubbish then, doesn't it?' she asked, her eyes darting from Jacobson to Kerr. 'Not rubbish at all.'

Chapter Twenty-Six

Vicky hadn't liked the place when the property agent had finally showed. It was big, fair enough. But it was on the ground floor – which meant no rooftop view – and there had been damp patches inexpertly concealed in the kitchen. The agents for the other two flats she'd arranged to see had at least turned up on time. But neither of those had grabbed her imagination either. She'd had a good look around the area in between the viewings though, had grabbed a late lunch in the Beehive, one of the new breed of Longtown pubs – panini and red wine edging out beer and pickled eggs. There were cool little shops to linger in as well. Original fashions, bric-a-brac, curios: a mini-Wynarth in the making. On the way back to her car she'd taken another look up at the attic flat from the evening before and made her decision there and then: this was the one – go for it. She could get the paperwork sorted today, they'd told her when she'd phoned, the office stayed open until five on Saturday afternoons. She'd parked in the NCP again, gone in and signed. She'd wandered into the Indoor Market in the shopping centre after that, browsing the second-hand book stalls but not finding anything she especially wanted to buy. She stopped at Starbucks on her way out, might've lingered longer over her coffee if she hadn't had to fend off a clumsy attempt at a chat-up from a bloke she dimly remembered from her schooldays. He wasn't too bad looking in an over-groomed kind of way. A pity really that his conversational skills didn't seem to extend very far beyond his work – some weaselly job to do with personnel management – and the latest prospects for house prices. The original charisma bypass. No weapons of moderate desirability in sight.

It was still raining when she emerged on to the High Street but she had the little umbrella with her that she always kept in her car. She was approaching the pedestrianised square at the top end when her mobile rang: a policeman who called himself Jacobson said that her mother had given him her number, that it was urgent that he talked to her about Paul Shaw and Darren McGee. That was it, she thought. She'd just about had it with total strangers raking over the coals. But before she could speak or reply she drew level with the news stand, read the headlines on the placard: *Drowning – London Journalist Named As Victim*.

Mick Hume and DC Barber parked at the Divi and grabbed quick cups of tea in the canteen before they made a dash across the square for the Town Hall. The CCTV OCS – Operational Control Suite – was down in the basement. A series of purpose-built rooms that had replaced the archive storage which had been shunted out to the annexe behind the Town Hall proper. The duty security guard escorted them downstairs and the duty admin clerk led them through the main control room to the tape-viewing room. Compared with the amateur night set-up at the Riverside Hotel, Hume thought, this was a bit more like it. A hundred and twenty-odd cameras located around town feeding images down here twenty-four hours a day – and ten or so trained operators panning, tilting and zooming: watching out for known scumbags, sundry toerags and allied trades. Plus, whenever an incident looked to be in the offing, the oppos could switch immediately from lapsed-time recording over to real time, capture whatever was occurring in glorious

Technicolor. There was no wiping after twenty-four hours either. Images were stored for thirty-one days unless they came to official attention – in which case they were retained for as long as it took. If something went as far as the High Court and a conviction was handed down, the footage was kept until six months after the *end* of the sentence. The bleeding-heart *Guardian*-readers didn't know the half it. Which, as far as Hume could see, was probably just as well.

They discussed the Memorial Bridge and the possible routes in and out of town which connected to it with the deputy manager, a cold fish who went by the name of Jeremy Bentham. Bentham shared his surname with the Chief Constable but he was no relation as far anyone knew. It was just as well the do-gooders didn't know too much about types like him either. The current rumour around the Divisional building was that, despite (or because of) being married and a regular churchgoer, he always made sure he was on duty Friday and Saturday nights – when the voyeuristic possibilities provided by shop doorways and alleys reached their weekly peak. Bentham was efficient though, if nothing else. They worked out where and when the most useful footage would be likely to come from and Bentham went off to set it up for them. Which left Hume and Barber tapping their thumbs in front of the bank of monitors.

'I don't suppose we can get the racing results on here,' Hume said idly.

'Here's a thing about jokes, Mick,' Barber replied, without glancing up from the nearest screen, 'they work better when nobody's heard them before.'

Barber just wanted to get the viewing session over with. Jeremy Bentham gave him the creeps. This whole place in general gave him the creeps. As far as he was concerned, the jury was still out on surveillance systems. Sometimes they helped with the evidence for a conviction. Great. Especially when getting convictions was your job. But they'd been sold to the public as making the streets safer.

Tell that to the Bulger family, he thought. Or, right now, tell it to Linford and Edith Shaw. There was no camera anywhere quicker than a knife in your guts or a bottle, a fist or a boot in your face. Big Brother Was Watching You – and occasionally clocking the guilty. But he'd yet to lift a finger in the time frame when you actually needed it.

Jacobson arranged to visit Vicky Maxwell inside the hour. The news about Paul Shaw had clearly shaken her – that much was evident just from a mobile-to-mobile conversation – but she insisted she'd be fine to drive herself home. Before then, he needed to speak to Greg Salter. There were authorisations he needed to extract and even Jacobson had a limit to the amount of time he'd attempt to keep his senior officer in the dark. Salter never worked on the premises on Saturdays – or Sundays – if he could avoid it. But he couldn't avoid at least being on home stand-by when there was a serious inquiry underway within his bailiwick. Kerr dropped Jacobson off at the Flowers Street junction. The clouds had finally burst all they had to burst and were moving on. And in any case the Millennium Apartment Complex was less than two minutes' walk away, the Divisional building less than ten. He told Kerr he'd come and find him when he was ready. Kerr wanted to check on the Randeep Parmeer situation, maybe ring Parmeer from his office.

The MAC had been one of the first of the recent wave of upmarket town centre developments and was still holding its own as a prestige address. Jacobson noticed that a blue plaque had appeared on the wall near the entranceway since he'd last called round, commemorating the old Palace of Varieties which had once stood on the site. He spoke into the video entryphone and endured the non-dulcet tones of Chrissie, Salter's hawk-faced better half, as she buzzed him in. He crossed the mezzanine and took one of the fast lifts upwards. The Salters lived at the top of the building. A kind of eyrie, Jacobson always thought, where Chrissie lurked and Salter plotted his career moves.

'He was just on his way to the roof garden to do some planting and pruning, Frank,' Chrissie said, when she'd ushered him in. 'He'll be down in a jiffy. It's so good to see him de-stressing these days – with all the responsibilities he carries. Coffee, tea – something stronger?'

'A coffee would be fine, *Christine*,' Jacobson replied, playing his companion game to dubbing Greg as *sir*.

He stretched back on one of the Salters' irritatingly comfortable white sofas, watched the last of the clouds trailing eastwards through the wide skylight.

Greg Salter arrived at the same instant as the coffee. His wife left them to it, announced that it was high time she did her Pilates work-out in her yoga room. The high time would have been twenty years ago, Jacobson thought with trademark unkindness – before she'd needed the XL jogging bottoms. Salter, inches shorter than his wife and stones lighter, always seemed less nervous – in Jacobson's imagination at any rate – when Mrs Salter wasn't in the room. Like a rabbit relieved that it's not going to be cooked and eaten after all – or at least not immediately.

Jacobson brought Salter up to speed but emphasised for his benefit – or for the benefit of Jacobson getting what he needed out of him – that everything remained speculative at this stage. Circumstantial possibilities were starting to suggest themselves – but the forensic results remained key. Paul Shaw's death could still be a simple case of suicide, he pointed out – and a fraction of suicides every year were committed by men and women with no known previous history of mental disturbance.

'But you definitely want access to Wayne Parker's telephone records – and to put him on a national alert?' Salter asked.

'If it does go the other way – say, the blood spilled on the Memorial Bridge does turn out to be Shaw's – then Parker's the closest thing we've got to a potential suspect so far.'

Salter coughed up the necessary authorisations after a little more coaxing. He was wearing his off-duty Levis and a light blue Lacoste sports shirt but he looked even less convincingly casual than usual. If he'd reached the wrong conclusions in the Darren McGee inquiry then he'd made a bad blunder – and both Jacobson and Salter knew it. Jacobson finished his coffee and abandoned him to his rose bushes.

He phoned ahead and met Kerr in the Divi car park. Fifteen minutes later they were back outside Sharon and Vicky Maxwell's front door. They talked in the tidy kitchen, leaving Mrs Maxwell and her boyfriend, Stan, in the front room. Vicky Maxwell had her mother's dark hair and – even at this instant – dark, lively eyes. She'd fixed herself a brandy and now she was fixing a thin roll-up with licorice papers – a student habit she'd never quite got out of, she told them.

Jacobson offered her a light from his silver lighter but left his B & H packet in his pocket. He said that he needed to know whatever she could remember about her conversation with Paul Shaw.

'He claimed Darren had been murdered, that it hadn't been suicide.'

Her voice was clipped, editing out emotion.

'Did he say whether he had any proof?' Jacobson asked.

'He never told me any details – which didn't impress me – he just said that he was working on it, that he was sure whatever I could tell him about Darren would be a help.'

'But you weren't keen to talk to him?'

'Darren's dead and he's not coming back. And before he was dead, he was crazy. All I want to do is get on with my life – not constantly dig up the past. Don't forget I was there – in the room – the first time he tried to kill himself. He took a bread knife to both of his wrists. I was drenched in his blood from trying to stop the bleeding by the time the ambulance showed up. It wasn't exactly a surprise when I heard he'd drowned himself.'

She half-finished the brandy, found an ashtray for the roll-up.

'To be honest, I reckoned that madness must be a family trait when I listened to Paul Shaw trying to say different.'

'And now?'

It was hard to tell whether it was the shock of Shaw's unexpected death – or the memory of Darren's – that was getting to her. But something was.

'Looks like I could be right, doesn't it? Maybe he got so obsessed with what Darren had done that he ended up copying him.'

Jacobson didn't comment. Instead he rechecked certain facts from the witness statements she'd made to Greg Salter's investigation. She'd lived with Darren McGee for just over two years. *Yes*. Firstly in London, then in Barcelona, then briefly in London again. *Yes*. During their time together, Darren had been hospitalised for mental illness, had made two serious attempts on his life. *Yes*.

'And he'd put you in fear of your own life?'

Vicky stood up and turned around, away from the table, lifted her top over her head. Jacobson and Kerr stared at her. She was bra-less and perfectly slim around the waist. Yet what their eyes were drawn to was the almost-neat series of deep scars in the middle of her back – as if a maniac had been playing noughts and crosses. She pulled her top back down, turned to face them again.

'I never pressed charges but that was when I finally left him,' she said. 'The last straw. That's when I finally came to my senses.'

Her roll-up had gone out. She picked it up, re-lit it from a gas ring on the cooker.

'But he followed you here – to Crowby,' Jacobson observed.

It was all in the summary files, it was all what he already knew. But what was written down wasn't always the same as what had really happened.

'Not at first,' she said, 'I moved here in August – it was

the middle of December before I had any idea that he'd followed me.'

According to her witness statement, McGee had taken to hanging round the school gates watching for her, had done the same outside her mother's house, had followed her in the street a few times when he'd spied her in town, tried to talk to her.

Kerr asked her why she'd never invoked the injunction against him – which he'd potentially broken by even setting foot in Crowby, which he'd certainly broken by approaching her. Her voice unclipped itself at last.

'Yeah, well, it's not that easy is it? Not when you've loved somebody. And he wasn't threatening – just sad, pleading. In a way I suppose I was impressed. He was keeping himself together after all, even holding down a job. Eighty per cent of recurrent sufferers never work, did you know that? Can't get themselves organised enough for normal routines.'

She swigged her brandy right down to the dregs.

'I didn't like him near the school of course. I think if he'd done that even one more time then I *would* have reported him – of course there never was a next time.'

Jacobson brought her back to the major topic he needed to know about: her conversation earlier this week with Paul Shaw.

'He must have told you some details though, surely? He must have had some grounds for his theory after all.'

She maintained good eye-contact, he was thinking – for a young woman lying by some kind of omission to a senior, heavy-duty cop.

'He wanted to know if Darren had ever mentioned being threatened since he'd been in Crowby. But I had to tell him no – the conversations I had with Darren didn't last long enough, for one thing. Just him saying please, can't we just talk? And me saying no we can't, it's over, Darren, go away, leave me alone.'

Chapter Twenty-Seven

Nevil Drury's live-in shag turned up before Drury had got back himself.

'Wayne, is it?' she said, dumping her bag down on the table, sliding a pink leather jacket off her shoulders and slinging that on to the sofa. She was a looker, of course, mid-twenties and bottle-blond. But there was something earnest about her too, something that said she wasn't to be mucked around with. The fact that she worked for a living, didn't just sponge off Drury in exchange for bedroom favours, was part of it. But there was more, stuff he couldn't grasp immediately. He took the hint in any case when she mentioned the spare room, suggested he must be tired out from his journey. Too right, he told her, he could do with getting settled in, checking his stuff – he didn't want to get in anyone's way.

'Don't worry, it's not a problem,' she said, making it plain that it definitely was.

He followed her out into the hall and upstairs, lugging his rucksack over his right shoulder. He was impressed to find that the room was big, spacious. And it even had an en suite: toilet, generous handbasin, walk-in shower. Five minutes later, she came back, threw him a couple of soft, clean towels.

'Great, eh, Teresa,' Parker said, 'just what I could do with – a good clean-up.'

She gave him an unfriendly smile and closed the door behind her on the way out. He was used to strangers not liking him, finding nothing in him of particular interest, not realising that – most of the time – he felt exactly the same about them. He listened to her footsteps retreating downstairs, thought that he felt a little bit like a prisoner after lights-out – or, this was more accurate, like an inmate in one of those clinics where pop stars and TV personalities paid through the nose to dry out, to dump their various addictions. Banged up in comfort – but still banged up.

He decided to have a shower anyway. After that, it wouldn't do any harm either to get some of his clothes unpacked, get them on to hangers, maybe lose some of the creases. He stripped off and stepped in, adjusted the temperature until he had it right: warm but not too hot. Drury had been gone a fair old while, he thought. He'd told him an hour but it was more than two by now. Maybe Drury was already looking into whatever could be done for him, wasn't just out and about on his own business. If he was going to help him, it made sense to do it ASAP. That way he'd be gone, out of Drury's face, with the least risk to Drury. He found the remains of a bar of soap, worked a lather up over his skin then let the water run it off. *Get a life*, Drury had told him. And if you looked at Drury, compared how they were living, you had to admit that Drury had a point. A stash of cash and a nice bit of female company versus bog all: a crap job and a crap, rented flat – and having to watch what you said all the time, who you said it to. That was where idealism got you, wanting to do something for your race.

He stepped out again, dried himself, took a look out the window with the towel wrapped around his waist. He was at the back of the house, Drury's unworked garden underneath him. The rain had drained away to a steady Manchester drizzle. The ridiculous thing was that he was the one facing double figures when, at best, he was – what – an accomplice? A provider of information, an aider, an abetter. Drury, on the other hand, was the genuine article. A murderer. A killer. Drury had been in the same line of business then as he was now, had worked his way up until he was one of the biggest army dealers in Carrington, the barracks town down south where they'd both been stationed. Carrington wasn't an army centre on the scale of somewhere like Aldershot or Catterick. But it was a busy transit point – and that was what had given it a flourishing drugs scene. Lads passing through from all over. Jocks, Geordies, Scousers, Londoners. All of them bored shitless; all of them with money to burn. Eventually Drury had cornered enough good business to provoke a turf war. Riskily, he'd taken his main rival out himself, in person, *to encourage the others, Wayne* – a point-blank bullet in the head, a carefully wiped L85 rifle pressed into dead hands, another mysterious army suicide making a few newspaper headlines for a few days. The red filth from SIB had guessed who'd really done it, half the barracks had guessed, but Drury had his cast-iron alibi: Wayne Parker. According to Drury, they'd been drinking together on the night in question – at a country pub ten miles away. A pub conveniently remote and quiet enough that bribing the publican and a couple of rural alcoholics had been well within Drury's financial capacity. And Drury *had* been there anyway, had just left sooner than his bought-for witnesses had been prepared to admit. Parker had been Drury's ace in the hole. An ordinary, run-of-the-mill squaddie with a reasonable-enough record – and totally no involvement in Drury's business.

Parker unpacked his rucksack, took out clean underpants, a clean shirt, his best pair of jeans. He wondered how much it would piss Teresa off if he used her washing machine. Drury had paid him well enough at the time. But he'd said himself that it was a debt that went beyond cash, well beyond. *If you ever land yourself in any real shit, Wayne*, he'd told him, *let me know – I owe you, mate, understand?*

*

Kerr chauffeured Jacobson to the Divisional building and then drove off in the direction of Mill Street. Jacobson took the lift up to the fourth floor. He'd decided that it might be better for Kerr to check out the Bricklayers Arms on his own. One 'tec in a dodgy pub stood out less than two did, brought fewer conversations to an instant halt. The CID Resource Centre was a sea of abandoned computers and workstations. Five thirty pm on a Saturday was one of the few interludes in the week when there were more resources available than CID to use them, when the room was possessed by the weird sense of emptiness that big office spaces succumbed to after hours, the desperate sensation that there was a fantastic party going on somewhere else – and you weren't invited.

Emma Smith talked him through what she'd found out about Paul Shaw's previous investigations. Shaw's major stories had been nearly all about race or xenophobia. The mistreatment of asylum seekers in the detention centres, racist abuses in the prison service, dangerous conditions faced by illegal migrant workers in farming and the building trade. A lot of unpleasant people would have been highly pissed off by Shaw's exposés – but Jacobson really couldn't see a contract hit as an outcome. Shaw hadn't managed to do any of them enough personal damage for that to seem credible or likely.

'What's this about the Yardies, lass?' he asked, glancing over her shoulder at her computer screen.

'It's nowt, guv. Not in the way you mean anyway. Shaw wrote an article claiming that the Home Office were using the Yardie menace as an excuse to deny work permits to ordinary, law-abiding Jamaicans. He accused them of operating secret quotas.'

'I don't doubt it for a second, lass. Though what beats me is why anyone would *want* to come to this country, the piss-hole state it's in.'

His mobile rang: Mick Hume – there was a white Ford Transit that fitted the time frame, it had been caught on a traffic camera at the Flowers Street junction at twelve-forty am on Friday morning and then again – in the opposite direction – at one forty-six.

'The footage isn't great, more's the pity. Jeremy Bentham reckons there was a camera fault. It's been fixed since this morning according to him – but that's no bloody help to us. We think it's the same van both ways all the same. The real pig is the number plate – zero readability at every magnification we've tried.'

Jacobson traced the route in his mind. The journey time from Flowers Street out to the vicinity of the Memorial Bridge tallied nicely to the thirty-eight minute security camera switch-off at the Riverside Hotel – and also to Arlette Lefevre's testimony that she'd seen a white van parked on the bridge around one thirty.

'This could still be good news, Mick,' he said. 'Organise a police copy and then give Steve Horton a ring. If he's available for some Saturday night overtime then let's see what he can do in the way of computer enhancement. We definitely need that number plate.'

DC Williams turned up. The stills exercise was complete, he told them, but it had drawn a total blank – although probably that was to be expected if all the action had happened during the time that Wayne Parker had disabled the hotel's cameras.

'Precisely, old son,' Jacobson commented, 'so from the point of view of excluding other possibilities it was worth doing.'

He asked them to write up their reports. After that they might as well clock off – provided they stayed on stand-by in case they were needed later.

Jacobson left them to it. Williams waited until he was out of earshot.

'We need to talk, Emma,' he said. 'We screwed up last night – we should have spotted that there was a problem with the video recording straightaway.'

Emma Smith closed the files on her screen but didn't look up.

'I didn't screw up, Ray. I was the one trying to watch, remember? You were the one talking bollocks and making pathetic excuses instead. You're a wanker as a person, Ray – and you're a wanker as a copper.'

'But I told you about Cerys from Day One, Emma—'

'You told me about her all right – that it was over, that you'd split up for good. You just didn't bother to mention it when you got back together again. Must've slipped your mind I expect.'

To be fair to Williams, his long-running, off-on relationship with his fiancée in Swansea was well-known inside Crowby CID, was almost legendary. But the fact remained that it had been 'off' when Emma had started sleeping with him.

Ray Williams's face reddened.

'I was going to tell you, Em—'

She did look up this time.

'When? Before the wedding – or after the honeymoon? Or did you think you could help yourself to a bit on the side during the week and then bog off back to Cerys of the Valleys at the weekends?'

'Look, I'm sorry. I'm in the wrong,' Williams said weakly.

What worried him – what he knew worried both of them – was that he'd blown their working partnership. They'd joined CID in the same intake, had been co-opted into the Murder Squad pool at the same time, had established themselves as a part of Jacobson's trusted inner circle. And she was right of course. He'd just seen an opportunity and grabbed it. She was a nice-looking girl and half a dozen years younger than he was. He would've kept fucking her as well as Cerys if he could've got away with it.

Emma Smith logged out, started to gather her stuff together. She could write up her reports from the comfort of her flat as easily as here.

'What's supposed to happen now, Ray, is that I put in

for a transfer, isn't it? It's always the woman's career that has to suffer after all.'

'Well, it might be easier if—'

She stood up, resisted the strong temptation to slap him very, very hard.

'I'm staying put, Ray. I'm even prepared to go on working with you - provided you quit whingeing about how sorry you are - and provided you tell the DCI exactly *who* fucked up last night.'

DC Williams nodded, a little blankly. He watched her sweep out of the room. He'd chosen Cerys over her, had to wonder if he'd made anything like the right decision.

Jacobson used the lift again. Up to the police canteen on the seventh floor. He chose his customary egg and chips and glass of orange juice. Less typically, he added a plate of green salad on the side as a health measure, even opted not to drown it in mayonnaise. He called up Jim Webster after he'd eaten. Webster was officially off duty today but Jacobson knew he would be keeping track of developments via his spotlessly-clean telephone, would most probably have called into the Divi at some point earlier. Webster wore a regulation mask of weary disinterest but serious cases - rapes, murders, suicides that mightn't be suicides - grabbed the Chief SOCO's attention as much as they did his own. Webster's team would've pulled out the stops - and Webster would've made doubly sure that they did.

Webster's five-year-old daughter answered on the third ring. A teddy bear called Iris was somehow involved in the consultation as to whether Daddy was at home or not. It transpired after a moment or two that he was. Jacobson told him about the potential number plates and the missing thirty-eight minutes.

'Everything that needs to be with the FSS is with them, Frank,' Webster told him, reciprocating. 'Plus the burnout's secured in the vehicle workshop. There's a fire-autowreck specialist booked in for tomorrow morning.'

'And they're definitely fast-tracking on the possible blood sample?'

'Check. The biology guys are promising basic results by Monday lunchtime, the bridge stains included.'

Jacobson ended the call. The FSS – Forensic Science Service – laboratories in Birmingham were the largest in the country and covered all the major forensic specialisms. Crowby benefited from geographical proximity: crime scene materials could be physically couriered backwards and forwards in a fraction of the time it cost some other forces. He finished his orange juice and took stock. Steve Horton's computer skills. Whatever Kerr learned over at the Bricklayers Arms. The slender possibility that the all-forces alert on Wayne Parker yielded a quick result. That was pretty much it for now. He looked at his watch. Just under a minute to six. If he hurried downstairs, he should be able to catch the Radio Four news on the ancient portable he kept in his office. It would be useful to find out whether Shaw's death had generated national interest, as Henry Pelling had predicted, or not. So far, Pelling apart, he'd had no journos pestering him. But Shaw's name hadn't been publicly released until this morning and the inquest into his death wouldn't convene until Monday. He knew from experience – most of it bad – that press silence didn't always last, was frequently just the calm before the storm.

There was no such thing as a safe parking place in an area like this. Kerr pulled in where he could, just down from the bail hostel, and walked the hundred yards or so along Mill Street towards the Bricklayer's Arms. The place was busier than he'd expected for the time of day – when a lot of pubs were still trapped in the lull between afternoon drinking and the full-on Saturday evening session. A women's boxing tournament from Mexico was the current attraction on the giant-screen TV and might have been one part of the explanation – the other part was that a lot of the BA's regulars had nowhere else to go, were banned from other pubs closer to town. Kerr ordered a pint of Grolsch and supped it at the bar, clocking faces and scanning to see if anyone was clocking him.

The half-dozen who did recognise him seemed more than happy enough to ignore him – and the bar staff all looked new. Nobody worked behind the bar of the Bricklayers for long if they had a better offer elsewhere. The kid who'd served him had been a young Aussie, probably wouldn't be here the next time Kerr called by. He knew Parker – *oh yeah, the night porter guy* – but said he hadn't seen him for a few days. Parker had a habit of calling in early evening, he told Kerr: *He'll have a couple of pints and read the paper – but he keeps himself pretty much to himself.* When he'd drunk half of his pint, Kerr decided to check out the pool room. He moved away from the bar and slipped through the crowd. There were four tables, all of them in play. The figure hunched over the far table was none other than Gary Bowles. Engrossed in his game, Bowles didn't notice Kerr watching him. But he fluffed his shot anyway. His opponent was a hefty-looking lad but nimble enough with a cue. Kerr waited until he'd potted the black. Bowles cursed, finally spied Kerr only as Kerr crossed the room.

'Gaz,' Kerr said, 'you could do with a bit of coaching.'

'Who the fuck are you?' the hefty lad asked before Bowles had time to reply.

'I'm *fucking* Detective Sergeant Kerr, Crowby CID – and you are?'

'Tony Blair.'

Kerr eyeballed him.

'No – really,' Tony Blair said, fished in his inside pocket, produced a grubby driving licence: *Blair, Anthony Phillip, 14-05-83*.

'And you're a friend of Mr Bowles.'

Tony Blair No Relation shrugged.

'I don't know about that. I only come down here to play pool.'

Kerr didn't press it. But he committed Blair's details to memory before he handed him back his licence.

'We need to talk again, Gaz,' he said, pointing to the exit.

Bowles followed him through to the bar, probably thinking that at least it was noisy there, that at least every fucker in the room wouldn't overhear the conversation.

Kerr confronted him about the shit-dumping at the Viceroy Tandoori. Bowles denied any knowledge of anything, anywhere, anytime. He'd been at home last night and had stayed there. Him and Linda.

'You got a dog, Gaz?' Kerr asked him, thinking that if he didn't, it was generous of him to open up his front garden as a facility for the local canine population.

'Linda's mum's bull terrier's stopping with us. Linda flaming needs it with all the flaming al-Qaeda coons and foreigners we've got round our way.'

'Well, think about this, Gaz. Suppose I arrange for a scientific comparison between the dog crap in the Viceroy and the dog crap in your front garden?'

'You want to waste your time, you go ahead,' Bowles said, seeming confident enough about it. 'And my name's Gary. I keep telling you that.'

Kerr swallowed the last inch of his beer.

'Speaking of names, *Gaz*, Wayne Parker mean anything to you?'

Bowles didn't reply, took a swig of whatever he was drinking: lager mixed with cider and blackcurrant was Kerr's best guess.

'Drinks in here, works at the Riverside Hotel,' Kerr added, 'a quiet bloke by all accounts.'

Bowles tried to keep the smirk off his face.

'Sorry. I don't know the name. I can't help you.'

'That's too bad, *Gaz*. Because if you help me, I might be able to help you. And you're going to need help soon. That's a promise.'

Kerr found an empty table for his empty glass, sat it

down alongside half a dozen others which had been lined up next to an overflowing ashtray and a half-eaten, black-yolked scotch egg.

'I'd give that some thought, *Gaz,* if I were you.'

Chapter Twenty-Eight

Rick Cole phoned his wife. Their daughter, England, had been sick after teatime last night. Wendy reckoned it was nothing. She'd eaten too much or she'd eaten too quickly. But Cole had told her to get the doctor involved if she still didn't seem good today. You couldn't be too careful, he'd told her.

'She's fine, Rick, just fine,' Wendy Cole said, 'apart from missing her daddy.'

Cole's wife put his daughter on the line for a moment.

'Love you, Daddy,' she said.

'And Daddy loves you, doll. Be good.'

Cole walked back into the barn that was being used for the dinner. The tables had been re-arranged since lunchtime, had been pushed together until they formed two long rows, *bierkeller* style, plus a much shorter top table for the leadership. Cole sat down between the Stuart brothers and Martin Kesey. There was a free bar for beer and spirits. To look like he was part of things, Cole had accepted a pint of something called Black Sheep – real ale was officially regarded as patriotic – yet he knew that he wouldn't accept another, didn't like his mind to fuzz out. The barn was big, wasn't wholly converted as a living space yet. But it was already clean and comfy enough. A new stone floor, storage heaters and a decent lighting system. Like everything else that Sutherland forked out for, all the labour would have come from sound, reliable white firms. And why not? It was what the Pakis and the Jews did – always put business the way of their own people. Cole sipped his beer, only half-listening to John Stuart enthusing about some talk or other he'd been to. The Party's training days always divided neatly into two halves. Something physical – fighting techniques or weapons handling – followed by informational sessions: political strategy, political theory, international developments, etcetera. Big John had listened to some Yank from Oregon giving an update on the US White Power scene. *The fucking weapons they can get hold of over there, Rick*, he was saying, *you would not fucking believe*. Cole just nodded. However many they had it wasn't even a fraction of a fraction of what the ZOG army, the FBI and the CIA had, he thought.

The Party's attitude to armed struggle still wasn't clear enough for Cole's liking. It was sensible that the Party's elite, its *cadre*, were weapons-trained and capable of looking after themselves in a ruck. And everybody knew that the Collapse was coming sooner or later – the void that only the Party would be able to fill when the System finally fell apart under the weight of its own contradictions. Yet short term, the goal was supposed to be about building a mainstream power base. The Party would set out real solutions on immigration and law and order – no compromises – but it would use modern methods: focus groups and slick advertising. The BNP had attempted something similar and had botched it. Mainly because the BNP was more of a drop-in club for social inadequates than a serious political organisation – you didn't join *this* party unless you had a proper job and no serious criminal record (if you were too stupid not to get caught, you were too stupid to lead, Matthew Sutherland was fond of saying). And the BNP lacked sufficient access to the generous funds and the wealthy, committed backers necessary to do the job properly. When everything was ready, they'd been told, the Party would be 'rolled out' to the nation exactly like the latest must-have brand of washing powder. So why were they regularly spending half their Saturdays fannying about with police armour and AK47s when next year, or the year after, they were supposed to be putting themselves forward as prospective councillors, MPs and MEPs? Especially as nearly all of them had already proven themselves in the field at one time or another anyway.

Cole sensed a hush descending. Matthew Sutherland was banging a gavel on the top table and somebody else was dimming the lights. A screen was lowered on the far wall. *Building the Future*, the Party's closely guarded 'internal' propaganda video, was about to be shown, signalling that the after-dinner speeches would be following. Cole had been privileged to see it four times now. But to be honest he still wasn't bored by it. Not with Skrewdriver, Death in June and Wagner all on the soundtrack. Not with its rapid-fire history of the movement. *Kristallnacht*, the death camps, an SS warrior demonstrating the correct method with a meat hook, unknown English patriots trashing a Paki corner shop. There were southern lynchings too – and the real, hardcore footage from the Abu Ghraib prison. As usual, you had to be able to read the subtext since the voice-over was sweetness and light, the purest bullshit: evil things had happened because of the dominance of unnatural, decadent philosophies – the way to prevent a future that repeated the mistakes of the past was for the races to go their own ways, each to his own – and for the white race to reclaim its inheritance.

The barn erupted into applause when the video ended. Cheering, footstomping, hands slapping the trestle tables. Matthew Sutherland waited until the noise subsided before he rose again to speak. Cole had heard a rumour that the big man – the leader – would be here in person today. But later he'd been told that he was still fund raising overseas. It was a pity – although Sutherland was no mean speaker in his own right.

'Thank you all for the dedication and commitment you've

shown again today. I know a lot of you are impatient, thinking that the Party must seize the time. But softly softly catchee monkey. When you do go out there to win this country back for its people you will be ready – like no party before you ever has.'

Sutherland paused, making sure that he had their full attention before he continued.

'And I'll tell you this – your days of action are coming soon. The so-called respectable politicians are doing our groundwork for us. So are the newspapers. The more they make concessions to us on crime and immigration, the more ordinary, decent people say fair enough – *fair enough but not far enough*. But this party *will* go far enough. You will not hear speakers from this party talk about *voluntary* repatriation. You will not hear them say that rapists and muggers and foreign pimps need to be *understood*. The only thing scum need to understand is that there is a noose and a gallows waiting for them—'

Noose. Noose. Noose. Noose. Noose. Noose.

Cole put down his beer, chanted with the rest. He glanced at the Stuarts, carried away now, whooping and stomping, certain local difficulties forgotten for the time being. Cole felt his own doubts melting. He was only a middle-ranker, couldn't expect to understand every tactical detail. Mussolini's Action Squads had a slogan – *Believe, Obey, Fight* – that was worth taking to heart. He was in a room full of secrets after all – and meanings that were buried underneath the surfaces of words. When you looked at it that way, the Crowby contingent were already ahead of the game. Very well ahead.

Jacobson switched off his radio when the bulletin got to the sports stories. There had been no mention of Paul Shaw's death. Mick Hume rang in: they'd got the CCTV footage copied over OK but there was a problem about Steve Horton. Apparently, Horton had clocked off at lunchtime – as soon as he'd got the hotel security stills ready for DC

Williams – and then disappeared to Birmingham. Some mates of his were on a stag weekend and Horton had planned on joining them. His mobile was switched off and – even if it wasn't – Hume reckoned that Horton would be rat-arsed by now, pub-crawling his way along Broad Street. Hume had left him a voicemail message but so far there'd been no response. Jacobson asked Hume to text Horton as well in that case, just to make sure: if tonight was out, then tomorrow morning would have to do.

He found his B & H packet and the silver lighter that Janice had given him a lifetime ago. He'd been doing quite well today on the no-smoking front but this was frustrating news. He lit up and stood up, crossed over to the window. Horton was a civilian employed Monday to Friday, nine to five. He was always eager and willing to help out in exchange for overtime. But Jacobson hadn't asked him to go on stand-by so there was no reason in the world why he shouldn't currently be ogling pole dancers, fending off drunken women and downing tequila slammers. Jacobson knew that it was his own fault if it was anyone's. He still hadn't got it into his luddite skull how important computers – and the geeks who understood them – were becoming for police work. He thought about asking Kerr or Emma Smith to have a go – but decided on balance that it would probably be better to wait for the expert.

He'd had a message earlier from Sergeant Ince in the control room: the telephone records he'd requested wouldn't be available until tomorrow either. The mobile phone companies, Ince reminded him, were fielding half a million police data requests a year – or struggling to field them, especially on a weekend. BT had installed a direct police link to its billing databases which, in theory, meant that there should have been less of a problem in regard to Wayne Parker's land line. But there was a server update scheduled overnight and access was intermittent and currently non-existent. Jacobson took a deep draw, watched half a dozen kids skateboarding recklessly across the square. You could only push an investigation up to a point. Investigations were journeys. And there was nothing you could do when they got bogged down with delays – other than put up with it and keep an eye on your blood pressure.

After a minute, he phoned Hume back.

'You lads might as well call it a day, Mick. But keep your own phones switched on. Just in case.'

He tried DS Kerr next. Kerr told him he was on his way back from Mill Street – he'd talked to a few toerags at the Bricklayer's Arms who were prepared to say that they knew Parker as an occasional drinker there. But that was all they'd been prepared to say. None of them had seen him for a couple of days, none of them seemed bothered at the loss. Jacobson arranged to meet Kerr in the Divi car park:

'We'll give Bradley's gaff another spin, Ian. Then maybe leave it there till tomorrow.'

Bradley's two long-serving tenants were at home this time. Or as at home as two confirmed users were ever likely to be. Billy Marsden and his latest woman, Rhea, had been dossed in Derby Crescent for more than a year. They were on maintenance scripts that they were more or less sticking to. Rhea was out of it. She was fully dressed but snoring blissfully on top of the bed. Marsden, though, was up and about, cooking something on the two-ring Baby Belling that involved mixing packets of dried soup with real-life leeks, carrots and button mushrooms. Jacobson had never met him before but Kerr knew him, although he hadn't seen him in a while.

'Been down the veg market, Mr Kerr. They give it all away cheap the last half-hour.'

Kerr nodded, gave him a half-smile. Marsden and Rhea were living on the top floor, in the room that had been next to Darren McGee's.

'Smells good, Billy,' he said, thinking that he couldn't abide Marsden's life for a day, even without his drug problem.

He was over-sensitive to cooking smells for one thing,

hated it if they clung to his clothes or penetrated to other parts of the house beyond the kitchen. But Marsden did everything in one poky room. Cooked, ate, washed, enjoyed junkie sex.

Kerr told him why they'd called.

'Yeah, yeah. I read about that in the paper when I was in town.'

Marsden lifted the pan he'd been stirring off the heat and found Paul Shaw's business card amongst the chaos on top of a small chest of drawers near the bed. He showed it to Kerr and Jacobson like he was pleased about it, like it connected him in some way to something important.

'So Shaw wanted to know about Darren McGee?' Kerr asked.

'Yeah, yeah. Darren. Another lonesome soul on the lost highway. He was all right, Darren – all right.'

Marsden was tall, even broad shouldered, but his movements were precarious – as if falling over was always an imminent possibility. He was pushing forty, had spent nearly half his life on gear. He hovered in front of his tiny cooker again, began to stir the pan as soon as he'd put it back on the ring.

'The general view seems to be that he was mad as a hatter,' Kerr said.

'What's mad, Mr Kerr? William Blake talked to the angels and they said he was a genius once he'd snuffed it, stuck his shit in museums. Darren saw stuff, heard stuff – but he had it under control. It's about walking between the worlds, isn't it? You gotta keep a careful balance.'

Kerr reminded him of his witness statement to Greg Salter's inquiry. McGee talking to his voices, telling Marsden to be careful of Rhea because she had the 'mark of the beast' on her.

'Yeah, well she has. 666. Darren was right about that. It's on her left arm, had it done years ago – when she was shacked up with a Satanist biker.'

The other thing the room stank of was paint – from

Marsden's piled-up canvases. He'd gone to art school, Kerr knew, was regarded by some as a wasted, destroyed talent. He'd been in a couple of bands as well – but had always made sure he screwed up any time it looked like he might be in any danger of being successful. Kerr noticed that he still had a couple of cheap, shitty-looking amps stuffed in a corner next to his battered Stratocaster-copy.

He asked him again what Shaw had said to them, what he'd wanted to know.

'He knew they'd done it, he said, just needed the proof, yeah.'

Marsden peered at his soup, turned the gas down, stuck a lid haphazardly on the pan.

'They?' Kerr asked.

'Fascists. Blue Meanies. He said they'd killed Darren deliberate, wanted to know if we'd seen anybody hassling him.'

'But you hadn't?'

'There were a couple of young kids had a go at him one time that I saw – over in the Londis shop in Mill Street – they reckoned he'd skipped past them in the queue. Told him to *eff off you black B*. But I mean that's just everyday stuff, isn't? Man's inhumanity to man, yeah.'

Jacobson was fascinated by the canvas leaning against the wall nearest to him. Dark, angry oils and an ambiguous, androgynous figure slashing a painting of another figure slashing a painting of another figure – and on and on until your eyes were dizzy from the effect.

'What about here, Mr Marsden?' he asked, pulling his gaze away.

'It's mainly youngsters in this gaff as well, mate. Eighteen, nineteen, twenty. What do they know? A lot of them were on his case. Especially after the time he barricaded himself in the bathroom. But what Paul Shaw was saying about death threats? Nah, nothing like that.'

'Did Darren ever tell you himself that he was being seriously threatened?'

'He said to me once that he'd been told to get out of town, yeah. But when I asked him who by, he went off on one of his raps, told me it was the four riders of the apocalypse that were after him.'

Rhea coughed in her sleep. The lid rattled on Marsden's soup pan.

'Did Paul Shaw offer cash if you did recall something more useful?' Kerr asked.

'That's right, yeah. Only I told him that money's no good to me. The more I have, the more damage I do. Straight into my arm, mate. Straight into my effing arm.'

Matthew Sutherland introduced Martin Kesey to Dave Gill, the Party's North-West organiser. The speeches were finished and a general drinks session was underway.

'*Dr* Kesey gave an excellent talk the other night, Dave,' Sutherland said, emphasising Kesey's title, 'fucking first rate.'

Gill shook him by the hand.

'Welcome on board. That's what this party's all about. Blokes with real calibre, blokes with something special to contribute.'

Kesey smiled, returned Gill's over-vigorous grip, ounce for ounce.

'It's been a great day,' he said. 'Too bad the top man's not here.'

'Well, that's the way it goes. The next cadre day's not till June. The London region's turn. Hopefully he'll be back from the US of A by then. You've not heard him speak before I take it?'

Kesey said that he hadn't.

'You're in for a treat then, lad. 'Course you don't want to be sitting next to him on these occasions if you can help it. Him and his bloody cigars – smokes more than an Auschwitz chimney.'

Kesey laughed louder than either Sutherland or Gill did – as if he'd never heard the ancient joke before.

When they'd moved on – *doing the rounds*, Sutherland said – Kesey grabbed a refill at the bar and looked for Rick Cole and the Stuarts. He'd spent most of the day in their company and he'd picked up on an undercurrent running between them. Something they obviously wanted to keep to themselves. Something that might be important to know about. He'd noticed that Cole hardly touched alcohol. But John and Phil did. And drink, in Kesey's experience, usually helped to fuddle the fascist brain and loosen the fascist tongue.

Chapter Twenty-Nine

Kerr dropped Jacobson outside the Bellevue on Riverside Walk and drove off in the direction of the North Crowby bypass and the Bovis estate. Jacobson's car was waiting for him in the car park. He took half a dozen steps towards it – enough time for Kerr's Peugeot to disappear around the corner – and brusquely redirected his feet.

He found Alison Taylor behind the reception desk in the Riverside Hotel. A middle-aged couple were complaining about their room and the receptionist was too busy checking in late arrivals for an anniversary party to deal with them. The husband was the pompous, overbearing variant on upper class that could make you wish the Russian Revolution had been a more successful export – and Britain's ancient families had been comprehensively shoved up against the nearest wall. They talked in her office once she'd sorted out the problem.

'I'd've been tempted to tell them exactly where to stick it,' Jacobson told her.

There was no police reason for his visit and she hadn't asked him for one.

'The very first rule, Inspector, is never take it personally.'

'Frank,' Jacobson heard himself saying, 'my name's Frank.'

'Well, never take it personally, *Frank*, then.'

From somewhere inside her desk, she produced a full bottle of a Jura malt – one that Jacobson wasn't familiar with – along with two cut crystal glasses.

'A rep's sample,' she said, pouring out two measures, one more generous than the other. She handed the fuller glass to Jacobson.

'That's not bad,' he said after the first peaty mouthful. 'But don't they ever let you go home from this place?'

'Hotels don't run from nine to five unfortunately, Frank. But I'm off Sundays and Mondays at the moment.'

She wasn't married, she smiled at him when she talked, she smoked, she even drank whisky.

'I was wondering—' he started to say.

'Tomorrow night, if you like. Around eight o'clock? You bring the wine and I'll cook. It's how it's usually done, isn't it?'

He tried to keep the spring out of his step as he walked back to his car. He knew he should've explained that he might not be able to make it, that his hours weren't predictable when he was working on a serious case. But he hadn't wanted to chance it, hadn't wanted to risk screwing up before there was even something *to* screw up. Just about the only thing he found believable if he ever watched a police show on TV was that the cops' personal lives were always a disaster. Things never worked out. Things never ended happily. He drove back to the Divi, sifted through the Darren McGee paperwork and picked out certain files he wanted to look at more closely. It was still only eight thirty by the time he'd got to Wellington Drive. Tomorrow night might conceivably turn out to be different – but tonight would follow his usual, solitary routine. He stopped at the Yellow River, the Chinese takeaway on the corner, and ordered his default selection – beef kung po and fried rice. He'd eat, take a shower and then get to work. And if that failed, he thought, there was always Schopenhauer.

Vicky poured a supersize-me ration of her mum's Remy

Martin into a mug and retreated to her bedroom. Sharon and Stan were going out again – some kind of special karaoke night – and she'd have the house to herself later, although she doubted if she'd stir very much from her own room. There was stuff she needed to think about, even reach decisions about. But not yet. Not straightaway. She switched on her laptop and the little red study lamp that had survived back here since she'd been a teenager. She sat down, took a swig. She wasn't especially keen on brandy but it was the conventional prescription for shock and so far it seemed to be doing the trick.

She brought up her American History resources and the folder she was using for her sixth-form class. She wanted to put something together on the origins of lynching to tie in with the Liverpool case study. At least get it into a few heads who Colonel Charles *Lynch* was. It was a straightforward task. All it took was ten minutes' judicious cutting and pasting and she'd produced a reasonable-enough handout. She swigged the brandy again. There were other teaching-related odds and ends she could be getting on with, other useful distractions. It was how she'd been spending a lot of her evenings, taking her work home, taking pains over it. But maybe tonight, she realised, her displacement methods were finally running out of steam.

She'd been thinking about Barbara during the day too, ever since she'd heard Moby on the radio. Barbara was back in the States now, working on her doctorate. Vicky thought about giving her a call. It would be sometime in the afternoon in New York – she could never get her mind around the time difference – but Barbara would either be at home or she wouldn't be, would either answer or she wouldn't. No, she decided after a moment, not now. Not when I don't even know what to think anymore, what to believe. They'd only kept in touch sporadically anyway, exchanged Christmas cards and the occasional email. A few days before Darren's funeral, Barbara had phoned her and said she was going to fly over – *to be there for you, Vix.*

But in the end she hadn't showed. And Vicky had endured it on her own. Darren's mother had barely tolerated her presence, even though she'd only attended the burial, had avoided the Baptist service which had preceded it. His uncle and aunt had been OK though, had spared her a few kind words. It had occurred to her later that Barbara might feel guilty even though, if she did, she was being as irrational as Vicky was in blaming her.

She gave up on the laptop, put on some music. Dido again. The blander – the more mundane – the better. She made two licorice-paper roll-ups so that she could smoke one straight after the other if she felt like it. Yet Barbara couldn't have foreseen the consequences any more than anyone else. How could she? Barbara, like many visitors before her, had developed a fascination with the history of London in its most famous recent decade, the 1960s. Although maybe she'd become more fascinated than most. Maybe Barbara's interest had become just the slightest little bit fanatical. She'd certainly progressed well beyond the standard tourist itinerary: Abbey Road, Heddon Street (where the cover of *Ziggy Stardust* had been shot – though not until 1972, as Barbara liked to point out pedantically), the Marquee's old site in Wardour Street – and all that. Instead, Barbara had got into near-enough serious research, had even started to refer to herself as a chronicler. *Somebody needs to get stuff down, Vix*, she'd say, *before it's lost*. She'd disappear for whole days, persuading the bemused owners of sushi bars and tanning salons to allow her into their backrooms and cellars, seeking out the legacy of long-forgotten clubs and 'scenes'. She'd be note-taking, videoing, interviewing. *I found where the Middle Earth club really started out, before they moved over to Covent Garden* – the kind of thing she'd say to Vicky and Darren when she'd eventually return to the flat. For a while, she was letting a malodorous fifty-something dosser kip in the spare room because he'd lyingly claimed to have been the 'head' who'd introduced Mark Bolan to Mickey Finn in a pub near the Roundhouse. The same pub – another false claim – where he'd said the Pink Fairies had played their first gig.

She'd got into acid then too – in the same kind of weird, retro-obsessed way. She started reading Aldous Huxley, the Shulgins, Timothy Leary. People didn't take drugs seriously anymore, she complained. They *did* them in a major way – but it was just for a laugh, just as an adjunct to sex or a night out. Psychedelics were sacraments, portals to other levels of consciousness, other states of being. That was what had been understood back then, that was the knowledge that had been lost, trampled on. Vicky hadn't bothered to argue – it rarely seemed worth arguing when Barbara took up an enthusiasm. Especially as she couldn't really care less either way. She was happy enough to try something new from curiosity, once, maybe twice, then leave it at that. It was Darren who hadn't been cool with it. He'd seen too many basket cases on the streets for that, he told them. A spliff was one thing, but head-tripping wasn't for him. He liked calmness, the place in his mind he could go to when he juggled, he didn't need to see the face of God right now, if it was all the same to them. *God give you your brain the way it is, Barbara, why'd you want to fuck with it?*

Barbara had fucked with it. She'd found a second-hand copy of Leary's *The Psychedelic Experience* in Camden Market and proceeded to re-decorate the front room into an approximation of a Notting Hill squat, circa 1967. She'd even recruited a handful of other students who'd more or less become her followers for a time. They'd light candles, shove on some dross New Age music and Barbara would guide them through their all-night trips. Vicky and Darren had stayed well out of it, under the duvet in their bedroom. Or had tried to anyway.

One Sunday morning, nine months after Darren had moved in, Barbara had presented them with breakfast in bed. A peace offering, she'd said. They'd rowed about the dosser a few days before – after Darren had effectively kicked him out behind Barbara's back, had told him to get lost if he knew what was good for him. You could hide a couple of microdots in anything really. Especially if you'd sprinkled cracked wheat and various assorted health shop seeds on to bowls of muesli. The first thing Vicky had known about it was when she was getting up, getting dressed. Suddenly, the walls and furniture were miles away, racing across a desert of red, swirling sand. Darren hadn't actually seemed to mind all that much at first. He'd put on the telly, wanted to see what it looked like under the influence. They'd spent the day lost in their inner landscapes, lying on the bed, holding hands, Vicky smiling idiotically. She'd let herself go into it – there was nothing else she could do in any case. Time fell away and returned. Then fell away again. It was dark when she started to come down. She'd got finished dressing at last, went in search of a glass of water. Barbara wasn't at home, had maybe regretted the daft prank, made herself scarce.

Darren looked at her unblinking when she came back into the room.

'I gotta get outside,' he said.

He pulled on his jeans, his boots, grabbed his jacket, knocking Vicky and Vicky's glass of water flying as he rushed out the door and bolted along the hall. When Barbara did finally show her face, she helped Vicky to look for him. They scoured the streets and tried the pubs he was known to favour. The Alma, the Nag's Head, half a dozen others. Eventually, close on midnight, when they were giving up for now and walking back home, they found him pacing up and down on Islington Green, shadowed by the trees.

'I gotta get outside,' he told them.

Vicky let Barbara try to work on him, try and draw out of him whatever reality he thought he was experiencing.

'He's inside and he wants to be outside,' Barbara said portentously.

Vicky slapped her. The comment had made her want to laugh – but she knew that there was nothing remotely funny going on.

She sat with Darren around the clock for two days after the

bad trip, never left him on his own. Barbara pretty much did the same, trying to make up for her stupid joke. Everybody knew that acid was a bad idea for some people, could unmask – unleash – latent psychoses. She'd just never seen Darren as vulnerable in that way. But even then, neither of them were really worried. The effects wore off, everybody told them, faded, didn't last. The thing about acid, Barbara kept saying, was that it amplified your relationship to your environment. It could literally make you feel at one with the universe. But it could also make you feel totally alone and isolated: the only human cog in a vast, terrifying, impersonal machine. Other people ceased to be real or you saw them as soulless, lifeless manikins. Gradually, Darren came out of the worst of it. Yet he wasn't exactly how he'd been before. He spent hours in the flat, not wanting to go out, never even looking at his clubs. Barbara tried to get him to talk to a therapist she'd found, somebody who was supposed to be good, but Darren refused point blank. He moved into the spare room, stopped sleeping with Vicky. He became obsessive about doors and locks and the idea of confinement. She'd hear him in the middle of the night, wandering around the flat, opening windows, checking and rechecking that the front door hadn't been boarded-up while he'd been trying to sleep.

Barbara abandoned her interests in the '60s and in inner voyaging as abruptly as she'd taken them up. Their Finals weren't far off and both of them – Barbara and Vicky – were spending more and more of their time in the Senate House library, burrowing into their textbooks. Vicky didn't know what else to do really. Her hope was that she'd just wake up one morning and everything would be all right again. But on the night they'd called the police and the ambulance, on the night she'd betrayed him – and that was still, irrationally, how she saw it – they'd come back to St Peter's Street and found Darren in the bathroom with a kitchen knife, hacking at his wrists. There was a slur in his voice but they understood what he was saying all the same. *I gotta get outside, girl, I gotta get outside.*

Chapter Thirty

When she'd finished the brandy, Vicky raided the kitchen again. She couldn't face any more spirits but she had some bottles of her own around somewhere. Wine mainly. She picked out an Australian Shiraz. One of the other teachers had thrown a house-warming party, everyone invited. She'd bought it intending to go along but then hadn't, had changed her mind at the last minute. She found a cork screw, still didn't bother with a glass. She put Dido on repeat when she went back upstairs: she knew what too much alcohol could do to her, didn't want to find herself sentimentally digging something else out, something nostalgic with a capital N.

Darren had been hospitalised for a month while the psychiatrists argued about his diagnosis. He'd made a second wrist-slashing attempt during the first week. But after that he'd seemed to get used to the regime. He'd self-harmed before, it transpired – in his early teens, when he'd still been living at home with his mother, Tilda. And there had been a possible arson incident then as well, although he'd never been charged. Darren seemed a lot better when he came out – at first. He was taking Clozapine, one of the newer type of antipsychotic drugs ('atypicals' was the medical classification, Vicky learned, swiftly reading everything she could find on mental illness) – but probably only because Barbara had paid up for private consultations and private prescriptions. The standard NHS treatment tended to depend on older drugs – largactil, for instance – for the non-Hippocratic reason that they were a lot cheaper to prescribe. Atypicals on the other hand had far fewer side effects. The worst one with Clozapine was the possibility of weight gain. But tall, gangly Darren had escaped that too. Barbara and Vicky had finished their exams by the time he was back with them. A 2:1 each. Good enough for postgrad research in Barbara's case – where money wasn't an issue – but disappointing for Vicky. She'd be able to register for a master's or a doctorate but, without a First, she just wasn't in the running for any kind of supporting grant or scholarship.

Barbara planned on returning to America at the end of the summer and she wanted to see more of the UK outside London. She hired a car and the three of them toured the country on the tourist trail. Eventually, they headed down to Pilton for that year's Glastonbury Festival and carried on from there to Cornwall, which chimed with Barbara's latest fads: stone circles and the legends of King Arthur. The problem was what Darren and Vicky would do when Barbara went back home. They could stay in the flat short term, Barbara said, but her father would be putting it up for sale as soon as Barbara moved out. And Darren was still hearing stuff, still having difficulty motivating himself through an ordinary day, even though he understood what was happening to him – and understood that his voices weren't 'real'. Then one afternoon in August Vicky found the solution pinned to a noticeboard in the Students' Union: Barcelona. An English language school over there was offering an intensive training course followed by guaranteed temporary work.

Vicky persuaded herself it was the answer to everything. Academic research might've been one thing but she certainly wasn't ready for a serious nine-to-five career yet, wasn't sure she'd ever be ready, and Darren needed to get away. He'd spent his whole life in London. First with his weird, control-freak mother and then out on its unfriendly streets. A new environment - one with no negative associations - could only be a good thing, couldn't it? And for a while it was good, was almost a new beginning. Darren's mood had visibly brightened the first time they'd wandered down the Ramblas in the sunshine amongst the flower stalls, bird sellers and café terraces. They'd found a room in a pensión near the Plaça Reial with a rent that they could just about afford. And they'd fucked the first night they'd slept there. On the old, solid bed. The first time in a long time.

Clozapine could also have a sedative effect and the recommendation was that you took your daily fix last thing at night. But Vicky and Darren established their own routine that suited them better. Darren would dose himself in the mornings and spend much of the day asleep while Vicky did her language training and, later on, the work assignments that the language school found for her. They'd both rest up in the early part of the evening and then - towards dusk - they'd go out into the city's teeming street life. Darren liked the spaciousness of the Plaça Reial, liked to watch the moon rising over its palm trees and its famously ornate lamp posts. Occasionally he felt up to fire juggling again and, when he did, he usually attracted a decent crowd. They were making a circle of acquaintances too. A mix of other street entertainers and the friends Vicky made via the language school. If they were feeling energetic enough, they'd get away from the world's tourists in the Old Town and head over to the Barrio de Gràcia where the customers in the bars spoke Catalan first, Castilian second - and English only if they had to. Autumn turned into winter and winter turned into spring. Vicky started to believe that her life was taking shape at last. London had buried Crowby and now Barcelona was burying London. When she'd finally put Darren back together again, they'd both of them be free of the past. And free for whatever future they chose.

Jude became Vicky's closest Barça friend. A tall Australian girl with a wicked laugh. On a Friday night in May, a big group met up to mourn and celebrate the fact that Jude was leaving that weekend - moving on to Budapest, the next staging post in her year-out travels. It was a special event and Darren made a special effort, donning an elegant Pedro Morago suit he'd bought cheap from a hard-up thief in the Barri Xines. The main item on the agenda was a slap-up meal in the Restaurant Egipte, near the Boqueria, where Vicky loved the *arroz negro* with squid. Jordi was there of course. Jude's boyfriend with his dream-black eyes and even blacker hair. There was an attraction there every time they met that Vicky had no intention of doing anything about. And Jordi never had either - before tonight. Some men were like that, she supposed, couldn't stand to be without something good to look at on their arm for more than thirty seconds maximum. Goodbye Jude, hello Vicky - basically.

Darren hadn't seemed to notice at first. That was one of the problems for him the way he was now. He could miss the subtleties and nuances of conversations and body language entirely. Or else he'd read them the wrong way. There was a plan to go on to a night club later but immediately after the meal, they'd piled across the Ramblas to the Café de L'Opéra. It was the first bar Jude had ever visited in the city, she was telling everyone, so she wanted to include it on her last night also. Not that Jordi had been especially subtle. Somehow he'd contrived to sit at their table, wedged himself next to Vicky. He'd made his play while Jude had been distracted - having her photo taken with a couple of the Opéra's habitués - and while Darren was visiting the gents. Vicky told Jordi to fuck off in three languages but he was still leering at her, still had his hand hovering over hers when Darren was suddenly back beside them.

Vicky uncorked the Shiraz, filled the mug up to the brim. She still thought that the explosion of anger wasn't just about Jordi. That Darren's mother, Darren's schooling, everything bad that had ever happened to him, had melded together in his mind in that one moment. He swooped Jordi out of his seat before Jordi had even glimpsed what was coming, dragging him by the lapels and propelling him head first through the door into the street. There were spilled drinks, overturned tables and broken glass everywhere. And then there was the solid thud of Darren's toecap against Jordi's skull as Jordi hit the pavement. Darren kicked him half a dozen more times before Vicky, with the strength that sometimes finds the desperate, shoved him away through the slowly-gathering crowd. And then they were both running, disappearing down into the Liceu metro station and boarding the first train that presented itself. Vicky always carried both their passports with her in her bag because Darren obsessed about losing his, about not being able to prove who he was. They got out on the Avenguda Diagonal and Vicky found a taxi. She tidied Darren up on the way, even wiping the flecks of blood from his right shoe. There was no time or prospect to go back to the pensión. Vicky saw one chance of keeping Darren with her, out of jail or hospital, and took it. The fact that Darren looked distressed wasn't a disadvantage for once. He'd had bad news from London, she told the clerk on the British Airways desk, his father was dangerously ill, they needed to take the very first flight out that they could get. Vicky sank a couple of vodkas after take-off to get her nerves under control. She was picturing the scene at the Opéra. The ambulance arriving, the police taking statements, the filing of names and addresses. Her mind raced from one extreme to the other. Everything was computerised now, just a matter of checking flights and ticket sales and passenger lists. The police would be waiting for them when they landed, wouldn't they? Come off it, girl, she'd tell herself in the next second. It was only a pub brawl, one of hundreds surely on the busiest night of the week. It would be Saturday or Sunday, or even Monday, before a couple of bored policías would call at the pensión, ask in a bored way if the young English couple were still in residence.

It was gone one in the morning when the plane had slouched into Heathrow and of course there'd been no police. The customs hall was empty and there was only a single, tired-looking woman behind the EC entry desk. She'd barely glanced at them or their passports. Vicky paid the rip-off taxi fare back into London and they'd checked into a cheap hotel in Paddington where they knew Darren because he'd shifted in the kitchen a few times when he'd been on the streets. Vicky had locked the rickety door and they'd both fallen into a long, exhausted sleep.

Kerr knew he wouldn't go straight home after he dropped Jacobson off, had known it all day. Cathy would be waiting and probably so would the twins, kept up beyond their bedtime so that they could see him. Yet sometimes not even his son and his daughter weighed as much in his mind as convention said that they should. He slowed down when he approached the turn-off for the Bovis estate, as if he might change his mind at the last minute, but he kept straight on, picked his speed back up. He'd phoned Rachel twice already – her home number and her mobile – but she hadn't answered, hadn't returned his messages. He drove on along the Wynarth Road, too focused on the issue even to bother shoving music on to the in-car.

The hub of Wynarth was the market square with the war memorial in its centre. The square functioned as a car park in the evenings and on non-market days. Driving around it, he noticed the Viceroy's home delivery van parked in one of the spaces that faced directly on to the restaurant. He considered calling in, having another word with Randeep Parmeer. He could make his visit legitimate that way, even abandon it, turn the car back towards Crowby after he'd spoken to him. Instead he turned the corner into Thomas Holt Street. Rachel's flat was above an antique shop near the Looking East Gallery. Kerr drove along the street and then turned at the end, cruised back. He pulled in between a gleaming Mini and a mud-splattered Kawasaki motorcycle. He was on the other side of the street and maybe thirty yards away from Rachel's. Close enough to see her door and her window. Too far away to be noticed at a casual glance. He tried both her numbers again but this time he didn't leave any messages when she didn't answer. He still had the key she'd given him to her flat. A symbol of trust, a symbol that they were supposed to be serious about each other. He'd never used it without her knowledge before, had never even considered the possibility until right now. He saw that the light was on up in her front room. But although the curtains hadn't been closed yet, there wasn't much that he could see of the interior from down here in the street. He tried to put the idea out of his head. Walking in on her uninvited - whatever was she was doing - would finish it for good. He sat where he was, drumming his fingers on the steering wheel.

The light went out. Three minutes later - Kerr counted each of them on his dashboard clock - her door opened. Rachel came out into the street followed by Tony Scruton. Scruton said something to her that made her smile, that made her run her hand lightly down his arm and kiss him on the mouth. Kerr watched them walk off in the direction of the market square, watched Scruton slide his arm around her shoulders, pulling her tightly towards him. He got out of his car, banged the door shut. Rachel heard the noise and looked round, just stopped and gaped at him.

'It's not what you think,' she said when he caught up with them.

'Isn't it?'

Scruton still had his arm defiantly around her.

'What're you going to do, fit me up?'

Scruton's voice always sounded deeper than Kerr expected. As if a choirboy had been force fed forty high-tar king-size a day. Kerr pushed him away from Rachel, lifting him off his feet and pinning him against the plate glass of the Looking East's front window. Behind Scruton's head there was a poster announcing the gallery's next exhibition: *Images of Varanasi*. Kerr kept him dangling there for a few seconds and then let him drop to the ground.

There was probably something smart or clever to say but, whatever it was, Kerr couldn't find the words. He dug deep into his inside pocket, found Rachel's key and pressed it into her hand. Neither of them spoke - and Kerr turned swiftly away, walked purposefully back to his car.

Chapter Thirty-One

Sunday April 24th

Jacobson listened to the Radio Four eight o'clock news while he yawned and brewed his coffee. Paul Shaw still wasn't a feature. He'd been dreaming when he woke up, something involving Billy Marsden's angry painting come to life. The four names were written on the canvas but every time Jacobson tried to read them, the figure from the painting plunged a knife through it, tearing it to shreds. He made himself something to eat after he'd drank his first cupful. Scrambled eggs on toast. The news bulletin had turned into the religious service and he'd switched his radio off, cooking and then eating in silence.

He'd trawled through the Darren McGee files he'd brought home late into the night. But the exercise hadn't thrown up anything fresh. Procedurally, all you could say was that Greg Salter had done a reasonable enough job. The problem was that he'd also committed the cardinal sin for a detective: he'd started from his conclusion and worked backwards, putting all his effort into proving that McGee had taken his own life. It hadn't helped either that his team had lacked suitable experience. Mick Hume and DC Barber had been back from holiday leave in time to work on the last couple of days of the investigation. But by then the suicide theory had become an unchallengeable orthodoxy –

and before then Salter had been co-opting officers with virtually no Murder Squad background. The brightest of the bunch had been Amanda Singh. But no matter how capable you were, you had to learn to walk before you could run.

Salter hadn't left himself much choice of course. DS Kerr had been in Florida and Ray Williams and Emma Smith had been on leave too, although presumably not together. Jacobson poured himself out his second cup of coffee, lit his wake-up B & H, and wandered through to his lounge. He drew back his curtains and let in more sunlight than he was entirely ready for. Amazingly, Salter had agreed to his own last-minute request for a couple of weeks away. Salter should have kicked off about it, should have insisted that the force's senior officer with special responsibility for homicide and serious crimes against the person stay put over Christmas and New Year – a favourite time, as every policeman knew, for night club fracas that got out of hand and for domestic arguments that got taken too far. But Smoothie Greg had just smiled, had signed Jacobson's leave form on the spot – with his personalised gold nib pen. Later, of course, Jacobson had realised that if he'd been looking forward to a fortnight without Salter, then Salter had been looking forward just as much to a fortnight without him.

Jacobson had spent ten days in Tunisia, a specialised tour visiting the Carthaginian and Roman remains. He was learning to make do with arrivistes like the Romans. The way the rulers of the world were fucking up their bright new century, he believed he'd never set foot on the truly ancient sites that he really wanted to see – Ur, Nineveh, Babylon. Or that, if and when he did, nothing worth seeing would have survived.

He tried Crowby FM, enduring a commercial break and a mindless phone-in competition to hear the eight-thirty local news headlines. Shaw's death was the fourth story even though the newsreader had nothing new to say: the inquest would convene on Monday, the police were still investigating the incident. He finished his coffee and his cigarette and then took a shave with the ageing electric razor he was thinking about replacing.

He stopped at the newsagents next door to the Yellow River on his way into town. He bought copies of all the Sunday papers, except for the *Sport*, made sure that he pocketed the till receipt. He dumped the pile down on his desk when he got to his office. He took the broadsheets first and then the tabloids, scanning the news pages and trying not to get sidetracked by wars, famines and the details of which celebrities were hot in bed and which weren't. It took him half an hour. And then he skimmed through again just to make sure. The *Observer* and the *Independent on Sunday* had run brief obituaries (*Paul Shaw was a talented investigative reporter who tirelessly pursued the theme of racism at home and abroad*, according to the former) but they hadn't carried Shaw's death as a news story - and neither had the other papers. Maybe Henry Pelling was losing his touch as a stringer, he thought. But at least it looked as if the national media weren't going to get in the way of his investigation after all. He stacked the newspapers next to his wastebasket - for which extra weight the cleaners would really love him - and took the back stairs down to the second floor: Steve Horton's office. Assuming Horton had showed up yet.

Vicky woke up with the hangover from hell. She'd polished off two bottles of wine in the end, had a vague memory of even mixing in more of the Remy Martin at a certain point. With an effort of will, she made it down to the kitchen, swallowed a couple of aspirins and drank a glass of water. At least her mum and Stan weren't up and about yet. She had another vague idea that she'd heard them when they'd come in. Stan murdering Elvis and Sharon whispering at him to keep quiet. She went upstairs again, crawled back into her bed. She'd wanted to think about the elements of the situation: what had happened in Crowby, what Paul Shaw had wanted to know, what his death signified. But her mind was stuck on involuntary repeat, kept replaying Darren – and Darren, in a sense, wasn't actually relevant. She buried her thumping head into her pillow. But realised she probably wouldn't get back to sleep, which was the only real hangover cure she knew.

Nothing had gone right when they'd got back to London. Nothing. Barbara was gone and so was the big Islington flat. A friend of a friend from UCL took pity on them – or on Vicky anyway – put them on to a place in Brixton where there was a room going. Money was tight to non-existent. Vicky took on two waitressing jobs just to meet the rent. Darren stayed in the room and rarely left it, spent most of his time just staring out into the street. He wrote down the details of Vicky's shifts in a notebook and watched anxiously every night for her to return, took to quizzing her loudly if she got back any time that he considered to be late. His fire clubs had been abandoned in Barcelona and he showed no inclination to replace them.

She phoned Jude's mobile from a call box on Acre Lane, ten days after they'd left Spain. It had been a narrow escape for Jordi, Jude told her. Darren had kicked him unconscious and there'd been a fear, which fortunately turned out to be unfounded, that he might have sustained brain damage. He'd been a prat, Jude said, yet he'd scarcely deserved what Darren had done to him. She didn't know how seriously the Spanish police were pursuing the case but Darren would be a real fool, obviously, if he went anywhere near a border control for a while.

The rest of the people in the Brixton house were the usual graduate mix, busy all day, trying to get their careers off the ground. Most of them were suspicious of Vicky's Weird Boyfriend, as they started to refer to him behind his back. Vicky just tried to keep going, tried to keep it together. It actually helped that she was working long hours, was always dog-tired when she got home, ready to fall fast asleep. On some level, she believed now, she must have understood that it couldn't last, that there would be a day when she'd have to give up, have to get away. But she still didn't know whether it was a strength or a weakness in her character that she'd struggled on for so long. At least Darren had kept his prescription up – although Vicky started to think that he was sporadically forgetting – or omitting – to dose himself.

She turned her head the other way, away from the sunshine streaming in despite the curtains. All she'd done 'wrong' the night it had finally finished was to stay later than usual in the restaurant where she was working. It was the chef's birthday and there'd been a cake and a few drinks. Darren had been waiting for her outside the tube station. She'd smiled at him at first, pleased to see him out and about. But once they were away from the main streets, he'd pulled her into the garden of an empty house, had told her she was evil – *the devil's slag, girl* – had forced her to the ground and taken the knife to her back. Even then she'd protected him. She'd refused to press charges, had settled for an injunction. There'd been no shortage of housemates willing to testify on her behalf that Darren had menaced her, threatened her. He'd disappeared by then anyway – back to living rough or even, conceivably, back to his mother's. Vicky had told herself she didn't care. A few weeks later she'd gone back to Crowby. She was sick of waitressing, sick of London. She'd needed to lie low, needed to let all her different kinds of scars heal. Only now, of all the bad, screwed-up decisions she'd made, coming back here seemed like the very worst, the very stupidest.

Rick Cole drove over to the Stuarts' place. The Stuarts ran a building firm and often put work Cole's way. So there was no difficulty, no suspicions, with the three of them keeping in regular contact. Old man Stuart had built the firm up and the Stuarts had knocked it back down again – although not so much that they weren't making a healthy enough living. Stuart senior and his wife had died in a road accident when John Stuart had been nineteen and his brother, Phil, seventeen. Cole had been at school with them

– they went as far back as that. Their house was on a self-build plot not far from the Bovis estate. It was big, spacious. But the Stuarts took little care of it. The lawn was overgrown and the gravel drive was an obstacle race of builder's supplies and equipment. John Stuart's wife had left him a year or so ago and Phil's girlfriends had been few and far between. Phil was the thinker really, the one who'd sold it all to John and Rick in the first place: graduating them from death metal and an interest in the occult – Atlantis, vampires, Charles Manson – towards darker fare – Himmler, the Spear of Destiny, the Thule Society – and ultimately, towards the orbit of the Party.

Cole slowed to steer past several pallets of masonry bricks. Wendy wasn't best pleased, had complained that she'd hardly seen him over the last few days, had wanted them to have a lie-in together. But he'd told her that it couldn't be helped, that he wouldn't be long. And besides Wendy was a mouse. Not to look at, certainly not in that way, but deep inside her head. She was compliant, submissive, liked to be kept in line. It was why he'd picked her out really. The kind of woman who didn't mind being at home, bringing up your kids, giving you the support you needed. There were some cars he didn't recognise next to the Stuarts' white Transit 280. Hardly unusual though – the Stuarts had a minor subsidiary trade in buying up vehicles, fixing them, and then selling them on. Cole parked on the end of the line. Phil Stuart opened the front door as Cole was walking towards it. He had two muzzled Alsatians at his feet.

'We're in the kitchen, Rick,' he said.

He shunted the dogs out into the garden and closed the door again after Cole had stepped in. Cole knew the way through. John Stuart's bulky arms were in the sink and the room still stank from the morning fry-up.

'You got back all right then?' Cole asked.

He'd left Matthew Sutherland's country gaff around ten o'clock the previous evening, when the boozing had still been in full swing.

'Yeah, we buggered off around midnight. We would've left earlier only we got talking to that Kesey bloke – he's all right for a poncehead intellectual, I reckon.'

'I hope you watched *what* you were saying, John.'

'Course we fucking did. We just hinted a bit that we'd seen proper action, that was all. No word from Parker then?'

'Not a whisper. You?'

Big John shook his head.

'I was giving it thought on the way over,' Cole said. 'He must've said something to one of us at sometime – something that might give us a clue where he's headed.'

Phil sat back down at the table, stirred sugar into his mug of tea.

'He didn't though, did he? He was in the army, he'd worked in London – that's as much as I know. That's as much as John knows.'

'The Party holds a profile on every member – every job you've had, every address you've stayed at, your next of kin,' Cole commented, suddenly thinking that the answer to the puzzle was probably contained in the Party's well-hidden, well-encrypted computer records. You handed over your life history when you joined, right down to details like your bank account and national insurance numbers. It was all about the Party checking you out, making sure you were who you said you were.

Phil allowed himself a tight little laugh.

'We can hardly ask the Party though, can we? Oh by the way, Matthew, we've done a couple of darkies and we need to find Wayne Parker before he shops us. Everybody knows that kind of stuff goes on – but you can't talk about it, can't make it official.'

Cole continued thinking out loud:

'We can't tell them the whole story obviously. But we could tell them something close enough. Suppose we tell Sutherland we think Parker's an infiltrator – one of those red twats from the SWP or whatever. You know how paranoid the leadership is in that direction. We could say we confronted him with it – and now he's done a runner.'

Phil sipped his tea, Big John stacked soapy plates on to the dish rack.

'That could work, Rick,' Phil said after a moment. 'The difficulty is they might want to deal with it higher up – or involve some other unit.'

Cole smiled now – Phil was hot on theory and history and ideas but he wasn't a tactician, wasn't practical.

'Exactly, Phil. Which means we win either way. Either Sutherland says it's your mess, you deal with it. Or – end of problem – he takes it out of our hands, passes it on elsewhere.'

Steve Horton's office door was open and Horton was already hunched over one of his several keyboards. For once in his life he looked less than pin-up perfect: bleary-eyed, unshaven, clothes that might conceivably have been slept in.

'A good night then, I take it, old son?'

'At the time yeah,' Horton replied, 'but my advice is don't mix vodka, whisky and lager. Or not in the same glass anyway.'

'I'll bear that in mind,' Jacobson said, grimacing at the concept.

DS Kerr appeared in the doorway and then managed to squeeze himself into the cramped room. Horton booted up his main machine and brought the Flowers Street traffic footage up on to the screen.

'Oh right. A fair bit of periodic noise,' he said, 'but not too much of a problem.'

'So you think you can do something with it, Steve?' Jacobson asked.

'A piece of the proverbial, Mr Jacobson. I wish I could get rid of my bad head as easy.'

As easily, Jacobson thought. But kept the correction to himself: in the immediate context, computer knowhow topped grammatical rectitude by a big margin.

Horton treated them to his usual arcane commentary. He enjoyed an audience – another reason why Jacobson thought his true, unfulfilled destiny lay in showbiz instead of technical support.

'We'll convert over to grayscale obviously. Then we can FFT it.'

Jacobson made the mistake of glancing at Kerr.

'Fast Fourier Transforms,' Kerr said, as if he knew what he was talking about – although Jacobson suspected that Kerr was two per cent computer knowledge, ninety-eight per cent computer bullshit.

'Basically, I'm stripping the crap out, Mr Jacobson,' Horton explained, 'getting down to the undistorted information – if it's in there.'

Jacobson looked at the screen. You could see the rear end of the van more clearly in grey than in colour. But you still couldn't read the number plate.

'Okey dokey,' Horton said, 'we'll try and flatten the background next. And then we can zoom in on the specific area, try some more filters, maybe make some gamma adjustments.'

Jacobson glanced at Kerr again. But evidently Kerr hadn't got as far as 'gamma' in his bluffer's guide yet.

Jacobson phoned the control room while Horton worked on. There were two items of news. The uniformeds had drawn a blank in finding any witnesses to the burnout on the Woodlands but the North Wales police had located Wayne Parker's Fiesta at the Hollyhead ferry port. Parker had bought a ferry ticket although there were discrepancies in the records – it might be that he hadn't actually boarded the crossing. Somebody from Bangor CID was looking in to it.

The screen cleared, filled, cleared.

'That should do it,' Horton said, stretching his arms and trying not to yawn.

The screen filled again – revealing a full registration plate: every single letter, every single number.

Chapter Thirty-Two

The DVLC computer link coughed up the registered owner without too much of a struggle. They threw the name details – Phillip Alan Stuart – against the PNC and all of the local databases, Amanda Singh's included. Nothing came up. Total, absolute zero. Jacobson considered the options while Kerr watched Steve Horton continue to play with his toys. There were other vehicles recorded in the footage. Maybe one of them had a driver or a passenger who'd seen something. If Horton tracked the number plates and the owners now, it could save time later. Jacobson paced out of Horton's office and along the empty corridor. The narrow window at the end gave an uninspiring view across to the NCP car park, foregrounded by the Divisional building's fire escape.

In a more straightforward case – if Paul Shaw had been beaten to an obvious pulp, say, before he'd been chucked in the river – it would have been a good result. Jacobson would've disturbed Greg Salter's Sunday morning, always fun in itself, and requested authorisation for a full forensic examination of the van, even for a warranted search inside the owner's house. None of that was about to happen. A savvy journalist had met the same death as his demented cousin. His hotel room had been ransacked while the hotel cameras were conveniently switched off. The night porter who'd been on duty had vanished. Yet they needed something more, something that resembled hard *proof* – not just possible coincidence piled on possible coincidence. His best hope was that the forensics would do it when they came in. The problem was that Jacobson still couldn't say with any certainty that he was investigating a murder, let alone two related murders. And, strictly, all the law allowed him to do right now was to politely ask the owner where his van had been in the early hours of Friday morning. But at least, he thought, he could be sneaky about it. He took out his mobile, got DC Barber out of bed and Mick Hume out from under a leaking radiator in his spare room. The rendezvous point would be the Texaco garage at the start of the Wynarth Road – ASAP.

Jacobson smoked his second B & H of the day en route. Kerr wound down the driver's window but didn't comment otherwise. He was glad of action, glad of a reason not to be off duty, stewing in his juice. Cathy had persuaded him over to the Lonely Ploughboy when he'd got home. He hadn't argued, had just made sure that he drank more, and more quickly, than he usually did. Cathy seemed to know half the couples on the estate – or the wives anyway – since the twins had been born. And any time they went into the pub, they seemed to get further embroiled in the local networks of conversation and acquaintance. Kerr had listened and nodded on autopilot, even cracked a few jokes. Nobody could see behind your eyes and into your heart unless you let them. They'd had sex when they went home – full of Kerr's anger at Rachel that Cathy had mistaken as passion for her.

The Texaco forecourt was a hive of suburban activity when they got there. Queues for the petrol pumps and the car wash. Diligent drivers checking their tyre pressures. Kerr bought a tea for himself and a coffee for Jacobson from the garage shop after he'd parked near the air and water bays. By the time he got back to the car, Jacobson had mercifully finished his death-stick. Hume and Barber drove in ten minutes later, each in a separate car – just in case. Kerr talked them through the set-up. He knew the location of the house – barely a mile and a half from his own – and the local geography. There was a lay-by, he told them, which was probably close enough to function as an observation post. It would probably be busy as well – anglers used it to access a footpath which led down to a popular stretch of the Crow and Northern Canal. So they should be fairly invisible. Mick Hume nipped into the shop and came back with a packet of Maltesers and two pork pies in case it turned into a long haul.

The lay-by was crowded but Hume and Barber managed to find places, although Barber's back wheels ended up on the grass verge. Kerr watched them in his mirror then drove on to the address. Someone had started to build a gateway but hadn't finished it yet. The gates themselves were lying neglected on the ground behind the half-built wall. Two muzzled Alsatians had noticed them, started running wildly alongside. Kerr drove as far up the drive-way as he could, sounding his horn. The white van stood in the middle of half a dozen other vehicles. A haphazard line. Some of them had been jacked up and there were tools and engine parts strewn around the area. But their eyes would've been drawn straight towards the van even if they hadn't been looking for it. In contrast to the others, it was dazzlingly, brilliantly clean.

The porch door opened and a bulky figure peered out, called the dogs towards him. Jacobson and Kerr waited until he had them securely leashed before they stepped out.

'Phillip Stuart?' Jacobson asked.

'Who wants to know?' Big John retorted.

The Jehovah's Witnesses, Jacobson thought: have *you* given praise to the Lord on the Lord's Special Day? He fished his ID out his pocket, didn't actually say anything. Kerr did the same.

'Phil's my brother,' Big John said, didn't volunteer his own name.

They heard a voice from further inside.

'Who is it, John?'

John didn't bother to answer. When Phil joined him on the doorstep, Jacobson and Kerr showed their IDs again. Jacobson established that Phil was Phil, that the Ford Transit was his as far as the DVLC was concerned.

'We need a word, Mr Stuart,' Jacobson added.

It was the point where ninety per cent of the public, and even a high percentage of career criminals, invited you inside. But the Stuarts and their dogs didn't budge.

'We'd prefer to talk indoors,' Kerr said.

'You'd need a warrant for that,' Phil Stuart said, 'this is private property.'

'I *know* the law, old son,' Jacobson commented, 'but most people—'

'We're not most people. I'd prefer to talk here if it's all the same to you.'

Jacobson kept the irritation out of his voice.

'Have it your way. Where were you on Thursday night?'

'Why should I tell you? Why do you need to know?'

'Because that's the law too. I'm conducting a serious inquiry. I'm not obliged to tell you what into – but you're obliged not to *obstruct* it.'

'So arrest me,' Phil Stuart said, taking one of the dog leads from his brother so that now they had control of one dog each.

'I'm highly tempted to. But I'm asking you again first.'

Big John answered for his younger brother. A habit that might've started in the playground.

'He was here all night. We both were. We never went out, we watched TV, we went to bed early.'

'And there's only the two of you living here?'

'Since my slag of a wife fucked off, yeah.'

Jacobson told them he'd seen video footage that proved the Transit had been in the town centre around one in the morning.

Phil needed both hands to keep the dog by his side.

'That's not possible. The van was here. Must be one of

those computer errors you hear about.'

'Or somebody nicked it and brought it back,' Kerr suggested sarcastically, 'gave it a good clean while they were at it.'

'I was here and so was the van. That's all I've got to say.'

'And you've nothing else to add. No other explanation?'

Phil Stuart said that he hadn't, that he'd like to get on with his Sunday if that was all right.

'Be my guest,' Jacobson replied, 'enjoy it while you can.'

'What's that supposed to mean?' Big John asked.

'Whatever you think it means,' Jacobson said, almost enjoying himself.

Phil tried to nudge his brother, nearly dropping the dog lead in the process.

'Leave it, John,' he said.

Kerr and Jacobson climbed back into Kerr's car. He started the engine and did a careful U-turn, drove slowly back towards the half-constructed gateway.

'Well, at least we know that one of them was up to something the other night, Frank. Maybe both of them.'

'You're not wrong, old son. But the question is *what*. Statistically it's a lot more likely that they were nicking lead from church roofs than tipping investigative reporters off bridges.'

Wayne Parker tried not to listen to Drury and Teresa having noisy sex in Drury's bedroom, the big one that faced on to the street. He took a shower and then got dressed, wandered down to Drury's designer kitchen. He clicked on the kettle and looked for the tea bags, assuming that they weren't too downmarket an item to be in stock. Drury had been late coming back but he'd told him it had been sorted. It would be done by tomorrow night – Monday – and Parker could be on his way. All that was wanted was his mug shot plus the fee. Teresa had a digital camera, he said.

They'd use that in the morning, email the pics to the bloke who'd be needing them. *The wonders of modern technology, Wayne*, Drury had said. They'd gone to bed after that – cue noisy shagging – and Drury had sat up on his own, watching *Kill Bill* on one of the movie channels. Tarantino was fucking losing it, he'd thought. He'd started out as the outsider. But now that he'd made it big he was just another Hollywood liberal, bleating on about being anti-war and all that poncy shit.

The tea bags were in an old-fashioned red Oxo tin that Parker thought looked out of place but that maybe Drury thought added character. Or maybe Teresa did. Drury'd only known her a couple of months apparently – but she clearly had her feet well under the table. He found a mug and waited for the kettle to boil. For about the tenth time, he considered phoning Cole or the Stuarts to find out what was what. Like the other times, he decided against it. Telephone lines could be tapped, calls could be traced – and there was no telling how far the police investigation had got by now. Cole was living in a fool's paradise and had convinced the Stuarts to join him. The Darren McGee project had been one thing. Properly planned. Cleanly executed. But they'd done Paul Shaw in a hurry, had probably fucked up in ways they hadn't even realised. Cole thought all they had to do was sit tight, that even if the police got so far as suspecting them, they wouldn't be able to prove anything – or not enough. *That's the thing about water, Wayne, washes your sins away*. It was all very well for Cole of course. He wasn't the one in the firing line, the one who'd tampered with the hotel cameras, the one the police would definitely want to speak to unless they were total thickoes. Which was the other aspect – the final straw that had decided him in favour of legging it. He'd heard it on Crowby FM, Friday lunchtime. They had DCI Jacobson on the case. The exact opposite of a thicko, according to the local criminals Parker was on semi-familiar terms with from the Bricklayers Arms.

*

Cole had his work cut out to rally the troops after the police left. *They're on to us, Rick*, Big John kept saying. Phil didn't say much at all, just kept going upstairs, checking surreptitiously through the front bedroom window to see what he could see. They'd been arguing again even before the knock on the door: whether it would be smart or idiotic to involve the Party in any hunt for Parker, going over the whole thing once more – when Cole had thought that they'd already reached a decision.

'Look it's bad news, guys – I admit it. That DCI is definitely the one who's investigating the drowning. His name was in yesterday's paper – and the day before. But it doesn't mean he actually *knows* anything. They're obviously not sure yet that Shaw was topped deliberately. If they were sure, they'd be all over the van – and they never even went near it.'

'Yeah but what's going to happen if they do, Rick?' Big John asked.

They were in the lounge now. Big John and Cole plonked in armchairs, staring at each across a dusty, rarely used gaming table.

'They'll find nowt, that's what. You've cleaned that van inside and out three times now – or is it four?'

'Four. But don't you ever watch the telly? They've got all kinds of techniques these days – plus they might just decide to fit us up anyway.'

Phil walked in before Cole could reply, back from one of his upstairs sorties.

'There's no cars hanging about in the immediate vicinity as far as I can see. Although there's a fair few down at the lay-by.'

Cole shook his head.

'There always are on a Sunday, you know that, Phil – anglers and dog walkers. Honestly, unless they get to Parker, they've got nothing on us. Absolutely bog all.'

'And you definitely got rid of all our clothes from the other night?' Phil asked, sinking on to the sofa.

Cole treated them both to a smile. They were true warriors just like him. They always had been. But every now and again they needed encouragement - and he never did. It was the reason he'd always been their leader - even though Phil probably knew more stuff and John was twice as strong as him physically.

'They're all gone, mate, I promise you. I burned them with the garden refuse, Friday night. Then I bagged the ashes, chucked the bag out on the way over to Matthew Sutherland's yesterday. I took a detour into Solihull, found a half-empty skip in a street full of Pakis. It's what you call ironic, that is.'

He left soon after, drove back to Bovis-land, where you were supposed to live snug and tucked up, not ask too many questions, just work, consume, work, consume - for the greater good of the bankers and the secret world government. He put his tape of the real leader on to cheer himself up: the World Is On Fire speech. A rare, clandestine recording of something that didn't exist, never happened - as far as the brain-dead herd would ever be concerned. The top man had taken the kid gloves off for once, hadn't buried their mission in the subtext and the small print. Cole knew it virtually by heart. *The world is on fire. And we are the firemen. The Muslims lit the flames. The Jews lit the flames. The mud people from Africa lit the flames.* He slowed down at the entrance to the estate, signalling right, waiting for a gap in the traffic. *We will put those flames out. We will extinguish them. We must steel ourselves to step over dead bodies to create new life.*

Chapter Thirty-Three

Kerr steered the car though the entrance lane of the vehicle workshop, a couple of streets away from the Divisional building, and pulled up next to Jim Webster's immaculate Volvo estate. Webster had just ferried the FSS auto-firewreck examiner, who - weirdly - didn't drive, over from the railway station. Jacobson checked with the control room - no more news from North Wales - and clambered out of the passenger seat. The Sunday overtime bill was clocking up nicely, he thought. Hume and Barber on surveillance. Williams and Smith ploughing through the requisitioned telephone records, which were supposedly now available. Steve Horton still fast-fingering his keyboards. And that was before you added on Jacobson's and Kerr's own personal tallies plus, it now seemed, the Chief SOCO's. Greg Salter would be throwing a budget-driven, managerialist wobbly if it wasn't for the fact that he had something far worse to be worrying about: the growing possibility that he'd mistaken a racially motivated murder for suicide.

Forensic specialists came in all shapes and sizes. This one seemed human enough. He was thin and dapper in a tweedy, old-world kind of way. He got suited up and Webster walked over with him to the screened-off area where the burnout had been towed from the Woodlands. Kerr checked his mobile for messages (there were none) and Jacobson, in lieu of any wet paint to study, watched a fitter removing and replacing the exhaust pipe on an elderly patrol car.

Webster rejoined them five minutes later. He told them it was definitely the right model - from the GS300 series, which hadn't been confirmed before then - and the examiner was hopeful that he'd find something, maybe even a partial serial number, which would enable them to find out for certain if the trashed vehicle actually was Paul Shaw's. There also seemed to be traces of what Webster referred to as extraneous materials. Jacobson asked him for a translation into English.

'Electronic parts of some kind in this case, Frank - that would be my guess anyway. But you know what FSS are like, he won't commit to an interpretation until he's sure.'

Jacobson nodded, didn't say anything about pots calling kettles.

'I'll keep you posted,' Webster promised.

They drove back to the Divi, took the lift up to the CID Resource Centre. Williams and Smith were amongst the few DCs at home. Williams told them that they had finally accessed the information - but literally only in the last two minutes. Jacobson thought that maybe there was less of an atmosphere between them than there'd been yesterday. He hoped so anyway. They had three sets of records to play with: Paul Shaw's mobile plus Wayne Parker's home number and mobile. The last ten days in the case of Shaw, the last month in the case of Parker. Williams would work steadily through the data, essentially similar to the information on a domestic phone bill, trying to identify the other party on each call. Emma Smith would try a different tack, looking for any matching numbers between Shaw's records and Parker's. Jacobson had considered requisitioning the records for the Riverside Hotel reception desk during the hours of Parker's recent shifts. But he'd rejected it as too onerous an additional task for the time being. Looking again at the Darren McGee files last night, he'd noticed that

Parker had never been interviewed during Salter's inquiry because he'd been on leave over New Year's Eve and New Year's Day. The night porter on duty on the night of Darren McGee's death had been an agency temp who'd never worked at the hotel before.

His mobile rang. Mick Hume: a Vauxhall Astra had driven away from the address, DC Barber was tailing it on the off chance. Jacobson scribbled the licence number and Kerr put a call through to the control room for a PNC/DVLC check. When the details came back – nothing on the PNC – he switched on the nearest free terminal, checked the name and address against the local intelligence sources. Nothing again. A third of British men under the age of thirty had a criminal conviction for some offence or other but Richard Austin Cole apparently wasn't one of them. Kerr wondered if he knew him by sight – he didn't recognise the name – since the address was out on the Bovis estate, probably not much more than a five-minute walk from his own house. Since he was sitting in front of a computer screen, he ran a check on Tony Blair, Gary Bowles' snooker opponent. Blair didn't feature on Amanda Singh's hate crimes database but he was on the PNC: several minor convictions for dealing, mainly in coke and ecstasy by the looks of it.

Jacobson's mobile rang again – and Kerr's went off barely a second later. Messages from the control room in both cases. Randeep Parmeer was trying to get in touch with Kerr and there was a caller asking for Jacobson by name, claiming to have information pertaining to the death of Paul Shaw.

'Put him or her on,' Jacobson said, expecting a Looney Tunes merchant.

Deranged, malicious or simply mistaken members of the public were an occupational irritation for any serious investigation. The only reason there'd been none so far with regard to Shaw was probably because the case still wasn't a murder inquiry officially.

'Chief Inspector Jacobson?'

The voice surprised him a little. Calm, educated, no heavy breathing.

'Speaking.'

What it had to say surprised him a lot more.

Drury's house had four bedrooms. His own, the guest room and two others. One of them he kept locked, the other one he'd kitted out as a mini gym. Parker thought he might try and work out later if Drury didn't mind. It would kill a bit more time after all. Drury had nipped out when he'd finally emerged from his bedroom – *a bit of business, Wayne, won't be gone long*, he'd said – and Teresa was taking what appeared to be an endless bath. She seemed to have her phone with her in there as well. Parker had heard her gabbing away earlier, although he couldn't make out who to – or what about. He was sitting on his own in the front room, drinking more tea, idly skimming the pages of a two-day old copy of the *Manchester Evening News*. He was wondering how narked Teresa would be if he fixed himself a proper breakfast when he heard the sudden approach of wheels and a car engine. He got up and looked out through the bay window. Drury's vehicle pulled into the drive, followed by a Range Rover. Drury climbed out and unlocked the front door of the house. Two blokes emerged from the Range Rover and lifted a large packing case carefully out of the back, the kind you'd deliver a TV set or something like that in. White goods they called them. A term which, being a racist and proud of it, always amused Parker. Drury held the door open for them and pointed the way upstairs. He closed it again as soon as they were inside.

'I don't like this, guys, I don't like this one bit,' Drury was saying. 'Never on home premises – that's always been our rule and it's never let us down.'

One of the two newcomers was a Paki, Parker noticed – now that he was in the house and he could observe him close up. They were so many of them now, he thought, they'd become so common everywhere, that even a race warrior didn't always clock them straight off. Both of them were wearing decent suits that didn't really look the part for lugging deliveries around.

'It can't be helped, Nev,' the non-Paki said. 'We've had an inside tip-off, you know that. *Make alternative storage arrangements*. That was the advice. And it's only for the next hour or so – until we can get something else sorted.'

Drury didn't reply, just watched them struggle up to the landing with the case. Parker didn't think he'd ever seen him as agitated as this before. And certainly not on a particular evening back in Carrington. Once they had the case upstairs, Drury followed them. He unlocked the spare room and they stuck the case inside. Teresa was on the landing by now, wrapped in a dressing gown, a big pink towel around her head – shooting Drury daggers. Parker reminded himself it was none of his business. He'd been standing in the lounge doorway but now he returned to the sofa, slurped a mouthful of tea, took out his cigarette packet. The conversation carried on upstairs but it was muffled. It was even possible, he thought, that they were whispering. He lit up, started to look at the classified pages, which was a kind of pointless habit that he'd acquired. He never bought anything, just liked to see what was available – wherever he was, whatever newspaper he happened to be reading.

The first hefty bang against Drury's strengthened front door made him jump. But then his soldiering kicked in. He was headed for the kitchen and a possible exit route by the time – a few seconds only – that the third bang brought broad daylight and looming, swiftly moving figures into the hall.

Armed police. On the floor now.

Parker kept going. There was no time to fanny about with Drury's elaborate locking system. He picked up an expensive, steel-legged chair and threw it with all his strength at the kitchen window. Then he was flinging himself though the jagged gap into the garden. There were more of them outside of course. But evidently they hadn't covered reacting to the shock of an imploding window on their poxy training exercises – and at least he made them work for their money. He nearly reached the back wall before a big bastard tackled him rugby-style and felled him, shoving his head down needlessly into the muck so that he could hardly breathe.

They guarded them together in the front room while they carried out the search. Parker. Drury. Drury's two associates. Each one cuffed. Each one facing against a different part of the wall. Any time you turned your head even slightly a boot found your arse.

Face the front. Cunt.

They hadn't asked him who he was yet. Though there was hardly any need. His real driving licence and his real passport were upstairs in a side flap of his rucksack. He'd just say who he was when they did ask, nothing else. There was no point saying anything more until they interviewed him. Call it thinking time, a period of grace. He became aware of softer, lighter footsteps moving around the room. He turned his head to look, got another kick in the arse for his trouble. But it didn't prevent him from witnessing Teresa walking up to Drury. She was smiling, dressed and conspicuously uncuffed.

'I just wanted you to know this, Nev,' she said, talking straight into his ear, the palm of her hand pressing on the back of his head, shoving his face hard against the wall. 'You're not just the worst shag I've had in the line of duty – you're the worst shag I've had full stop.'

Chapter Thirty-Four

Kerr parked in the market square, tried not to think about Rachel around the corner in her flat in Thomas Holt Street or who might be there with her or what they might be doing. He locked his car and walked across the square in the direction of the Bank House. Randeep Parmeer's latest problems were apparent even at a distance. Somebody in possession of a large quantity of white paint had used the front window of the Viceroy Tandoori as a giant sketch pad. Swastikas. *Sieg Heil*s. All the usual, dreary slogans: *Paki Scum*, *Terrorists*, *Race War Now*.

Randeep Parmeer was standing behind the counter of his bar. There were two younger men present. Parmeer introduced them: his son, Ashraf, home for the weekend apparently, and Ramesh, the waiter who'd opened the door to let Kerr in. For some reason, the Viceroy's owner looked pleased with himself. Kerr noticed a portable TV perched on the counter next to a digital video camera. Ashraf connected a lead between the camera and the front of the television.

'I thought you'd want to see this on a reasonable-sized screen, Sergeant,' Parmeer said, virtually beaming.

Ashraf pressed the play button. Kerr watched three figures approach the outside of the Viceroy. While one kept an anxious look-out, the second opened up the tins of paint and the third started daubing rapidly at the window. The time in the corner of the screen read 5.45 am: just before sunrise. Parmeer explained what had happened while the recording played on.

'I made some inquiries about CCTV yesterday – I'm getting a system installed this week. But this was Ashraf's idea in the meantime. The two of them parked the delivery van in the square, made sure they had a clear view of the restaurant, sat up in it all night.'

'We were lucky to catch them,' Ashraf said, 'I'd already nodded off but Ramesh managed to stay awake.'

'This is good evidence, isn't it?' his father asked.

'It's certainly that all right,' Kerr said, more than a little impressed. 'But why wait until now to call me – why not first thing?'

Parmeer exchanged a look with his son. Then:

'Ashraf thought that we should be dealing with it ourselves now we know who's responsible. There, eh, was a family debate before we contacted the police station.'

Kerr nodded but didn't comment. He pointed towards the screen.

'That's Gary Bowles with the paint brush, the character you picked out on Friday. The one holding the paint cans is a toerag by the name of Tony Blair. What I *don't* know is who the third customer is.'

Randeep Parmeer's smile returned to his face.

'That's not a problem though,' he said, patting the shoulders of Ashraf and Ramesh in turn, 'because *we* do.'

Jacobson drove out to the university campus on his own. There was no need for Kerr to be there when there was a development in his hate crime case to pursue. Especially since any current racist activity in the area was looking more and more potentially relevant to the deaths of Paul Shaw and Darren McGee. He parked in the main car park and, following the signposts, made his way amongst the brutalist concrete and tokenist shrubbery to the Sociology and Media Studies building. He stopped outside the wide glass-fronted entrance, checked the details he'd scribbled into his notebook: room 219, second floor. There was an out-of-order notice on the lift so he was stuck with taking the stairs up. The long corridor was weekend-quiet although there were unexpected signs of life in a small handful of rooms: lecturers or researchers or whatever beavering away at their books and their computer screens as if the survival of civilisation depended on their efforts. Or maybe, Jacobson thought unkindly, just their promotion prospects. He found the room he wanted and walked in.

Dr Martin Kesey stood up, offered Jacobson a chair, shut the door firmly before sitting back down behind his desk. He was a big lad, Jacobson thought, well over six feet. He wore his office like an ill-fitting shirt that had shrunk even more in the wash. All apart from the giant film poster that took up most of the wall behind him. *Der Blaue Engel*, 1930: Emil Jannings letching at Marlene Dietrich. Jacobson had suggested the nearest police station or Kesey's home address or any pub of his choice now that they were into opening time. But Kesey had been adamant: the university was the safest place for them to meet – *or safer for me, anyway*, he'd said. Jacobson had been writing him off at that point as a Looney Tuner after all, albeit an unusually articulate one. But then Kesey had mentioned the six magic words that proved he knew something that was worth knowing: Rick Cole, John Stuart, Phil Stuart.

'The best thing would probably be if you just start at the beginning, Dr Kesey.'

'Fine, MAFN,' Kesey said, shoving his chair right back, trying to find some extra room for his legs.

'MAFN?'

'The Midlands Anti Fascist Network. It's a coalition group, campaigning against the BNP and the far right in general.'

Jacobson nodded. Now that Kesey had spelled it out, the acronym did sound slightly familiar.

'What about it?' he asked.

'MAFN's mainly known for its public work. Demos, leafleting, education. All the usual stuff. But there's another aspect to it – infiltration, finding out what the Nazis are up to from the *inside*. I'm part of that other work – I have been for several years – and that's how I know what I think I know about Paul Shaw.'

'You mean the BNP's involved?'

'No, absolutely not. I'm talking about the New Nationalists – that's their official name. A group that's staying more or less clandestine at the moment until it has built up the strength of numbers it needs to go public. The NN's still in what the leadership calls the *poaching* phase, recruiting disaffected members from other groups, provided they're of sufficient calibre in NN terms. Which basically means three things. One: they're out and out racists. Two: they've got no significant criminal record – and certainly don't have any *race-related* criminal record. Three: they understand that what a party says in public to stay within the law and how it's prepared to act in secret are two very different things.'

'And the three names you've mentioned – they're members of this set-up?'

Kesey tried his chair at a different angle but didn't appear to create any extra leg room.

'They're the local unit. There's one or two others I'm not certain about yet. But Cole and the Stuarts are the major players.'

He pulled open a desk drawer, took out a creased magazine.

'This is the kind of stuff the NN's peddling on the quiet.'

Jacobson glanced at the first few pages. Although there was scarcely any need to look beyond the front cover: a photograph of worshippers leaving a mosque, framed through a rifle sight. He rubbed at a patch of stubble under his chin that his worn-out shaver must have missed.

'A question before you go any further. How the hell does

a sociology lecturer blend in with a bunch of – according to your description – racist thugs?'

Kesey half-smiled.

'They're thugs all right, Inspector – but they're intelligent, well-organised, well-financed thugs. Academics, teachers, lawyers, doctors – anyone with a good, middle-class front scores highly as NN candidate material. And I'm afraid it's a patronising, ill-informed *Guardian*-reader's illusion that fascism only appeals to the poor and the disadvantaged. It was never true historically – and it's certainly not true now. You only need to look at some of the supporters of the Countryside Alliance. It also helps that I've taken the trouble to publish a few ambiguous, deliberately misleading articles in a couple of obscure right-wing journals. So I scrub up pretty well as an Aryan extremist intellectual – or at least as a liberal sinner who's seen the light of repentance.'

'And Paul Shaw?' Jacobson asked, fascinated but needing to keep to the point.

Kesey gave up on his chair, stood up again and found a leaning space between his filing cabinet and his window.

'I'm assuming, Mr Jacobson, that Rick Cole and the Stuart brothers have already come up in your inquiries?'

'And what makes you think that?'

'Because otherwise you wouldn't be here – you'd have dismissed me as some kind of mad conspiracy nut.'

Jacobson returned the half-smile.

'As you say, Dr Kesey – I'm here.'

'And that makes me think I'm on to something,' Kesey replied, resting one hand on a pile of unmarked student essays which had been stacked on top of the filing cabinet.

He told Jacobson that he'd spent a lot of time the day before with Rick Cole and the two Stuarts, without going into all the details of where and why, and that he'd happened to see a copy of yesterday's *Argus* at breakfast this morning. He didn't go into all the details of that either: lazily scanning the pages in Karen Mott's bed while Karen padded into the kitchen and came back with burnt toast and too-weak instant coffee.

'It's the fact that he was black that got me thinking. That and the link the *Argus* made to the drowning earlier in the year. They were cousins, right?'

Jacobson nodded again.

'The Stuarts were fairly pissed up last night. John Stuart in particular. *Have you got the real stuff, Martin?* he kept asking me, *can you walk it as well as talk it? We know we can, Martin. Rick and Phil and me. We knew it on New Year's Eve and we knew it just the other night*. His brother told him to shut it. But he kept on, kept coming back to it. *See ya Martin*, he said when I was about to go. *We've got it, Martin. Whoosh, Martin. Ker-plop. Splash.*'

Chapter Thirty-Five

There was no immediate luck with Tony Blair. A patrol car visited his current address, a bedsit near Mill Street, but he wasn't at home when they called. All that could be done immediately was to put his name on the local alert list. The same went for the look-out man. According to his neighbours, he'd been seen loading his family – a wife and two kids – into the Espace, was presumed to have taken off for the day on a Sunday outing. Gary Bowles was the opposite case. His girlfriend, Linda, made a half-hearted attempt to keep the uniformeds on the doorstep and the bull terrier did its fair share of yapping. But by the time Bowles had roused himself from the sofa, where he'd crashed out on his return from Wynarth, it was already too late. As soon as he'd been processed, Kerr arranged the formal interview, dragooning a bored duty solicitor who'd been headed out of the Divisional building as Kerr had been headed into it.

The custody suite upgrade had been completed at last. Fifty per cent of the interview rooms – although this wasn't one of them – now had video facilities. As well as chairs that didn't dig into your arse. But all the rooms still stank tangibly of tobacco. And still reeked intangibly of lies, deceit and fifty-seven varieties of human regret and despair. Bowles, on the other hand, was cultivating a pose of defiance: *Fuck you, pal.*

Kerr told him he'd been caught on camera. He was busted, stuffed, washed-up:

'The only question, Gaz, is *why*?'

'No comment,' Bowles replied, staring beyond Kerr to the wall.

'The courts take this stuff seriously nowadays, Gaz. A bit of graffiti's one thing. But there's been death threats made to Randeep Parmeer and his family. What do you reckon to conspiracy to murder, Gaz? You could be looking at ten years if it goes to that.'

'That's bollocks and you know it.'

'Is it, Gaz? I don't think I do. You're working out at the retirement flats complex on the Wynarth Road. Skivvying for the painters. You and your mate, Tony, likewise. How you met up, maybe. Why you were handy anyway when Clive Rushton was looking for a couple of mugs to help him with his dirty work.'

'No frigging comment.'

'So you're saying you don't know Clive Rushton?'

'No comment.'

'For the tape record, Clive Rushton is a partner – with his father – in a property development and estate agency business. The Rushton firm are handling the sales for the retirement complex. Clive Rushton is a frequent and regular visitor to the site. Along with Mr Bowles and Mr Blair, Clive Rushton was filmed this morning vandalising the Viceroy Tandoori.'

Kerr paused for a moment, watched Bowles affecting a yawn.

'The thing about the Viceroy Tandoori, Gaz, is that it's located in the Bank House building, smack in the middle of Wynarth, yes?'

Bowles chewed a thumbnail but didn't reply.

'The other half's occupied by Rushtons Ltd, Gaz. Randeep Parmeer tells me that recently the Rushtons have been pressuring him to sell up and move on, which would give *them* control of the entire property – plus the full profit from any future sale or redevelopment. A conversion into luxury dwellings for instance.'

Bowles shrugged.

'I don't know what you're on about, mate.'

'You know all right, Gaz. Because that's where you fit in, isn't it? Trying to *scare* Randeep Parmeer off?'

'No comment, and my name is Gary.'

'OK then, *Gary*. We'll leave it there for now. I'll talk to you again when I've made some more inquiries.'

Kerr stated the time - one fifty-two pm - and switched off the tape recorder.

'So I can go then?' Bowles asked, glancing at the duty solicitor who seemed to be doing a convincing job of sleeping with his eyes open.

'You can go back to your cell, yes,' Kerr said, pressing the button for the custody officers. 'I'm not joking about conspiracy to murder. You want to think about how far you were involved - and how all these "no comments" are going to look in court.'

Another thing Kerr disliked about the custody suite - and which the upgrade hadn't changed - were the low ceilings. There was always the real, uneasy sensation that the whole weight of the building was pressing down on you. He took the stairs up to the ground level as soon as he could, glad to see daylight again. If they did bring conspiracy charges, they probably wouldn't stretch as far as murder. But if racist murders were being committed in Crowby, and Bowles had got a whisper about them, then it wouldn't do any harm to put the fear of God into him.

The house was empty again. Sharon and Stan were worse than teenagers. They came home late, slept late, and then they went straight out partying again. The Sunday afternoon line-dancing club this time, according to the note Sharon had scribbled and left on the kitchen table. Vicky swallowed another couple of aspirins and washed them down with the last third of a carton of orange juice. She took slow, headachy steps back upstairs to the bathroom and hung her dressing gown on the hook behind the door. She stepped into the shower and turned it on full. Her mother hadn't always been so carefree of course. And her dad maybe never had. Vicky found it difficult to recall what he looked like without the aid of a photograph. Not to really recall him, the way an artist could set down every feature of a face, every line and blemish and wrinkle. Sharon had 'borrowed' her shower lotion again – well, she had 'borrowed' Sharon's brandy – but the warm jets of water cascading down her body felt pleasant enough unscented. She stayed under the shower maybe ten minutes and then stepped out, dried herself with the towel that she kept in her bedroom out of Sharon's and Stan's way. What she mainly remembered about her dad were his brown eyes, melancholy with hope and fear. He hadn't asked for much from life and that was exactly what it had given him. Twenty years of drudgery that had killed him before his time, a house full of anonymous, mass-market possessions, a handful of cheap, foreign holidays – and a wife whose life had blossomed – flourished – after he'd died. None of that had happened overnight of course. First there'd been the two years it had taken him to die. Sharon had been strict with her really before that, overprotective. But then she'd started to spend hours on end at the hospital, coming back home too blank and too exhausted to care anymore. A lot of the rest of the time she'd just sit in the lounge and stare at the television, nothing on the screen actually registering. Vicky was fourteen when her dad's cancer was diagnosed, sixteen when he died. She pretty much took over the cooking and the housework from her mum, supervised her own homework – and then, free to please herself, she'd take off into the wild night: pills, booze and boys.

She'd thought Cole had been handsome back then. Tall and brooding. It had been her dad's last summer when they met, the summer – for Vicky – of *Wonderwall* and *Firestarter*. Vicky hadn't liked him at first, had thought he was cocksure, big-headed. But then she'd fooled herself that there was vulnerability too, a place behind his eyes, waiting to be reached. She was working in Virgin on the High Street, needing to be out of the tidy, gloomy house. The holiday relief girl. She thought he was funny, too, at first. Maybe mad. Even on the hottest days he'd wear his long leather coat, his big boots. Cole and the Stuart brothers. Every lunchtime they'd come in, poring over the racks, rarely buying anything. They had a band, he told her one day, Scuzz. They hadn't played any gigs yet but they rehearsed Thursdays nights in the YMCA. She didn't turn up the first week that he told her this. Nor the second week. As if she already knew not to hurry the bits of life that mattered, knew to scroll them all into her memory, knew not to lose them too easily to whatever would come next.

The YMCA building was a Victorian mansion, red Midlands brick, but under-repaired and falling apart. Unkempt trees swamped the pot-holed driveway like litter. Any night after dark you could have used it as the set for a teenage horror flick. Appropriately, it was barely a quarter of a mile away from the municipal cemetery. That was where he'd walked her that first night. And where they often went back. He'd wanted to do it up against a gravestone. But that was something she'd refused at first. Scuzz were rubbish of course. Phil Stuart peering at his bass guitar through his beer-bottle-thick specs, his fingers fumbling on the strings; John Stuart always bashing the drums to the last number but one, never managing to keep up. Only Cole himself showed anything like ability, prowling the stage, shrieking and howling. 'Vampire Hell' was their one almost-classic number. *Gonna take you to hell, gonna take you to hell, gonna take you to heh-ell.*

She had a sudden urge to dress in black, which had been her uniform in those days, found an old pair of black jeans and an even older black T-shirt at the back of her wardrobe. She couldn't blame her mum and dad really. It was what you did at that age, showed two fingers to the grown-up world. And Vicky had been a rebel with the smallest *r* anyway. Cole had packed in school on his sixteenth birthday - as a choice, nothing at all to do with lack of ability - wanted her to do the same. She'd never considered it for more than two seconds. As if she was already a compromised adult, already dividing her life into neat compartments. School by day, Cole by night - reality and fantasy, packaged and separate. Cole never bothered to try. Which was why, after Scuzz got totally nowhere, it was almost funny, even after everything else, maybe even now, that Cole had trained as a plumber, had ended up with a wife and a baby and a semi on the Bovis estate. Cole - whose big thing, encouraged by Phil Stuart, had been his adolescent misreading of Nietzsche - one law for the slave herd, no law - no limits - for the Superman. And something else just as badly misunderstood by them: to discover what your morals really were, all you had to do was *act*.

Chapter Thirty-Six

It took an hour to obtain duly signed search warrants and to assemble the necessary personnel. Greg Salter, to his rare credit, didn't really try to stand in the way, just asked to be kept informed. Mick Hume and DC Barber maintained the surveillance on both addresses in the meantime. Barber had loosely tailed Cole all the way back to the Bovis estate, hanging back in the traffic, making sure that Cole couldn't notice him. It had been a relief each time he'd cruised past the end of Cole's street, clocked that Cole's Astra was still standing there on his driveway in front of his blue work van. And it was a relief now: watching the police convoy drive on to the estate. Jacobson, DC Williams and Emma Smith in Kerr's Peugeot. Kerr behind the wheel, disregarding the prescribed hierarchical etiquette. Two patrol cars with two uniformeds a piece. Plus a SOCO in the second car. The searches couldn't be forensic searches yet – but at least the SOCO could try and ensure that nobody did anything drastically stupid in the way of compromising or contaminating potential sources of evidence.

Rick Cole's wife, Wendy, kept her daughter tight at her side in the front room. Cole managed a cool front, exercising his right to keep an eye on the process, roaming from room to room to watch them at work. The interior décor of the house was standard issue – mid-price suburban – until you walked into the box room that Cole had kitted out as his den. Jacobson had anticipated the Nazi flag and the replica SS paraphernalia. But the sheer volume of the collection surprised him. Plus posters and blown-up photographs on every free inch of wall: the Oklahoma bomber, Timothy McVeigh, the London nailbomber, David Copeland, Himmler, Himmler's castle at Wewelsburg, Blood and Honour gig lists and artwork. There was even an old Anti-Nazi League poster that showed a pile of concentration camp corpses and the slogan 'never again' - except that Cole (presumably) had scored over the 'never' with a neat red swastika. The bookshelves were full too. David Irving, Savitri Devi, Julius Evola, *The Turner Diaries*. Plus multiple copies of the magazine Martin Kesey had shown him, most of the contents - the raison d'être of the search warrants - almost certainly illegal under the relevant sections (17 to 29) of the 1986 Public Order Act. Jacobson stuffed a representative sample into a large-size evidence bag.

'A right little shrine to evil, old son,' he said.

Kerr nodded, riffling through Cole's cupboard drawers. His computer would be taken for examination anyway but it was always possible that there was an incriminating floppy disk or two lying around somewhere as well. Cole asked for a moment with his wife when, downstairs again, Jacobson cautioned him. If he'd meant in private, tough. Jacobson just stood there, didn't budge. Cole lifted up England, told her to be good, told his wife not to speak to the police or anyone else:

'And remember, doll, I love you.'

He passed his daughter back to Wendy and didn't resist when two of the uniformeds cuffed him and led him out to one of the patrol cars.

They repeated the process at the Stuarts' place. They'd lost the two plods who were taking Cole into custody but they'd gained Mick Hume's solid presence. Eight police in all, if you included the SOCO. The Alsatians knew that something was up, maybe the kind of thing they'd been trained – or mis-trained – for. But the SOCO tricked them into the unused greenhouse and shut the door on them. There was no specific shrine this time but there were bundles of the same magazine – plus others – in a cupboard under the stairs, along with a horde of white power music CDs.

Jacobson cautioned the two brothers in their front room and the uniformeds produced their cuffs.

'Is that necessary? On a bullshit charge like this?' Phil Stuart demanded.

'Why bullshit, old son?' Jacobson retorted. 'Something else on your mind, maybe? Something more serious?'

Stuart clammed up then, held out his wrists. Big John took a long, slow look around the room. A tracking shot, weighing up the situation. Probably discounting Jacobson and the woman. But still left with odds of six to one against. He made a show of making it difficult for the two uniformeds when they stepped forward yet didn't seriously try to stop them.

Jacobson wasn't through with the house, though, wanted every single room searched, even the loft. They tackled the kitchen last, the Stuarts, guarded by one of the plods, watching from the hallway. Jacobson kept himself in the thick of it. He got down uncomfortably on his knees, started carefully emptying out the contents of a freezer compartment.

'This is a joke, this is,' Phil Stuart shouted, 'a fucking joke.'

His brother didn't say a word. Jacobson pulled out a hefty-looking frozen chicken and half a dozen Marks and Spencer ready meals.

'Their lasagne's not bad, I always think,' he commented, 'but I don't really rate their Indian range – certainly not their jalfreji anyway.'

He reached in again, pulled out something oblong-shaped, wrapped up in a red and white tea towel. He placed it on the floor and unwrapped it: a faux-leather case of the sort your granny might have stored her best knives and forks in. Jacobson opened it and looked inside: a Walther PPK lying next to a full round of seven bullets.

Wayne Parker stared across the desk at his interrogators and weighed up his dwindling options. Option singular really: talk or don't talk. They'd provided him with a plastic cup of instant tea. He took a slow sip as a delaying tactic. He'd declined the offer of a dozy duty solicitor, reckoned he was better off without. Every town and city in the country had its favoured firm of criminal defence specialists, the one you asked for if you were in the know. Parker knew who that was in Crowby – Alan Slingsby and Associates – but here in Manchester he didn't have a clue. And the North West Regional Crime Squad weren't about to enlighten him.

He took a second, even slower sip. There was a tall one and a short one. Both male, both white, both hardly seeming old enough to be detective sergeants, which apparently both of them were. The short one always coughed before he spoke, some kind of nervous tic maybe.

'For the second time, Wayne, did you see any evidence of drug dealing while you were under Nevil Drury's roof? If you help us then—'

Shortarse's voice trailed off. There was no need to waste his breath spelling out the completely obvious. Parker willed his brain to stay calm, to analyse the situation dispassionately. How much had Teresa, or whatever her real name was, overheard or guessed? She hadn't been there when he'd mentioned murder to Drury. But who knew how talkative Drury was in bed in the brief intervals between shags? Would Drury think it worth his while to trade what he knew? Or was he in such deep shit anyway that a trade-off would make no real difference?

Talk or don't talk? And if talk – what about? The NN recruited healthily from the prison service. He'd be taking his life in his hands if he went inside as a known informer. But he'd probably *get* life if he didn't inform on Cole and company. On the other hand, Nevil Drury was involved with some heavy-duty customers too, was affiliated to one of the biggest supply chains in the country. If it was made clear that he'd kept silent on that front, there might be a level of protection forthcoming once he was banged up. Quid pro quo, they called it. He took another mouthful of the piss-awful tea. Then:

'No, I didn't see any drug dealing. I didn't see any drugs full stop. If you ask me, you've got the wrong man - either that or you're fitting Nevil up for some reason or other of your own.'

Chapter Thirty-Seven

Six o'clock. Jacobson enjoyed, as he always did, the sonorous chiming of the clock on the Town Hall's art deco white tower. He'd skipped the idea of a meal break on the increasingly theoretical grounds that he might still be able to make his date with Alison Taylor. *Date*. The word could have made him smile if the circumstances had been different. Teenagers went on dates. Young, carefree people. And now he had one too – only he'd have to call his off, fall at the first hurdle. The whole afternoon had vanished in the searches and the preparation for the searches. And in a second conversation with Martin Kesey. Now they were into the interviews. Three in a row. Plus Wayne Parker was on his way from Manchester, was being ferried by patrol car down the M6. Instead of something to eat, he'd smoked an illicit B & H, drunk a cup of black, instant coffee – and stared out of his office window for ten, peaceful minutes. He should have called her really. But he'd bottled it and right now there wasn't time. He straightened his tie on the sixth chime and walked out of his office towards the lifts. Kerr was waiting there, pressed the button when he saw Jacobson approaching.

Rick Cole had already been brought to the interview room, was sitting as far back from the table as the fixed-to-the-floor chair allowed, his arms folded jauntily across his chest. Kerr made sure that the video equipment was running properly. Jacobson sat down and made the usual statement of what the time was and who was present. Cole had declined his right to a duty solicitor or to a solicitor of his own choosing. Jacobson checked again if that was still his preference.

'I'd prefer to be at home with my wife and my daughter. But I don't need some brain-dead legal wanker earning a fat fee at my expense. I'd rather talk for myself.'

Jacobson ran through the possible charges that Cole was facing.

'You're looking at two years if it goes beyond possession to distribution or intent to distribute.'

'And I thought this was a free country.'

'And I thought people like you thought that was the problem with it,' Kerr said, sliding into the chair next to Jacobson.

'Oh, a humorist,' Cole smirked. 'I know you, don't I? I've seen you out with your little 'uns on the estate. A decent, white, family man – you should be thanking me for what I do, not harassing me.'

Kerr didn't recognise him. But their addresses were only a few streets apart. Cole could easily have seen him out and about, easily seen Cathy and the twins too.

'My family's not your business, Mr Cole. And that better be the way it's staying.'

Cole didn't reply, just kept up his jaunty posturing.

'And what exactly *is* it that you do, old son?' Jacobson asked. 'This stuff that DS Kerr should be thanking you for?'

'I'm standing up for the white race, mate. The way you should, the way everybody should.'

Jacobson spread a copy of one of the seized magazines out on the table.

'This muck goes beyond any standing up. The way I read it, it's calling for race war.'

'Prosecute away then – if you think you can prove anything. Find me one person who's bought a copy off me – or even seen a copy.'

'For the moment, I'm more interested in where *you* got the copies, old son.'

'No comment,' Cole replied.

'I take it you've known John and Phil Stuart a long time, for instance?'

'I know John and Phil, yeah. They went to the same school as me. They've got a building firm, they throw a bit of subcontracting my way.'

'And now you're all pals together in the New Nationalists?'

'No comment.'

'My sources say that all three of you certainly are members. You spent all of yesterday at a Party training day, including the illegal handling of firearms - and you spent Thursday night at a Party meeting out past Wynarth.'

The human body was a sieve - constantly leaking information about the human brain. Jacobson watched Cole unfold his arms at last, scratch the side of his head as if for inspiration. Whatever Cole had thought that the police knew, it was clear that he'd never thought it was as much as this.

'I've just spoken to the landlord of the Bideford Arms, Mr Cole. He tells me that your meeting broke up around nine thirty. I'm wondering exactly what you and your old schoolmates got up to after that. DS Kerr's wondering the same thing, I expect.'

Cole scratched the side of his head again.

'I don't think you can ask me that - I don't think it's relevant to the charges. That's why I'm changing my mind. I do want a solicitor here - and I'm saying nothing else till I get one.'

Jacobson, conscious of the video camera and the courtroom audience that might lie beyond it, kept his voice even and his gaze steady.

'No problem, Mr Cole. I'll ask the custody sergeant to arrange it and then we'll talk again.'

Jacobson pressed for the custody officers and Kerr stopped the recording.

'Does the name Paul Shaw mean anything to you, old son?' Jacobson asked, rising to go – he didn't expect an answer just wanted to spell Cole's predicament – if that's what it was – out to him, help him to sweat and worry.

Cole kept his mouth shut and his head down, studying the bland, pine surface of the newly commissioned table.

'Or Darren McGee?' Jacobson persisted. 'No? They're the kind of people your in-house magazine really doesn't seem to like.'

Kerr stood up too.

'Well, they *were* anyway, Rick,' he said, 'past tense, if you follow me.'

They took the lift back up to the fifth floor. Jacobson felt the need for another cigarette but he didn't want to succumb. So they talked in Kerr's office – where Jacobson knew Kerr would never stand for it.

'You don't think you gave too much away then, Frank?'

'Well, either they did it – if there is an *it* – or they didn't. If they did, they've probably been feeling fairly confident up until now. Don't forget that poor old Darren McGee didn't even get flagged up *as* a murder victim. The more they think we know, the more one of them might decide to talk. That's the beauty with conspiracies – there's usually one party or another looking for a way to bail out when it comes to the endgame.'

'But if there isn't on this occasion?'

Jacobson sunk himself into the chair used by Kerr's rarely seen room-mate, DS Tyler.

'The incitement to racial hatred charges are looking solid enough, Ian. Plus there's the Walther PPK in the case of Little and Large. We can hold all three of them for the full twenty-four hours if we need to. Then it's all about the forensics coming in on time – and containing something positive.'

'So what's next – carry on and interview the brothers?'

Jacobson glanced at his watch, executed some hazy mental arithmetic, shot to his feet.

'Yes, old son, the brothers. John Stuart first as we agreed. Set it up with custody and I'll join you - say ten minutes. I need to make, ehm, a personal call first.'

Kerr gaped at him. It wasn't a typical Jacobson utterance. But the latter had exited from his office, practically bolted from it, before Kerr could formulate any kind of response.

Vicky was still occasionally mistaken as being much younger than her real age. One of the first times she'd walked in to the staff room at Simon De Montfort, a soon-to-retire geography teacher had complained to her that pupils weren't allowed there, not even sixth formers. She'd had a similar experience earlier today when she'd stopped her car outside an off-licence on the way out of town. The middle-aged woman behind the counter had wanted ID before she'd been prepared to hand over the litre bottle of vodka that Vicky had asked for. She'd shown her driving licence triumphally, enjoyed watching the cow gawping at it, gawping at her, gawping back at the licence again. A big part of the explanation, she'd decided afterwards, was the adolescent way she'd got dressed - for God's knows what reason. All in black. And thick black eye-liner as well. Even the spiky dog collar she'd used to wear sometimes in the days when she'd hung out with Cole, standing loyally at the side of the stage when Scuzz played their gigs - few and far between - in their usual shitty venues. She'd bought a bottle of White Lightning too, another old teenage habit, although she'd no intention of drinking it, had just wanted to irritate the suspicious old bat a little bit more.

After that she'd taken the winding road out here: Crow Hill. Crowby's beauty spot. Or as close as Crowby got to one. She'd parked in the woodland clearing at the foot of the hill, hiked up the waymarked trail all the way to the top. There'd been a quite a few people around then - in the middle of the afternoon - but now, gone six o'clock, there was scarcely anybody else here. The Sunday picnickers and dog walkers had gone home for tea. And it wouldn't be until after sunset that the couples would arrive who used the car park as a lovers' lane.

Vicky was sitting on an outcrop of rock, gazing across Crowby to the motorway in the distance. She was halfway through the vodka, had promised herself in the last half-hour that she wouldn't leave until she'd finished the bottle. She took another swig, stowed it carefully at her feet while she rolled a thin cigarette with her licorice papers. The thing she'd learned to appreciate about vodka was the purity of its intention. The way it cut through every pretence about alcohol like a sharp razor. Vodka, undiluted, had no taste, no flavour, no bullshit aesthetics. You drank it solely in order to get pissed: to get deeply, inwardly, profoundly drunk. Drunk enough not to care about anything. Or only to care about whatever you really did care about.

Chapter Thirty-Eight

The interview with John Stuart and the interview with Phil Stuart followed a similar pattern to the interview with Rick Cole. Each of them blustered and 'no commented' about the possession of material likely to incite racial hatred. Each of them denied he'd ever seen the Walther PPK or the ammunition before. At first they didn't want solicitors - *agents of the Zionist Occupation Government*, according to Phil Stuart - but then, exactly like Cole, they changed their minds when the subtext of the questioning started to point towards their whereabouts late on Thursday night. All three of them had asked for representation by Alan Slingsby and associates. Jacobson used the delay to check the progress of the rest of his team. He took the lift to the second floor first of all. Steve Horton had somehow found space for the computer equipment removed from Cole's den and from the back bedroom *chez* Stuart. But so far it looked like he hadn't started to examine any of it.

'This is strange stuff, Mr Jacobson,' Horton said, ending a telephone conversation as Jacobson walked in.

'What is, Steve?' Jacobson asked.

Horton explained as non-technically as he could.

'Paul Shaw had a website, right? Used it as a contact point for anyone who had a story to tell him. Plus, in his line of business, he was frequently away from home, living out of a suitcase.'

Jacobson nodded.

'The thing is, if that was me – and if I had information I didn't want to lose – I'd probably upload it to the private area on my web space on a regular basis. It's common practice for all kinds of professionals – I'd've thought especially for an investigative journalist.'

Jacobson nodded again, started to see Horton's drift: even though Shaw's laptop had vanished, it was possible he was regularly filing virtual copies of his reports and discoveries elsewhere.

'Anyway, I thought it might be worth tracing the ISP who hosted the site. That's who I was just speaking to – the guy on their service desk. Obviously, we need authorisation to take it any further but usually they're willing to give you a hint as to whether it's likely to be worthwhile or not. One geek to another, you know?'

Jacobson didn't know – but he kept on nodding anyway. Horton turned to one of his keyboards, fast-typed something and then hit the *enter* key. Jacobson looked over Horton's shoulder, read the message that appeared on the screen:

The page cannot be displayed.

'You've lost me now, Steve,' he said.

'What it is, Mr Jacobson, I've just tried to access Shaw's site. But – as you can see – it's not there anymore. According to his site provider, his entire web space has disappeared. It looks as if somebody who knew the system administrator password has logged on in the last couple of hours and deleted the lot. The public pages, the private storage – and all his email archives. Whoever it was, it obviously wasn't Paul Shaw.'

'And it wasn't Cole or the Brothers Stuart either – not if you're certain about the time frame.'

'I'm certain all right. The service desk guy's going to phone me back with a precise time and any other info he can get.'

'Thanks Steve,' Jacobson said, puzzled. 'Better keep me posted.'

He took the stairs up the two flights to the fourth floor, thinking about Horton's news, thinking about the interviews, thinking about Alison Taylor. *Too bad*, she'd said when he'd phoned her, *too bad*. But Jacobson, whose job was to see underneath the surface of the words that people said to him, realised that he had no idea what she'd really meant, what she'd really felt. He paused for breath halfway. Not even the slightest inkling of an idea.

Emma Smith, Ray Williams and DS Kerr - takeaway canteen tea in hand - were the sole occupants of the CID Resource Centre. Smith and Williams had finished their trawl through Shaw's and Wayne Parker's telephone records and were collating their report. Kerr talked Jacobson through the most obviously important results. Parker had phoned Rick Cole and the Stuarts on a very few occasions, had taken calls from them as well. Plus they now knew something about the last telephone conversation Paul Shaw had ever had. Jane Spencer had already told them that Shaw had received a call late on Thursday night. Around about ten thirty according to her; actually at ten thirty-seven according to the records. The pig, Kerr told him, was that the call had been made from a public phone box in a quiet street in Wynarth.

Jacobson didn't comment immediately. It was a possibility worth looking into that a passer-by or a local curtain twitcher would have a memory of it, even a description of the caller. But it wasn't something you'd want to bet something you cared about on. Your health, if you did care about it, or your wife, if you still had one. Likewise, it was good news that they could *prove* there'd been contact between Parker and the other three. But making phone calls didn't automatically make them murderers.

'I don't suppose there's any matches between Shaw's records and Parker's, old son?' he asked finally.

Kerr didn't answer this time, decided to let Smith and

Williams take the credit for their own work. Emma Smith looked up from her computer screen.

'Just the one match, guv. Paul Shaw phoned Pete Bradley's gaff in Derby Crescent on Saturday and, again, on Monday. The times tally with the visits we know he made there – talking to Bradley and Billy Marsden. But here's the thing – on Tuesday afternoon, Pete Bradley phoned Wayne Parker.'

'What time, lass?'

'Three minutes past three. They talked for five minutes.'

'And this is definitely on Bradley's own land line? Not a coinbox for his tenants or something like that?'

'Definitely,' Emma Smith replied, 'we checked that out.'

'Fine, good work,' Jacobson said. 'It could be something or nothing though. Anything really dodgy, anything Bradley doesn't have an easy cover for, you'd think he'd use an unregistered mobile, try and avoid leaving a trail.'

Kerr finished his tea, flung the empty plastic cup neatly into the nearest wastebin.

'Tuesday was before the murder though – if it was a murder. He mightn't have known then that he needed to be careful to that extent. And don't forget that Bradley and Parker live in the same area of town. They're not that far apart in age. Plus Parker's a regular in the Bricklayer's Arms – and it's hard to believe that a toerag like Bradley *doesn't* get in there from time to time.'

'I can't see Pete Bradley as a racist though,' DC Williams observed, 'not an active one anyway – not unless there's free cash or free sex in it.'

Emma Smith shot him a dirty look when he mentioned sex but she didn't make any verbal comment.

'There's only one way to find out,' Jacobson said. 'It won't do the Third Reich – or Alan Slingsby's slimeballs – any harm to cool their heels for a while before we resume the interviews.'

The drive took barely ten minutes in the quiet, Sunday

evening traffic. En route, Jacobson set Hume and Barber the task of tracking down any possible sightings of whoever had phoned Paul Shaw from the Wynarth call box. Kerr pulled in behind Bradley's rusting beamer when they reached Derby Crescent. Jacobson clambered out and Kerr followed him up the short path to the paint-peeled front door. Bradley was still in his dressing gown and so was the teenage girl who disappeared quickly, but not quickly enough, back into Bradley's bedroom.

'We need a word, Pete,' Jacobson said, but didn't explain further.

Bradley ushered them into his lounge. There'd been some kind of tidy-up effort since their last visit and this time Jacobson plonked himself on the sofa, although it seemed that Kerr still preferred to stand.

'Who's the girl, Pete?' he asked.

'It's not what you think, mate. She turned up on the doorstep last night, nowhere else to kip.'

'Yeah, you're a virtual saint to the homeless, Pete,' Kerr sneered. 'I expect she can prove she's over-age?'

'She's seventeen, mate, got her birth certificate and everything with her.'

'Everything except common sense,' Kerr commented.

Bradley disappeared for a minute, came back in a pair of jeans and pulling a yellow T-shirt over his head. He found the packet containing his last cigarette under a pile of car magazines, took it out, gestured at Jacobson.

'I don't suppose?'

Jacobson produced his lighter. When he'd lit Bradley's cigarette, he took out a B & H for himself and lit that too.

'Wayne Parker, Pete,' he said, when they were both done, 'a friend of yours, I take it?'

Bradley didn't reply, tried hard to look blank.

'Cut the crap, Pete,' Jacobson said. 'He lives off Midland Road, drinks in the Bricklayers, works as the night porter at the Riverside Hotel.'

'Parker,' Bradley mumbled, 'Parker, Parker—'

'You phoned him on Tuesday afternoon, Pete,' Kerr cut in, 'just after three o'clock.'

Bradley inhaled, exhaled, inhaled again. What he looked like now was someone who'd like to be somewhere far, far away. Kerr coughed, although the room stank permanently of nicotine anyway.

'Oh yeah, *that* Parker,' Bradley replied eventually. 'He's been pestering me about picking up a few day shifts on the minicabs. I phoned him up to say there was nothing doing. Custom ain't great, I've hardly enough work for the regulars – never mind anybody else.'

Jacobson laughed in his face.

'Cab shifts my arse. You weren't giving us the full card yesterday, Pete. And you're lying your head off today. This business about Paul Shaw and Darren McGee could turn into a full-scale murder inquiry at any minute. If I were you I'd start again at the beginning – tell us *exactly* what you know.'

The girl – her name was Janine apparently – stuck her head nervously around the door. She was doe-eyed and ridiculously beautiful to be sharing Pete Bradley's manky bed. Bradley told her not to worry: there were pizzas in the fridge in the kitchen if she was hungry, a Smirnoff Ice too if she wanted it.

'Are you really sure about her age?' Kerr asked when she'd gone again. 'Feel like gambling on a visit from the child protection team?'

'And then there's your door licence worries,' Jacobson said, 'which could easily become your cab licence worries. Or maybe you've got something a lot nastier on your plate – a couple of race killings for instance.'

Bradley wiped the sweat away from his forehead.

'OK. OK. You could help me about the frigging door licence though, couldn't you, mate?'

'That depends, old son,' Jacobson said, tipping his ash on to a copy of *What Car?* in the absence of an ashtray.

'And I'm only talking off the record, yeah? I ain't going to make a statement or nothing.'

'I'll make do with that for now, Pete. But if I end up needing your statement, you'd better let me have it.'

'Otherwise we might stick you on the sex offenders intelligence database just for the sake of it – even if the lass's age *does* check out,' Kerr added, knowing that Bradley's details were already logged there anyway.

Bradley wandered through to his kitchen, came back – fag in mouth – with a whisky glass and a bottle of Jack Daniel's, two-thirds empty. He filled the glass to the brim, stuck his cigarette on the edge of his mantelpiece, took a couple of quick, deep swigs.

'What I told you yesterday – about never seeing Darren being threatened? Well, I did see it once really. Over on Mill Street – the alley that leads the back way into Hayle Close?'

Jacobson nodded: *go on*.

'Four of 'em had him up against the wall. They weren't really hurting him from what I could see, more like he was being given a warning. *Get out of town or else*, that's what they were telling him – *get out or you're dead meat, nigger*. Well I knew who two of them were – and, eh, Paul Shaw paid me for the names.'

'How much?' Kerr asked.

'Does that matter?'

'You lied to us yesterday, Pete. We're only giving you *one* more chance.'

Bradley took another swig. Then:

'Two thousand cash. A thou upfront – and I was to get the other half if it led him anywhere. I'm still waiting for that bit.'

'Who were the two you knew, Pete?' Jacobson asked.

'Wayne Parker – like you say I know him from the Bricklayer's Arms. And Rick Cole the plumber. He's done a bit of work for me now and again. The other two looked familiar – but I couldn't put a name to them.'

'Two thou's a lot of cash for two names and one relatively minor incident, Pete,' Kerr commented.

'Yeah, well I'd seen the four of them hanging about together in the vicinity a few other times as well, as if they were on the look-out for somebody.'

'And you told that to Paul Shaw too?'

'Yeah, I did,' Bradley admitted.

'So what was your phone call to Wayne Parker *really* about?' Jacobson asked.

Bradley's cigarette had all but gone out. Jacobson chucked him a B & H and Bradley lit the fresh stick from the remains of its predecessor.

'I just told him that Paul Shaw was snooping around, asking questions about what happened to his cousin. Kind of a double-bluff, yeah? I told Parker I'd told Shaw to eff off. So if anything came of it, Parker and company wouldn't think it was me that Shaw got his information from.'

'A brain like yours, you should have gone in for nuclear physics, Pete,' Jacobson said, thinking that Bradley might've saved his own skin at the expense of signing Paul Shaw's death warrant.

He asked Bradley if he'd ever heard of the New Nationalists.

'Nope. Is that the fuckers Shaw was banging on about? Nazis or whatever. I told him I didn't know anything about that kind of shit. I've never even voted, mate. No point, is there?'

Chapter Thirty-Nine

Jacobson's mobile rang as they were walking across the police car park towards the rear entrance of the Divisional building. Greg Salter: *I need to speak you, Frank. Urgently. I've come in to my office especially.*

'Can't it wait, *Greg*?' Jacobson asked. 'We were about to restart the interviews.'

No, it couldn't wait, Salter told him flatly.

Kerr got out of the lift at the fifth floor, planned on chasing up the Randeep Parmeer situation in the interim. Jacobson carried on to the eighth floor, the senior management enclave, wondering what the hell was going on. Whatever Salter wanted, it had to be serious to lure him away from his penthouse lifestyle on a Sunday evening in April. He walked into Salter's office without knocking, was surprised to find that Crowby's Detective Chief Superintendent wasn't alone.

'Frank, please, have a seat,' Salter said, indicating the untaken third chair at the low, oval table in his famous 'informal interchange' area.

Jacobson had closed the door behind him but, for some reason, Salter got up and checked that it was firmly shut.

The visitor was young, barely thirty in Jacobson's instant estimate. But his hair was short in a non-modern, non-fashionable way and his face receded into his neck without the intercession of a chin.

'This is Commander Ashbury, SO12, Frank,' Salter said, sitting back down. 'He got in from London an hour ago.'

Jacobson nodded non-committally, pleased with himself that he was managing not to look completely astonished. SO12 was one of the Metropolitan Police's special operations units. The one that was better known to the general public as the Special Branch. Ashbury leant across the table, gave Jacobson a fleeting handshake. His palm felt faintly wet, faintly unpleasant.

'I've already said this to your DCS, Inspector, but now I'm saying it directly to you. Everything about the conversation we're about to have is covered by the Official Secrets Act. *Nothing* gets repeated outside this room without my express permission. If either of you break that simple rule, you'll be off the force without a pension.'

'Pleased to meet you too—' Jacobson started.

But Ashbury wasn't finished.

'That's the best-case scenario. The worst is something that earns you a stretch into the bargain. Maybe we set you up as being on the take – or maybe we stuff something embarrassing and illegal on to your home computer.'

'I don't have a home computer,' Jacobson said, rallying a little from the unexpected onslaught.

Ashbury allowed himself a microscopic grin.

'Believe me, Inspector – that wouldn't pose a problem.'

Jacobson didn't reply. He glanced at Greg Salter. But Salter didn't utter a word either, just carried on looking forlorn and uncomfortable. Like a hyena who can't get near the carcass for all the lions.

'Good,' Ashbury said briskly, evidently satisfied that he'd dealt with the preliminaries.

His accent was purest ruling-class Oxbridge: polite to the point of total malice. The Special Branch was known to recruit from the widest spectrum these days – it was the only way it could get its dirty work done – but, if Ashbury was anything to go by, the public schoolboys were still running the show at the top level. Jacobson watched him fidget with the knot on what was conceivably a regimental tie. Ashbury cleared his throat and threw down his gauntlet.

'The race hate charges you're considering, Inspector – drop them. Drop them now. Get rid of every shred of relevant documentation. And let the suspects go home.'

Jacobson couldn't mask his surprise this time.

'What?'

Ashbury micro-smiled again.

'The New Nationalists are off limits, I'm afraid. In fact, the New Nationalists at this moment in time are pretty much a state secret. No mentions permitted in the press – and certainly no mentions permitted in the public courts.'

Jacobson suddenly saw patterns where before there'd only been discrete facts. Henry Pelling failing to sell his Paul Shaw exclusive to Fleet Street. Steve Horton discovering that Shaw's computer space had been recently and mysteriously deleted.

'Is that why the national media aren't carrying Paul Shaw's death as a news story?' he asked, thinking he was starting to get a glimpse of a wider picture.

'That's absolutely why. Paul Shaw's work – how can I put this? – has been of interest to us for some time. He seems to have got wind of the NN when he was in the States. Maybe he stumbled across one of their American connections. Anyway, there's been an intercept on his phones and his email for the last couple of months. The minute he turned up dead, there was a Defence Advisory notice slapped on the topic. There's been a few breaches locally, I understand, but thank goodness there's been absolutely fuck all at the national level.'

Jacobson half-smiled himself. It was something about the way Ashbury mangled the pronunciation of 'fuck all': '*fuhck awl*'.

Ashbury cleared his throat again. Then:

'That's one side of it. Shaw sticking his nose in. The

other side – the more important side – is that the NN are a highly *infiltrated* organisation. SO12 are undercover right up to the highest layers, have been ever since day one.'

Jacobson shook his head.

'So I can't follow up a possible double murder because it might blow your security operation?'

Greg Salter made his mouth work at last.

'We still don't know that they *are* murders, Frank. But anyway that's *not* what's being said. Not at all. If your suspects have committed murder you can bring them to book in the usual way. What you can't do is make use of the New Nationalist background as any part of your case. You're going to have *prove* the charges without that – if you can.'

'It's been done before, believe me,' Ashbury commented. 'Play up the lone nutcase angle, play down any suggestion of links to organised groups. Although in this case, Inspector, it's not a matter of playing down – it's a matter of saying absolutely nothing at all.'

'And I'm off the force if I don't go along with this?'

'I thought I'd already explained your – eh – options. The operation against the NN has authority right up at Cabinet level. They're a honey trap for God's sake, drawing away the country's worst racists into one nice, well-organised, easily monitored falange.'

'And if I can't make a case without referring to them, then the fact that two men might have been murdered doesn't come in to it?'

Ashbury looked down at the thick wad of notes he had in front of him.

'Your positive vetting file says "*interested in philosophy*", Inspector. I'm sure you remember the Greatest Happiness principle – sacrificing the individual for the good of the many?'

Jacobson didn't say anything for a minute. He didn't even know he'd been positively vetted although – as Ashbury confided later – it was covert Home Office policy for all appointments from the rank of inspector upwards. Between obedience and whistleblowing there was a third option that Ashbury hadn't mentioned: straightforward resignation, walking away, finally calling his police career a day. He took out a B & H, lit up, guessed correctly that in the circumstances Greg Salter wouldn't raise an objection.

'Mum's the word then,' he said finally, as sarcastically as he could.

'Good,' Ashbury replied, 'that's agreed. I'll be staying on in, eh, Crowby for a couple of days. Any developments in the case, all the paperwork – everything gets told to me and everything gets copied to me. And I mean everything.'

He didn't bother to look up, seemed to be preoccupied with putting his notes back in order. At least he only said *good*, Jacobson thought. Not *good man*. Not – worst of all – *good chap*.

Vicky maintained a driving commentary to herself second by second, spoke it out loud as an extra stimulus to alertness. What gear she was in, what she could see in the mirror, whether she'd signalled before she'd changed lanes, what direction she'd take at the junction up ahead. There was actually nothing particularly difficult about driving drunk anyway, she reminded herself. Nothing at all. A piece of total and utter piss. The art of it was just the art of living in general. Staying *conscious*, staying aware, staying in the absolute purity of the here and now. When she'd turned off the main road, she parked up for a moment: *put in neutral, yes – hand brake applied, yes – turn engine off*. She'd drained the bottle before she'd left Crow Hill and she'd got all this way without a mishap. She'd even braked in time when that taxi had appeared out of nowhere, the arse behind the wheel honking and shaking his fist like it was *her* fault. The fat arse. The fat, taxi-driving arse. She thought about another roll-up and decided she couldn't be bothered, couldn't be arsed, ha, ha. She'd just sit here and take stock. She noticed that it was virtually dark now – and the moon was out above the houses. She'd need to remember to turn on the lights this time when she drove off again: further into zombie-land, further into the dead zone.

It really was hard to believe that Cole had ended up here – in a cosy box with Sky TV and a patio. Cole with his thousand outlandish schemes for the future. Cole with his strange hopes and twisted dreams. Cole with his endless plans. And one plan that had apparently come off exactly as he'd wished – at the Death Head's Festival: a bank holiday weekend in a godforsaken field in Lincolnshire, barely a year after they'd met. John Stuart had 'borrowed' one of his dad's vans to get them there, had stuffed Scuzz's gear in where the cement bags usually lived. In the end, their vaguely promised stage slot hadn't materialised. But none of the three of them had seemed to mind all that much, had seemed happy enough just to be soaking up the atmosphere. It had been the first time they'd seen the tents decorated with swastikas. The first time they'd heard the bands who went beyond death metal and black metal. Well beyond. And kids from all over it seemed too. Belgium, Germany, Scandinavia. Cole had loved all of it. The slashing speed chords and bellowed lyrics. The books and pamphlets Phil Stuart kept acquiring. *Adolf Hitler: Occult Master*, *The Nazi Search for Atlantis, Exposing the Holocaust Industry*. Vicky had told herself they were only being ironic, only striking a pose. You pretended you believed in nothing, of course you did, that you wanted death and destruction and chaos – anything that wasn't acquiescence, that could deliver you from terminal, grown-up boredom. Do What Thou Wilt Shall Be The Whole of The Law. And Cole, she'd told herself also, wasn't stupid, wasn't a fool. Even now, she still knew that was true.

She reached behind her to the back seat. Fuck it, she'd have the White Lightning too. Well, why the fuck not? Then they'd been driving home, back to Crowby, taking the

A roads to avoid the motorway traffic. Then there'd been a lay-by somewhere outside Grantham. Quiet, pitch black, broken-streetlamped. And Cole's voice, laughing like the Devil in the darkness. *Grab her arms, Phil, keep the bitch still. That's it, hold her down. You can go first, John.*

Chapter Forty

Half past nine. Jacobson assembled together everyone who was involved in the investigation, used one of the meeting rooms on the third floor for the purpose. He'd persuaded Ashbury to speak to them, to do his own bullying. Ashbury went into less detail - a lot less detail - than he'd done for Jacobson and Salter. But the message was identical: forget everything you've guessed or learned about the New Nationalists, delete any kind of record you've made, don't whisper so much as a '*fuhcking*' word to anyone not currently present.

Jacobson took reports back after Ashbury had finished. Hume and Barber hadn't found anyone in the vicinity of the Wynarth call box with any kind of useful memory of who'd been using it at ten thirty-seven on Thursday night. A young couple who'd been wending their way home from the Wynarth Arms had said they thought they might've seen 'a man' making a call around about that kind of time. But that, unhelpfully, had been it: 'a man'. The bloke had remembered him as tall, well-built. His girlfriend had said no, he'd only been average height and weedy: *definitely weedy*. Steve Horton announced that he'd found his way into Rick Cole's computer but was still running his password de-encryption utility against the machine which had been taken away from the Stuarts' place. It looked like there was a fair bit of material relating to the New Nationalists and there'd been email contact between Cole, the Stuarts and Wayne Parker – but there didn't seem to be any specific reference to either Darren McGee or Paul Shaw. Ashbury reminded Horton that SO12 would need full copies of both hard disks in due course and that nothing that even *hinted* at the existence of the NN could form part of the chain of evidence. Ray Williams handed round printed summaries of the phone record data. There were no new surprises – except maybe his insistence on crediting Emma Smith with the bulk of the collation.

Jacobson thanked them for their efforts – *over the odds, as usual* – and told them, all apart from Kerr, that they could call it a night.

'Only keep your phones switched on. Just in case.'

Ashbury left too: to sort out his hotel room. Predictably, Jacobson thought, he'd booked himself in to the Riverside Hotel. He asked Kerr for an update on the Randeep Parmeer case. Clive Rushton and Tony Blair had been picked up at last, Kerr told him, he was planning on interviewing them next.

'Unless you want me to sit in on Wayne Parker, Frank.'

Jacobson shook his head.

'No need. Besides we want all the background we can get on the local race-hate idiots even if we can't be upfront anymore about this, eh, NN group.'

They walked out of the meeting room and along the corridor together. But Kerr wanted to use the stairs so they separated at the lifts.

Back in his office, Jacobson lit up a B & H, promised himself it would be the last one today. He ran through the sequence of questions in his mind that he needed to put to Wayne Parker. He'd successfully negotiated with Ashbury not to have Rick Cole released until after he'd had a chance to interview Parker. Reluctantly, Ashbury had also agreed that the Stuart brothers could continue to be held overnight in relation to the possibility of unconnected firearms charges. The Walther PPK needed proper forensic examination but at first glance it looked as if it had never been fired. Ashbury hadn't been able to argue against the reasonable likelihood that the Stuarts had acquired the gun independently of their racist activities. You could pick one up easily enough in Birmingham if you knew the right pubs to go to, the right people to see. Walthers had become fashion accessories for young street criminals - and were starting to make market in-roads into the paranoid, property-owning classes (store in your beer fridge until needed). Jacobson reckoned he could do them for it without making the slightest allusion to race and politics. He smoked his cigarette with his feet up on his desk. *Maybe another time*, Alison Taylor had said. But how was he supposed to know if she meant it or not? His desk phone rang, wiping the mystery of the female psyche from his brain. The control room: something had just been faxed in for him from the Forensic Science Service - did he want them to send it up now? Or would it keep to the morning?

Vicky lurched the car to a halt and read the street sign - she'd overshot again. The Bovis estate was a rabbit warren of drives and courts and cul-de-sacs, most of them indistinguishable from each other. And she only half-remembered the address anyway. She hadn't really being paying complete attention when she'd looked it up in Sharon's telephone directory. It had only been a game then. An imagined, possible game. Which maybe it still was really. She drove on again, passed the pub for the third time. The Lonely Ploughboy. Sitting on his lonely arse, ha, ha. She tried a right at the mini-mart and then another right. *Signalling right, yes - nothing coming either way, no, - easy on the pedal, yes*. She'd found it at last. The second house in. The blue van - well, black in this light - on the narrow parking strip, stuck behind a saloon of some kind. Only don't ask me what make. She cut the engine, cut the lights, just sat there. Sober up and go home, girl. Just sober up and go home.

She climbed out with exaggerated slowness, didn't shut the door properly, didn't want it to bang. Bang, bang, you're drowned. Nobody nicked cars round here anyway. Nobody did anything round here. She walked carefully up the garden path. Keep steady. She could ring the bell or not ring the bell. Bell the ring or not bell the ring. Ha, ha. There were no lights on at the front, only the porch light. Maybe round the back then. She squeezed between the garage door and the rear of the van. Maybe they kept another vehicle locked inside. The three-car family. The three-chord trick. Three-card brag. Three against one.

The path was narrow along the side. She nearly tripped once, had to steady herself against the wall. Keep steady. There was a wooden garden bench beyond the patio, near the foot of the lawn, but facing back towards the house. Vicky sat down, making the slats creak, hearing the creak like a roar. But nobody had seemed to notice her. The kitchen was where the lights were on. Vicky could see all the way in. All the way right in. The wife was doing something, domestic-ing something, even had a white pinnie on over her pink top and her short, dark, pleated skirt. Something with her hands, something that bent her forwards over the table. The little girl was there too, sitting up on a kitchen chair – watching mummy. There was no sign of Cole – Cole didn't seem to be home. Vicky crossed her arms tightly, caressing them with her fingertips, feeling the night chill a little.

Bread, that was it. Wifey was baking fucking bread – greasing the oven tray, kneading the dough. The little girl yawned, said something. Wifey looked at her, smiled. She walked over to the sink, ran her hands under the tap, then dried them casually down the front of the pinnie. It was liking watching a play – or being God, present everywhere.

She lost them then for a while. Then a light came on at the top of the stairs. Then another light, in what might have been a bathroom. Finally a bedroom light – and wifey pulling the curtains shut. Vicky shivered, the worst of the drunkenness wearing off – or getting to the point where it no longer controlled you, where you felt you had some options about what you thought, what you did. Wifey came back downstairs on her own. She had a phone in her hand, not speaking but listening, and then putting it down somewhere that Vicky couldn't see. Back to the bread after that, more kneading, more fussing, checking the temperature of her oven. Vicky stole towards the patio doors. She thought about knocking hard or calling out. Then she thought that wifey wasn't small, that wifey probably wasn't six sheets to the wind either. Not tanked, not trolleyed, not half-juiced, not half-slated. Not rat-arsed.

Ha, ha. There was a stone tortoise on the grass. Decorative, *très amusant*. Not too big to pick up and probably just about the right sort of weight. You could chip a stone at the window first maybe. Get attention that way. And be round the side obviously. Readyish.

Chapter Forty-One

Jacobson grabbed a cup of what passed for coffee in the police canteen. This late in the evening, his system needed caffeine, regardless of the source, if he was to get his head round the latest turn of events. SO12, it transpired, had clout with the Forensic Science Service that a provincial police division didn't. Not even one like Crowby, with its relative proximity to the FSS HQ in Birmingham. Ashbury, obnoxious in so many ways, had nevertheless made arrangements earlier in the day to get the preliminary forensic analyses *super*-fast-tracked. Although he'd probably only done so in the hope of kicking Jacobson's inquiry (irritating and petty from the SO12 point of view) into touch. Jacobson forced down a mouthful of brown liquid. Which was exactly what might be about to happen.

The kind-of-good news was that there *were* foreign fibres clinging to Paul Shaw's clothes. Fibres that might very well match later on to the fibre samples lifted from his hotel room – thus showing a link to the ransacking there – and, ultimately, back to the clothes or the habitual environments of his attackers. The bad news was that the blood traces discovered on the Memorial Bridge definitely *weren't* from Shaw. That didn't mean of course that they weren't from someone he'd been in a struggle with. But Jacobson had to face the fact that it was every bit as likely that their origin lay in some other, completely unconnected incident. He took a second mouthful, then a third. The devastating news had been something else that the tests on Shaw's blood samples had thrown up: ketamine – better known to its mainly youthful aficionados as *ket* or *Special K*. Ket, from the little Jacobson knew about it, had a powerful, hallucinogenic effect on the brain. Something about the chemistry involved temporarily dissociated the mind from the body. Yet Jacobson thought he understood enough to appreciate that it was precisely the kind of mind-fuck substance that could put you on a bridge after midnight and whisper into your head that you could do anything – step off and fly like an angel or step off and soar like a bird.

He'd really only gone through the motions with Wayne Parker after that. All the time in the interview he'd been thinking *I got it wrong, I put two and two together and I came up with six*. Not that Parker wasn't lying, not that something dodgy hadn't occurred in the Riverside Hotel, Room 315, Thursday night. The question was, what exactly? Parker had just 'no commented' like the rest when it suited him – and talked nonsense the rest of the time. It had just been a daft impulse to take a few days off work. He'd been in a rut, needed to get away. He'd planned to go to Dublin and then changed his mind at the last minute, decided to look up his old army mate instead. He'd no idea that Nevil Drury was involved in drug dealing. Why would he? And the missing half-hour or so on the Riverside Hotel's CCTV tape had just been the result of a simple mistake. He'd shut the system down by accident, had switched it back on again as soon as he'd realised. He hadn't a clue how Paul Shaw's room had been broken into, hadn't seen the slightest thing unusual or suspicious. Plus who could say for certain that the break-in had happened during his shift anyway?

It was a crock of shit. Except that, for the time being, Jacobson had let it go. He'd sent him back to the cells, could at least hold on to him overnight. But it looked as if, sometime tomorrow, Wayne Parker would be walking out of the Divi's revolving front doors without a charge against him. Jacobson had already let Rick Cole go, had no real option. John Stuart and Phil Stuart were still in custody of course. But illegal possession of a firearm was a far cry from a prosecution for double murder. He finished the 'coffee' and took the main stairs down the two flights to his fifth floor office. At this time of night on a Sunday there was no danger of running into someone he didn't want to talk to. There was hardly any danger of running into anybody at all.

He'd collect his coat, he decided, file the FSS report away for now, drive home and attempt to get a decent night's sleep. Ashbury had arranged a meeting for first thing in the morning. Just the three of them again. Jacobson, Salter and Lord Snooty of the Special Branch. If Paul Shaw's death could be put down to drug-related misadventure then that would be effing that as far as the hierarchy were concerned. Case closed – and Greg Salter still smelling of roses re Darren McGee after all. His mobile rang just as he was bundling the FSS paperwork together. He looked at his watch – a quarter to eleven – felt the temptation not to answer. But didn't feel it strongly enough.

'Hello Frank? Sorry. We were out visiting friends – I've just got back.'

'No need for apologies, Peter. Home life comes first,' Jacobson heard himself saying, like a banker extolling the virtues of communism.

He'd been trying to reach Peter Robinson for over an hour and not getting anywhere. They'd developed an informal routine where Robinson was always pleased to field any queries Jacobson had about the content of FSS reports on body samples and the like. Alasdair Merchant (deceased) would never have entertained a similar arrangement in a million years. You had to fit in with Merchant's schedule – he was frequently too busy to see you or to come to the phone. The difference was partly because Robinson was a decent bloke. And partly because he was an eternal student, endlessly keen and fascinated by his subject.

Jacobson read out what he took to be the highlights. There was a pause while Robinson scribbled down some hasty notes.

'Tell me about the norketamine again, Frank,' he said after a further moment.

Norketamine was the breakdown product of ketamine in the body, detectable in blood and urine for up to fourteen days after ingestion. Jacobson told him the volumes that had shown up in the lab test, quoted the paragraph which estimated the time of ingestion as somewhere between ten o'clock and midnight. Robinson went silent again. Then he asked Jacobson to repeat the figures.

'You're sure?'

Jacobson read them out a third time:

'That's what it says here, old son. Problem?'

'No problem, Frank. But I think you've jumped the gun a bit. I take it this is purely a preliminary report - no summary conclusions, no clear statement of what's possible and what's impossible.'

Jacobson, who'd been standing, pulled out his chair and sat down.

'That's right. More or less just the raw data.'

'OK. If these figures *are* accurate, Paul Shaw must have ingested somewhere in the region of 300mg of ket. That's a hell of an amount, Frank - straight through the K-hole and then some.'

'The K-hole?'

'Ket's a clubber's drug, as I'm sure you know. Popular with the coke and ecstasy crowd. On a low dose it's just another euphoria rush. But up at the top end it's seriously trippy - out-of-body experiences, the lot. The K-hole's what they call the peak effect - the high, basically.'

'And 300mg is top end then?'

'200mg is top end, Frank. And you need to be bloody careful with it. The medical use of ket is as an anaesthetic.

Walking around with it inside your system is problematic to say the least. Temporary paralysis is common – being literally unable to get up off the floor. More than 250mg, you're probably looking at a state of actual unconsciousness.'

'So you couldn't for instance climb up on to the parapet of a bridge? Or put up a fight if someone else was lifting you up on to it?'

'That's exactly the point I'm making. Ket's a relatively short trip regardless of the dose. But for ninety minutes or so, Paul Shaw would have been as helpless as a kitten with four broken legs.'

'They snort it, don't they?' Jacobson asked, feeling like the apocryphal judge who'd had to ask who the Beatles were.

'That's right,' Robinson replied. 'You do a line just like coke – zap it through the mucous membranes and straight into the blood stream.'

Kerr had to get out of the house. Cathy was all over him, still misinterpreting the night before. He told her he was stressed, reminded her that he'd put in a long day, had put in three long days in a row. If she didn't mind, he'd just take a walk around the block, clear his head before he went up to bed. *The job, Ian, is it really worth it?* she asked him. Only she spoke gently, wasn't warming up for a shouting match. She was trying to be understanding, supportive, which only made him feel worse about the stuff she didn't know about, couldn't know about. He told her he wouldn't be long, grabbed his jacket from its hook in the hall, tried not to stumble over the cat, who'd followed him out from the lounge, as he did so. She'd probably thought he was going into the kitchen, gave a plaintive meow when she saw he was headed out the front door instead.

He was too late for the pub but he thought he might walk over in that direction anyway. It didn't really matter. The purpose of the walk was just to be on his own. Alone with the thoughts and images he needed to lose: Rachel in the company of smug, up-his-own-arse Tony Scruton. At least he'd told Cathy the truth about his long day. Long and frustrating as far as the drownings were concerned. Although he was getting somewhere with the trouble at the Viceroy Tandoori. He'd left all three of them – Bowles, Blair and Rushton – banged up for the night, would take his time putting the charges in the morning. They'd probably get bail when they made their court appearances. So Kerr figured one night in the cells wouldn't do them the least harm. Clive Rushton in particular. The other two were hardly strangers to detention but Rushton was – and it might concentrate his mind a little bit more. He'd admitted that he knew Rick Cole when Kerr had mentioned the name, more or less idly, when the tape had been switched off – although only, he'd claimed, as a contractor that his firm sometimes made use of. Bowles and Blair, of course, had said they'd never heard of him. Which meant absolutely nothing either way. Not that it would prove anything if they *did* know him. They were all involved in the building trade one way or another, so why shouldn't they be acquainted with each other? And only Bowles gave the impression of possessing genuine, heavy-duty racist attitudes. Their plan was just a business ploy as far as Rushton was concerned – and an easy cash-in-hand job for Blair.

Kerr turned his collar up, passing the mini-mart. It was cold for April, he thought. A clear, starry night. He crossed from one empty pavement to the other, suddenly realising where he was actually going. It was really just from curiosity, he supposed. A bloke who lived in a house just like his – and only a few, mundane streets away – with his head full of twisted hate. Not somebody at the bottom of the heap either, shat on and excluded, the way you were always led to believe they were. But a bloke with a decent enough job, a nice enough house, a wife and a kiddie.

There was nothing to see of course. Apart from that it

was night time, nothing looked any different now than it had when they'd searched the place this afternoon. The front was in darkness apart from the porch light. Exactly the same as the houses around it. Kerr might not have noticed the Clio parked outside if it hadn't been parked so badly – at least a foot from the kerb and at a weird, skewed angle. He looked at the car again, something recently familiar about it he was sure. But not from here. He memorised the number plate then turned on his heel. What he'd do on his way back home, he decided, would be to call up the control room. Ask them to run a check – just on the off chance.

Chapter Forty-Two

Rick Cole paid off the taxi but didn't give a tip. The driver was an Asian as per usual. White taxi drivers, he thought, were becoming an endangered species, like virgin brides and non-Paki doctors. He scowled at the badly parked car directly outside his front pathway but didn't think any more about it. All he wanted to do was get indoors, maybe take a shower, get the stink of the police cells off him. He smiled to himself, finding his key. The police had sod all, exactly like he'd predicted. Otherwise he wouldn't be standing here right now. John and Phil might be in the shit of course – if the search at their gaff had been as thorough as the one here. He'd warned them about that idiotic pistol more than once. But they wouldn't listen, especially not Phil. He'd got it into his head that they needed protection from low-life burglars and prowlers. Yeah, right. Protection more than two mad Alsatians and a brother the size of a brick shithouse. He opened the door, stepped in, closed it softly behind him. England would be fast asleep by now, he didn't want to risk waking her. But an unused pistol wasn't too much for them to worry about. Not compared to what they were getting away with.

The smell of baking bread hit his nostrils. Wendy must have waited up for him just like she'd said she would. She was probably still cooking or tidying then, keeping herself busy. He put on the light, hung up his jacket, walked along the hall. Nonchalantly, he opened the door into the kitchen.

'*What the—*'

'Shut it, Rick,' Vicky said, 'you don't want to wake the street, do you?'

Cole gaped at the scene. His wife, Wendy, was tied into a kitchen chair. Her arms, bound at the wrists, had been thrust forwards over the table. There was a gash of plumbers' duct tape across her mouth and an untreated wound on her forehead, crusting over where it must have been bleeding fairly recently. Vicky Maxwell was standing behind her, holding a kitchen knife to Wendy's throat.

He made as if to pounce at her but she pressed the edge of the blade closer to his wife's neck. He stopped short at the other end of the table, just stood there. For some reason it came to him that the white pine surface was precisely the same shade as the table in the police interview room.

'Where's my daughter? Where's England? If you—'

'Your daughter's fine, Rick. She's asleep in her bedroom. Isn't she, Mrs Cole?'

He couldn't really read his wife's face, distorted and tightened by the tape. But he saw her nodding some kind of assent.

'Sit down, Rick,' Vicky said, indicating the chair nearest to Cole with the point of the knife. 'You did say we should get together one of these nights. Catch up – I think that was the phrase you used.'

Cole sat down slowly. Like someone in a bad dream, sure they're going to wake up any minute.

'What's all this about?' he asked.

'I want to know why you killed Darren. I want to know how you killed him as well.'

Wendy Cole made a noise that might have been a groan or a whimper.

'Leave it out, you mad bitch,' Cole said.

Vicky pressed the blade to Wendy's neck again.

'I mean it. Tell me.'

Cole glared at her.

'Because you're mine, bitch. Because I fucking own you.'

Vicky felt calm, lifting the knife away from the wife's throat. She ran the point carefully down the length of the left forearm, watched the blood gush gently in its wake: tiny red rivers.

'No-You-Don't,' she said, as if each word was a sentence. 'You never did. Not even when—'

Cole found it in him somewhere to laugh.

'You loved that, you slag. Three blokes and both holes.'

Vicky could have stuck the knife right into her then. This thick, stupid woman who didn't know what she was living with – or didn't care.

'No-I-Didn't. You raped me. The three of you raped me.'

But still keeping control, cutting a second, parallel line, careful not to go too deep.

'So why didn't you go to the police then? You mad cow.'

'What? And be raped a second time by the courts? Everybody I knew, everybody at school, would've known who it was, would've known what had been done to me. I wasn't having that, Rick. I did something better for my revenge – I got out of this dreary, dead-end shithole. I got a *life*.'

'I own you, you know I do. Why I couldn't have McGee following you around, making me into a laughing stock. A fucking darkie getting his hands on my property.'

Wendy Cole was crying now. It was hard to hear the sobs because of the duct tape. But Vicky could see the tears in her eyes at least. She brought the knife back to her throat.

'How did you fucking do it, Rick?'

'Easy peasy, doll, we—'

Vicky took the knife away slightly, slapped the side of Wendy's head.

'Don't-Call-Me-Doll.'

Cole grinned at her. There was no point to this, no

danger, no reason not to humour her.

'OK. OK. We had inside info from where he worked. What his shifts were, when he went home, the route he took. We just sat outside and waited for him. And it wasn't like we didn't fucking warn him, didn't give him a chance to go away.'

Vicky slapped Wendy's head again. Maybe not so angrily this time.

'I planned it out from the telly really. Saw one of those programmes about the police. Forensics and all that. How if you could get somebody into water quickly enough, just get them in without a struggle, it would probably look like an accident or suicide. That's all we did – wait for him and chuck him in. Superior force. Three against one.'

'But he – he must've fought back, surely?'

'Well, that's a strange thing, Vix. That's what we expected – and we had something prepared for it. But he just stood there and waited when we got out the van. I swear to God he just held his arms out for us when he realised what we were about. Like he *wanted* it.'

Vicky stared at Cole, evaluating what he'd said, still trying to see behind his blasted eyes.

They heard a noise from out in the garden. Just an animal most probably. A neighbourhood fox maybe. Vicky was distracted for just a second too long. Cole leapt from the chair and flung it at her. It caught his wife too but it did the trick. Vicky reeled backwards and he had her. Grabbing the knife away from her. Punching her hard in the face. Watching her fall, deflated, to the floor. He straddled her, not sure what he'd do next.

Kerr used the first thing he could find. A stone hare. He broke the glass near one of the handles, slid one of the doors far enough to gain entry. Cole had time to see him coming, got up off Vicky, kept a hold of the knife.

'Stay back – or I'll slice the both of them.'

From somewhere upstairs, Kerr thought he could hear a child calling out: *Mummy*.

You couldn't get a knife off a grown man without getting cut. It was as simple as that. You took the risk or you walked away.

'Stay back – I'm warning you, you plonker.'

Kerr kept moving forwards. Cole stood his ground, swung the knife at him as soon as he was within reach. He'd aimed for his face, a slashing blow, and Kerr had swerved back from it. Cole reversed the lunge and caught Kerr this time – on the upper arm he'd raised instinctively to protect himself. Cole pulled the knife back, maybe preparing to plunge it into Kerr's stomach or his heart. But Kerr just kept going forward, remembering from somewhere some idea about getting *inside* the arc of the assailant. He managed one hand, and then two, around the wrist of Cole's knife arm, knowing that all that mattered in the world was maintaining the grip, keeping the knife from its work. They were staggering around the kitchen now, Cole trying to get the knife free, Kerr trying to stop him. Somehow, he worked one of his legs behind Cole's ankles, tripped him off balance. The knife dropped to the floor and Kerr kicked it away. Then he was on him, holding him for risky seconds in the banned neck lock that dangerously constricted the windpipe. While Cole caught his breath, Kerr spun him round and banged his head down hard into the table. Again. And then again. Cole slumped to the floor. No longer a current threat.

Vicky Maxwell roused herself to a sitting position.

'You all right?' Kerr asked her.

Her voice was hardly a whisper:

'Yeah.'

Kerr glanced at Wendy Cole, still trussed into the chair and staring down, dazed, at her bleeding arm. His own arm hurt like hell and he didn't know how deep the cut was. He'd untie her in a minute, he thought, get the tape off her mouth. But first he took his mobile out of his jacket pocket, dialled the control room again, called it in.

Chapter Forty-Three

Sunday May 1st

Jacobson had shaved twice after his shower, hadn't been satisfied with the closeness the first time. He'd even dabbed on aftershave, an ancient Christmas present from his daughter, Sally, that he'd never used before. He was wearing an open-collar shirt – no tie – with his linen jacket. He'd even thought about buying a pair of jeans, worried that he should look casual, off duty. But in the end he'd ditched that unlikely idea in favour of a pair of chinos that Sally had chosen for him the last time she'd twisted his arm into buying himself some new clothes. When he was finally ready, he wandered through to his kitchen and took the bottle of white out of the fridge and sat it next to the red. That had been another agony. Whether to take one bottle or two. And running a hotel, she'd know more about wine than Jacobson could ever be bothered to find out. Still, he reminded himself, people either liked you or they didn't. The odd, wrong detail wouldn't put her off if she didn't want to be put off. All he had to do was relax, really. The idea, old son, was to *enjoy* the evening.

He found a carrier bag, put both bottles inside and then walked back through to his lounge, taking the bag with him. Just one more task and he'd be sorted – and it would be time to get going. His half-finished investigating officer's report was spread out on the table. He could have done with carrying on with it tonight really. But he wasn't going to risk cancelling a second time. Definitely not. *Ahb-so-lutely* not, as Julian Ashbury would no doubt say. Plus there were loose ends being tied up almost daily; it wouldn't help to run too far ahead of himself. Although the main chain of evidence was more or less in place.

Vicky Maxwell had broken a silence that had lasted for near enough eight years. Once she'd started talking, her story had been like a torrent. It didn't matter whether her rape allegations were true or false. Half of Crowby in her age group seemed to remember her stormy relationship with Rick Cole: the basis of the fixation, on Cole's part, that even a sleepy CPS barrister could probably persuade a jury had led to the first murder. Which followed neatly on to the concept of the second murder as a straightforward attempt to silence Paul Shaw before he could do the murderers any real damage. Wayne Parker had spilled the beans when he saw where the investigation was going. Although he hadn't looked happy about it, had seemed to be hyper-obsessed by how long a prison term he'd get for his role as an accessory – keeping tabs on Darren McGee's movements, facilitating the break-in to Paul Shaw's hotel room. It was Parker who'd put them on to Tony Blair as the source of the ketamine hydrochloride that Cole had planned on using on McGee but had ended up over-using on Paul Shaw. Blair had coughed too – in exchange for lesser charges than Gary Bowles and Clive Rushton would have to face for their campaign against Randeep Parmeer. Blair had drugs charges pending anyway, would be doing a stretch soon enough. The Stuart brothers had made a reasonable job of valeting their van. But there had been traces of the ket in an interior side panel – and the latest forensic fibre analyses proved that material from the bottom of their wardrobes (as well as from Rick Cole's) matched samples lifted from Paul Shaw's hotel room and from his river-soaked clothes.

The padded envelope Jacobson had bought in WH Smith's was lying on the table next to his unfinished paperwork. He stuck on the stamps and then took the computer disk from its hiding place on his bookshelf - behind Copleston's *History of Philosophy*, Volume 7. Steve Horton had copied it for him. The highlights from Cole's and the Stuarts' computers. He put the disk inside the envelope and sealed it. Finally he printed the address on the front with untypical neatness:

Dr Martin Kesey
Senior Lecturer
Department of Sociology and Media Studies
University of Crowby

He checked the post code in his notebook and added it to the last line. Fine. He was done. He bunged the envelope into the carrier bag, intended posting it on his drive over to Alison Taylor's. Kesey would find a use for the content, might even find a way of getting some of it out to the public. At least shed a scintilla of light somewhere.

Author's Note

Schizophrenia is a widely misunderstood illness. Despite the vast army of 'mad' killers in the pages of crime fiction, the overwhelming majority of schizophrenic sufferers pose no violent threat either to their families or to strangers. The following websites are reliable UK sources of information on schizophrenia and other mental illnesses: www.rethink.org, www.mind.org.uk. On the specific topic of LSD and psychosis, there is a useful primer for the scientifically inclined on the University of Iowa's 'virtual hospital' site:
www.vh.org/adult/provider/psychiatry/CPS/28.html

The best anti-racist news and intelligence resource on the British far right continues to be the indefatigable magazine, *Searchlight* www.searchlightmagazine.com.

I am unable to take the original 'credit' for the Auschwitz 'joke' in Chapter 28. A BBC transcript attributes it to Nick Griffin, the chairman of the British National Party at the time of writing.

Iain McDowall www.crowby.co.uk